CRIES OF THE CHILDREN

CRIES OF THE CHILDREN

Clare McNally

INNER CIRCLE

This one is for my mom.
You may be far away, but our hearts
are always close. I love you!

1

SAMANTHA WINSTEAD'S DAY had been a long one. She knew she shouldn't have agreed to take a double shift at the hospital, and as one A.M. brought sixteen straight hours of work to an end, complete exhaustion was creeping into every joint of her five-foot-one frame. She winced, rolling her neck and closing her stinging eyes as she waited for the elevator.

"I thought only residents slept on their feet," a familiar voice said.

Samantha looked up at Barbara Huston, her friend since medical school and a coworker for six years. As usual, Barbara looked gorgeous—tall, blond, and glamorous—making Samantha feel even grimier.

"It's been a hell of a day," Samantha said, running a hand through her shoulder-length brown hair.

"That's what you get for telling John you'd do his shift for him," Barbara said.

The elevator opened and they stepped on, barely finding space in the crowd of workers going off duty. They resumed their conversation in the downstairs lobby.

"Well, John had to go to a wedding," Samantha said. "And he did fill in for me when I had the flu last winter."

She yawned.

"But I don't want to do this again in the near future," she said. "Double shifts are for the young."

"Are we old?" Barbara asked with a frown. "Last I looked, I was only twenty-eight."

Samantha pushed her way through the front door into the cool April night.

"Sometimes I feel old," Samantha said. "I guess it's just fatigue. And we're thirty-five, dear heart. Not twenty-eight. Sorry."

"And here I was living in blissful ignorance," Barbara

sighed. "Well, maybe you ought to come up to the maternity ward sometime. The sight of all those babies bundled up like little pink and blue burritos is rejuvenating."

Samantha smiled wearily. "Burritos. I always thought they looked like potatoes."

"Well, at least your vacation starts next week," Barbara pointed out.

"I wish it started right now," Samantha said, "but I have to come in just one more day to tie up a few things."

"Then two whole weeks to yourself," Barbara said. "Any plans?"

"I thought I might drive into Denver," Samantha said. "To do some shopping and sightseeing."

Samantha's divorce had cut off any ties she had to a family, since her parents had died when she was very young. Barbara wished she had some time off herself, to keep her friend company. The only girl among five children, she considered Samantha the closest thing she'd ever had to a sister.

They had reached Samantha's truck, a denim-blue Bronco II. The hospital was on the edge of the town, and there were virtually no buildings between it and the mountains. Ashleigh Creek was situated just west of Pueblo, in the valley formed by the Front Range and the Sangre de Cristo Range. The snowcapped peaks of the Front Range loomed majestically in the distance, a virtually unbroken line of the Rockies that cuts through the center of Colorado. To Samantha's stinging, weary eyes, they might as well have been the terrain of a distant planet.

"Enjoy yourself," Barbara said as Samantha jumped into the truck. "I'll see you when you get back."

"So long," Samantha said, yawning again.

"Put on the radio," Barbara suggested. "You have to stay awake."

"I will, I promise!" Samantha said.

Though the Front Range is the most densely populated area of Colorado, the twisting mountain roads were virtually deserted at this late hour, and she passed only a few cars as she made the half-hour trip home. The sight of her garage was a welcome one.

She pulled the truck to a stop, opened the garage door

with a remote, then rolled the truck inside. As she got out, the garage door started sliding back down all by itself. There was an override switch at the back, and she jumped from the truck to press it, but the door continued its descent, leaving Samantha in darkness when it stopped.

She let out an annoyed groan and felt her way along the wall to the back door. She tried her key. The click was satisfying, but the door wouldn't budge. Samantha fought a growing sense of claustrophobia, forcing herself to see that she had turned the key the wrong way. She tried again, heard a click, but still the door wouldn't open.

Just then Samantha heard the barking of her dogs. Attuned to the pair of animals that she'd had for five years, she knew at once something was wrong. The barking was shrill and frightened. Was there an intruder on her property? Maybe someone had purposefully tampered with the doors!

She breathed in heavily and peered into the dim room at her rusty tools. There . . . an ax was just what she needed! Maybe if she shattered all the glass on the back door, and smashed the frame, she could crawl out.

The barking rose to a frenzied pitch as she pulled the ax down from the wall.

Something shifted on the other side of the room. Samantha froze, the ax held tightly in her white-knuckled hands. There was someone else in here. . . .

It seemed her heart had stopped beating. She moved on stiff legs to the back door. Then, forcing herself to pretend there was no one watching from behind, she swung at the windows. Glass flew out onto the pathway that led to her house. Cool air blasted through the new opening, and Samantha began to scream. She knew no one would hear her, but she couldn't stop. Again and again she swung the ax.

"Samantha . . ."

The voice was soft, hard to identify as male or female. Samantha spun around, raising the ax to use as a weapon. She barely had time to register a pair of dark eyes as the ax was wrenched from her grip. Even as the dogs barked, a sweet-smelling mist as cold as snow struck Samantha in the face. Everything faded to black.

2

THE FIRST OF Samantha's senses to return was smell. She breathed in the aroma of freshly laundered sheets, Rocky Mountain columbines, and coffee. She couldn't remember making coffee. She remembered driving home from work; the garage . . .

"Are you awake yet?"

Bolting upright, Samantha found herself staring into the wide eyes of a little girl. For a moment she could do nothing but gape, dumbfounded. It took a few seconds to take it all in. She was in a strange room. The girl, who seemed to be eight or nine, tucked a rippling strand of long brown hair behind her ear.

"Are you going to get up?"

Samantha blinked.

"Who . . . who are you?" she asked.

She looked around. The mustard-gold curtains, drawn tightly now, and the matching bedspread indicated a motel room. There was no door on the closet, and the hangers were permanently attached. A vase of purple and white columbines had been set on the nightstand, as well as a small tray with a cup of coffee, a croissant, and fruit.

The little girl laughed.

"You're funny when you wake up," she said. "Look, I went down to the restaurant and brought up breakfast. The coffee has two teaspoons of sugar and a little cream, just like you told me yesterday."

"Yesterday?"

Samantha rubbed her head, feeling a dull ache. Yesterday she had worked a double shift and Barbara Huston had walked her out to her car. She'd driven home, and then something had gone wrong with the garage door, and . . .

"I'm . . . I don't know what's happening," she said. "Where am I?"

"We're in the Miner's Hotel, of course," the child said.

"The what?"

The little girl opened the dresser drawer and pulled out a piece of stationery. Samantha read the letterhead and gasped. It said: "MINER'S HOTEL. EST. 1902, DURANGO, COLORADO."

"Durango!" she gasped. "But that must be a hundred miles from Ashleigh Creek! How on earth did I get here?"

Panicking, Samantha got out of bed. She was surprised that she was dressed in her own nightgown. A suitcase lay open on the dresser at the opposite side of the room. Samantha recognized her own clothes, folded neatly, as if she'd planned this trip. She turned to the child.

"Look, I don't know what's going on here," she said in a harsh tone, "but if this is someone's idea of a joke, it isn't very funny."

The child backed away from her, genuine fear filling her green eyes.

"Why are you yelling at me?" she asked. "You're scaring me!"

"I'm scaring *you*?" Samantha said. "I just woke up in a strange motel room and I don't know how I got here!"

The little girl moved carefully to the breakfast tray. She picked up the cup of coffee and handed it to Samantha.

"Maybe . . . maybe you'd better drink this," she said.

Samantha took a sip. The coffee was perfect, just the way she liked it. But she hadn't told this child how to make it.

"What's your name?" she asked, trying to calm herself. It was obvious the little girl was as befuddled as she.

"That's a silly question," the child said. "You know what my name is."

Samantha shook her head, cradling the warm cup between her hands to steady them.

"No, no, I don't," she said. "Something's happened to me. Please help me, little girl."

The child straightened herself. "I'm not little. I'm nine. And my name is Julie."

"Julie what?"

Julie frowned at her.

"I . . . I can't . . ."

"You can't remember?" Samantha prodded. "Julie, how did you come to be here?"

"Mr. Henley brought me," Julie said. "From the Cliffside Home. You talked to him, signed some papers, and we had a nice day together. Don't you remember? We took a ride on the Durango and Silverton Narrow Gauge Railroad. You bought me a piece of aquamarine from an Indian man."

Unable to recall any of this, Samantha sat down on the edge of the bed. She didn't speak for a few moments as she finished her coffee.

"Julie," she said at last, "how long have we been here?"

"In Durango?" Julie asked. "Just since last night. We met Mr. Henley at the home the day before that."

"Where's the home?"

"In Tacoma," Julie said.

Tacoma. Samantha had never been there.

"Wait a second," she said. She opened the nightstand and pulled out a phone book. "Cliffside . . . Cliffside . . ."

But there was no listing for a Cliffside Home.

"Did Mr. Henley leave a number?"

Julie shrugged.

"Well, I don't understand any of this," Samantha said. "We've got to call the police. Maybe they can help me find this Mr. Henley."

There was a plastic tent-card next to the phone, listing local restaurants, movie theaters, and emergency numbers. No sooner had she dialed two numbers than her hand froze. She felt something like electricity running through her body, as if she were being shocked.

I'll die if I call the police. I can't talk to them.

The thought came through loud and clear, like a piece of rote learned to perfection. With a cry, she threw the phone away from herself and stared at the dangling receiver.

"What . . . what's wrong?" Julie asked.

When Samantha looked up to answer, her face was pale and her voice husky.

"I don't know," she croaked. "I got some kind of shock from the line."

But it was more than that. Samantha felt an overwhelming sense of dread at the thought of trying to call the police again.

"But I'm going to find out," she went on. "Julie, pack your things. We're going home. And when we get there, I'm going to find out who you belong to!"

"But I belong to you now!" Julie insisted. "To you!"

Samantha met the child's gaze. Julie's green eyes were filling. Samantha felt a sudden urge to run and put her arms around the child. She wanted to hold her close and comfort her and tell her everything was going to be all right.

But it wasn't all right. And nothing would be all right until she figured out what the hell was going on.

3

WITH A SWEEP of her conductor's baton, Rachel Freleng brought the *William Tell Overture* to a finish, thus ending the John Glenn High School Orchestra's Spring Festival. She turned and bowed to the cheering audience. At last, when the clapping ceased, she gathered up her music and made her way to the dressing room backstage.

"Mommy!"

Rachel crouched down and opened her arms to greet her two daughters. When six-year-old Tatiana and eight-year-old Olivia ran up to her, she caught them both in a loving embrace.

"It was so pretty, Mommy," Tatiana said. "And I didn't fall asleep once!"

"Oh, I'm so glad you liked it, Tati," Rachel said, kissing the child's brown curls. "How about you, Olivia?"

Olivia smiled sweetly. "Yes, Mom. I liked the part where that boy was playing the flute. It really did sound like bees."

" 'Flight of the Bumblebee,' " Rachel told her. She hugged the girls tightly. "It means so much to me to have you as fans."

Tatiana and Olivia were actually her husband's children. Eric had full custody of them, and had made it clear he'd never give them up when he asked Rachel to marry him. She'd assured him such a thing would never be acceptable to her either. In the years she and Eric had been married, she'd grown to love these two girls as if she'd given birth to them herself. Rachel had no relatives herself, and to come backstage tonight and find a family was like a dream come true.

She saw her husband now, holding a can of diet soda. She stood up as he moved through the crowd of students

14

and parents. Eric handed her the soda at the same time he stopped to kiss her.

"It was wonderful," he said. "These kids get better every year. The school board was smart to make you head of the music department."

A young boy cradling a tuba sidled past them with a quick greeting to his music teacher. Rachel waved to him.

"I'm very proud of my students," she said. She took a long sip of soda, then handed it down to Tatiana. "Eric, I have a few things to wrap up. Why don't I meet you and the children in the lobby?"

"Sure, honey," Eric said. He put his arms around her and kissed her warmly. "Tell Mommy we'll see her in a few minutes, girls."

"See you, Mommy!" Tatiana cried.

Olivia just waved.

Rachel entered her office. Once the door was closed, it seemed as if the noisy world outside did not exist. She shut her eyes and worked her neck and shoulders in a stretching exercise, trying to relieve some of the ache she felt after two hours of conducting.

When she opened her eyes, someone was standing in front of her desk.

"Who . . . ?"

A strange, cold sensation against her face arrested any attempt at speaking. Rachel had a brief thought about icy rain before everything went black.

When she awoke again, she was still sitting at her desk, her head resting in her arms. She looked up slowly, feeling shaky inside. No one was in the room now, but she had a vague sensation that someone had been there. It was like the last vestiges of a dream.

She rubbed her eyes, and as she drew her hands away, she noticed they were dirty.

She must have passed out. Sheer exhaustion, that's all. Maybe she only dreamed someone was in the office. But she was certain Eric would be worried about her if she didn't hurry and get her things together.

She filed away that night's music and gathered up some songsheets she hoped to practice that weekend. Then she opened her office door and left, locking it behind her.

Rachel was immediately aware that something was

wrong. It was dark in the hallway, and so *quiet*. Where had all the students gone? Where were their families?

She quickened her pace to a half-run, her high heels rapping on the tiled floor. There wasn't another person in sight, not another sound but those she made herself. She reached the lobby, expecting to see her family waiting. But Eric and her daughters weren't there.

A soft click made her cry out in fear. She swung around, expecting to see someone behind her. Instead, her eyes were drawn to the big clock on the wall. In the daytime, with so much noise in the school, she never would have heard the click of the moving minute hand. But what startled her more was the time: 1:10 A.M.

"But the concert was over at eleven!"

What had happened to her in those missing hours? Where was her family?

Clutching the folder of music as if it were a shield, she hurried down the hall to the administration office. As she had expected, it was locked tight. She opened her purse, found a handful of change, and went to call home on the pay phone. Eric answered on the first ring.

"Rachel?" he said. "Thank God! Where are you?"

"At the school," Rachel said. "Eric, I don't know what happened!"

"You just wait there," Eric said. "I'm coming to get you."

The Freleng house was on the outskirts of Columbus, Ohio, just two miles away from the high school. Eric was there within minutes, running to take a frightened and confused Rachel into his arms.

"We've been looking everywhere for you," he said, leading her to their car. "Honey, where were you?"

"I . . . I think I passed out," Rachel said. "But when I woke up, I was in my office."

Eric backed away, resting his hand against her face. Under the lamplight, his dark fingers were a sharp contrast to the café-au-lait color of his wife's skin. Her gray-green eyes were filled with tears, a show of both relief and fear.

"When I came to," Rachel said, "no one was here! Eric, why did you leave without me?"

Eric shook his head.

"But we checked your office. We looked everywhere—

and then we had a few people help with the search. The janitor even let us into the boiler room . . ."

He hugged her again. "God, I was so scared. I thought something terrible had happened to you."

"What about the girls?" Rachel asked.

"They couldn't get to bed when we got home," Eric said. "Tati was afraid of having nightmares. She hears so many stories about missing people. The poor kid probably thought you were going to end up on a milk carton. Olivia didn't say a word, but you could tell by her eyes that she was frightened too. They'll be glad to see you."

He opened the car door and helped her inside. Then he went around himself.

"Do you feel okay?" he asked. "Are you hurt anywhere?"

"I think I'm fine," Rachel said. "I just feel a little dizzy. But, Eric, more than two hours of my day are missing!"

Eric started the car, and they drove home through the well-lit streets. "I'll call the police when we get home. They didn't consider you missing long enough to conduct a search, but they should know something happened to you."

Rachel's grip was so tight that Eric nearly steered the car off the road.

"No!" she cried. "Please don't call the police!"

"Rachel," Eric said with concern, "all indications point to the fact that you were kidnapped tonight. We have to report this!"

"No, we don't," Rachel said. "I'm fine, really. I don't know what happened to me, but that doesn't mean we have to include the authorities in the matter."

"But, Rachel—"

"Damm it, Eric!" Rachel snapped. "I'm fine! I don't think I was kidnapped, and I don't need for you to start worrying. Can we end this, please?"

Eric had never seen her so hostile in the four years they had been married, and the revelation that she could express such fear and anger surprised him.

"All . . . all right," he stammered. "I won't call the police. But, Rachel, if you feel anything at all—any pain, I mean—promise me you'll call a doctor."

"I promise," Rachel said, fixing her eyes on the road ahead.

For a long time Rachel was silent. Eric thought to himself that this was the first time he'd ever seen her so introverted. It was her outgoing personality that had attracted him to her in the first place. They'd met at a faculty meeting. Rachel was new to the music department then, while Eric had been a gym teacher for three years. Friends had steered them toward each other. Though they had enjoyed the ensuing conversation, nothing had come of the evening. But Eric's friends, worried about him raising two girls on his own, insisted he ask Rachel out again. Eric had given in, only because he thought Rachel was the most beautiful woman he'd ever seen. What started as infatuation turned into love when he saw Rachel's warm reaction to his two young daughters. He asked her to marry him, and she'd accepted. It had been a strangely one-sided wedding, with only his family present. Rachel said she had no living relatives.

When they reached the long driveway that led up to their house, Rachel finally spoke again.

"Don't tell the girls about your kidnapping idea," she said.

"Of course I won't," Eric promised, shutting off the engine.

"We'll just say I went for a walk to get some fresh air," Rachel said, "and because I was so tired, I passed out."

Olivia, relieved to see her mother was home and safe, willingly accepted the explanation. But Tatiana scrutinized Rachel as if trying to bore into her mind and learn the truth. Rachel caught the child's gaze and felt a chill run through her. She managed a smile and patted Tatiana on the head.

"Everything's all right now," she said. "You go on up to bed."

"Aren't you going to kiss me good night?" Tatiana asked.

For a moment Rachel simply stared. Then she blinked a few times and said, "Oh, yes, yes! Of course!"

Tatiana accepted a kiss on her brown cheek.

"Your mother's worn out," Eric explained. "Go on,

now, up to bed. You've got ballet class tomorrow and you'll never be up to it."

Tatiana took Olivia's hand and walked with her up the staircase that cut through the middle of the colonial house. At the top, she looked back over her shoulder. Her parents were hugging each other.

"Something's wrong with Mommy," she said softly.

"Don't be silly," Olivia answered. "Mommy's fine. Come on, it's late. Let's get some sleep."

Each girl went to her own room. Despite Olivia's reassurances, Tati still worried that there was something different about their mother. It was a long time before she fell asleep that night.

4

MOVING WITH THE quickness of a startled mouse, the little girl pulled herself back into the shadows cast where the city streetlamp washed over a tall pile of garbage bags. She didn't notice the rotting smell of food left wrapped in dark plastic under the warm sun. Her nose was too stuffed up from crying. She wanted to run to someplace safe. If only she could remember where it was she was supposed to go.

If only she knew something more than her name.

"Lorraine," read the gold chain she wore around her chubby little neck. There was no other clue to her identity, not even in the two small suitcases she had with her. The only thing she was sure of was that she was in a frightening, unfamiliar place. There were stores with great metal doors pulled down over them. Trash littered the streets, blown down abandoned sidewalks. Lorraine had been alone for the last hour, ever since she "woke up" to find herself wandering down a dark and deserted road. When she'd heard voices, she'd felt relief. Maybe someone would help her find her family.

But when she saw the group of teenagers moving toward her, she knew instinctively that they were trouble. The sight of a knife in one boy's hand closed the most recently formed gap in her memory. She knew who they were. She could close her eyes and see them approaching her, laughing and threatening and sneering.

"What you got in that suitcase, man?"

No, they weren't talking to her. They were talking to . . .

Whom?

Who had she been with?

"Step aside," said the figure next to her. In her mind,

20

she tried to see who it was. It spoke in a man's voice, but the image was no more than a silhouette.

"Who are you?" Lorraine asked in her mind.

But there was no answer.

"You step aside, shithead," one of the boys said. *"You step aside or . . ."*

Suddenly the silhouette produced a gun. In a flash, one of the gang members pulled out his own weapon. There was a gunshot, and cries of dismay, and a scream.

Did I scream? Lorraine wondered.

She remembered now that she had started running, both small suitcases clutched firmly in her pudgy hands. Overwhelming fear embraced her so completely that it began to block out all her memories. She ran on and on, unseen on the empty streets, a small figure lost in the shadows. By the time she stopped, all that was left to her was her name.

It was easy to hide. She was just a very little girl. She waited, biting her lip to keep from crying aloud, until the gang passed by. They never even noticed her.

Time moved slowly, and she felt herself drifting off to sleep. She awoke with a jolt when something warm and furry brushed her cheek. With a cry, she jumped up. Night had fallen completely by now, and the street was black and eerie.

Lorraine moved out of her hiding place as if in a trance, too exhausted to feel fear any longer. She walked like a little robot with no destination. When she turned the corner she saw movement under a lamp halfway up the block. Someone dressed in a big coat was hunched over a trashcan, exploring the inside. Lorraine walked toward this person, feeling none of the apprehension she had sensed when the gang passed her. She didn't understand why the person was looking in a trashcan, but she was too young to worry about such behavior. She only knew she needed help, and this might be her only hope.

Up ahead, the ragged figure froze, her arm still reaching into the bin. Her fingers were wrapped around a partially eaten hero sandwich. Bettina heard footsteps behind her. They were tiny footsteps, but she knew how tricky these gang kids could be. They'd try to sneak up on her, and if they caught her, they'd beat her. But she wouldn't let them do that. Bettina might have been a "crazy old lady," but she had the keen hearing of a much younger person. The footsteps were drawing closer now. She held fast to the hero—nothing would make her give up the only food she'd found in hours. With her other hand she reached deep into the pocket of her tattered raincoat and felt the comforting smoothness of her weapon. She'd found a broken knife behind a restaurant once and had wrapped it with bits of masking tape. Now, as the footsteps stopped directly behind her, she whipped out the knife and swung around with a cry.

But the cry turned to a gasp of horror at the sight of the little girl.

"Holy Mother!" she cried.

She shoved the knife quickly into her pocket. She'd almost stabbed a child! Injuring a mugger was one thing, but hurting an innocent would mean an eternity in hell! Bettina could feel her heart pounding in her frail chest, and she pressed her hand against it. It took a number of deep breaths to calm herself.

"What in the name of the Lord are you doing out here, child?"

The little girl's eyes were the oddest shade of gray-green Bettina had ever seen. They went very round now, and tears began spilling from them.

"I . . . I'm lost," Lorraine wailed. "I don't know where I am!"

Bettina turned for a moment to the overstuffed shopping cart behind her. She put her sandwich in it, then looked at the child again. The necklace she wore glistened in the lamplight, so she knew at once the child's name was Lorraine. She seemed to be no more than five or six. Bettina knelt down to her height.

"Your name is Lorraine?"

The child nodded, her lower lip quivering as she fought another bout of tears.

"What's your last name?"

"I don't know."

"Do you know where you come from?"

The little girl shook her head.

"Well, you sure ain't from this area," Bettina said. "Ain't no kids around here who dress like this."

She indicated the matching slacks and top Lorraine wore, a fancy outfit decorated with eyelet and ribbons.

It was dirty now, and a bit of the trim was dangling from the hem, but Bettina knew boutique clothing when she saw it. Many years ago she'd worked in the garment district.

Now Bettina noticed the two suitcases Lorraine was carrying. Could there be a clue in them? There were no tags on the outside.

"May I look into the bags?" she asked.

Trustingly Lorraine nodded. That was another thing that indicated she didn't belong here. No child born in this area would trust a complete stranger.

Bettina looked around to be certain they were alone. She, too, had noticed the gang earlier.

One bag held more of the same type of clothing, the stuff only rich people dressed their kids in. And the other bag proved Lorraine really was rich, while adding to the mystery of this lost child. What on earth was she doing walking around the Lower East Side of Manhattan with a suitcase stuffed with twenty-dollar bills? Bettina gasped at the sight of the money. There had to be more than a thousand dollars in here!

Quickly she closed it. Temptation was coming down on her, making her want to steal this from the innocent child. Bettina didn't want to burn in hell, so she stood up and put her dirty hand gently on the child's.

"You stick with me, sweet Lorraine," she said. "You stick with old Bettina. She'll take care of you."

5

NIGHT HAD FALLEN by the time Samantha saw the exit sign for Ashleigh Creek. Soon she'd be back home, where she could begin to piece together the missing days.

She had spent the better part of the drive questioning Julie. The child answered as best as she could, which usually meant a shrug or an "I don't know." Julie's past was a mystery. The only information she could provide was that she had lived in an orphanage. Somehow, even the names of the people who had cared for her (other than Mr. Henley) had been blanked from her mind. Most disconcerting about all this was that the child took it so readily. Samantha thought a normal kid would be very upset. But Julie seemed to accept being with Samantha as if it were the most natural thing on earth.

When Samantha pulled up to her garage, she sensed the danger she'd felt the last time she'd been here. Much as she wanted to push the frightful thoughts from her mind, she welcomed them instead as a way of getting to the truth. She aimed the garage-door remote and tried to make its actions bring back memories of that day. But everything in the garage was as it was supposed to be, mundane and nonthreatening.

Everything but the shattered back-door window. Leaving Julie sound asleep, Samantha turned off the engine and got out. Her feet crunched on bits of broken glass. There was an ax lying on the floor just inside the door. Samantha picked it up carefully. The feelings that came to her were instantaneous, and so frightening she threw the tool down. She had a brief flash of memory, of swinging the ax at the door in a desperate attempt to get away from . . . something.

She tried to push her fears away and let the ax help

24

her remember what had happened. But at that moment Julie suddenly began to scream.

"No! Don't put me in that!"

Samantha hurried to the truck. Julie was sitting as far forward as her seat belt would allow, staring at something Samantha couldn't see. Her arms were flailing, as if she were fighting someone.

"No! No! No!"

"Julie!"

Samantha reached around the wildcat child and unfastened her seat belt. It took all her strength to control her. Julie screamed and fought, seeming unaware of her real surroundings.

"Julie, wake up!"

The girl took in a huge gulp of air. She began coughing, focusing at last on Samantha with wild eyes. Then she blinked a few times, and Samantha understood that the little girl was finally seeing *her*.

"You had a bad dream, sweetie," Samantha said. "But it's over now."

"Someone was trying to put me in a box," Julie said.

Samantha shivered at the image. What kind of dream was this for a little girl? Had her previous life been so terrible that she forced it out of her memory?

Julie snuggled against her.

"It's okay now," Samantha said. "Look, we're home now. Let's go inside."

Julie stopped at the door, staring for a moment at the broken window. Finally she said, "You did that."

"How do you know?"

But Julie was already walking down the path to the house. The outside light worked on a timer, and it had come on a short while earlier. Julie didn't continue on the path, but veered in the direction of the kennel. Samantha was suddenly reminded of her dogs. They'd been left alone for almost two days!

"The dogs need you!" Julie called. "Hurry!"

"Damn," Samantha said. "How could I have forgotten them?"

She hurried into the kennel.

"Lady! Sunday!"

Her calls were answered by soft whimpering. Samantha opened the inner door and gasped. Sunday and Lady, two chocolate Labradors, were huddled on a pile of hay in the corner of the room. Samantha hurried to them and stroked their matted fur.

"Oh, my God," she whispered. "You poor things! You've been cooped up here without food and water!"

"But look," Julie said from the back of the room, "someone did leave them food and water."

Samantha stood up. To her surprise, the water trough and food trays were full. Whoever had kidnapped her the other night had also seen to it that the dogs were taken care of. It was an odd show of humanity from a mysterious stranger. But it also put things into a different perspective. If the kidnapper had wanted to hurt her, why bother caring for the dogs?

She noticed now that Sunday and Lady had pulled away from her and were staring at Julie with their cocoa-colored eyes. Julie returned the stares. It was like a tableau, a moment of frozen time. Samantha wondered why the dogs didn't run to greet the new stranger in the frolicking, barking way they always did. They seemed to be studying Julie, sizing her up.

"Julie?" she said softly. "These are my dogs, Sunday and Lady."

"I know," Julie said. She opened her arms and the dogs ran to her. Each one licked a hand with a warm, wet tongue.

Samantha shook her head.

"That's amazing," she said. "Those two are usually a pair of maniacs, especially around kids."

She leaned down a little to speak to the dogs.

"What's up, you guys?" she asked. "Why are you behaving so nicely?"

The dogs didn't even acknowledge her voice, another first. She straightened.

"Sorry," she said. "I'm really sorry you were cooped up in here. It's not my fault."

Julie bent down and whispered something in Sunday's ear. Instantly the dog turned around and ran to Samantha. He jumped up, putting his big paws on her shoulders. She hugged and petted him as he licked her.

"Good boy!" she said. "What a good boy!"

Lady followed suit, and in moments all was forgiven.

Samantha led the dogs outside to run a bit. Julie stood in the doorway and said, "I'm glad they're okay."

"So am I," Samantha said. "But, Julie, how did you know about the dogs?"

"I heard them," Julie said.

"But they weren't barking."

Julie came out of the garage, her eyes fixed on the pair of brown animals that romped under the floodlight.

"I heard them scratching," she said.

Samantha had to accept this, because there was no other logical explanation. Julie was yawning, and it was obvious all these questions were wearing her out.

"You can sleep in the guest bedroom," Samantha said. "Let's take your suitcase inside."

Upstairs, Samantha opened Julie's suitcase and found a nightgown and toothbrush. There were several more changes of clothes and another pair of shoes. *Someone* had seen to it that the child was well prepared; too bad they only thought of the material things Julie would need.

"The bathroom is just down the hall," Samantha said. "I'll wait in here until you're ready."

When Julie returned, all washed up and dressed in her nightgown, she came to Samantha and put her arms around her.

"I'm so glad you didn't make me go back," she said. "I really like you, Samantha."

She looked up at Samantha with such loving eyes that the woman felt her heart skip a beat. For an instant she felt as if she really *knew* this child. But that was impossible, of course. She was just feeling sympathetic toward someone in need.

"Would you like to hear a story?" she asked.

"Okay," Julie said.

There was a shelf of books on the wall, a collection of romances, science fiction, and mysteries. Samantha looked them over, then sighed.

"I'm sorry," she said. "None of these seem right for a little girl."

"I don't mind," Julie said. She pointed to a book with a ringed planet on its spine. "What's that one?"

Samantha took it down. It was a collection of short

stories by some of the greatest science-fiction writers of all times: Heinlein, Asimov, Bradbury, Clarke.

"I'll read a short one to you," she said.

They sat down on the bed together, and Samantha began to read. By the end of the ten-page story, Julie's eyes were closed. Samantha helped her under the covers. Then, as if she had done it every night, she bent over and kissed Julie's cheek. Julie sighed but did not awaken.

For a long time Samantha stood at her bedside. A twinge of worry began to knit inside of her, worry that perhaps she might become too attached to the child. In the few hours she'd known Julie, she'd come to feel very, very close to her. Was it more than the camaraderie of two victims? she wondered.

No matter, she had to do what was right.

She would call the police, no matter how difficult it was.

But she'd wait until morning to do it, because tonight she was too afraid.

6

AFTER HER ORDEAL the previous night, Rachel was relieved when Eric volunteered to drive the girls to their Saturday ballet class. The day had been rife with tension from the moment they woke up; Eric wanted to discuss what had happened, Rachel refused. Instead, she kept herself busy until it was time for Eric and their daughters to leave. She met them in the foyer downstairs, dressed in a multi-colored neon exercise outfit. Her softly waved brown hair was pulled up into a bun.

"I'm going to work out for an hour or two," she said. "I need something to push this tension from my muscles."

"Just be careful," Eric said.

"Oh, Eric," Rachel said, "I've been working out three times a week ever since you've known me."

"Yes, but . . ."

Rachel glanced down at the girls, then gave her husband a warning look. He silenced himself, and after a quick good-bye they all parted company.

The Frelengs' house was a large colonial, and a room in the back corner had been converted to a mini-gym. Rachel was an athletic woman, balancing the rather sedentary life of a musician with regular exercise. She headed now for their personal stairmaster. Within half an hour she was so deep in concentration that she did not hear Eric return. When he tapped her on the arm, she gasped in surprise.

"Sorry!" he called over the din of the machine's levers and pulleys. "There's someone here to see you."

Rachel stopped pumping.

"It's Nina Blair," Eric said. "You know, the social worker who comes down to the high school on occasion?"

Rachel grabbed for a towel and wiped the sweat from the back of her neck.

"What does she want with me?" she asked.

"She said she wanted to discuss something with both of us," Eric replied.

Nina was waiting on the black-and-floral chintz couch in the living room. She looked up at them with glassy brown eyes, a small-boned woman with lackluster hair. Rachel had often thought she'd be a perfect Agnes Gooch if the school's Faculty Players ever put on a production of *Mame*.

"Hello, Mrs. Blair," Rachel said. "What can I do for you?"

Nina stood up.

"Oh, Mrs. Freleng," she said, "I've come to ask for a very, very big favor. If you say no, I'll understand, but please listen to everything before you make a decision."

"Sit down," Eric said as he and Rachel took seats on the opposite couch.

"A few nights ago," Nina said, "the police brought a black boy of about ten years old to the Children's Shelter. He'd been wandering alone down 315 South. When I spoke to him for a while, I knew you would be the perfect family to take him in for a few days."

Eric shook his head.

"I don't understand," he said. "Where is this child's family? And why on earth would you pick us—out of all the people in Columbus—to take him in?"

"That's the trouble," Nina said. "We don't know who his family is. The child is suffering from amnesia and remembers only a little of his past. But wait until you hear why I decided to take a chance that you might have room for him. Mr. Freleng, it would only be for a few days, and a sensitive, talented child like Steven shouldn't be kept in an institution. This child is the most musically gifted boy I have ever heard in my life. I thought . . . I thought that perhaps, through Mrs. Freleng's own musical talents, you could help him open up."

Rachel was silent for a few moments. A strange sense of *déjà vu* washed over her, chilling her to the bone. She'd had this conversation before, but when? Consciously she was certain she'd never heard about a child named Steven. And yet . . .

"Where . . . where is the boy now?" she asked softly.

"Rachel . . ." Eric cautioned.

"He's at the shelter," Nina said. "You could pick him up this afternoon."

Eric held up both hands. "Wait a minute! We haven't agreed to this!"

"Oh, Eric," Rachel said, "Mrs. Blair said it would only be for a few days. And we have so much room here."

Nina turned to Eric, her eyes moist.

"I know how busy you must be with two little girls," she said. "I'm asking an awful lot from you, but I'm sure you'll be rewarded. Steven is a good boy, I can tell. He'll be no trouble at all."

"But what about . . . ?"

"Eric, please!"

Rachel's tone was almost begging. It was so unlike her that Eric frowned. Rachel had never made such a snap decision before.

"What about Tati and Olivia?" he asked. "Have you thought what they'll feel like, having a perfect stranger enter our home?"

"Oh, Eric, stop it," Rachel snapped. "He's a ten-year-old boy. Nina thinks we can help him, and if you ask me, it's high time we shared some of our good fortune."

Nina was silent, looking from one to the other. She could tell Eric wasn't at all happy with the idea, but there was a steely determination in Rachel's eyes that promised she'd win in the end. It was almost as if someone else had come here to prepare her for Steven's arrival.

"Okay, okay," Eric said. "If it's only for a few days, I suppose I can put up with it."

"Thank you!" Rachel said, throwing her arms around him.

"Thank you, Mr. Freleng," Nina said, relief in her tone. "I'll be in touch."

Nina drove through Columbus in a sort of fugue, some inborn homing device keeping her eyes on the road when her mind was elsewhere. She'd been like this for several days now, losing bits and pieces of time. Nina was a mousy-looking woman, but she'd always been an efficient one. Blacking out was devastating, and embarrassing. It was not until she was in downtown Columbus, passing the relatively congested area of One Nation Plaza, that something snapped. The blare of a horn behind her made her realize she hadn't moved when the light turned green.

She gripped the steering wheel and forced her eyes on the road ahead. She had to get hold of herself!

Well, she reasoned, she probably had a lot on her mind. After all, placing Steven with the Frelengs had been her idea, and if it went wrong, it would cost her her job.

Nina had lived on a farm outside the city limits since childhood. She had been alone there ever since her mother had died. When she got home, she was grateful to be in comfortable, familiar surroundings. She parked her car and looked around at the barn and silo, the rusting old tractor, the broken-down hay wagon. None of these things had been in use for fifteen years. Her father had done most of the farmwork, and when he died her mother had not kept up with it. None of the fields bore crops, and all of the animals had been sold through the years. All but one—Nina's Appaloosa horse.

She went to Miracle's stall now, took down a brush, and began to stroke his spotted hide.

"Let's take a ride, Mir," she said. "I need to clear my head."

Usually nothing would have worked better to get her thoughts in order than a brisk ride over the grass that grew tall and wild on her land. But she was no more than halfway across the acreage when Miracle suddenly reared up, whinnying in panic. Nina gripped the reins and called to him.

"Whoa! Easy, Miracle! Whoa!"

But the horse kept backing away in fear.

"What is it? Is it a fox?"

Nina steered the horse around and galloped away. Almost at once the animal calmed down, as if it knew it was out of danger. Nina left him in his paddock, then headed back across the field to see if she could find out what had frightened him so much.

The grass was waist-high in places, the result of her having neither the time nor the desire to trim it down. Nina followed the path her horse's hooves had made until she came to the spot where Miracle had panicked. There was nothing to be seen. But when she walked about four yards farther, she came across something half-buried in the ground. Nina walked over to it and knelt down. It was a box shaped something like a canoe, and she was certain she had never seen it before. She stared at the jagged surface of the wood.

Something was staring back at her.

She gasped, and the odd black eyes that had locked with hers were instantly gone.

"A field mouse," she told herself.

Nina ran her hands over the rough wood. Instantly an image of Steven came to her mind. She sensed this thing had something to do with that little boy. Perhaps, if she looked carefully, she would find an explanation for what had been happening to her these past few days.

She noticed a little door on the front of the box. Maybe there was something inside that would help. She worked at it until, finally, it popped open. Something dark and green came oozing out.

Nina pulled her hand back with a cry of disgust, slightly shaking the box. The action caused another panel to come off. This time, there was nothing inside that she could see. She looked into the small black void. In a few moments something within it began to glow bright and orange. The light drew her to itself, as unrelenting as a magnet pulling steel. Nina leaned closer to the newly opened panel, peering in at the orange glow. It smelled strangely, at first like almond extract, then flowery, and finally like nothing she'd ever experienced. She felt very warm all of a sudden.

She felt a strange tingling all over her skin; she ignored it. The tingling grew more intense, until finally she had to acknowledge pain. With a cry, Nina fell forward. She hurt, badly, all over. It was as if she had been burned.

She looked at the hand where the green ooze had touched her skin.

But there was no skin.

Nina stared down at her arms and hands. Instead of skin, she could see glistening bloody flesh.

Nina began to scream, but in that vast field no one heard her. She tried desperately to run back to her house. It was just a nightmare! She couldn't even remember how she'd gotten here! It wasn't real! The pain wasn't real! She had skin!

Her legs gave out, and she fell to the ground. Tips of bone protruded through the ends of the fingers that grabbed for the weeds.

Nina Blair was disappearing.

7

SOME CHILDREN ARE awakened by the sound of birds singing outside their windows. Lorraine dreamed of birds, strange birds with multicolored feathers, but it was the squeal of a garbage truck's brakes that awakened her. Her first sight was a dingy beige wall. The bed she had slept on felt lumpy. For a few minutes the little girl didn't move; she was bewildered by her surroundings. Then slowly she began to recall the previous night. She remembered the gang, the deserted streets, and Bettina.

Lorraine had spent the night in an old appliance box. Her "bed" was a pile of old clothes.

Rubbing her eyes with chubby fists, Lorraine sat up. She pushed a ragged coat off herself and crawled out of the box. Rising to her feet, she gazed out the litter-strewn alley at the people who were walking by.

There was no sign of the old woman. Her two suitcases were propped against the inside back of the box. She found herself too hungry to think about checking to be certain the money was still there. Instead, she plunked herself down on an upturned box and buried her face in her hands. She was a pathetic little sight, a small child in the midst of all that filth, but no one turned to look at her.

Presently she felt a hand on top of her head.

"Here, now, child," a voice said, "did you think old Bettina had deserted you?"

Lorraine looked up to see the woman standing before her, a white paper bag held tightly in one fist. She opened it and pulled out a buttered bagel and a pint of milk. Lorraine accepted them and ate as if she were starved.

"I talked to Jesus last night," Bettina said, pulling another crate to sit beside her, "and he told me it'd be all

35

right just to borrow some money from your suitcase. I went to the Y and had a shower. This morning, while you slept, I got rid of my old rags and bought this dress from a street vendor."

Lorraine sucked hard at the straw, making gurgling noises as the milk disappeared.

"That's a nice dress," she said. "And I don't mind at all that you borrowed some money."

Bettina smiled.

"You're sweet," she said. "It isn't that I don't have good intentions. We're going to have to find a better place to live, and there's no hotel that's gonna rent to a ragged old bag lady."

She paused for a moment, her vision seeming to focus on a delivery truck that had parked at the curb. Finally she spoke again.

"Well, you work on your breakfast," she said. "Then we'll dress you up and look for a room."

"Are you going to help me find my family?"

"Of course," Bettina said. "But we have to have a place to stay in the meantime, don't we? It isn't proper for a little girl to live on the streets."

Lorraine nodded and finished her breakfast. Bettina opened the suitcase with clothes in it and found a yellow T-shirt dress for the child to wear. There was a pair of yellow barrettes to match, and a hairbrush. The child stood quietly as Bettina fixed her hair.

Lorraine, Bettina noted, wasn't exactly a pretty child. But there was *something* about her. Her almond eyes were a queer gray-green color, and seemed to be watching everything very carefully. Her hair was the blackest Bettina had ever seen on a white child. There was still baby fat clinging to her, and her small teeth were smooth along the edges—an indication they were still baby teeth. For this reason, Bettina guessed that she wasn't quite six years old.

They spent the morning looking for a place to stay. The desk clerk stared at Lorraine in such a way that the child instinctively felt he was not to be trusted. She took Bettina's hand.

"Don't pay attention to him," Bettina said as they climbed the stairs. "You ignore him, and don't talk to anyone else either."

"Why?" Lorraine asked. "What if someone knows me and can help me find my family?"

Bettina gave her head a rough shake.

"No one in this neighborhood would know a nice little girl like you," she said. "You leave finding your family up to me. I'll call the police as soon as we're settled."

Bettina pushed into the apartment. It was a studio, with a minimal amount of furniture. There was a small kitchen at the back. Bettina found that the refrigerator had been unplugged and opened it to air it out. As Lorraine stood near the door, she checked the sofa.

"Sleeper," Bettina said. "Big enough for two. You've probably slept in better, but at least you won't be on the street tonight."

She bent closer to it, wondering if there were bugs hidden inside the foam cushions. She didn't mention this out loud; no point scaring the child.

"Well, we'll need a few things to make this place livable," she said.

"Are we going to stay very long?"

There was such worry in the child's voice that Bettina knew at once what her thoughts were. She probably wondered why the old woman wasn't calling the police right now. The truth was that only Bettina knew about the child. She hadn't told anyone, not her friends in the streets or at the homeless shelter. And as far as finding Lorraine's parents, well, what kind of monsters left a baby to wander the dangerous streets of the city? With a suitcase full of money, no less! Let them stew about her for a week. Maybe then, when Bettina brought her back, they'd appreciate the child.

"Of course not," she said at last. "Just until we find your folks. Now, let's check out that bathroom. I hope it's clean. . . ."

When she came out, she was surprised to see Lorraine on the sofa. The money suitcase was open next to her.

"We have one thousand, two hundred, and twenty dollars," Lorraine announced.

Bettina laughed. "How do you know?"

"I counted it," Lorraine said matter-of-factly.

"But, child!" Bettina cried. "You didn't have enough time. And you don't seem old enough to count that high."

"But I did," Lorraine answered.

"You just let Bettina have a look."

Sometime later, Bettina turned to the little girl with fascination in her expression.

"That's amazing."

"I guess I'm good with numbers," Lorraine said with a shrug.

"I guess you are," Bettina agreed in awe.

Lorraine began to fidget. "I'm hungry."

Bettina opened the other suitcase. found a sweater, and turned to put it on the child.

"We've had a long morning," she said. "And heaven knows when you last had a decent meal. But we can't spend a lot, you know. I know how fast money goes. I've been without a home for almost a year now."

"Really?" Lorraine asked in disbelief. "Did you lose your family too?"

Bettina laughed bitterly. "Yes, and good riddance to all of them. When my husband's business failed, no one came forward to help. It killed him. So they can all rot in . . ."

She saw the worried look on Lorraine's face and stopped herself.

"Don't fret about that," she said. "Come on. I know a nice Chinese restaurant with a special luncheon menu."

A short subway ride later, they walked through the red door of a restaurant called Jade Garden. Bettina had not been there since her husband's death. But today, wearing a clean new dress, she walked in with her head held high. Yes, there was a reason the Lord had sent Lorraine to her.

The maître d', a handsome middle-aged Chinese man in a black suit, smiled broadly as he greeted them.

"Mrs. Norwich," he said. "It's been a long time."

Bettina's grey eyebrows went up.

"You remember me?"

"Of course," said the Chinese. "I never forget anyone."

He looked down at the child with questioning eyes.

"Oh, this is my grandniece," Bettina lied. "Lorraine. She's visiting me."

"Welcome, little girl," the man said. "I'll show you to a table."

He handed them menus and walked away.

"Do you want me to read it to you?" Bettina asked.

"I can read," Lorraine said. "I'll have this."

She turned her menu around and pointed to an item. Bettina laughed.

"Lorraine, that's written in Chinese!"

Lorraine read the words out loud.

"It means 'chicken with peanuts', " she said.

Quickly Bettina thumbed through the extensive menu until she found the number that matched the Chinese translation. Sure enough, it described a dish with chicken and peanuts. She shook her head.

"I'm amazed," she said. "You count faster than anyone I've ever met, and you read Chinese. I wonder what else you can do."

"I don't know," Lorraine said. "But my family will tell me."

"When we find them," Bettina said noncommittally.

Their meal came and they enjoyed it immensely. When they were finished and had paid the bill, they said goodbye to the kind maître d' and left. With the lunch-hour rush behind them, the platform down in the subway was all but deserted. Bettina dropped two tokens in the turnstile and helped Lorraine push through. It was dark down here, all the lights dimmed by a coating of greasy dust. Bettina saw that the change booth was empty.

"When will the train come?" Lorraine asked, looking down the tracks into the dark tunnel.

"Any minute now," Bettina said. "Let's sit on that bench."

As they approached the seat, they suddenly heard a whooping holler. With amazing speed, like rats scurrying out of water pipes, nearly a dozen tough-looking hoods raced down the stairs and jumped over the turnstiles. Lorraine moved closer to Bettina, fear making her tremble.

"I saw them the other night!" she whispered. "They were in the street when I woke up!"

Bettina moved quickly.

"Hide under here," she said, pushing Lorraine off the seat.

Lorraine obeyed instantly. Bettina felt deep in her

pocket for the tape-wrapped knife blade she kept as a weapon.

"Yo! Bitch!" one boy yelled.

From her hiding place Lorraine heard the sound of running feet, yelling . . . and what seemed to be Bettina's screams. She curled herself up and wished it all to be a nightmare. It had to be, because she was certain she'd never been so scared.

They're gonna kill us!

Her young mind screamed in terror.

And suddenly a voice cut into her silent cries.

No! You're stronger! You can control them!

Lorraine opened her eyes. Where had the voice come from? There was no one looking under the bench. She could see only scuffling feet—most in sneakers, Bettina's pumps among them.

Close your eyes.

Bewildered, but too frightened to protest, the little girl did as the voice commanded. She realized now that it wasn't from outside, but from within her own mind.

Who . . . who're you?

My name is Marty. I'm here to help you, Lorraine.

You know my name!

I have heard you thinking it.

Bettina's screams brought the child back to reality. She didn't know how this strange voice came to be in her head, but she was too young to separate it as fantasy. To her the voice was very, very real.

Help me, Marty! I'm scared!

Crawl out from under the bench.

No!

You have to! It's the only way. Crawl out and look one of them straight in the eyes. You can control them!

Shaking all over, but almost powerless to resist the voice in her head, Lorraine crawled out from under the bench. She glanced quickly at Bettina, who lay unconscious on the platform.

Look at the biggest one!

Lorraine's head snapped up, her gray-green eyes as round as if she were in a trance. She found the biggest, most evil-looking member of the gang and fixed her gaze on him. He said something to her she didn't really hear or understand. With Marty's words encouraging her, she continued to stare at him. Another hood pulled out a knife and moved toward the child, but the big one snapped a commanding hand to keep him away.

"That's the little bitch we saw the other night," he said. "She's *mine*."

Just keep looking at him. Don't move. I'll help you.

Lorraine tried to draw strength from Marty's words.

Menacingly the big boy moved toward the little girl. Lorraine, though her knees were wobbling, held her ground.

Tell him he's a coward!

"You're a coward," Lorraine said in a grim little voice.

Some of the other boys laughed. But without warning or explanation, the big thug stopped in his tracks. His eyes widened and he screamed.

"No! No! Oh, shit, man! N-n-n-n-o-o-o-o!"

"Whazzamatter?" someone yelled.

None of the other kids could see anything.

The gang leader backed away in horror, his whole body going into convulsions of fear. It was as if he were seeing something that no one else could. He tripped over his untied shoelaces and landed hard on the platform, screaming and crawling away from Lorraine crab-style.

"What the hell's wrong with him?" someone shouted.

The boy rolled over on his stomach and began to retch. Humiliated, he dragged himself to his feet and wiped blood from his nose with the back of his hand.

"Let's get the hell out of here," he commanded.

"What're you so afraid of, Royce?"

"Shut up!" Royce screamed, pushing through the revolving gate and running upstairs.

The other gang members followed, and the subway platform was silent once more.

Lorraine fell to her knees and began to cry.

It's over. You stopped them.

I don't understand what I did.

You brought out his worst, deepest emotion—fear. He's been humiliated. He'll never bother you again.

Who are you, Marty? Where do you come from?

I can only tell you the name they gave me. Marty. The less you know, the safer you'll be. When the time is right, when everything is ready, I'll contact you. I have to go now. You stay with the old woman. She won't harm you.

Don't go away! Please, I'm so scared!

But her mind was a blank. As clearly as she had heard the boy speak, she now heard only silence. After a moment, though, she opened her eyes to the sound of moaning. Bettina was pulling herself to her feet, holding her head. Lorraine ran to help her.

"Are . . . are you okay, child?"

"Uh-huh," Lorraine confirmed with a nod. "But you're hurt!"

Bettina fished through the pockets of her coat until she found a handkerchief. She pressed it to her head.

"Bettina . . ."

Bettina turned to the child.

"Just a little blood," she said. "I wasn't really passed out, you know. It was a trick to make 'em stop. I didn't dare open my eyes. But what was that kid screaming about?"

Lorraine didn't really know the answer to that, so she simply shook her head.

"I want to go home," she said.

Bettina took her hand. At that moment a train rumbled into the station. Together they got on board.

Bettina did not even look at the transit cop who was riding in the car.

8

SAMANTHA'S HOUSE had been built a hundred years earlier by the owner of a mining company. It was situated on two and a half acres at the base of the Sangre de Cristo Range. Much of this was wooded, but a small yard had been cleared behind the house. Springtime brought lavender wisteria blooms, dripping over the surrounding split-rail fence, pink blossoms on a flowering Japanese cherry tree, and countless bright tulips and daffodils. This bright morning, the array of colors and scents seemed to give the yard the charming effect of a secret garden.

"Oh, it's so pretty out here!" Julie cried as they walked toward the kennel. "So many beautiful flowers! Do you know the names?"

"Some of them," Samantha said. "But not all. We could probably get a field guide, if you'd like."

Julie nodded eagerly.

"It smells so good!"

Samantha breathed in deeply. The scented air was calming, and yet somehow the contrast between this natural beauty and the troubles she was having made her situation all the more difficult to handle.

She opened the kennel and let the dogs out for a run. Immediately they circled around Julie, licking her hands and wagging their tails. Julie picked up a stick and threw it. Sunday raced ahead of Lady, grabbed it, and brought it back. Lady, however, had started down a path that cut through the nearby trees.

"Where does that go?" Julie asked.

"That's a surprise," Samantha said, pushing her worries aside for the moment. "You follow it and see."

The path was a narrow one, inlaid with odd-shaped pieces of bluestone. Lavender and white columbine grew up in the cracks, and tall yellow pines sheltered it from the sun. At its end, tucked into a clearing, was a tiny adobe-style house.

"Oh!"

"Isn't it cute?" Samantha asked. "It's the reason I fell in love with this property. I'm told the first owners built it for their children, a hundred years ago."

Julie didn't hear her. She had already run up to the Lilliputian dwelling and was through the wooden door before Samantha could catch up with her. There was one room inside, empty now except for a few forgotten flowerpots and a battered old trunk. The walls had been painted white, and several niches had been cut for shelves. Two small windows were situated to either side of the front door, and each remaining wall had one window. A loft had been molded into the back wall, and there was a fireplace in one corner, decorated with an Indian motif.

"We'll clean it up for you," Samantha said. "And we'll get some furniture, and toys . . ."

Something in the sensible part of her brain told her to stop acting as if Julie was going to be here forever. But she pushed it aside, as she had tried to push away the idea of reporting Julie to the police.

"Well," she said, "you have fun. There's a trunk back there with some old dishes and things if you want to play pretend. I've got to catch up on some chores before I go back to work tomorrow."

Julie nodded. "Okay."

The first thing Samantha planned to do was groom the dogs. But when she opened the door and called to them, they refused to budge from Julie's side.

"Sunday, Lady, come on!" she called. "I want to brush your fur."

The dogs whimpered, and Lady moved a little closer to Julie.

"I think they want to stay with me," she said.

"I think you're right," Samantha said in wonder.

She left the child and the dogs, shaking her head. She'd had those dogs for five years, and never before had they refused to come to her.

Leaving the dogs to be groomed later, she went to her office to catch up on some files she'd been meaning to organize. When lunchtime came around, Julie returned to the house with a bouquet of wildflowers.

"Aren't those pretty?" Samantha said.

"For you," Julie said, handing them to her.

As she came into the office, she noticed a human skeleton hanging in one corner.

"Oh, look at him!"

"He isn't real," Samantha admitted. "I couldn't afford a real human skeleton. But he's an exact life-size replica. Isn't he something?"

Instantly the names of the bones came into Samantha's mind: *mandible, maxilla.*

"That's his mandible, and that's his maxilla," Julie said. She pointed to the lower arm. "This is the ulna and the radius and the . . ."

"How do you know all this?" Samantha asked with surprise. It was almost as if Julie had read her mind.

Julie turned to look at her. "How come I remember things like bones, but I don't remember where I came from?"

"Sometimes memory loss is like that," Samantha said. "But obviously someone went to the trouble of teaching you. I have an anatomy coloring book that a young patient gave me. Do you want to use it?"

"Sure!"

Samantha took down the coloring book. She set Julie up at her desk with colored pencils and soon the child was busy at work.

Strange how she'd come to be with a kid who had an interest in anatomy when she herself was a doctor. Was it just coincidence? she wondered.

Samantha knew the right thing to do. She *had* to call the police. Surely what had happened in the motel was just a moment of anxiety, perhaps brought on by whatever had made her lose her memory.

"Have fun," she said, patting Julie's shoulder. Then she left the room and headed for the kitchen telephone. This time, she wouldn't be stopped. This time, she'd dial the number, and she'd talk to Ari. No anxiety attacks, no backing down.

She settled onto one of the three-legged stools lined up along her kitchen counter, then reached up for the phone. There was a sticker on the receiver, with the numbers of the police and fire departments printed in bold black letters. Just seven numbers. Easy enough to dial.

She couldn't do it. She got as far as putting her finger on the first button, but as soon as she pressed it down, a pain began to grow within her stomach. It started as a slightly cold feeling, then grew until it became so unbearable she started to tremble all over. She watched the receiver, waiting for it to become monstrous. For a moment she was completely mesmerized by the black plastic. But she caught hold of herself and threw the hateful thing the way someone might brush off a hideous spider. It bounced once against the red counter and swung back and forth like a hanged man.

I can't do this. I can't! I'm too afraid!

She grabbed for the edge of the counter, gripping it to steady herself. Beneath her, her trembling body was actually making the stool quake. She shut her eyes, trying desperately to get control of herself.

She could feel the room spinning. It was like being on a very scary ride in an amusement park, feeling yourself being thrown around instead of seeing the ride in motion, because you are too afraid to open your eyes. There was no controlling it. Samantha could only hold fast to the counter and pray the feeling would soon pass. She felt tears streaming down her tightly shut eyes as her body continued to tremble.

She thought she was going to die.

"Look what I did!"

With the sound of that sweet young voice, Samantha's ordeal came to an end. Everything was still once more. Continuing to hold fast to the counter, afraid to let go, she opened her eyes and breathed in deeply. There was no time to wonder about the anxiety attack, because Julie was crossing the kitchen to her. Quickly she dried her eyes.

"I colored this picture," Julie said. "I picked it out because some blood is red and some is blue and I like those colors."

Slowly, barely hearing what the child was saying, Samantha took the anatomy coloring book and looked at the picture the child had colored. She braved a smile, not wanting Julie to know something was wrong. There was still an ice cube in the pit of her stomach. She could see the phone receiver from the corner of her eye, but she didn't reach to hang it up.

"Did I do it right?"

"Huh?"

Julie pointed at the coloring book.

"Did I get the colors right?"

Samantha tried to concentrate on the child's picture, forcing away the coldness she felt inside. For a moment she merely stared at the page without really seeing it. But when at last her eyes focused, her mouth dropped open in amazement. Not only had the child colored an extremely detailed picture without flaw, she had also chosen the proper shades. She'd chosen red for the arteries and blue for the veins, and hadn't mixed them up!

"How . . . ?"

Julie took the book away from her.

"I'd like to color another picture," she said. "Okay?"

"Sure," Samantha said. "Sure, you go right ahead."

Julie skipped out of the room. Samantha watched her go, wondering what to make of her. She couldn't begin to figure the child out, let alone the situation in which they had both found themselves. She couldn't bear living inside a mystery a moment longer. She had to talk to someone!

And if she couldn't call the police, there was someone she could call: Barbara Huston.

For a moment Samantha hesitated to pick up the fallen receiver. Then she grabbed it, and as soon as she realized it hadn't burned her, she began to dial Barbara's number. After a few rings Barbara's answering machine picked up the line. Samantha left a message.

"Barbara, it's Samantha and I'm in trouble. I think I was kidnapped last night, and—"

Another voice cut in, more animated than the first. "Hold on! Hold on!"

There was a click, and then the real Barbara came on the line.

"It's me!" Barbara said. "I was just screening my calls. I've been getting a barrage of calls from people trying to sell me things. Now, explain this to me. You think you were kidnapped?"

Samantha related what she could remember, beginning

with her ride home and ending with finding Julie in the
motel room. Barbara made some thinking noises, then
said:

"The last thing you remember before waking up is
being in your garage?"

"Sort of," Samantha said. "I get a feeling something
happened to me when I got out of the truck, but it's not
clear."

"Have you tried calling the police?"

"Of course I have," Samantha said. "Sheriff Sirtos is
a friend, you know. But every time I attempt to dial that
number, something terrible happens to me. This overwhelming sense of panic takes hold of me, and for a few
moments I'm too frightened to even move."

"Of what?"

"Of calling the police, I guess," Samantha said. "I
don't know! I've never been afraid of anyone in my life."

For a moment, thoughts of her mother threatened to
make a liar of her. She *had* been afraid of that woman.
But that was beside the point now.

"Anyway," she went on, "I'm stuck here with a little
girl who can't remember her past. The only thing she can
figure is that a man named Mr. Henley brought her to
that motel room. Apparently I signed some papers making me Julie's legal guardian."

Barbara was silent for a moment.

"Do you still have those papers?" she asked.

"Sure I do," Samantha said. "I'm holding on to them
for dear life, because if this kid's family ever does show
up, it may be the only thing that saves me from a kidnapping charge. Barbara, what am I going to do? Julie can't
remember where she came from, and every time I try to
call the police, something stops me."

"Samantha, can I say something to you?" Barbara inquired. "As a caring friend?"

"Sure . . ." Samantha was doubtful.

"Well, you know you've had problems in your life,"
Barbara said. "Considering the kind of childhood you
had, couldn't it be possible that something has . . . well
'snapped'? Could it be possible you *did* kidnap this
child?"

"Barbara, I would never . . . !"

She could almost see Barbara holding up a hand.

"Wait. I'm not making accusations. It's just something to consider. For lack of a better phrase, maybe there was a moment of 'temporary insanity' that made you snatch this kid."

"From a hundred miles away?"

"I can't explain that," Barbara said. "All I can suggest is that you keep her to yourself until you do some research. Look, the kid herself doesn't seem to remember where she came from. So she may be as much of a victim of a hoax as you. But you have to be certain."

"I don't want to go to jail," Samantha said, almost to herself.

"Then find out where Julie is really from," Barbara said.

Samantha thought for a few moments.

"This may sound crazy," she said, "but I'm growing very attached to this little girl. She's so much like me! It's almost like we were meant to be together, and yet I know she'll eventually have to go back to her own family."

"And that bothers you?"

Samantha began to twist the phone cord.

"A little," she said.

In truth, it bothered her a lot, though she couldn't say why. After all, Julie wasn't her child, not even a relation or a friend. She hardly knew her. But somehow she felt protective of her.

"Julie is too intelligent to be lost in the shuffle of the system," she said at last. "They'd put her in some institution until her family was found. I don't think it would benefit her. No, I'm going to have to handle this in some other way."

"When do you plan to do all this?" Barbara asked. "When's your next shift?"

"Monday afternoon," she said. "So you can see I don't have a lot of time to deal with this. I certainly can't bring Julie to the hospital with me."

"Why not?" Barbara asked. "The way you described her, she sounds like a miniature doctor already. A sort of female Doogie Howser."

Samantha laughed. "Well, I guess I'll do what I have to. It's my last day before vacation, so I'm sure no one will mind her being there. Oh, I hear her coming back now. I'll have to hang up. Good-bye, Barbara."

She set the receiver back on its hook and turned to Julie with a smile. The smile quickly faded when she saw the look on Julie's face. Her face was drawn, her eyes glazed over. Beads of sweat had broken out on her forehead.

"Julie!"

"I . . . I had another bad dream," Julie said. "I fell asleep drawing."

Samantha went to take the child in her arms.

"You shouldn't be falling asleep so much," she said. "You're too young."

Dear Lord, she thought, on top of everything else don't let this child get sick on me!

She felt her forehead and took a close look at her.

"You don't seem to have a fever," she said. "But let me check you out. Come back to my office. I've got my medical bag in there."

In the office she sat Julie down on a comfortable chair and began to check her over very carefully. By now the child's color had come back to her and her eyes had cleared. Everything else about her was normal, as far as Samantha could tell.

"Maybe you're just worn out from this ordeal," Samantha said, tucking her stethoscope back into her bag. "But if this happens again, I'm taking you over to the hospital for further tests."

Julie looked up at her, wide-eyed.

"Tests? I don't want to have any tests! They'll hurt!"

"Well, maybe there'll be a little prick for the blood test," Samantha said honestly. "But it won't be too bad. I'll be right there, and—"

"No!" Julie screamed, jumping up from the chair. "No! No more tests!"

She ran from the room, then from the house, screaming this over and over. Samantha watched her through the window as she headed toward the path to the playhouse. Chills ran through her as she wondered what sort of hell the child had been through to make her so terrified.

Out on the path, Julie raced toward the relative sanctuary of the little adobe. She didn't know what she was

going to do there, or why it made her feel safe. Lady
and Sunday, thinking it was a game, barked playfully and
followed her to the building. Julie seemed unaware of
them. She huddled up against the toy chest and buried
her face in her knees. Her whole body shook with fear.
She didn't want to go to any hospital! She didn't want
anyone doing more tests on her!

Befuddled, wondering if the running game was over,
the dogs whimpered and nudged her. Absently Julie
began to stroke Lady's fur.

For a few moments she just sat there, her mind a flood
of unconnected thoughts. But after a while she began to
calm down, and to think as reasonably as a young girl
could. She was afraid of tests, so that meant someone
had actually done tests on her. But why? Who had done
them? Was it the man she kept seeing in her "dreams"?

It hadn't really been a dream that sent her out of Samantha's office. It had been a kind of vision, a picture
of being forced into a little box.

Sunday's warm tongue washed her small hand. But he
stopped suddenly, making Julie open her eyes to see
what was wrong.

Somehow, she wasn't in the playhouse anymore. The
dogs had also vanished. She stood in a long hallway. It
stretched without end into a dark oblivion that seemed
to hide all sorts of childish nightmares. Julie looked at
the door she was standing before and read "NO ADMIT-
TANCE" on the brass plate. Now she heard footsteps approaching. Suddenly a voice bellowed:

"What are you doing here?"

With a silent gasp, Julie swung around, and found herself nose-to-chest with a strange creature. It was shaped
like a man, but all covered up by a helmeted white suit.
She backed away in fear, thinking he looked like some
kind of outer-space creature.

"I asked you a question," the man said. His voice
sounded strange from behind the black visor of his
helmet.

He made a grab for her, but she turned and ran away
as fast as she could.

"Get back here!" bellowed the man in white.

And then there was another voice. Someone she
couldn't see was calling to her. He had a young voice,

one filled with kindness. Carefully Julie stopped and turned. The corridor was gone now. All that remained was a soft blue light that obliterated any possible view. In the distance she could see a shape that was vaguely like a young person's.

"Don't be afraid of him," a boy said in a kind voice that immediately reassured Julie. "He can't hurt you."

"Who . . . where . . . ?"

"The 'who' is Marty," the boy said. His silhouette opened out its arms and turned a slow circle. "The 'where' is . . . well, I'm not sure. I don't remember being brought here, or where I was before. It's a building of some kind, with labs and strange rooms. They do tests here. They think I'm sleeping now. They don't know when I walk around."

Julie gazed at the blueness.

"I don't see anything at all," she said.

"That's because *you're* not really here," Marty told her. "I am, but you're not. Only your mind is here. I heard you screaming—"

"I didn't scream."

"You screamed in your mind," Marty insisted. "That's why I heard you. Somehow, we can talk with our minds."

"We? Who are 'we'?"

"I don't know," Marty said. "But there are others like us, I'm sure. We *need* each other, or we'll never stop what is happening here."

"What do you mean 'like us'?" Julie answered. "I'm not 'like' anything!"

"Oh, yes you are," Marty insisted. "You're special."

"I am not!" Julie cried, suddenly as fearful of this soft-spoken boy as she was of the creature in white. "And I'm not going to listen to you. You aren't real! You're just a vision!"

"I'm as real as you," Marty said. "You'll see. You'll see. You need me."

"I *don't!*"

Instantly the blue dissolved away, like dissipating clouds. Julie found herself in the playhouse once more. For a few moments she studied her surroundings to make sure she was really here. The dogs backed away from her, hackles risen stiffly. Julie regarded them, wondering what they had seen. Then she raced back up to the house, suddenly needing the comfort of Samantha's presence.

In her office, Samantha had had a sudden feeling that Julie was in danger. She had closed her eyes to bring about a sense of reason, but instead had seen the frightening image of a man in a white cleanroom suit chasing her young friend. Trusting her instincts, she went looking for the child. The moment she entered the kitchen, Julie walked in the door.

"Are . . . are you all right?" Samantha asked uncertainly.

How do you tell a child about instincts?

Julie shook her head.

"I'm scared, Samantha," she said. "I'm really scared."

Samantha opened her arms and Julie ran to hug her. At the moment, there was no need for words.

9

As SOON AS Nina had gone, Rachel left the living room to go upstairs and take a shower. Eric followed her, shaking his head.

"I'm overwhelmed," he said. "I can't believe what we just did."

"We agreed to help a little boy in trouble," Rachel said, stopping at the foot of the stairs. "I know it was a quick decision, but I feel really good about it. Don't you?"

Eric wasn't exactly sure how he felt, but he smiled for his wife. Rachel wasn't given to making snap decisions, so if she felt in her heart this was the right thing to do, well, then, it was.

He followed her up the stairs. Her exercise clothes showed off her body very well, and he couldn't help admiring her. She was a beautiful woman, with the most perfect face and body he'd ever seen. There didn't seem to be a single flaw in her. And her beauty was complete, mental and spiritual as well as physical. She'd certainly proved that a few minutes ago by opening up her home to a needy stranger.

"Have a good workout this morning?" he asked.

"I ended earlier than expected," she said, "but I feel good. Are you going to pick up the girls?"

"I just wanted to comb my hair," Eric said.

"You just wanted to see me in the buff," Rachel teased as she got undressed.

He made grab for her, but she laughed and disappeared into the bathroom.

"I'm all sweaty!" she cried. "You go on and get the girls!"

Eric moaned, but turned to leave. It was a relief to see Rachel smiling again, after what had happened last night. Maybe it was a blessing that Nina had showed up on their doorstep that particular morning. With her mind on a new "member" of the family, Rachel might be able to forget about it.

By the time Rachel had showered and dressed, Eric was home again. Tatiana came racing up the stairs.

"Mommy!" she cried. "What's the news? Daddy says we have news!"

Eric and Olivia caught up with her.

Olivia stood back and observed this with twinkling eyes, keeping as much dignity as an eight-year-old could muster.

"We're going to get you a brother," Eric said.

"Oh, my," Olivia said in awe. "Mama, are you gonna have a baby?"

Rachel laughed.

"No," she said. "We're going to take a little boy into our home and care for him for a while. You see, he's lost his family, and until the police can find them, it's best he lives in a real home."

Tatiana frowned worriedly.

"How did he lose them, Mommy?" she asked.

"No one really knows," Rachel told her. "He has a little trouble remembering. But maybe we can help him. What do you say?"

"I'd like a brother," Olivia said. "How old is he?"

"Nine or ten," Rachel said. "His name is Steven. Right now, that's all I know about him."

"Nine or ten," Olivia repeated. "That would make him a *big* brother, wouldn't it? My friend Laurie has a big brother and he always teases her."

"Well, don't judge Steven until you meet him," Rachel said.

"When, Mommy?" Tatiana asked. "When?"

Rachel looked at Eric as if to ask the same question.

"Nina said we could pick him up this afternoon," Eric said.

"I'll call and make an appointment after brunch," Rachel said. "Come on, guys. I smell crepes suzette."

Tatiana got to the dining room first, with Olivia walking just in front of her parents. When they entered, Tati was bounding around the housekeeper and telling her about the little boy.

"We're taking in a foster child," Eric explained. "A ten-year-old named Steven."

Helga gasped, throwing up her arms. "And what am I to do with a boy?"

She exited the dining room, where she'd laid out platters of wonderful brunch food, then came back with a pitcher of orange juice. The Freleng family enjoyed their meal, talking excitedly about the new addition to their family. When they were finished, Rachel got up to make a phone call to Children's Services, while the girls went off to play and Eric opened a copy of the *Dispatch*.

A few minutes later, Rachel came back into the dining room.

"We're set up for one o'clock," she said.

At one o'clock that afternoon Mr. and Mrs. Eric Freleng sat in an office at Children's Services, nervously anticipating their first meeting with Steven. The woman who came out to help them had a friendly smile and seemed very pleased with their presence.

"We were expecting Nina Blair," Rachel said. "She came to our house this morning to talk to us."

"Nina told me all about you," Kathy Mayer said. "I'm so thrilled that Steven will be going into such a fine home. But I'm also surprised she went directly to your house. We usually do all our initial work from here. And Nina hasn't shown up for work yet. That's not like her."

Kathy seemed worried, but Rachel hardly heard her. She was more concerned about meeting Steven.

"When do we see the boy?" she asked eagerly.

"The children are just finishing lunch," Kathy said. "He'll be brought out shortly."

They entered the office, where Kathy offered them seats. She sat behind a desk, took out a folder, and opened it.

"Steven's been with us for three days," she read. "We don't have a last name on him. I don't know how much Nina told you . . ."

"I know he's lost his memory," Rachel offered. "And I know he's nine or ten years old."

"That's correct," Kathy said. "He's a quiet, shy boy, but I have a feeling there's quite a little mind inside that head. Keeping him in an institutional setting is wrong.

Nina was adamant that we move him as soon as possible."

Eric leaned forward, folding his hands on the desktop. "Just a question," he said. "Doesn't it usually take a long time to process these children? Don't we have to go through some kind of screening?"

"Nina recommended you highly," Kathy said. "That would be good enough for me. And since it is only temporary, I see no reason to make a big production out of it."

She shoved a paper across the desk. "Now, let's see about signing these forms . . ."

Rachel thought the session would never end. She didn't care about forms or legal mumbo jumbo. She only cared about meeting her new "son." At last there was a knock on the door and a grandmotherly woman poked her head in.

"Steven's ready," she said. "Everything okay in here?"

"Bring him in, Dorothy," Kathy said.

The door opened farther and in stepped a wisp of a boy. His hair was a little too short, indicating it had been freshly cut. Small hips did nothing to keep his pants up around his waist, and a thin line of white underwear showed over the waistband. He wore a neon-print T-shirt and seemed to be completely absorbed in his red high-top sneakers, because he never took his eyes off them.

"Come on in, Steven," Kathy said. "Don't be afraid. I want you to meet Mr. and Mrs. Freleng."

"Hi, Steven," Rachel said, encouragement in her voice.

"H'lo," Steven mumbled.

He was a handsome child, she noted, with large brown eyes and a small straight nose. His skin was coffee-and-cream-colored like her own. Maybe, if she'd had a son, he might have looked just like Steven.

"We'd like you to stay with us for a while," Rachel said.

"I think you'll enjoy living with the Frelengs," Kathy said. "Would you like them to take care of you until your family comes for you?"

Steven nodded eagerly. Then suddenly he ran to Rachel and threw his arms around her waist. Rachel hugged

him back, looking over him at Eric. She was smiling like
a woman who had just found a long-lost son.

Eric turned to Kathy.

"If all the papers are in order," he said, "then we'd
like to take Steven home."

"We sure would," Rachel said with an eager nod.

Kathy smiled. "You're all set. We'll be calling you in
a day or so to check up on your progress. And of course,
if anything turns up regarding his identification, we'll call
immediately."

"Of course," Eric said.

Kathy wished them luck, and soon they were on their
way. Steven sat in the front seat between Eric and Rachel. Rachel kept an arm across the back of the seat, as
if to protect the young boy.

"I'm so excited," she said, her gray-green eyes sparkling. "We're going to have so much fun together."

"You bet," Eric agreed. "We've got a huge backyard,
and there are lots of kids your age in the neighborhood."

Rachel looked up at her husband.

"One thing at a time, Eric," she said. "Steven doesn't
need to be bombarded with other kids."

"I'd like to make new friends," Steven said in a soft
voice.

"So you can talk," Eric teased.

Rachel shot him a dirty look, but he was too busy
watching the road to notice. A short time later they
pulled up in the driveway of their house. Two little faces
were peering through the beveled-glass door. As soon as
Eric stopped the car, the door swung wide open and the
girls came running out.

"What's your name?" Tati asked Steven as he exited
the car. "How old are you? Do you know how to play
baseball?"

"Tati, let him get settled in before you bombard him!"
Rachel cried.

"*I* know his name is Steven," Olivia said. "You forgot,
Tati."

"I did not!" Tati protested. "I just wanted to hear him
say it!"

Steven watched all this with huge eyes. It was not exactly a look of fear, but there was apprehension in his

face. He felt Rachel's reassuring hand on his shoulder and moved a step closer to her.

"Don't let Tati overwhelm you," Rachel said with a laugh. "She's just very excited to meet you. Tatiana, Olivia, this is Steven."

"Hi, Steven," Olivia said politely.

"You have a nice haircut," Tati said, pointing.

Olivia pushed her sister's hand down firmly.

"Don't point."

Steven ran his fingers through his dark hair.

"I think it's too short," he said softly.

"It's just fine," Rachel said. "Come on, let's go inside. It's been a long morning and you must be exhausted."

"Ten-year-old boys don't get exhausted. Rachel," Eric pointed out. "Do you want to play baseball, like my daughter suggested?"

"I don't really like baseball," Steven admitted.

"But I'll bet you'd like a nice cold drink," Rachel said. "We have a cook, Helga, who makes wonderful lemonade."

"Okay," Steven said.

Steven's eyes wandered in a hundred different directions as they passed through the house. His mouth hung open in amazement to see the beautiful antique furniture and stone fireplace. There was a huge harp in one corner of the living room, and a grand piano set to the other side. Noticing it had caught his attention, Rachel said:

"I understand you play, Steven."

"I like music," Steven said.

"You can use any instrument in the house," Eric said, "as long as you respect it."

"You never let me touch the harp!" Tatiana protested.

"That's because *you* just yank on the strings," Olivia said.

Eric put a hand on each girl's shoulder and steered them toward the kitchen.

"We can talk about this later," he said. "Right now, a cold drink sounds good to me too."

In the kitchen Helga was listening to a country/western station. The sight of this blond braided woman singing a Judd's tune in a German accent was amusing. Steven watched her in fascination as he drank his glass of lemonade.

"Helga enjoys singing," Rachel said with a slight air of apology in her voice.

"And what is wrong with that?" Helga asked. "It is good music."

A new song came on. Steven turned to the radio, then said, "That's Tammy Wynette."

"Do you like country music?" Eric asked.

"I like all kinds of music," Steven said. "I play classical most of all, though."

"Maybe you could play for us," Rachel suggested.

Steven pushed his chair back from the kitchen table. Without a word, he turned and hurried from the room.

"Now you've scared him," Eric said. "Kids don't like being put on the spot like that."

Rachel glared at her husband.

"I did not put him on the spot," she said. "And don't tell me what kids like, as if I don't know anything about them. The girls are my—"

Her words were cut off by the sounds of the *Moonlight Sonata* being played so flawlessly that all of them were rendered speechless. When the music stopped, Eric and Rachel sat staring at each other.

"My God," Eric whispered, "how can a child play like that?"

Rachel nodded. "Nina wasn't joking when she said he was musically gifted."

Helga, who had stopped in the middle of washing dishes to listen, said, "It will be a pleasure to hear such music. I'm glad that the boy is staying."

Tatiana jumped from her chair, racing from the room. "I want to hear something else!" she cried.

When she reached the living room, she found Steven standing behind the open piano bench going through the music. He pulled out a book of opera favorites and chose to play the "Habañera" from *Carmen*. It was as beautiful and perfect as the first piece he'd played. As he went through it, Eric stared at his wife. In turn, she was watching Steven carefully. There was such admiration in her eyes that Eric might have guessed Steven was her own flesh and blood, not a child who was staying with them only temporarily.

The admiration in her eyes scared him, although he really wasn't sure why.

10

COMPLETELY SHAKEN by what had happened, Lorraine did not speak again until she and Bettina were safely locked inside the apartment. Bettina helped her wash away the dirt from the subway platform, and the warm water had a calming effect. Bits of memory had come back to her during the subway ride home, and now she told Bettina about them.

"Bettina," she said as the woman brushed her hair, "one of those boys knew me. I remember something now. I was with a man last night. A man who had a gun. He said he was on . . ."

She paused to remember his words.

"On 'official business,' " she said.

Bettina turned her around and looked at her with concern.

"He had a gun?"

"I . . . I think so," Lorraine said. "I can sort of see him pointing something black. I think he shot someone, but I'm not sure."

Bettina sighed. "No wonder that gang went after you."

She wondered if the man had been the child's father, some Mafia hoodlum who didn't care that he put his child's life in danger.

"Was he your father?" she asked.

Lorraine shook her head. "I don't think so. I mean, I don't remember. But he didn't *feel* like my father when I remembered him. He didn't feel like I knew him at all."

At once Bettina's mind changed and she imagined a kidnapper. The money in the valise was ransom! But why such a small amount? And why wasn't there a story in the news about this?

61

Lorraine touched her arm. "Why do you look so worried? Are you okay?"

Bettina smiled at her. "I'll be fine," she said. "You know what? We need some groceries. Why don't you take a nap on the sofa while I go to that little market on the corner?"

"But I don't want to stay here alone, Bettina," Lorraine said.

"I'll be only a few minutes," Bettina promised. "And I think you're safer up here. What if that gang is around?"

"Please?"

"I'm sorry," Bettina said in a firm voice. "This is best."

She took some money, then turned and left the apartment. The sound of the clicking lock echoed in the almost empty apartment like a ghost.

Obediently Lorraine went back to the couch and climbed onto the cushions. She wasn't tired, and bounced up and down a few times. Then she climbed up onto the back, walking across it like a tightrope. Bettina would have been amazed once more, this time by Lorraine's sense of balance. But Lorraine was quickly bored with this. She left the couch and went to the window. She pulled aside the blinds and looked out at the street below. It was a flurry of activity, and she had fun watching all the different characters that passed by.

Though she was several stories above street level, Lorraine could clearly see the people's faces. There were people of dark skin and people of light skin. Any one of them could be her mother or father, coming to look for her. What if they passed by without realizing she was up here?

Lorraine decided to see how many men and how many women there were. Her perception of the crowd was almost instantaneous, and she knew there were nine men and three women below. Did she know any of them? She tried to concentrate on faces, but nothing came back to her.

Discouraged, she was about to turn away from the window when a man turned the corner. He was so ordinary that the people in the street didn't even glance his way. But something about his face, something about those dark eyes and stony features, made a sour lump congeal in Lorraine's stomach.

She knew him. She couldn't exactly place him, but thought he might be the man she remembered from the previous night. For some reason, he terrified her.

She dropped the blinds again and hurried to the couch. Gathering herself up into a tight little ball, she tried to put the man's image out of her mind.

She saw him coming at her with something sharp, looking for blood. She tried to move away, but found she had been strapped to a table. He was going to hurt her!

Bettina opened the door to the sound of the child's screams.

"What's wrong?" she cried, running to her. She took hold of her, trying to calm the hysterical little girl.

"Lorraine! Lorraine!"

Bettina's voice helped calm Lorraine, and she gave the old woman a fierce hug.

"You were gone so long!" Lorraine cried. "I saw a man on the street, and he scared me!"

"The man from the other night?"

"I . . . I . . . I don't know," Lorraine stammered between sobs.

Bettina stroked her cheek.

"Slow down, child," she said, "catch your breath."

Lorraine concentrated on the kindly old face. It helped her forget the horrible vision she had just experienced.

"I was looking out the window," she said, calmer now. "It was fun watching all the people. Then he came around the corner, and I felt so scared!"

Bettina seemed to understand the hurt the child was feeling. Mumbling words of consolation, she held her close and stroked her long black hair. She began to wonder more about the child's background. Lorraine's thoughts of someone trying to hurt her was a very telling thing regarding her loss of memory. Maybe she had been so badly abused she blocked everything from her mind as a sort of defense mechanism. Bettina did not know any psychology, but she did have a good deal of "people sense." And she sensed this little girl had run away from a deplorable life.

"Well, sweet Lorraine," she said, "that man will never find you up here. I have a plan."

She let go of the child and walked to the two bags of groceries she had set down by the front door.

"I've stocked up on supplies," she said. "I have eggs, cheese, milk, and bread. Lots of crackers, peanut butter and jelly, some canned vegetables and fruit, some soup . . ."

She counted things off as she pulled them out. There was even a special kid's cereal for Lorraine's breakfast and a few puzzles and toys.

"We'll hide out for a while," Bettina said, "at least until it is safe for us to leave."

"But why?" Lorraine said. "Won't the police come to talk to me?"

Bettina shook her head.

"They're working very hard," she lied, hating herself for the necessity of it, "but they feel you are safest here with me. That man you saw might want to hurt you."

She took Lorraine by the shoulders.

"Listen to me carefully, child," she said. "The streets are dangerous. I can't let anything happen to you. Why, if those boys in the subway had hurt you . . ."

"They didn't," Lorraine said in a small voice, "but you are."

Bettina pulled her hands away and gazed at them with a stricken expression. She hadn't realized how tightly she was gripping Lorraine's arms.

"I'm sorry!" she cried. "But this is so important! We have to hide out here for a while. The police will contact us when they find your family, but in the meantime we have to stay safe. That man on the street must never find you."

Lorraine nodded, but she felt uneasy. Something about Bettina's words seemed wrong, and it wasn't just the fact that she wanted to hide out. But Lorraine decided not to let it worry her. She accepted the fact that she was safe here, away from that loathsome man on the street below.

Whoever he was, she never wanted to go back with him.

11

TATIANA SAT WITH an elbow propped on the kitchen table, her cheek resting against her fist. It was late evening, a time set aside for homework.

She pouted down at the workbook that was opened before her.

"I hate subtraction," she grumbled. "I hate math."

"That's just first-grade math," Olivia pointed out. "Wait until you're in third grade. Then it really gets hard."

Steven was sitting at the table too, looking through a book about the Civil War. He glanced up now.

"Maybe I can help you, Tatiana," he said.

"Everybody calls me 'Tati,' " the little girl told him with a smile. "Okay, help me."

Steven closed the book and turned around in his chair until he could see Helga working in the kitchen.

"Helga, do you have anything we can count?" he asked. "Like beans or raisins . . ."

"I want raisins!" Tati interrupted.

"They aren't for eating, Tati," Olivia said.

"Who asked you?"

Helga opened a cupboard and took down a mason jar.

"Sorry, no raisins," she said. "I have some peas."
She handed them to Steven.

"Just don't make a mess," she warned.

Steven promised they wouldn't, and opened the jar. He dumped a small mound of peas on the table.

"We can use these for the examples," Steven said. "What's the first problem?"

Down the hall, in the den, Rachel looked up from the papers she was marking and said, "Isn't that sweet? He's helping Tati, just like a big brother."

65

Eric laughed. "If he was like any big brother I've ever known, he'd be teasing her."

"That just proves he's special," Rachel said.

"He's a remarkable, all right," Eric said. "I'm interested in meeting his parents and finding out what kind of people they are. He—"

The doorbell rang, and Eric went to answer it. A stocky bearded man with aviator glasses introduced himself.

"I'm Detective Mark Bristol," he said, opening a wallet to show a gleaming gold badge. "I'm here in reference to a woman named Nina Blair."

"I'm Eric Freleng," Eric said. "Please come in."

As he led Bristol into the hallway, he turned and said, "Nina was here earlier this morning. Has something happened?"

"I'm afraid so," Bristol said. "Ms. Blair has been killed in a suspicious accident."

Eric brought him into the living room and introduced Rachel. He offered the detective a seat, but the man remained standing.

"What happened to her?" Rachel asked.

"We're not sure," Mark said. "A neighbor found her just outside her barn."

He sighed, but his expression never wavered from deadpan.

"We identified the body through dental records," he said.

"Dental records?" Eric said in surprise. "Was there a fire?"

"It seems she was doused with an incredibly caustic chemical," Mark answered. "There wasn't much left of her but her skeleton."

Eric gasped. He turned to see his wife's reaction, but she only regarded the detective with cool interest.

Eric felt sick to his stomach, imagining the pain Nina must have suffered. That poor woman! But Rachel still just stared at the detective with neither sympathy nor horror in her expression. When she spoke, it was with almost clinical detachment.

"What does this have to do with us?" she demanded.

"Because Nina was a municipal employee," Bristol said, "it was easy to find out who she had spoken to today. We asked for a list of clients, and yours was the only name given."

Eric looked at Rachel, but she was staring hard at the detective. She seemed more annoyed by his presence than upset about Nina.

"We'll be happy to answer any questions," Eric said. "But I don't think we'll be of much help."

The detective opened his briefcase and pulled out a clipboard.

"I have a standard questionnaire," he said. "We use it in all these cases."

He began to ask generic questions relating to the Freleng's demographics. Eric answered them all, because Rachel didn't seem willing. But when Mark asked about their relationship with Nina Blair, Rachel blurted out:

"None."

Eric volunteered more.

"Well," he said, "nothing personal. In her capacity as social worker, Nina often came to the high school where Rachel and I work. I had some contact with her."

"I understand she came to talk to you about a foster child?"

Rachel nodded. "His name is Steven."

"Isn't it unusual for work like this to be done in someone's home?"

"You'll have to talk to Social Services about that," Rachel said. She glared at him, as if challenging him to contradict her.

Bristol did not take the bait. Instead, he went on to a few more questions. Finally he asked, "Can you account for your whereabouts in the past twenty-four hours?"

"Of course," Rachel said. "I spent most of yesterday teaching school. I stayed late to prepare for a concert we had last night. Then I came home, had supper, and got ready to go out again. I conducted the school orchestra, spoke to a few dozen people afterward, then came home and went to bed."

Eric felt a lump in his throat and fought to swallow it before it was his turn to speak. He'd never known Rachel to lie before. Why was she withholding the fact that she'd lost several hours last night?

"How about you, Mr. Freleng?"

"I was also at school yesterday," he said. "After

classes, I coached the baseball team. Rachel and I came home together. We ate dinner, went to the concert, and came home as a family."

"Look," Rachel interrupted. "I don't understand this line of questioning. Surely you don't think *we* murdered Nina Blair?"

"It's only routine, ma'am," Bristol said, never losing his cool, professional demeanor. "No accusations are being made. We're just trying to paint a picture of Nina Blair's last hours."

Eric winced. Whatever that picture might be, he knew it was a hideous one. He couldn't imagine who would hurt Nina Blair, and he said so.

"Of course I don't know any of her acquaintances," he said. "We didn't run in the same social circles. But she came across as a sweet woman who wouldn't hurt anyone."

Bristol nodded, closing his book.

"Thank you for your cooperation," he said. "Where will I be able to contact you if I need more information?"

"Right here," Eric said. "Or, as of Monday, at the school."

He shook his head. "It's a terrible tragedy."

"Yes, it is," Bristol said.

They walked him to the front door. "Good-bye, Mr. and Mrs. Freleng. Thank you again."

Eric watched the detective's silhouette through the beveled window. He heard Rachel's footsteps clicking away behind him.

"I'm going to tell Steven he'll be with us awhile longer," she said. "I think he'll be pleased."

Eric swung around. "Rachel, wait!"

She stopped and turned. Her face had a quizzical expression.

"Is that it?" Eric asked. "No words of sympathy for Nina? Don't you even wonder who did that to her?"

"I'm sorry for her," Rachel said. "But I can't bring her back to life, and I have a child who needs me."

"Rachel," Eric said quietly, "why did you lie about the hours you disappeared last night?"

"I didn't lie," Rachel said. "I withheld information. I don't see what this has to do with Nina, and I didn't feel like answering a bunch of stupid questions."

"But, honey . . ."

"Eric, please leave me alone!" Rachel snapped, spinning around and hurrying down the hall.

Eric watched her disappear into the kitchen. He shook his head in dismay and headed into the den, where his baseball-card collection was waiting. He wanted to call Steven in to join him, father-son-like, but remembered the boy didn't like baseball. He wondered if the child liked any sports at all. Maybe, Eric thought, he came from a family of musical prodigies who frowned on sports.

It didn't matter, though. He couldn't concentrate on the cards. Thoughts of Nina filled his mind, but soon they were crowded out by thoughts of Rachel. Something was very wrong with her, and the answers were hidden somewhere in her memory of the previous night.

He heard Tatiana's voice from the kitchen. His daughter sounded angry about something being "not fair," and Eric put his concerns about Rachel aside to investigate. In the kitchen he found his wife and younger daughter face-to-face. Tatiana's eyes were hard, her fists clenched. Rachel had her hands on her hips and was bending down slightly toward the little girl. Eric noticed that Rachel had on the same cold, almost unhuman expression she'd had when Mark Bristol told them of Nina's death.

"What's going on in here?"

"Mom's making me give up my bedroom!" Tatiana cried. "It's not fair! It's *my* room!"

Eric looked at his wife.

"Rachel, this is rather sudden for the kid," he said. "I think you should have prepared her."

Steven was sitting sideways in one of the chairs, staring at his hands.

"It's okay," he said. "I can sleep on a couch."

"You most certainly won't," Rachel insisted. "After what you've been through, you need a proper bed. And, Eric, what time have I had to 'prepare' Tatiana? Things will be different around here for the next few days, and we'll all have to make sacrifices."

Tatiana pouted. "But I want my own room."

"You can double up with Olivia," Rachel said.

Olivia tried to smile for her little sister.

"It's only for a few days," she said. "Come on, it'll be fun. We can pretend we're having a sleepover."

"Will you tell me scary stories?"

Tatiana was beginning to accept the idea.

"Sure," Olivia promised.

Eric held up his hands.

"That's that," he said. "Now that we've settled sleeping arrangements, can you guys give Helga room to make our dessert?"

Helga, who had kept respectfully silent during the altercation, pointed to a strawberry pie on the counter.

"With homemade ice cream," she said.

"Wow!" Tatiana cried.

"Have you ever had strawberry pie, Steven?" Rachel asked.

"I don't know," Steven said quietly. He still felt bad about taking Tatiana's room, but since the conversation seemed to be closed now, he didn't bring up his feelings.

Eric patted his shoulder. "Well, you've never tasted any like Helga's, that's for certain. Come on, let's get ourselves around the dining-room table."

The family enjoyed dessert, and on the surface their troubles seemed forgotten. But every once in a while Eric would glance at Rachel, trying to read her thoughts. Tatiana made faces at Steven when no one was looking, and Steven tried hard to fit in with this new family.

At last, at bedtime, Rachel offered to escort Steven upstairs.

"I think the kid's old enough to put himself to bed," Eric pointed out.

Rachel gave him an icy glance, then said, "He's in a new house. He needs help getting settled."

Steven followed Rachel up the stairs to Tatiana's room, where he found pajamas in his suitcase while she folded down the bedcovers.

"You can dress in the bathroom," Rachel said. "You'd better get in there before the girls come up."

"Okay," Steven said.

He washed and dressed in the bathroom. As he turned to leave, he saw his reflection in the mirror on the back of the door. There was a logo on the shirt of his pajamas, a yellow oval with a black bat in the middle. Steven studied it for a few moments, trying to make himself remember it. But it meant nothing to him; no thoughts of superheroes came to his head, not Batman or anyone else. It was as elusive as his recollection of a family.

Steven sighed and opened the bathroom door. He'd been trying so hard to remember what had happened in the past few days, but nothing would come to him. And he was terribly, terribly worn out right now. He welcomed the thought of a comfortable bed, even if he was unhappy about taking it from Tatiana.

Rachel was waiting for him.

"Do you want to hear a story?" she asked.

"That's okay," Steven said. "I just want to go to sleep."

He climbed into the bed and Rachel tucked the covers around him. She smiled warmly at him, and he felt good for the moment.

"Thank you," he said.

"For what?"

"For letting me stay here," Steven said. "I like you."

"I like you too, Steven," Rachel said. "Don't you worry about a thing. You can stay here as long as you'd like. Does that make you happy, Steven? . . . Steven?"

But Steven, exhausted by his long day, was fast asleep.

Rachel met Eric in the hall.

"The girls want you to come say good night," he said. "They missed you."

"They missed me for ten minutes?" Rachel asked in a tone of slight disbelief.

She went to Olivia's room, where the girls were lying side by side in the bed. Tatiana's small brown head was cuddled against Olivia's shoulder.

"Good night, girls," Rachel said from the doorway.

"Aren't you going to come in and kiss us?" Tatiana asked.

Rachel seemed to hesitate, but just a moment. She walked into the room and kissed each girl on the forehead.

"I want a hug!" Tatiana demanded.

But Rachel had already left the room. Bewildered, Tati propped herself up on an elbow.

"She didn't hug me," she said in an offended tone.

"She's just tired out," Olivia defended Rachel. She reached for her nightstand and turned off the light.

"But—"

"Go to sleep, Tati!"

Tatiana mumbled something. Olivia didn't reply, but she had also been surprised at the quick, almost unloving way their mother had said good night.

Well, she told herself, her mother was probably worn out after all that had happened that day. She told herself that it would be for only a few days. Once Steven's family was found, everything would be normal again.

12

SAMANTHA WAS DREAMING. She was lying in a coffin, staring up through a bluish mist at two figures. One of them bent down and whispered something to her, but she did not understand the words. His face was hidden in the fog. He laid a hand on her chest; it felt cold.

They began to close the lid to the coffin, but somehow she was not afraid. It was a glass lid, and she could see through it. The blue mist vanished, taking along the two figures. Samantha could see up to the night sky, to the stars.

She did not feel afraid, but someone else in the dream did. She heard screaming.

And instantly she was out of the dream and sitting up in her bed. The screams had been real, coming from Julie's room. Samantha threw aside her covers and hurried to see what was wrong. Julie was pounding on her door, the sound reverberating like thunder down the hall. Samantha jerked the door open.

"Julie!"

The child stood with her fists up in the air, ready to strike the door again. Her eyes seemed focused on something behind Samantha. Samantha even started to turn around, but quickly stopped herself. Instead, she grabbed Julie by the wrists and fought until the child calmed down.

"Julie, wake up! Wake up!"

"I don't want to go in there! No box! No!"

"Julie, please!"

Suddenly Julie went limp in Samantha's arms. Samantha sank to the floor with her, holding her tightly and rocking her.

"God, how can I make these nightmares stop?" she asked.

Julie didn't answer. Samantha could hear her breathing steadily as she drifted back to sleep again. It wasn't the first time Julie's dreams had involved some kind of box. Samantha was reminded of her own dream, but she couldn't make a direct connection. Most important, in her dream she had felt at peace, as if she *belonged* in the coffinlike structure. Was it only coincidence, then, that they both dreamed of being in small boxes?

"You don't have to worry," she said, struggling to her feet with the little girl in her arms. "No one will harm you as long as I'm around."

She took Julie to the bed and settled her under the covers again. For a few moments she stood looking down at the child. Samantha wasn't certain, but she thought the warm feeling rushing through her right now had to be mother love. Maybe God had seen to it that she and her ex-husband never had a baby, but he had sent this little girl instead.

It wasn't until she was downstairs in the brightly lit kitchen, fixing herself a calming cup of tea, that reality hit her.

"Stop yourself, Samantha," she said firmly. "You can't let yourself get too attached to that child. She has a family!"

Really, she thought, what had she done to help find those people? Something was preventing her from going to the police. Did the Mr. Henley Julie had mentioned that first day have anything to do with it?

Samantha wished it wasn't three o'clock in the morning. She wished she had somebody to talk to. Barbara hadn't been much help, suggesting she keep Julie hidden until she could figure out what had happened. That could take months, or years. No, she had to get help for Julie in some other way.

Her eyes stung, and she was surprised to find tears brimming. She almost felt as if she was giving up her own flesh and blood. But how could this be? How could she become so attached to a child she didn't know in such a short period of time?

She pushed aside the almost full cup of tea.

"Tomorrow, at work," she vowed. "That's where I'll get help. Maybe one of my colleagues has an idea."

* * *

At seven o'clock the next morning, Julie entered Sangre de Cristo Hospital with Samantha. She looked everywhere, taking in all the activity of the emergency room.

"What's wrong with all those people?" she asked Samantha.

"That's what I'm here to find out," Samantha said, taking a file from a rack at the nurse's station.

The triage nurse smiled at Samantha. Her name tag said Maria Rivera.

"And who is this, Dr. Winstead?"

"My name is Julie," the child answered. "Samantha's my—"

"I'm taking care of Julie for a while," Samantha interrupted. "Would you mind if I set her up in the nurses' lounge?"

"Go right ahead," Maria said. "Nanette Belfield is in there now, tidying up."

Nanette was on the maintenance staff. She was a grandmotherly woman, and when she heard that Samantha was taking care of Julie, she put her hands on the child's cheeks and said in a lilting Southern drawl, "Don't you fret one minute 'bout this little darlin', Dr. Winstead. I'll see to it that she's taken care of while you work."

"I appreciate it, Mrs. Belfield," Samantha said. She put a hand on Julie's shoulder. "I'll be quite busy for the next few hours. There's milk and juice in the fridge, and you can have a doughnut. Do you have the things we bought at the Quick Shop?"

"Right here," Julie said, holding up a brown paper bag filled with activities to occupy her morning.

"Good," Samantha said. She smiled. "I'll be back later."

She left Julie in the care of Mrs. Belfield, who fussed over her like a mother hen. Samantha felt a tugging inside, as if something was drawing her back to Julie. But duty called, and she forced Julie out of her mind until she completed her morning rounds. As an emergency-room doctor she knew very few dull moments, so there was little opportunity in the next two hours to even think of Julie. When at last she was able to get a break, she found Nanette pushing a cart of linens down the hall.

"How is Julie?" she asked. "Has she been much trouble?"

"Trouble?" Nanette asked, her white eyebrows rising. "That child is an angel! She jes' sat herself down with her things to do, and we've barely heard a peep from her."

The triage nurse waved Samantha down.

"Julie drew a picture for me," Maria said, holding it out. "How old is that child? Isn't this rather advanced for her?"

"Julie is . . . nine," Samantha said, hesitating as she realized she didn't exactly know Julie's age.

She took the picture from the nurse. It depicted a yellow house with a green roof, on a seashore. The waves had been drawn and colored so carefully that they actually seemed to be moving. There was a black dog running along the beach, holding a stick. A little girl was chasing him, the wind blowing her hair across her face. In the distance, Julie had drawn a concession stand, complete with an awning surrounded by blue dolphins.

Samantha studied the picture a few moments, feeling a little strange. Something was familiar about it, but she couldn't decide what. When Maria spoke again, she pushed the feeling aside and handed her the picture.

"It's pretty amazing," she said. "But Julie is a remarkable child. She's a genius."

"I believe it," Maria said.

Samantha found Julie busy drawing more pictures—with both hands. Samantha's surprised gasp announced her presence. Julie turned around, then smiled.

"Hi," she said cheerily. "Do you want to see the drawings I made?"

"I'd love to," Samantha said, walking to the table. She shook her head in wonder. "That's amazing. I'm ambidextrous myself, but I certainly can't use both hands at exactly the same time."

Julie thought a moment, then spoke as if she were reading from a dictionary.

"Am-bi-dex-trous. Capable of using both hands equally well."

"That's right." Samantha nodded. She laughed. "You'll be able to do two homework assignments at one time."

"Am I going to school soon?" Julie asked. "I'd like to meet some other children."

"Oh, no," Samantha said. "I'm sure you'll return to school once we find your family. But there's no need to worry about it for now."

She quickly changed the subject.

"So, what have you been doing all morning? These drawings are lovely."

She studied each picture, amazed at the details. It was as if a much older person had drawn them, instead of a child of nine. She half-expected the feeling of *déjà vu* she'd experienced with the beach picture to come back, but it never did.

"I've been drawing a lot," Julie said. "And I did half the crosswords in that book."

"Half!" Samantha cried. She picked up the book and glanced through it. Sure enough, most of the crosswords were finished, and what little she could scan showed they were done correctly. "Julie, you finished fourteen crosswords in just a few hours, on top of everything else?"

Julie wasn't impressed with herself. "I would have done them all, but sometimes the nurses would come in and talk. It was more fun listening to them. One nurse had come down from upstairs, and she was telling her friend about twin babies that were delivered this morning. One of them was transverse breach, so they had to come out by cesarean."

Samantha nearly dropped the crossword book.

"Do you understand any of that?"

"Sure," Julie said. "Transverse means the baby's back was pointing down instead of his head. And cesarean means—"

"I know what it means, sweetie," Samantha said. This little girl would never fail to amaze her. "Julie, do you like babies?"

Julie nodded eagerly. "Maybe there's a baby in my family?"

"That could be," Samantha said, wondering if this was another piece to the Julie puzzle. "But I was wondering: would you like to see the babies upstairs?"

"Oh, yes!"

Samantha smiled at Julie's eagerness. "Well, my good friend Dr. Huston works up there. Maybe she's the one

who delivered the twins. I have just a few more patients
to see before my lunch break. Then we can go upstairs
together, and you can take a peek in the nursery."

"I'd like that a lot," Julie said.

Samantha patted her head gently.

"Then it's settled," she said. She looked at the para-
phernalia on the table. "Can you hold out for just another hour?"

"Sure."

"I'll be back for you when I'm finished with my morning rounds," Samantha said. "See you later."

When Samantha left, Julie went to the refrigerator and
took out a container of juice. She poured some into a
paper cup, returned the carton, and sat down again. As
she drank the juice, she began to work on another
puzzle.

She had noticed how astonished all the adults were
when they saw the things she could do.

Am I really that different? she asked herself. She
didn't *feel* different.

Suddenly she remembered the boy named Marty.
When he had rescued her in that crazy dream, he had
said there were other children like her.

Julie did not consider Marty to be merely part of her
vision. To her he was as real as the nurses who walked
in and out of this lounge. She wondered if she would
ever hear from him again, and if she'd ever meet the
others he had mentioned. He had said she was special,
but what did he mean?

She closed her eyes and tried to call him, but he did
not answer. Sighing, she returned to the puzzle book.

Before she knew it, an hour had gone by. Throughout
this time, Julie's concentration was never broken by the
sound of voices over the PA system or screaming ambu-
lance sirens. She was able to block out these distractions
without effort.

Expecting Samantha to return any moment to take her
up to the nursery, she began to clean up the table. Once
this job was finished, she went to the door and opened
it. The emergency room was a flurry of activity, people
rushing to and fro with serious, determined expressions.
Maria, the triage nurse, was busy interviewing people.

There were about fifteen teenagers here, some crying, some dazed, others being carried swiftly on stretchers.

"What happened?" Julie asked. Maria did not seem to notice her.

She felt a hand on her shoulder.

"Don't you fret, little one," Nanette said. "There's been a bus acs'dent. Your . . . Dr. Winstead will be busy for a while."

"But it's lunchtime," Julie protested. "We were going to see the babies."

"I'm sure you'll see them later," Nanette promised. "In the meantime, it ain't fittin' for a little girl to go hungry. Would you like me to take you up to the lunchroom?"

Julie hesitated.

"I'm sure Dr. Winstead won't mind."

"Okay," Julie said.

A short while later, Julie was set up with a lunch tray in the cafeteria. Nanette excused herself, saying she had to get back to work. Left alone, Julie ate her lunch in silence, studying the people around her. No one paid much attention to her. When she finished, she decided to make her way back to the emergency room.

While waiting for the elevator, she read the floor directory. She noticed that the maternity ward was just one flight up.

Maybe I can just go up myself, Julie thought. Samantha won't mind. I'll look for that Dr. Huston. I won't get in anyone's way.

Maybe, she decided, justifying her actions, Samantha was already up there waiting for her.

Since visiting hours hadn't begun, the elevator was empty. When she stepped onto the second floor, no one noticed her. Samantha read the visiting-hours sign on the metallic doors. It wasn't anywhere near one o'clock, but she didn't let that stop her. Instead, she pushed open the door and went off in search of babies.

She saw a nurse working at a desk, and heard the distant moans of a woman in labor. But then she heard a baby's cry, and turned in the opposite direction. The walls of the maternity ward were painted a soft blue, with murals depicting scenes from Mother Goose. Julie read a sign marked "Nursery" and followed the arrow around a hallway. To her disappointment, the shades were drawn in the nursery windows. She could hear babies crying, but try as she might, she couldn't catch a glimpse of the newborns.

Sighing, she turned around and decided she'd better wait until Samantha brought her up. But as she rounded the hall, she noticed a windowed door she hadn't seen before. She went up to it and looked in, but all she could see was strange machinery.

The sign on the door said "NO ADMITTANCE. HOSPITAL PERSONNEL ONLY."

Well, she thought, that couldn't apply to her. She was *supposed* to see the babies—Samantha said so. Without a moment's hesitation, she pushed open the unlocked door, and unwittingly entered the preemie ward. It was actually a group of rooms, all encased in glass and all with similar machinery. There were glass boxes too, which Samantha didn't recognize. The ones in this particular room were currently empty. Through the windows Julie saw two nurses, about three rooms away, talking. In the room directly next to this one, a man and woman stood over a glass box, looking very sad. Julie wondered what they were sad about. But she was more interested in finding the babies.

There didn't seem to be any in this room, so she decided to search elsewhere. But then a tiny mouselike cry made her turn sharply. She realized at once it had come from behind a curtain. Slowly, curious, she walked over to it. She pulled the curtain aside to find a glass box that held an impossibly tiny infant. For a moment Julie kept her distance. She felt scared suddenly, as if something bad was going to happen.

But it's just a baby! she told herself firmly.

She made herself walk closer, made herself look down at the doll-like infant. It had a little white knit cap on its head, and wore a simple cotton undershirt and diaper. Blue-violet light shone down on it, to help fight jaundice.

Julie smiled at the tiny but beautiful infant. But her smile quickly faded when she noticed the wires attached to various parts of the baby's body.

As if she'd been struck, she fell back against the curtain, knocking over a chair. This wasn't a good thing. It was bad, terribly bad. . . .

Wires. Something bad about the wires. Someone was yelling at her to get in the box or she would die.

Julie had to get away. She had to find a safe place. She had to run, to hide.

She raced from the nursery as fast as she could, drawing the attention of a doctor making rounds. Barbara Huston called out to the little girl, but Julie did not hear her. She simply ran blindly, trying desperately to get away from the wires and glass boxes.

13

LORRAINE SLEPT SOUNDLY all the night, and was awakened the next morning by clanking sounds. She sat up in the sofa bed, rubbed her eyes with chubby fists, and looked across the room. Bettina was fixing breakfast.

"Good morning, child," she said. "Come have some eggs."

Lorraine joined the old woman at the rickety table.

"Did you sleep well last night?" Bettina asked.

Lorraine shook her head.

"I had a bad dream," she said. "I kept dreaming about that man I saw."

Bettina thought a moment before speaking.

"Maybe he's a member of your family," she suggested. "He could be a mean stepfather—or even your real father. There must be some reason why you know him, and why he frightens you. Maybe he was cruel, and beat you."

"I don't know," Lorraine said doubtfully. "It didn't feel like I was looking at my father, or anybody like that. He just looked like someone I know, someone bad."

She stared into her Cheerios for a few moments, then bopped her head up quickly, her eyes wide.

"I know!"

"You know?" Bettina echoed. "Do you mean you remember?"

Lorraine frowned. "No, I wish I did. But maybe that man down there is a kidnapper! Maybe he stole me away from my family and gave me bad medicine to make me forget everything. Maybe there's a ransom!"

Bettina laughed.

"No, really!" Lorraine insisted. "You said I had nice clothes, didn't you? Maybe I come from a really nice family and they're looking for me! And if you bring me back, you'll get a big reward and you'll never be poor again."

"Oh, child," Bettina said. "What an imagination! Surely, if you were a rich family's child, they would have found you by now."

"But they don't know where to look!"

"There hasn't been anything in the newspaper," Bettina said. "Or on television. And the police do know where to find us if your family turns up. Don't you remember, I called them?"

Lorraine's face fell. Her hopes of being reunited with her family were destroyed for the moment, and tears welled up in her eyes.

"I just want to go home, no matter where it is!"

"Please don't cry," Bettina said, pushing her chair back. It made a screeching noise across the tile floor. "Look! I bought a few things for you at the store last night. I don't want you to be bored."

She lifted a paper bag onto the table.

"Look: crayons, paper, puzzles, a book. And here's a little doll you can dress up."

Lorraine took the doll box in her hands. It was an inexpensive plastic teen doll, and it came with a wardrobe of minuscule fashions.

"We'll only hide out for a few days," Bettina promised. "It will be okay, you'll see. You trust me, don't you?"

Lorraine nodded.

"Then dry your tears and finish your breakfast," Bettina ordered. 'And when we're through cleaning up, we can enjoy our little home together. Our safe little home."

Lorraine did as she was told, then took the fashion doll out of the box and began to play with it. Bettina produced a pair of knitting needles and some yarn that she had also purchased the night before. She took these to the couch and soon the bare room was filled with the sound of clicking needles. In time, the steady noise, accompanied by boredom, made Lorraine's head nod forward. She fell fast asleep on the table.

But it was a quick sleep, interrupted by a scratching at the window. Groggily, hardly aware of Bettina sitting on the couch, Lorraine shuffled over to see what was making the noise. When she saw a cat on the fire escape, sympathy filled her heart, and she began to unlatch the window. The cat went on scratching and meowing.

"Don't worry," Lorraine said. Her voice sounded

strange to her, as if she were speaking in a tunnel. "I'll save you."

She turned to look at Bettina, wondering if the old woman would disapprove. But Bettina did not seem to hear her.

Lorraine turned and pulled open the window. She reached out for the cat . . .

. . . but it was a human hand that grabbed her. The man from the street was on the fire escape! Lorraine screamed, pulling away from him. He held fast, and somehow she pulled him right into the room with her! He laughed, holding up a black cord.

"Bettina! Bettina!"

But the old woman still did not answer.

Lorraine screamed and fought as the man wordlessly began to tie her with the cord. Why wasn't Bettina helping her?

Wake up, you're dreaming!

"Bettina!"

Lorraine, it's Marty. Wake up. You're just having a dream. Wake up. Wake up!

Lorraine spoke to him in her mind.

It's not a dream. He's real!

No, he isn't. You're just remembering a bad person.

From where?

I can't tell you yet. Just wake up and you'll be okay.

Marty, I'm scared! He's hurting me!

Then listen to me! Wake up and he'll stop!

At last the strange boy's words got through to the terrified little girl. She jolted herself awake, and found she was still sitting at the kitchen table, doll clothes strewn all around her. Hearing Lorraine's gasp, Bettina turned around.

"What is it, child?"

"I . . . I guess I fell asleep."

"So early in the day?" Bettina asked worriedly. "I hope you aren't ill."

"I'm fine," Lorraine said, forcing a smile.

"Well, all right . . ."

Bettina returned to her knitting. Lorraine tried to call Marty back to her, but he was gone again.

Who was he? the little girl wondered. And who was that terrible man?

14

EVERYTHING SEEMED to be back to normal when Tati woke up the next morning. She could hear Helga singing in the kitchen, and the house was full of wonderful breakfast smells. While Olivia went on sleeping, Tatiana crept quietly from the room and downstairs. She hoped she had beat Steven awake, so she could have a few minutes with her parents. When she entered the kitchen and saw no sign of Steven, she began to believe this was going to be an okay day.

"Good morning, Tati," her father said. "Did you sleep okay last night?"

"I guess so," Tatiana said.

She sat down and Helga put a plate of blintzes in front of her. They were Tatiana's favorite kind, made with bits of fruit. She smiled at Helga, and the German woman stroked her cheek for just a moment before returning to work.

Tatiana looked around.

"Did Steven go home this morning?" she asked. "Did you find his family?"

"It's a little early in the morning for that," Eric said. "Steven is asleep upstairs."

Tatiana tried to be annoyed about this, but everything was going so well that she couldn't.

"Well, I decided something," she announced. "It's okay for Steven to have my bed. I know it's only for a few days."

Rachel put her coffee cup down and turned to look at her daughter.

"You don't understand, do you?" she said. "Steven may be here much longer than a few days. It could take months to find his family."

"Months?" There was worry in Tatiana's voice. It

85

wasn't that she didn't like Steven—he'd been nice to help her with her homework—it was just that she wanted things to be the way they'd always been.

Her father sensed her bewilderment. He poured a glass of milk for her and said, "We're doing the best we can to find his family. They must be looking for him too. Between all of us I'm sure we'll have this . . . this situation resolved shortly enough."

Rachel slammed her coffee cup down into its saucer. She pushed her chair back and left the room. Tatiana stared at her retreating figure.

"Why is Mommy so mad?" she asked.

"I don't know, honey," Eric said. "Don't you worry about it. Finish your breakfast so you can get ready for Mass."

He left the kitchen, passing Olivia on his way to the master bedroom. She was already dressed, and she gave him a good-morning kiss. Upstairs, Eric found Rachel sitting at her vanity, putting on makeup with short, angry gestures.

"Why did you say that?" she demanded.

"What?" Eric asked, opening the closet to find a suit. "I don't understand what made you angry, Rachel."

"You called Steven a 'situation'!"

Eric carried his suit to the bed.

"Don't twist my words," he said. "Having Steven here as a guest is a 'situation.' I certainly didn't mean to insult the child. He's a nice kid. But it bothers me that you seem to think you'll have him indefinitely. He isn't our child, Rachel. You can't let yourself become too attached to him."

Rachel turned on him, a tube of mascara held like a weapon.

"Someone has to care for him!" she cried. "At least I have feelings. The poor child is all alone!"

Eric was silent for a moment. His voice was soft when he spoke again.

"Yes, I suppose he is," he said. "Especially now that Nina Blair is dead."

"She didn't mean anything to him," Rachel said. "She wasn't his mother."

Eric was about to say "neither are you." But he

thought better of it and concentrated on dressing. When he finished, he said, "I'll go down and get the car ready."

Neither of the adults realized their voices had carried out the vent in their wall and into Tatiana's room. Steven lay awake on the bed, listening to them. They were fighting about him, and he was worried. Even though he had been here only a day, it seemed he was already causing trouble for this family. But how could that be? He just *knew* that somehow he belonged to these people! He only wished he could remember more.

The door opened just then, and Tatiana came in. Steven quickly blinked away the tears that were rising in his brown eyes. Tati looked at him.

"You're lucky," she said. "You don't have to go to Mass. I think church is boring."

Steven sat up on the bed.

"I think I'd like church," he said.

"Yeah, I guess you would," Tati said almost accusingly. "You probably know all the music."

She opened her drawers and put an outfit together.

"Can you go away?" she asked. "I don't want any boy looking at me when I'm getting dressed!"

"Sorry," Steven said, getting up from the bed.

He found his suitcase and pulled out some clothes. When he'd been found a few days earlier, he'd had this suitcase with him and little else. He took his clothes into the bathroom and dressed.

When he came out, Rachel was standing in the hall. She had a beige suit on, with a brown-and-yellow print blouse. The jacket lapel was decorated with a golden musical note. Steven noticed she held a pile of sheet music in her arms.

"I sing in the choir," she said.

"Can I come along?"

"Not this time, Steven," Rachel said. "I think meeting all those people would be too overwhelming. But don't worry, Helga is here if you need anything."

From downstairs Olivia called to her mother and sister.

"Tati! Mama! Hurry! Daddy's waiting!"

Tatiana raced by Rachel and Steven like a small tornado.

Rachel smiled at Steven.

"We'll be back in about an hour," she said. "Just

enjoy yourself. The backyard is plenty big enough for exploring."

After Rachel left, Steven went to the kitchen and had breakfast.

"Please don't dillydally," Helga said. "I have much to do, and I am not used to having a boy in the house."

"Mrs. Freleng said I can play outside," Steven said.

"This is good," Helga said with a nod.

Steven finished his breakfast quickly, sensing she didn't want him underfoot. There were plenty of outdoor toys to enjoy, but after a while he grew bored with them. He felt very lonely, and in his solitude he recalled the fight Rachel and Eric had had.

He couldn't drive their words from his mind, no matter how hard he tried. Maybe he could play music. . . .

No, Helga had made it clear he was to stay away.

At that moment he heard an unusual bird cry. Curious about what creature would make such a melodious sound, he decided to investigate the woods that marked the farther boundary of the huge backyard.

The pine scent of evergreens was laced through with the smell of spring blossoms. Steven was able to identify a number of scents separately, although he did not do this consciously. His brain registered juniper, blue spruce, lilacs, heather, and more. But there was one that did not seem to belong here: an unpleasant, burny smell.

At once Steven knew what it must be: fire. He broke into a run, tracking the scent as easily as a hunting dog. It was a physical ability like his penchant for math and music, and he did it without much thought. He stopped short in a small clearing, where a boy who seemed to be a little older than he sat smoking. The boy turned around so fast that Steven stepped back.

"Get lost!" the boy demanded.

Steven stared at the cigarette, not exactly sure what it was. The boy sucked on it and the tip glowed red.

"You're going to start a fire," Steven said.

"I said 'get lost,' " the boy, Ralphie Mercken, snapped. "It's none of your effin' business what I do."

Steven wouldn't be put off.

"But what *are* you doing?" he asked, curious. "What's that thing in your hand?"

"Well, it sure as hell ain't my . . . ."

Ralphie stopped, looked down at the cigarette, then back at Steven in disbelief.

"You're kidding, right?"

Steven shook his head.

"What are you, dumb or something?" he asked, "It's a cigarette, stupid."

He flicked the butt onto the ground.

"And this," he said, indicating the clearing, "is my private place. So just turn yourself around and get out."

Steven thought about it, then shook his head.

"I don't think so," he said. "I think this is still the Freleng's property. So you're the one who must leave."

Ralphie came up to Steven with his fists balled. He stood a head taller and weighed at least twenty pounds more than the younger boy.

"Are you gonna make me?"

Without waiting for an answer, he grabbed Steven by the shirt collar and lifted the boy until they were nose-to-nose. Steven did not waste a moment. In one fluid motion he brought his fists down on both of the boy's shoulders, and his knee up into the bully's groin. Ralphie screamed, letting him go. Steven backed away and watched him thrash on the ground, amazed at what he had just done.

The bully looked up at Steven with brimming eyes.

"You know effin' karate?"

"What's that?"

"Jerk," Ralphie growled. "I'm gonna kill you for this!"

Steven just stood and watched him. It didn't occur to him to turn and run away. In his mind, he had more right to be here than the bigger boy.

Suddenly Ralphie found his strength. He picked up a fallen branch and came running after Steven, ready to hurt him. Steven backed away now, but too late. The branch swung toward him . . .

. . . and somehow stopped just inches from his head.

"What the . . . ?"

Ralphie struggled to move his arm, still wielding the stick up high, but he couldn't. It was as if some invisible hand had taken hold of his wrist.

"What are you doing to me?" he cried. "Cut it out!"

"I'm not . . ."

The wind began to blow, gently at first, tossing the detritus on the forest floor. But within seconds it began to pick up speed, rocking small branches and knocking leaves from the trees. And as Steven stood watching him, Ralphie Mercken went completely ashen. Something dark and nameless began to surround him, a sense of fear so palpable it seemed to be carried on the wind itself.

Ralphie, never so terrified in his life, began to scream. *Something's coming for me! Something's coming to get me!*

"I'm gonna die!'

The wind blew furiously, knocking the stick from Ralphie's hand. Inexplicable fear had turned him from a bully to a frightened little boy, and he gazed at Steven with pleading eyes.

"Don't let it hurt me! Stop it! Stop!"

Ralphie felt something knock him to the ground. All the nightmares he'd ever had, all the fears of being hurt by his unloving parents, all the dark and evil threats he'd ever heard, seemed to be whirling around him, waiting to tear him apart.

Steven watched all this in wonder, afraid because of Ralphie's behavior and yet unable to understand what had turned the bully into the screaming boy who thrashed about on the forest floor.

And then he heard another scream, from behind him. He turned quickly and saw Tatiana, still dressed in her church clothes, gazing at Ralphie with a shocked expression.

"What's going on?" she cried, her voice barely louder than the wind. "What's wrong with him?"

"Nothing!" Steven yelled. "It's a trick! Go home! Go away!"

Tatiana glared at him. Fear of the scene before her was momentarily pushed aside by indignation. How dare this newcomer chase her from her own property?

"I'm telling my father!"

She turned to run back to the house, leaving Ralphie screaming. Steven began to run after her.

"Wait! You'll ruin everything! Don't go!"

But Tatiana was too far ahead to hear him. Steven tried to run after her, but something grabbed hold of him. There was nothing there. Steven stopped, expecting the same thing to happen to him that had happened to Ralphie Mercken. But the pressure on his arm stopped, and at the very same moment, so did the wind. Ralphie was silent, lying quietly on the ground.

Steven heard a voice. It seemed to come from inside his head, and yet, at the same time, from all around him.

Don't be afraid.

Who said that?

Steven was surprised he answered from within his mind.

I'm a friend. I'm here to help you.

Did you . . . did you make that happen?

Though his eyes were open, his mind still formed the vague image of a boy.

I didn't really make anything happen. It's all illusion. You can do it too.

Steven thought for a moment. Somehow the voice in his head seemed natural, and he wasn't afraid of it. But he was full of questions.

Why can't I see you?

We're too far from each other. But you will, one day soon. You can call me Marty, Steven.

Steven felt his heart skip a beat.

How did you know my name?

I have always known you. Steven, you told the girl she'd 'ruin everything.' Why did you say that? What do you know of all this?

I . . . I don't remember saying that. I don't know what it means.

In truth, he did remember his words. But the thought of saying something that made no sense was too much to deal with. Instead, he walked to Ralphie's unconscious form.

Is he dead? Did you kill him?

No, but he'll never bother you again. I've been looking for you, Steven. When that boy tried to hurt you, your emotions were so strong I was able to find you.

Why were you trying to find me?

There are others like us. We'll be meeting each other soon. You're a very special person, Steven. But you must not let anyone know this. You mustn't tell anyone what happened here in the woods.

What about Ralphie?

Ralphie created his own fears. I only brought them out. He'll push them away again and remember nothing.

But Tatiana—she's going to tell her father what she saw.

He won't believe her. No one will. Brush yourself off, go home, and act as if nothing happened. I'll come again soon.

Marty, wait!

But Marty had instantly vanished from his thoughts. Steven did as instructed, cleaning himself up and heading home. Rachel was waiting for him on the back steps, her arms open wide. She grabbed Steven into them and hugged him fiercely.

Then she stepped back and looked him over.

"You don't seem hurt," she said. "Tatiana said something happened in the woods."

Steven managed a bewildered expression.

"Nothing happened," he said. "I don't know what Tatiana is talking about. She came into the woods, to a clearing I found, and then she got really angry at me. She said I had no right to be there."

Tatiana had come out onto the deck, and now she stamped her foot.

"I did not say that!" she cried. "You did something to Ralphie Mercken. He was screaming like crazy, and the wind was blowing."

Rachel frowned at her.

"There is no wind today, Tatiana," she said.

"There was in the woods!" Tatiana insisted. "It was blowing and blowing. It knocked down leaves. And Ralphie was screaming!"

Rachel knew that every word Tatiana said was true. She had been sitting at the piano, playing a medley of Rodgers and Hammerstein tunes, when she'd been struck by a feeling something was happening to Steven. And then the sheet music had disappeared, replaced by a small holographic tableau of the woods. She'd *seen* Steven and Tatiana and an unfamiliar white boy in that clearing. She'd seen the white boy's mouth open wide in a scream, seen the wind blowing fiercely.

It had lasted only a half-minute, but it was enough to send her running out here to find out what was wrong.

Tatiana hadn't had a chance to tell her anything was wrong.

Only she knew the whole thing was crazy. Rachel would never admit, especially to a six-year-old, that she'd had a psychic experience. She would never tell *anyone*.

"Stop it right now, Tatiana," she said. "You're just jealous and want to get Steven into trouble. Well, you're the one in trouble now. Go to your room, and don't come out until dinnertime."

"Daddy will believe me," Tatiana blubbered.

"Daddy's gone to the hardware store," Rachel said almost triumphantly.

Tatiana's eyes were brimming. Rachel had never been so mean to her! But she could tell by the angry look on her mother's face that this was no idle command. Shaking, she ran up to her room.

No, it wasn't her room now. It belonged to Steven. She hated him. *Hated him!*

She went to the window and looked out. Rachel and Steven were still in the yard, their arms around each other's shoulders. Tatiana cried and cried.

The night her mother had come home late, she had felt there was something different about her. Now she knew it was true. Rachel was changing into something mean and ugly, and no one could see it but her.

15

IT WAS MORE than an hour before the situation in the emergency room was under enough control for Samantha to break away. She was worried about Julie. Had the child eaten? Was she upset because Samantha hadn't returned when promised?

Nanette Belfield easily read the concern on the doctor's face.

"Don't fret, Dr. Winstead," she said. "I've taken good care of Julie. I knew you'd be busy, so I took her to the cafeteria myself. She's probably there now, finishing her lunch."

Samantha sighed with relief. "Thank you, Mrs. Belfield. I'll go right up there."

In the cafeteria the lunch crowd had diminished considerably, but there was no sign of Julie. A quick check of the lavatory didn't produce her either. Samantha headed back to the elevator. As she was about to press the button, she heard her name over the intercom.

"Another emergency?" she thought aloud, stepping into the elevator.

"You are wanted on the second floor. Dr. Winstead, you are wanted on the second floor."

The second floor? Why?

Samantha realized what had happened. The maternity ward was on the second floor. Julie must have gone up by herself!

When she stepped off the elevator, Barbara Huston was there to greet her.

"You'd better come with me, Samantha," she said.

"Is it Julie?"

Barbara nodded.

"You really shouldn't have let her wander around by herself," Barbara said. "I saw her coming out of the preemie ward, and she looked like she was scared to death about something."

"I'm sorry," Samantha answered. "It's been crazy downstairs. I suppose the sight of those tiny babies was a shock to her. Most adults can't handle it, let alone a child!"

Barbara opened a door to a waiting room. Julie was sitting on the couch, her knees drawn up to her chest and her arms wrapped around herself. Her head was bent down, so that her long brown hair fell all around her shoulders.

"She ran from me," Barbara said. "I found her hiding under the sink in the maintenance closet."

"Julie, what happened?" Samantha asked.

At the sound of her voice, Julie's head snapped up. Samantha sat down and put her arms around her.

"I was so scared!" she cried. "When I saw the baby in the glass box, it made me remember something terrible!"

"Can you tell me about it?"

Julie just hugged her tighter and shook her head. Samantha looked across the room at Barbara.

"Now do you see why it's so important to find out who she really is?"

"But aren't you afraid of—?"

"I'm more afraid of the damage my keeping silent is doing to her," Samantha interrupted. "Barbara, I need your help. I have to do *something*."

"You said you can't go to the police," Barbara pointed out. "It could be because you're somehow involved in all this. You could be an accessory to a kidnapping and not be aware of it!"

"That's crazy," Samantha said, "but I guess it's possible. And not knowing is hurting both Julie and me."

She extricated herself from Julie's embrace.

"Come on, sweetie," she said. "I'll see if I can get someone to stand in for me. I'm going to take you home."

Barbara sighed. "I still think you should let things happen on their own. The answers will come, and only then will you be prepared to face the police—and the child's family."

Samantha took Julie by the hand and left the room without answering Barbara.

"Are we going?" Julie asked. "I don't like it here."

They walked to the elevator.

"You know, you'd feel better if you told me exactly what happened."

Julie stared down at her pink sneakers.

"There was a baby in a glass box," she began. "I . . ."

The elevator door opened and they walked inside. Julie clammed up immediately, refusing to speak in front of the other people there. Samantha decided to wait until they were alone before pressing the matter.

When they got off the elevator, Samantha noticed a friend, Dr. John Brightman. She called to him, and his face lit up with a bright smile.

"Hi, Sam," he said. He was the only person who ever called her by that masculine diminutive. "Thanks for taking over for me the other night. You really saved my neck."

"Did you enjoy the wedding?"

"It was great," John said. "And Kelly appreciates that I was able to take her after all. I still can't believe I got the date mixed up. If I can return the favor . . ."

"As a matter of fact," Samantha said. "You can return it right now." She explained the situation to him, claiming Julie had taken ill.

John looked down at Julie, who smiled shyly.

"Hi, pretty thing," he said. "It's nice to meet you. I'm sorry to hear you aren't feeling well."

He turned back to Samantha again.

"Maybe you should have Chris Webster up in pediatrics take a look at her."

Samantha didn't reply. She seemed to be thinking. John sensed she was bothered by something. He had only been working at Sangre de Cristo General for a year, but in that time he'd come to know Samantha like a good friend.

"Samantha, you aren't in trouble, are you?"

Samantha hesitated. She'd confided in her best friend, but Barbara really hadn't given her any practical advice. Should she involve another person? It really wasn't fair to include John in all this.

He touched her elbow.

"Sam, I'm your friend," he said. "If there's anything I can do . . ."

Samantha sighed. Yes, he *was* a friend, and she needed all the advice she could get.

"Julie, would you go on to the nurses' station and pack all your things?"

Julie looked nervous, but Samantha smiled reassuringly and said, "It's okay. Maria is there, and I'll be along in a minute."

Julie left the two adults. Samantha turned to John and said, "Yes, I'm in trouble. Something strange has happened, and I don't know what to do about it."

"Why don't you tell me?" John suggested.

"Well, okay," Samantha said. "It started the night I took over your shift. The last thing I remember clearly is driving up the road to my house . . ."

John listened attentively until she finished her story. He whistled softly.

"That's bizarre," he said. "You can't imagine who did this to you?"

Samantha shook her head.

"What about a relative?" John suggested.

"I don't have any relatives that I know of," Samantha said. "For that matter, I don't think I have any enemies. None of this makes even a bit of sense."

John thought a moment.

"The things you've told me indicate you might have been brainwashed."

"Why?"

"To get you to take the child without protest," John said. "That's why you're so afraid every time you try to call the police. They fixed it so you wouldn't report her!"

Samantha thought a moment.

"I'll buy that," she said. "It's the only explanation that makes sense. But, for heaven's sake, why? And why doesn't Julie remember anything either?"

"You have a lot of questions," John said. "What you need is a private detective."

"Oh, no!" Samantha said. "No police."

"A PI isn't exactly the police," John said. "And I happen to know one. A good friend of mine, Wil Sherer, retired from the force about eight years ago. He has a private agency now."

"Well, I suppose I could try," Samantha said. "It's a logical next step. I'll call him."

John pulled a small black book from his back pocket. He tore a page from it, found a pen, and copied a number. He handed this to Samantha and said, "Promise me you'll call."

"I promise," Samantha said. "Thanks, John."

But as she held the number in her hand, fear began to rise in her. Despite everything John said, a private eye *was* a little too close to a police officer for comfort. If she tried to dial the number, would something terrible happen?

16

TATIANA WAS AWAKENED from a fitful sleep by a soft knock at her door. She sat up and opened her eyes. It took a moment to focus them, they were so sore from crying. Her voice was hoarse when she called:

"Come in."

Olivia entered. She looked at her younger sister sadly, then came to the bed and put her arms around her.

"Tati," she said softly. "I heard what happened. I'm sorry you got in trouble."

"She called me a liar," Tatiana said. "But I didn't lie, really! Something scared me!"

"What, Tati?" Olivia asked with concern.

Tatiana hung her head. How could she explain, even to the sister who loved her, about the unnamed fear that had gripped her in those woods? She hadn't seen anything monstrous, she hadn't heard anything. It was just a . . . a *feeling*.

"I don't know," she whispered.

"Maybe it was shadows in the woods," Olivia suggested. "Or maybe it was that mean Ralphie Mercken playing a trick."

Tatiana pulled away. She stared at her sister with huge chocolate-colored eyes.

"Olivia, I'm scared. Something bad is happening. Things are changing ever since Steven came here."

Olivia clicked her tongue. "That's ridiculous, Tati. How could Steven make things change?"

"Mommy's never been so mean," Tatiana said. She looked up at her sister again. "What was our other mommy like?"

"I don't remember her," Olivia admitted. "You were just a baby and I was only two when she left."

"Maybe she's nice," Tatiana said. "Maybe, if she knew what nice girls she left, she'd come back."

Olivia stood up. "Tati, that's just crazy talk. You know Rachel is our mother now. Anyway, I came up to tell you she wants you to move all your things out of here and into my room."

"What?" Tatiana was shocked.

"This is going to be Steven's room," Olivia said with an apologetic shrug.

"But he isn't staying!" Tatiana cried. "They said it would only be for a few days!"

"I guess he'll be here longer," Olivia said. "I have to go now. Katherine and Michelle are waiting to play."

She closed the door as she left the room. Tatiana grabbed the nearest stuffed animal and threw it with all her might. The toy dog hit the wall with a soft but satisfying thud, then fell in a twisted heap to the floor. Tatiana jumped from the bed and ran to pick it up.

"Bear!" she cried. She picked up the floppy dog and hugged it close. "Did I hurt you?"

Bear, of course, did not answer.

Tatiana held him tightly, feeling anger beyond her years. It wasn't fair! It just wasn't fair! If they'd been in the woods, they'd know Steven was up to something! Then her mommy (her second mommy—not her *real* mommy, she decided) would know she wasn't a liar at all.

She began to throw all her things into the center of her bedspread, planning to gather it all up together like a hobo's bundle. No way was she going to leave one item in here for stupid Steven to mess up!

One by one, each of her belongings went into the pile. Her anger grew until at last she threw a doll with such force that it bounced against the headboard and landed with a flattened nose. At once Tatiana ran around the bed to pick up the injured doll. She hugged it close and began to cry loudly.

"It isn't fair, Daisy! It isn't fair!"

Downstairs, Eric had come home from the hardware store. When he walked into the house, he stood at the bottom of the stairs and called up.

"Rachel?"

Instead of his wife, he heard Tatiana's loud wails.

Wondering what had made the child so miserable, he hurried up to her room. Eric found his daughter sitting with her back against the side of her bed, her "Daisy" doll clutched tightly in her arms.

"Tati? What's wrong, honey?"

Tatiana looked up at him with red, brimming eyes.

"She's making me give my whole room to Steven," she complained. "Olivia says Mommy wants me to take everything out of my room and give it to him, forever!"

Eric crouched down.

"Honey, you must have misunderstood," he said. "Nobody's going to make you give up your room forever!"

"But . . ."

Eric helped her to her feet.

"Come on," he said. "We'll find your mother, and she'll explain things. Everything will be all right, you'll see."

Sniffling, Tatiana wiped her nose on the back of her sleeve. Eric found a box of tissues on her dresser and handed some to her. Then they went downstairs together.

They found Helga ironing in the laundry room.

"Mrs. Freleng went out?" Eric asked.

"She went shopping," Helga said. She nodded her head toward Tatiana. "She is not supposed to be out of her room."

Eric frowned at his daughter. "You didn't tell me that. What happened, exactly?"

Tatiana hung her head. "Something got Ralphie Mercken in the woods, and Steven did it, and when I told Mommy, she didn't believe me, and now I'm in trouble."

"What do you mean, 'something got Ralphie Mercken in the woods'?" Eric repeated.

Tatiana told him what she'd told Rachel. When she finished, Eric looked to Helga for clarification, but the German woman only shrugged.

"Do you believe me?" Tatiana asked hopefully.

Eric sighed. "I know you don't tell lies, Tatiana. But maybe you were mistaken. If Ralphie had bullied Steven, why would he lie about it?"

"Mr. Freleng," Helga said, "if I may say something? You were a boy once. Would you tell when someone was stronger than you?"

Eric thought about this, then nodded.

"Steven was too embarrassed to admit what happened," he said. He looked down at Tatiana. "But it's hard for me to buy that part about the wind."

"It's true!"

"If it had really happened," Eric pointed out, "then there would be leaves and branches down in this whole area."

He pointed out the window, across the back field.

"But look at the edge of the woods," he said. "Not a broken branch or fallen leaf to be seen!"

Tatiana's lower lip began to tremble.

"You don't believe me either," she said.

Eric picked her up and hugged her.

"Honey, I don't think you're lying," he said. "I think you have an overactive imagination. And I think that you should respect Steven's wishes for privacy. If he wants to talk about what Ralphie did, he will."

They heard the front door open and close.

"Come on, your mother is home," Eric said as he put his daughter down again. "Let's talk with her."

"Daddy, I'm scared . . ."

"Of what?" Eric asked. "She's your mother, and she loves you. She'd never hurt you!"

But she already did, Tatiana thought. She wanted to tell her father this, but she was just too young to put the concept of emotional hurt into words.

Rachel and Steven were halfway up the stairs, both burdened with packages, when Eric stopped them. Rachel turned around and gave Tatiana a hard look.

"You weren't supposed to leave your room," she said. "Eric, did Tatiana tell you she's been a bad girl? She was sent to her room for lying."

"She told me what happened," Eric said. "I think we need to talk."

"Steven," Rachel said, "take these up to your room and unpack them. I'll come up in a few minutes to help you put them away."

"Okay," Steven said. "But I can just leave them in the bags. I don't want to take any of Tatiana's drawers away."

He turned to the little girl, but Tatiana only stuck her tongue out at him.

"Did you see that?" Rachel cried. "That child is becoming a brat! She needs to be punished, Eric! She's selfish and spoiled and—"

"That's enough, Rachel!" Eric snapped. He put an arm around Tatiana.

"You go on outside and play, honey," he said. "Forget about what happened. You let me handle everything."

Tatiana opened her mouth to say something, but decided she'd better not press her luck. Instead, she opened the front door and ran from the house. At that moment she wanted to be as far away from stupid-old-Steven, and her mother too, as possible.

Not to be outdone, Rachel looked at Steven.

"Go on up," she said. "And don't worry about the drawers."

Steven hurried up the stairs, grateful to be away from a family altercation.

17

SAMANTHA SETTLED Julie in front of a cartoon show with a cup of hot chocolate. Then she took the paper John had given her upstairs to her room. She sat on the edge of her bed, staring at the phone for a long time. She wondered if the horrible feeling of dread would overcome her again, freezing up her insides and making her want to scream.

She didn't give herself much more time to dwell on the possibility. Her hand shot out and grabbed the receiver, punching in the numbers as if afraid that, any second now, something would make her fingers stop moving.

Nothing happened. It was going to be all right.

She had let the line ring about fifteen times and was about to hang up when a voice answered with words she couldn't decipher.

"Pardon me?" she asked. "Is this the Sherer Detective Agency?"

There was a moan, and a moment later a voice said, "This is Wil Sherer. Sorry. I was sleeping."

Sleeping, in the middle of the day? Samantha wondered how good a detective he could be if he had so little to do.

"Uh, what can I do for you?" Sherer asked.

"My name is Samantha Winstead. We have a mutual friend, John Brightman?" Samantha introduced herself. She heard an acknowledging sort of noise from the other end of the line. "I have a problem, and he told me you might be of help. You see, I—"

"Wait," the detective said. "I don't discuss business over the phone. Can you meet me this afternoon?"

Samantha looked toward her door, as if she could see downstairs to where Julie sat watching television.

"I don't know," she said. "I have a child here. Well, I could try to get a baby-sitter."

"I like kids," Sherer said. "You can bring him along."

"It's a girl," Samantha said. "She's the object of all this. And I'd prefer not to bring her."

She felt that Julie had been upset enough that day.

"Well, you make arrangements," Sherer said. "I'm just off a case, so I'm pretty free for the next few days. Just give me a call."

He hung up before Samantha could say another word. She looked at her alarm clock. According to the time, Barbara Huston was off-duty. If she hadn't gone out after work, she'd be home by now.

"Wishful thinking," Samantha said. "Barbara's probably got a date. Even if it is a week night."

But Barbara was her only choice. She prayed her friend would be home, and willing to baby-sit. Samantha was certain that if she didn't meet Wil Sherer this afternoon, she'd never meet him. Her fear of anything to do with the police promised that.

She dialed Barbara's number and was delighted when her friend answered the phone.

"Hi, Barbara," she said. "Are you busy this afternoon?"

"Not until eight," Barbara said. "Hang on, I have to switch ears."

A moment later: "I'm cooking here. Fred Matlin is coming for dinner."

"Who's that?"

"One of the guys from the lab," Barbara said. "Why do you want to know if I'm busy?"

Samantha felt like an intruder. "Forget it. I was going to ask you to watch Julie, but . . ."

"Where are you going?"

Samantha told her about Wil Sherer.

"Samantha, are you sure?" Barbara asked. "I mean, think of the way you reacted each time you tried to call the police!"

"It didn't happen this time," Samantha said. "I can't see any other way to solve this mystery."

"Well . . ." Barbara seemed to be thinking it over.

"Can you bring Julie to my apartment?"

"You'll watch her?" Samantha asked. "What about your date?"

"He doesn't get off until seven. You'll be back by then, won't you?"

"I should think so," Samantha said.

"Then bring Julie on over," Barbara said.

They agreed on a time, and hung up. Samantha immediately dialed Wil Sherer's number and made arrangements to see him within the hour. Then she went downstairs. The television was turned off, and Julie wasn't in the living room. Following the sound of running water, she traced the child's whereabouts to the kitchen.

"I'm rinsing out my cup," Julie said.

"That's nice of you," Samantha said. "Someone's taught you good manners."

Julie didn't respond, as if she was growing bored of this mysterious "someone."

"Can I go outside and play with the dogs?" she asked.

"Later," Samantha said. "Right now, I have someplace important to go. Barbara Huston said you could stay at her place for a few hours."

"She's the doctor from the maternity ward?"

"The very same," Samantha said. "Barbara's very nice. You had a bad scare, so you didn't really meet her."

Julie nodded, her hands holding fast to the edge of the sink. "It was scary, where the tiniest babies were."

"Can you talk about it now?"

Julie turned around. "I think so. I went up there looking for Dr. Huston, because you said she'd show me the babies."

"I'm sorry I couldn't keep my promise," Samantha said.

"There weren't many people there," Julie said. "I guess everyone was busy eating lunch. I took a look around, and I found the nursery."

She pouted. "They had the shades pulled down. I could hear crying, but I couldn't see a thing. Anyway, then I saw a window open down the hall."

She went on to tell how she'd crept into the preemie ward, but hadn't found any babies right away.

"Then I heard crying, and I looked behind a curtain."

She squeezed her eyes shut and shuddered visibly.

"It was terrible! I saw that baby in that glass box and I was so scared! It made me think of a bad thing, of being stuck in a glass box I couldn't get out of!"

Chills ran through Samantha as she tried to imagine what had happened to the child to make her think of such a thing.

"That is frightening," she said. "But don't you worry. You see, I'm going to see a private detective today. He's going to help us find out where you came from."

"Really?" Julie said. "What if it's a bad place? Will I have to go back?"

Samantha thought about this. The idea of giving Julie up was still too painful to contemplate.

"I don't know," she admitted. "But once we clear this up, someone is going to be in a lot of trouble. I don't think anyone will make you live with people who play mean tricks like this."

Julie put her arms around Samantha and gave her a big hug.

"Let's get going," Samantha said. "I have to be at the detective's office in an hour."

Actually, she was there in almost half that time. She found Wil Sherer's address on Laredo Street, one of a row of renovated Victorian houses. There was a small patch of pebble-covered land in front, decorated with various species of cactus. Dustballs and bits of scrap clung to the needles, blown by the wind. Forgotten newspapers, tattered and soggy, lay to either side of the walk. Samantha wondered what kind of detective kept his home in such disarray.

She climbed up the stone stairs onto a porch still strewn with last autumn's leaves. She located a bell next to the dark green storm door and pressed. There was an L-shaped tear in the screen. Behind it, the inside door stood open, allowing a view straight back to the kitchen. A figure, silhouetted by backlight pouring through a rear window, stood at a refrigerator tacking up a piece of paper.

"Come on in, Dr. Winstead," Wil Sherer called.

Samantha entered a small and dusky living room. The bare floor, patched with dull spots where the polyurethane finish had worn off, was littered with newspapers, clothing, and other domestic debris. Next to a television set stood a beautiful turn-of-the-century mission chair, its back resting in the rearmost notch of its arms. A slate-gray jacket had been tossed into it. The antique chair seemed out-of-place in this mess, as did the Shaker-style table that stood in front of it. A suitcase lay open and unpacked on the tabletop.

Samantha had never seen such a mess. She hoped Sherer proved to be a more efficient detective than he was a homemaker.

The man in question appeared at the living-room door.

"Sorry," he said, "I was weeding through messages my housekeeper left."

Like his home, Wil Sherer was a mix of styles. It was hard to guess his age: his eyes were marked with crow's-feet, but his light brown hair had no gray in it. He wore it in a punkish cut, short and raggy around the front and sides and long down the back. There was a three-day growth of beard on his face, outlined by heavy cheekbones. The T-shirt and whitewashed jeans he wore would have given him a James Dean look, except for the Top-Siders he wore. He stared quizzically with cobalt eyes, waiting for an answer.

Samantha was incredulous, and could only say, "You have a housekeeper?"

Wil's laugh was deep and hearty.

"Actually, a kid who came in to feed the animals," he said. "He answered a few calls too."

He held up a hand. "Wait a second."

He disappeared into what seemed to be a bedroom. Moments later he emerged wearing an ecru pullover shirt decorated across the chest with spice-colored Indian designs.

"Come on, let's go back in my office. It's more comfortable there."

He offered her a hand, as if she couldn't navigate solo through all the clutter. His grip was firm and warm.

"Sorry about the mess," Wil said. "I just got back from Africa two days ago."

"Africa," Samantha said. "How exciting! What did you do there?"

She expected to hear a glamorous story of a safari.

"Child-abduction case," Wil explained. "I've been working on this one for three years."

"Did you find the child?"

"Yeah, but it wasn't easy getting him," Wil said. "I had some mercenaries involved in 'rekidnapping' him. But it was worth it. He's home with his mother now."

Samantha smiled. How could anyone be so matter-of-fact about such an adventure?

"You must be glad when such a long case turns out successfully."

"You bet," Wil agreed.

Unlike the living room, Wil's office was neat and efficiently furnished. Samantha guessed Wil spent most of his time in here. An oak and black laminate computer center had been built around one corner of the room, well-lit by overhead track lights and two tall prairie windows. Books and other knickknacks filled some of the cubbies, but most were occupied by small cages and aquariums.

"You have so many pets!" she exclaimed. 'Julie would love it here."

Samantha neared one cage and searched among the rocks and branches inside. She couldn't see anything.

"Barney lives in there," Wil said. "He's a reticulated python. I don't think Julie would like him very much. He's got a bad temper."

Wil showed her the marks of a bite on the heel of his right hand.

"Is Julie your daughter?"

"Oh, no," Samantha said. "She's the reason I came to see you."

Wil swung a wheeled office chair around and pushed it toward her. She sat down. He started to do so himself, but stopped.

"Sorry," he said. "I've been out of touch with civilization for so long I've forgotten my manners. Do you want some coffee or tea or something?"

"No, thanks," Samantha said with a smile. As far as she could see, Wil's manners were just fine.

"Then let's get on with your story," he said. "What exactly do you want me to do?"

"I want you to find Julie's real family," Samantha said. "You see, I only met her a few days ago. I woke up in a strange motel room, and there she was."

"Did she say how she got there?"

Samantha shook her head.

"She said she came from some kind of home," Samantha said. "She can't remember anything else. At least, nothing concrete. She does have some frightening memories—almost 'daymares.'"

Wil sat back in his chair, rubbing his thumb along his jawline.

"Let me understand this," he said. "You've got some kid living with you that you don't know, have never seen before, and want to get rid of?"

"I didn't say that!" Samantha protested. "I really care about Julie. In truth, it's the very fact that I'm beginning to love her like a daughter that's brought me to you. I can't let myself become attached to this little girl if her family is waiting for her to come back. Detective Sherer, I need to find out who she is and where she came from. I need to know why she's been given to me, of all people."

"First of all, let's stop with the 'Detective' and 'Doctor' business, okay?"

"Okay. 'Samantha' will be fine."

"I guess you've called the police?" Wil asked.

He noted the sudden look of anxiety in his new client's eyes.

"No, I can't call the police," Samantha said. She began to twist her fingers together nervously. "Something bad will happen if I do."

"Like what?"

"I . . . I don't know," Samantha said. "But every time I try to call them, I become so terrified it's like falling off a ledge!"

Wil heard that the calm, strong voice she'd used when she first came in had been reduced to a tremulous, mouselike gasp.

"Hey, take it easy," he said.

Samantha shook her head, swallowing. "I'm fine, really."

"No, you're not fine," Wil said. "You won't be fine until we figure out what's happening here. So, why don't you start from the beginning?"

Samantha thought for a few moments, trying to find a starting point. Suddenly Wil got up.

"Wait a second," he said. "I want to put this on tape, if you don't mind."

"It's fine with me."

"Good, it'll make my job easier," Wil said. "Hang on a second."

He went to a door at the back of the room and opened it.

"The tape recorder's right here in the closet," Wil said, mostly to himself. "At least, I think it is."

Samantha watched him as he reached up and pulled a light cord.

When she saw the old police uniform hanging neatly by itself on the rack, she began to scream.

"Get it away! Get it away!"

Wil grabbed his tape recorder, turned off the light, and closed the door. He hurried to Samantha.

"What's the matter?" he asked. "What's wrong?"

Now that the closet was secured again, Samantha opened her tear-filled eyes and gasped for breath.

"What the *hell* was that all about?"

"The . . . the uniform," she said. "You're a cop?"

She gazed at him with wide eyes that begged him to say it wasn't true.

"Not these days," he said. He scratched his head, looking at the closet. "Someone's really done a number on you, Samantha. I don't know what this is all about, but I'm intrigued. Are you ready to talk to me? Or do you need a few minutes?"

Samantha shook her head. She wiped the tears from her eyes and straightened her shoulders.

"I'm ready," she said in a husky voice. "I'm ready to put an end to this craziness, once and for all. Make yourself comfortable. This is a long and crazy story. . . ."

For the next forty-five minutes Samantha told the detective all she could about her strange situation. The tape recorder hummed in the background, while various critters busied themselves in their small homes. When at last she finished, Wil reached over and pressed the Stop button. Then he glanced down at the pad where he'd also been taking notes.

"Let's see what we've got here," he said.

Samantha watched his full lips move silently as he read to himself. She felt uncomfortable that she'd had one of her "attacks" in front of a virtual stranger. He probably thought she was some kind of hysteric.

One of the animals began to fuss noisily. Samantha stood up and looked inside a cage to find a butterscotch-colored mop skimming around the cedar-chipped floor. Wil looked up at her, one arm resting on the oak top of his desk.

"That's a Peruvian guinea pig," he said. "Her name is Brandy."

"She's cute," Samantha said.

"Cuter than the python, anyway," Wil agreed.

Samantha returned to her seat and gazed hopefully at the detective.

"What do you think?" she asked.

"I think," Wil said, "that the very first thing we must do is locate the orphanage Julie came from. You said you looked it up in both Millersville and Ashleigh?"

Samantha nodded, her Dutch-boy hair bobbing.

"There wasn't any such place listed."

"Well, it may not even be in Colorado," Wil said. "I'll check with Social Services. Finding Henley is another matter entirely. I'd bet it was a pseudonym. Did the kid remember anything about him?"

"Not a thing," Samantha said. "But those dreams I told you about—maybe the man forcing her into a box is Mr. Henley?"

She became pensive. "I wonder if she was also brain-washed? I wonder if we've been 'programmed' to like each other?"

Wil leaned forward, taking both her hands in his. It was the gesture of a longtime friend. Samantha considered him with hazel eyes.

"You care about her," he said in soft, deep tones, "because you are a kind and caring person. I can tell that by the way you responded to my pets. I've worked on many child-abduction cases, and I've seen true evil. That's what people who did this to you are—true evil. But I think we can find them, and I know we can stop them."

For some reason, Samantha felt completely mesmerized. His words reached her as if through a dream. It was a few minutes after he had finished speaking before she managed to extract her hands from his.

"Uh, yes . . ." she stammered. She made a show of

looking at her watch. "Oh, it's late. Julie will be wondering about me."

"I'll need a picture of her," Wil said. "To run through Missing Persons."

Samantha looked worried.

"*You* may not be able to get to the police," Wil said, "but no one tampered with my mind."

"Of course," Samantha said.

She stood up. Wil did the same.

"When can I expect to hear from you?"

"Tomorrow morning," Wil said. "Are you working then?"

"Yes," Samantha said. "Ask for Marie. If I'm not available, she'll get a message to me."

She started out of the office. Wil hurried to precede her, kicking trash out of her way as they walked to the front door.

"I'm going to enjoy the challenge of working on this case," he said as he opened the door for Samantha.

"As long as you help end it," Samantha said. "Because I don't enjoy being someone's pawn."

18

LORRAINE WAS BEGINNING to feel restless. She'd exhausted all her activities, and though she held on to the fashion doll, she didn't really feel like playing with it. It was scary, being kept inside like this. She kept feeling she had to be on her way to . . . somewhere. If only she knew where to find her family!

She began to skip around the apartment, her shoes thudding loudly on the bare wooden floor. A moment later there was a pounding noise from beneath the floor. Someone was hitting the ceiling with a broom. Bettina looked up from her knitting.

"Don't do that, child," she said. "Sounds travel quickly in an old building like this."

Lorraine came to the couch and bounced into the cushions.

"There's nothing more to do," she said, frowning.

Bettina went on knitting. Lorraine thought the old woman was ignoring her. But after a few minutes she came to the end of a row and set the work aside.

"I know it's hard," she said. "But I promise you, we won't stay in here forever. We just have to be certain that man never learns where you are. I'm sure you're right to be afraid of him. The only safe thing to do is stay hidden for a while."

Lorraine shuddered, and moved closer to the old woman. Bettina put an arm around her.

"I don't know how to deal with such an intelligent child," Bettina said. "Your mind works too quickly. Most children would take days to complete the activities you've finished in a few hours."

She looked around herself at the barren apartment.

"It's too bad we don't have a television," she said. She snapped her fingers. "But why not? We certainly have enough money for a small set, don't we? I saw one in that electronics store down the block. It was only one-ninety-nine."

"Tax will make it about two-fifteen," Lorraine estimated. "Are you sure it's okay? I don't want to run out of money and have to go back to the streets again."

"We've paid a month in advance for this place," Bettina reassured her. "And I think the hours will pass more quickly with entertainment."

She stood up and went to the closet; actually, a doorless recess into the wall. Bettina pulled out her jacket and put it on. Then she took the case of money from its hiding place and removed some of it.

"Two hundred fifty dollars," Lorraine said, immediately aware of the amount.

"I thought perhaps I'd get a few board games too," Bettina said. "Surely a smart little girl like you is old enough to play with an adult."

She tucked it deep into her pocket.

"I'm going now," she said. "I won't be but a few minutes, so you keep the door locked tightly and don't let anyone in!"

She unlocked the door and stepped into the hall.

"Remember, I'll be back in a short while," she said. "Keep the door locked. And stay away from the window!"

"I will," Lorraine promised, having no desire to see that frightful stranger again.

She listened as the old woman descended the creaking staircase. The sound subsided after a few moments, but then Lorraine heard the very clear sound of the front door being slammed.

She went to the kitchen for a drink of water. A few minutes later, a knock beckoned her to the door, but she stopped in her tracks halfway across the room. Bettina had said not to let anyone inside. What if that bad man had gotten into the building?

"I know you're in there," a voice called. "Open the door."

Lorraine held her breath, not daring to move.

Go away!

"It's the landlord," the voice said. "We've got a problem I have to check out."

Lorraine went to the door.

"Are you really the landlord?" she asked.

The man said some words Lorraine didn't understand, and added in an exasperated tone, "You want to see an ID, kid? Open the door."

"I can't," Lorraine said. "Come back when Bettina is home."

"Hey, kid," the man said, "if we wait till Bettina comes home, there ain't gonna be no home. It's a gas problem. We traced a leak to this apartment."

Lorraine tried to understand this, but it didn't make sense to her.

"What do you mean?"

"I mean the apartment'll blow up!" the man cried. "Now, are you gonna open the door or do I get my key?"

Lorraine thought: If he has his own key, he'll get in anyway. She decided to open the door. The landlord was a frail man who seemed nearly ninety years old, but who was, in truth, just fifty. He brushed by her, leaving a trail of tobacco and liquor and after-shave-smells. Lorraine climbed up onto the couch, kneeling on the cushions and resting her elbows on the back while she watched him work at the stove. Pulling tools from a wooden box, he looked over his shoulder.

"Hey, kid," he said. "You wanna come here and hold something for me?"

"Okay," Lorraine said, jumping from the couch and bounding over to him. She was glad to have something new to do. "What do you want me to hold?"

"This," the man said.

He turned, one hand reaching into the unzipped fly of his pants. He took something out.

"Huh?" Lorraine asked, completely confused. She'd never seen anything like the pinkish-purplish thing in his hand.

"Hold it, kid," the man said. His voice sounded funny, rasping. His eyes had gone sleepy.

Lorraine backed away with a cry. Though many of her memories had been lost in the last few days, something deep down told her this was sick, a bad thing.

"Go away!" she cried. "You get out of here!"

"I said 'hold this,' you little . . ."

His hand shot toward her, fingers curled like talons to grab her long dark hair. Lorraine screamed, backing away and stumbling to the floor.

The man was about to shout something, but suddenly his words were obliterated by a sudden cry of pain. His face went completely pale, and his eyes grew so wide the whites showed all the way around. He began to make odd gasping noises, turning his body, with great effort, toward the stove. Confused, the little girl backed away and watched an impossible scene unfold.

The man had been resting his free hand on one of the cold burners of the stove. But now it had somehow changed, to become an iron shackle lined with sharp spikes. Lorraine watched, speechless, and the "cuff" grew tighter and tighter around her assailant's wrist. He screamed, trying to wrench it free. The more he struggled, the more blood gushed from the circle of wounds.

"Oh, shit!" the man screamed in agony. "Oh, *shit!*"

The landlord's view of the apartment faded away, replaced by waving blue and white light. In that light, he knew, lay all the most horrible, dangerous, vile things imaginable. And they were coming to get him. They were going to tear him apart.

I'm gonna die!

"What's wrong with you?" Lorraine demanded. "Stop doing that! Get out of here!"

The man went on screaming, waiting for the . . . *things* to get him.

"Go away!" he cried.

"You go away!" Lorraine shouted, not understanding.

At that moment the shackle became the top of the burner again, and the man was free. The blue-and-white mist faded away, but not the sense that the horrors within were waiting for him. But he wouldn't let them catch him, no sir. Without even looking at the child he'd come here to molest, he raced from the apartment, completely out of his mind.

Lorraine bent over, clutching her stomach to keep the sickness she felt from rising. She heard the man's screams all the way down the stairs. The door slammed, and seconds later Lorraine heard the man shouting something, followed by a screech of tires.

Where was Bettina? she wondered.

I'm scared! I'm so scared! What am I gonna do?

Lorraine? I'm here now, Lorraine. Don't be afraid.

The little girl kept herself rolled up in a shrimplike ball.

You're back again? Marty?

It's me.

Why did you do that? Why do you make scary things?

It wasn't me this time, Lorraine. It was you. You did it to make him stop.

I didn't!

I didn't realize it until now, but you have the same type of power that I have. We are not all as strong as this.

No, no, no, no . . .

Don't be afraid! It's all over. He was hit by a car. He won't hurt you again.

Lorraine's thoughts were silent for a moment.

I . . . I killed him? she asked uncertainly.

He killed himself. He ran into the street. They'll find drugs in his body and say he went insane. But you can't ever let anyone know what happened here. It will ruin our plans.

But . . . but Bettina . . .

Bettina can't know. She isn't one of us. You aren't supposed to be with her.

Who am I supposed to be with?

I don't know. Lorraine, you have to get up. You can't let the old lady see you crying. She'll ask questions.

Lorraine was about to reply when the door suddenly burst open. Bettina came rushing in, accompanied by a young man carrying a boxed TV set.

"Oh, you're safe!" Bettina cried, rushing to take the child in her arms. "Thank God, you're safe."

"Man, I never saw anything like that," the delivery boy said. "It was like he was crazy or somethin', yellin' stuff about monsters in the building."

Marty, will people come up here now?

But Marty was gone.

"You're shaking like a leaf," Bettina said. She looked at the child. "Did that man do something to you?"

"No!" Lorraine cried. She realized it came out too strongly, and to cover herself said: "I was looking out the window. I saw that man die!"

"Poor child," Bettina said. "What a terrible thing for young eyes to witness."

The delivery boy stepped forward. "Where do you want the TV? I gotta go back."

Bettina waved her hand toward one corner. The boy unpacked the box and arranged the small set up on top of an old dresser. He left without a word.

"Are you sure nothing happened?"

Lorraine felt that Bettina knew she was hiding something. She held the woman tightly, wishing she could tell her everything, but knowing she never could.

Outside, someone else had heard the man's strange talk of monsters. He was a very nondescript man: a plain pale face with small round glasses perched on a stubby nose; fine receding brown hair, mundane gray suit. He stood among the crowd of people waiting for the police to arrive at the accident scene. His eyes were focused on the apartment building from which the man had come running.

A few days ago he had foolishly lost a very important item. Now he was more than convinced he'd found it again.

"I know you're up there," he whispered, as if Lorraine could hear him.

He'd be glad to get her back and placed with the right family. Walter LaBerge had said this was his last chance to redeem the mistake he'd made. The man was absolutely determined not to blow it this time.

With determination marking his stride, he pushed his way across the street and entered the apartment building.

19

IT DIDN'T SURPRISE Samantha that she felt better just for having spoken to Wil Sherer. He was an eccentric, but she could tell he had a good heart and was dedicated to his work. If anyone could help her, it seemed he could.

The sun was setting as she drove to Barbara's house, pink and purple cirrus clouds waving like banners over the mountains. It gave the blue spruce a violet cast. There was a dreamy quality to the landscape now, like something from a Victorian watercolor. But Samantha, filled with thoughts of her conversation with Wil, hardly noticed it.

Barbara lived on the second floor of a colonial house in a modest apartment furnished from catalogs. She didn't spend much time there, always off on a date with somebody or other. Samantha remembered she had a dinner date tonight, and hoped Julie wasn't getting in the way. She'd find that hard to believe, but a couple having dinner might think the very presence of a child was a nuisance.

She climbed the brick steps and pressed the top doorbell. A light came on over her head, and a moment later she heard footsteps on the stairs. Barbara opened the door.

"Hi!" she said. "How'd it go?"

"He's going to help me," Samantha said, following her up the staircase to the apartment.

"Oh," Barbara said without much enthusiasm.

"You could be more encouraging," Samantha said.

Barbara sighed, turning to look at her friend as she entered the apartment.

"It's just that I'm so afraid of you being accused of something you didn't do," she said. "That detective will eventually have to work through the police, and I'm not sure they'll believe your reasons for not contacting them."

"Detectives work independently," Samantha said. "And in confidence."

She looked around. They were standing in a short hallway, the Navajo-print wallpaper decorated with dozens of small paintings in terra-cotta frames. Barbara dabbled in acrylics on the side, and had designated one of the apartment's four rooms as a sort of office/studio. Samantha could almost guess that's where she'd find Julie, but she asked anyway.

"She's painting," Barbara said. "That kid's got talent. But she keeps painting the same things. Always beach scenes, and always with a yellow house."

Samantha felt her heart skip a beat. She ignored the sense of uneasiness and headed toward the back room.

Julie was wearing an old flannel shirt. She peeked around the corner of an easel and grinned at the sight of Samantha.

"Hi!" she said.

She put down the paintbrush and ran to give her caretaker a hug.

"How've you been doing?" Samantha asked. "Barbara says you were painting."

She made no move to look at the child's work.

"It's been fun," Julie said. "Barbara's really nice. We made peanut-butter cookies too."

Samantha gave her friend a surprised look.

"*You* made peanut-butter cookies?" she asked. "I thought you hated baking."

"Well, there weren't any snacks in the house," Barbara admitted. "And Fred likes them too."

"I was worried he might be here already," Samantha said. "That Julie might be in your way."

"Not at all!" Barbara insisted. "And he likes kids, really. Besides, he'd have to like Julie. She did most of the baking herself. I've never met a kid like you, Julie. You're amazing. Is there anything you can't do?"

Julie laughed in a self-deprecating way. She looked down at her toes. Yes, there was something she couldn't do. She couldn't remember where she came from. But she didn't say this.

"Julie, why don't you clean up the paintbrushes?" Samantha said. "We'll be leaving in a few minutes. Would you like to go out to dinner?"

"Okay," Julie said.

The doorbell rang. Barbara excused himself to go down and answer it. As Julie began to clean up, she handed Samantha a large piece of paper.

"This is for you," she said. "It's the first one I did, so it's sort of dry."

Samantha studied the painting. It was a beach scene, broad and virtually empty. The strangely familiar yellow house with green shutters stood to one side, a triangle of light brightening one half of it as the sun shone down. On the other side of the painting Julie had depicted a concession stand. Samantha remembered the pictures she had drawn at the hospital. In those, the concession stand was also decorated with blue dolphins. This, too, looked familiar. Something about the blue-and-white awning stirred such memories in Samantha that she could almost hear it flapping in the summer breeze. There was a sign leaning against it: "HAYBROOK'S."

"It's beautiful," Samantha said, wondering why that name sounded so familiar. "Is it a place you've been to?"

"I don't know," Julie said.

But maybe I've been there myself. I'm sure I've heard that name before!

Julie pointed. "Do you see the little girl on the beach?"

She pointed to the picture's only living being. A young girl with long dark hair stood with her back to the viewer. She wore a one-piece shortall of red and white gingham, and held a red metal bucket by its broken handle. There was a picture of a fat white crab painted on the bucket's side.

Samantha felt a chill rush over her. There was something very, very familiar about that bucket. . . .

"Samantha!"

With a gasp, Samantha turned around at the sound of Barbara's voice. Barbara gave her an odd look, then said:

"This is Dr. Fred Matlin. Fred, I'd like you to meet my good friend Dr. Samantha Winstead. Fred also graduated from St. Francis."

Though Fred Matlin stood a good three inches shorter than Barbara, and barely an inch taller than Samantha, the confident way he threw back his shoulders seemed to heighten him considerably. He had a young, soft-featured face, his raggedy-cut hair the color of an old penny. Behind red-rimmed glasses his green eyes sparkled brightly.

"It's always exciting to meet an alumnus. What year?" Barbara giggled, sounding more like a child than Julie. "You aren't supposed to ask questions like that!"

What a flirt, Samantha thought.

"Sorry," Fred said. "I remember Barbara from several parties, although we weren't in any classes together. And I'm pretty certain I can remember seeing you around campus too, although I'm not so sure."

Samantha smiled. "I'm sorry that I don't remember you." She really didn't feel like idle chatter.

"Barbara, thanks so much for taking care of Julie," she said. "You're a life-saver!"

"She was great," Barbara said. "You can come anytime you want, Julie."

" 'Bye, Barbara!"

Samantha led Julie down the stairs and out of the house. In the truck, Julie tugged at her sleeve and asked:

"Is something wrong, Samantha?"

"Nothing, honey," Samantha said. "I'm just tired."

"We don't have to go out to dinner," Julie said. "I don't mind."

"I don't feel like cooking," Samantha said. But she really wasn't in the mood to face a crowded restaurant either. "Why don't we hit the drive-in at Pancho Pedro's? We could bring stuff home."

"All right," Julie said.

"What would you like?"

Julie shrugged. "I don't know. What do they have?"

Samantha started up the car and drove down the road, reciting the quasi-Mexican menu of Pancho Pedro's fast-food restaurant.

"I've heard of tacos," Julie said. "I think I know what a tostada is. But what's a burrito?"

Samantha laughed. "You're kidding."

"No, I'm not," Julie said. "I don't know what a burrito is."

It was such a mundane food product around this area that Samantha wondered if she'd stumbled upon another clue in Julie's mystery. Had she led an extremely sheltered life?

"Well, let me think," Samantha said. "You start with a soft flour tortilla, then you add meat and beans and . . ."

By the time she finished describing the food, Julie was rubbing her stomach.

"It sounds yummy," she said. "I'll try one of those."

A few moments on Interstate 25 took them to a row of fast-food places. They passed Burger King, Taco Bell, and Wendy's before finally pulling into the parking lot of a bright orange-and-green sombrero-shaped building. Samantha wondered why all fast-food places were orange. She maneuvered the Bronco up to the speaker, gave her order, then drove to the window. A few minutes later she drove out again with their dinner.

"Hand me one of those onion rings," she said to Julie.

"Can I have one too?" Julie asked.

"Sure."

"Ow! They're hot!"

The onion rings burned Samantha's tongue, but still the entire bag was finished by the time they reached Samantha's house. She walked with Julie into the house, then said:

"Let's eat in front of the TV. I'll set up the tray tables."

When Julie turned on the television, Alex Trebeck was introducing the guests of *Jeopardy*. There were a lawyer, a teacher, and a writer. The categories came up: Famous Faces, Starts with an E, Solar System, American History, and Potpourri.

"I love to try to guess the questions to these answers," Samantha said, unwrapping the taco salad she'd bought for herself.

The lawyer chose the first answer, American History, for one hundred dollars.

"Prior to the Revolutionary War," Trebeck said, "British soldiers fired at a crowd and killed five people in this famous clash."

"The Boston Massacre," Julie said.

Samantha turned to look at her, but Julie was staring, mesmerized, at the television.

The teacher buzzed in.

"What is the Boston Massacre," she said.

"Good for you, Julie!" Samantha said. "You must like history."

"Maybe," Julie said.

More clues . . .

Julie breezed through the American History category. The lawyer was up again. This time he chose Solar System.

"Nothing moves faster than this."

"The . . . what is 'the speed of light'?"

Julie was shaking her head. Samantha laughed.

"What's wrong?"

"That isn't the right answer," Julie said.

"Of course it is," Samantha said, a bit relieved to see Julie didn't really know *everything*. "Nothing moves faster than light."

Julie didn't say anything. They had gone on to the next answer. By the time the commercial came on, Julie had given the correct questions to almost all the answers.

"Barbara's right," Samantha said. "You are amazing. I wonder if—"

The phone rang just then. Samantha excused herself and went to answer it. Wil Sherer was on the other end.

"I've been checking with Social Services about any orphanages in the area," he said. "There are only a few in this state, and none of them list a man named Henley on their staff. Since you 'came to' in Durango, and it's so close to Four Corners, I'll check those nearby states."

Samantha was amazed. Four Corners was the only place in the USA where four states met. Colorado was joined by New Mexico, Arizona, and Utah.

"If we have to go that far," she said, "we may never find who we're looking for."

"Have faith," Wil said.

And suddenly Samantha did. After all, Wil had gone as far as Africa to find another child.

"I'll get back to you on it," Wil said. "But I thought you'd want to know. Try mentioning the other states to the kid. Maybe something will ring a bell."

"I will," Samantha promised.

As before, Wil hung up without saying good-bye. Samantha returned to the living room to find Julie breezing through Double Jeopardy. She was so brilliant, Samantha thought, that she almost seemed beyond human.

20

ONCE THE CHILDREN were out of the way, Eric requested that he and Rachel have a talk in the den.

"We need some privacy," he said.

"If you want," Rachel said without much interest. As far as she was concerned, this whole thing was being blown out of proportion.

When they'd shut the door, Eric spoke as gently as he could.

"Rachel, what's wrong?" he asked. "You've never been unreasonable, especially with the girls."

"Maybe that's the trouble," Rachel said. "They've gotten away with too much, especially Tatiana."

"They're good kids," Eric insisted. "You know that too. Rachel, I believe our daughter. I think Ralphie Mercken did cause some trouble, and Steven is too shy to talk about it. I respect his right to privacy, but you have to respect Tatiana's right to be believed. She isn't a liar!"

"Steven said nothing happened in the woods," Rachel said.

"I know what he said," Eric replied. "But it's only right to be on the side of my own flesh and blood before I believe a virtual stranger."

Rachel turned and gazed out the window. She could see Tatiana pushing one of the neighborhood kids on the swing in their yard.

"She really isn't my flesh and blood," Rachel said in a quiet tone.

Eric could not answer his wife, he was so stunned by her comment. When he finally did find his voice, he said, "I'm going upstairs, Rachel. I'm going to talk to Steven myself, man-to-man."

Rachel swung around so quickly that it seemed she might be ready to attack.

"You will not disturb that child!" she cried. "Hasn't he been through enough?"

"Rachel, it's the only way to learn the truth!"

"Let's forget it, Eric," Rachel insisted. "It isn't that important."

"It is to Tati."

They did not realize it, but at this point their voices had escalated enough to be carried through the heating ducts into the upstairs. Steven crouched near the vent, listening. He didn't mean to cause such trouble in this family. He felt inexplicably close to Rachel, yes, but he didn't want her to love him back so exclusively that everyone else resented it. He didn't want to be hated, but he thought that maybe Tatiana did hate him.

No, he had to tell Eric what he wanted to know. He had to set things right.

Steven pulled open the door and headed to the staircase.

Stop!

Steven froze instantly. He listened, expecting to hear one of the girls, or perhaps Helga, behind him. But the upstairs of the house was silent. He could still hear Eric and Rachel arguing below, but their voices had faded.

Steven turned around. The hall was empty. It had only been his imagination. He began to walk again.

You can't go down there! Wait!

Now Steven recognized the voice of the mysterious boy named Marty. He felt a chill rush over his skin, to think how easily the boy had picked up on his thoughts. He wrapped his arms around himself and stood still, his mind keenly alert to Marty's presence.

What are you doing here?

I've come to prepare you. It's time to join with us, Steven. You must come to us, tonight.

How am I going to do that? I don't even know where you are.

I will guide you. There is little time now. We must unite or die.

I'm not going to die! And I don't want to leave Rachel.

You will die if you don't leave her.

I'm staying. I want to find my family.

Steven's thoughts were defiant, the voice in his mind speaking in angry tones. Maybe Marty had rescued him from the boy in the woods, but that didn't give him the right to be so bossy.

You don't have a family.

Marty's words were so unexpected they barely registered in Steven's mind.

Did you hear me? I said you don't have a family.

Yes, I do!

No one abandoned you, Steven. There was no one to leave you behind. You are alone, except for me. And the others.

You're lying!

Why would I lie? What purpose would it serve? You don't have a family, and only I can help you.

Rachel . . .

Rachel cares deeply about you. There is something special about her but I can't say exactly what it is. But she must be left behind. You have to come to us. You have to leave, tonight!

I don't!

You have to!

"I don't have to!"

"Steven?"

The boy turned with a gasp. Instantly he sensed Marty was gone. Rachel and Eric were coming up the stairs, and he hadn't even heard them. He gazed at them, blinking his eyes.

"Poor kid," Rachel said. She shot Eric an annoyed look. "You probably upset him with your yelling."

"We were both yelling," Eric pointed out wearily. He looked at Steven, who returned his gaze with innocent brown eyes.

"Are you okay?" he asked.

"I . . . I was going to get a drink of water," Steven said.

He wanted to throw himself into Rachel's arms. He wanted to tell her everything that had happened in the woods, except that a vague but powerful force was preventing him.

Instead, he turned and headed back to his room.

"Are you sure you're okay?" Rachel asked.

"Uh-huh."

"Well, we'll call you at dinnertime," Rachel said.

"Okay," Steven mumbled.

He opened the door to his room and went to lie on the bed. Staring up at the ceiling, he tried to make Marty come back. He waited and waited, but there was no sign of the other boy.

Well, good, Steven thought. Because he isn't going to make me leave here!

Still, he lay there for a long time. His mind was full of questions. What place did Marty want him to come to? Who were the other people? And what did the boy in his mind mean when he said: "You have no family"?

21

LORRAINE AND BETTINA sat in front of the television set, eating soup and sandwiches for dinner. Bettina had brought over two of the kitchen chairs. She sat in one, and they used the other for a table. Lorraine had chosen to make herself comfortable on a cushion pulled from the couch.

The more Archie and Edith fought with each other, the easier it became to forget what had happened on the street below. Lorraine hadn't said a word about what the landlord had tried to do to her—and what she, in turn, had done to him. She really didn't believe she was the one who had made him so afraid. The little girl was convinced it was solely Marty's doing.

Someone knocked at the Bunkers' door on the television. But when neither character got up to answer it, and the knocking became louder, Lorraine realized it was someone at their own door. She wriggled around on the cushion and tugged at the hem of Bettina's long skirt. They frowned silently at each other, wondering who could be there. With the exception of a few delivery people, only the landlord had known they were here. And it certainly wasn't him.

"Bettina," Lorraine whispered anxiously, "what if . . . what if it's that strange man?"

Bettina patted the child's head. "How could it be?"

The pounding went on. Lorraine begged the unseen person to go away.

"Hide in the bathroom," Bettina suggested. "He won't go away unless I answer."

Lorraine shot Bettina a distressed look, then did as she was told. She locked the door behind her and pressed her ear against it, hoping to make out what was being said. Only a few words filtered through the wood:

"Police . . . young child . . . seen here . . ."

". . . mistake, officer. I'm alone."

In the living room, Bettina stood with her body wedged in the small opening allowed by the still-fastened chain. The man in the hall was dressed in a gray suit, not a uniform. He stared at her through wire-rimmed glasses with the hardest eyes she'd ever seen. They were like cold, unemotional pieces of coal.

If Lorraine belongs to the likes of you, she thought to herself, I'll never give her back!

Out loud she said: "I'm an old woman. I certainly don't have the energy to take care of a child."

"I know she's in this building," the man said. "Have you seen her?"

"No, I haven't," Bettina said. "And I'm in the middle of dinner. Good-bye, sir."

She backed up just a second to allow herself to close the door. But in that brief time the man was able to look over her shoulder into the apartment. He took in the double set of dishes, a doll lying on the floor, a small lavender jacket draped over the edge of the couch.

Instantly Bettina slammed the door shut and locked it.

"Open up! Open this door!" the man cried, in a fury no sane member of the law would ever exhibit.

Bettina turned herself around crazily. He was going to take Lorraine away from her! He was going to take away the only thing in her life that mattered! She had to save the child, no matter what!

She hurried to the bathroom and tried to open the door. When she found it was locked, she said in an urgent voice:

"Lorraine, it's Bettina! Open up!"

Lorraine unlocked the door and threw herself into Bettina's arms.

"What does he want?" she asked. "Who is he?"

"He says he's a cop," Bettina said, even as the pounding on the door increased. "But I don't believe him."

"Bettina, what if he's the man with the gun?"

A new sound joined the pounding, alternating with it. Bettina realized he was also *kicking* the door. The old wood might not hold up for long.

"We have to get out of here," Bettina said. "The only way is the fire escape. Hurry and get the money valise!"

In her mind, Lorraine cried out for Marty, but he did not answer her.

She crawled under the couch and pulled the valise from its hiding place. At the same time, Bettina went to the window and opened it. Then she took the valise from Lorraine and threw it out onto the platform.

"Open up! This is official business, damn you!"

Lorraine gasped to realize she remembered him saying those exact words to the gang of boys. It *was* the man with the gun, and she instinctively knew he was not to be trusted.

Bettina was already out the window. Lorraine climbed out onto the fire escape herself.

"I don't know what kind of place you came from," Bettina said, "but I'll die before I let you go back."

Together she and Lorraine began to hurry down the five flights of metal stairs that zigzagged alongside the old building. Bettina carried the valise. Burdened this way, she could not move as quickly as she wanted. Youth was on Lorraine's side, and when the valise came sailing by her, she suddenly realized she was a full flight ahead of Bettina. She stopped and turned. Bettina was sitting on one of the higher steps, her arms crossed over her chest. She had dropped the money suitcase over the railing.

"Bettina!" Lorraine called. "Don't stop! We have to get away!"

"I . . . I . . . my heart . . ." Bettina gasped.

Lorraine stared up at her. Bettina had gone very, very pale. Even from down here Lorraine could see her shaking. She ran up to her friend.

"No . . . you run . . . my . . ."

"Don't talk, Bettina," Lorraine begged. "You're hurt!"

Bettina tried to smile reassuringly, but it changed into a hideous grimace of pain. Fire burned over her entire chest, radiating down her left arm. She tried to focus on Lorraine, to gather strength from the loving gray-green eyes (*such strange eyes*). But the pain was too great.

It had been years since her last heart attack. It had happened just after her husband's death, perhaps brought on by the stress of losing him.

She had awakened in a bright and sparkling clean ward,

surrounded by a dozen other beds. She had cried out in indignation—a woman of her standing should not be subjected to a place like this. She wanted a private room!

"You can't afford a private room," her sister-in-law had said to her. "You can't afford a frigging apartment any longer. Good-bye, Bettina. You're on your own."

It was the last contact she'd had with any member of her family.

All this took place in her mind within microseconds. The pain was so great, so terrible . . .

No, there was no longer pain. Just a peaceful feeling. Bright light surrounded her. For a moment she thought she was in the emergency ward again. But she was on her feet, moving. She walked toward the light, the peaceful, painless light.

"Bettina, no!"

She heard the child's scream. She wanted to tell her it was all right, but she couldn't. Bettina could do nothing but give in to the light. She entered it, and succumbed.

On the fire escape, Lorraine realized to her horror what had happened. Bettina was dead! Her savior, her beloved Bettina, was dead!

"Don't do that!" Lorraine cried out. "Don't go away from me! I *need* you!"

She screamed these last words, but Bettina did not respond. An explosive noise from up above brought the child to her senses. The strange man had broken through the door!

With tears filling her eyes, she kissed the kind old woman's soft cheek and said good-bye. There was no time for more.

By the time the man appeared at the open window, she was on the ground, grabbing the suitcase Bettina had thrown. He shot at her, but missed. Lorraine wasn't about to give him another chance. She ran as fast as her small legs could carry her.

22

IT WAS AMAZING how fast a little kid could disappear off the face of the earth. Once he'd broken down the door to the old woman's apartment, Joe Trefill had seen the open window and had pursued his quarry out onto the fire escape. He'd paused a flight above the old woman, wondering if he was walking into a trap. He thought she might grab him, making him lose his balance and fall into the filthy alley below. From that viewpoint he could see the child. He'd fired off a warning shot, deliberately missing her. LaBerge had made it very clear she wasn't to be harmed. Well, if that fat pig thought he could get the kid without a little rough stuff, let *him* try!

He'd screwed up, royally. LaBerge had also let him know that, and had promised him nothing more than his hide intact if he fixed it all up and delivered the child as planned.

Trefill had tucked the gun into its holster again before racing down the fire escape. He was no longer wary of the old woman—she could be dead, for all he cared. But he couldn't lose sight of that child!

He crashed out of the alley and onto the street, nearly slamming into a bag lady. She yelled something at him, but he didn't hear her. His eyes were focused about two streets ahead, on a fading patch of bright red. It was the kid's shirt. If he ran, he'd catch up to her. No way was some six-year-old bitch gonna get away from him twice!

Joe Trefill had been working for Walter LaBerge for ten years, and in all that time he still hadn't learned what LaBerge's work was all about. Something to do with weapons, he thought, because it was based in a New Jersey factory where they made parts for airplanes. All that secret government stuff, the stuff LaBerge didn't believe Trefill had the right to know despite his years of faithful service, always pointed to military crap. Trefill wasn't treated with much more respect than a lackey. But this time, he thought as he raced along Eighth Avenue, there was a chance to prove his real worth.

And he'd screwed up, royally.

The crowd grew more dense, making it impossible to keep track of the child any longer. Trefill was forced to slow down to keep from bumping into people. He moved ahead with a quick, impatient stride. The kid would have to stop and rest sometime. If it took all night, he'd find her.

He couldn't imagine what a six-year-old girl had to do with LaBerge's work. They'd acted as if she was very important. LaBerge had given him a big speech about trust, about how vital it was that he deliver the kid as planned. When they'd found her, the only information she'd been able to give was the name of a couple living in New England. They'd traced the man and woman. Then they'd given Trefill a suitcase full of money and instructions to bribe the couple so that they'd explain everything about the child.

But Trefill had gotten off the wrong train and had ended up in a bad section of New York City. He'd been mugged, and the kid had run away. It had taken him days to find her.

Now he'd lost her once again, but this time he was determined to get her back right away.

Feeling as tense as a hungry tiger, he went off to find his prey.

Lorraine had wanted to run as fast as she could, as far as she could. But the streets surrounding the apartment building were filled with people. Clutching the valise tightly to her chest, she kept her chin tucked down and wove her way through the crowd. Without much conscious effort her mind registered the variety of shoes she saw: platform high heels, black shoes and brown shoes, sneakers with fluorescent laces. Twice, a face looked up at her from the sidewalk, filthy visages belonging to men who were too drunk to even stand. Lorraine ignored them all, and in turn, they ignored her. In a city that had to claim countless homeless families, the sight of a child on the streets at night was nothing unusual.

She didn't dare look back, for fear the action would bring the stranger into view. Lorraine had no idea how much of a head start she had on him. He'd been five flights above her when she reached the ground level of the building, but if he'd been running he might be right behind her, just inches away from reaching out and grabbing her.

Her heart pounded behind the shieldlike suitcase. She moved around a puddle that filled the gutter of one corner and dared a quick glance to be sure there were no cars coming.

Lorraine had no idea where she was going. She only knew that she had to get as far away from the stranger as possible. Maybe he knew who she really was, but she was too terrified of him to find out. There was no one she could trust now that Bettina was . . . was . . .

Lorraine realized she had turned into a deserted street. Exhausted, she huddled in the doorway of a wholesale fabric shop and buried her face in her knees. She cried long and hard, thinking of the kindly homeless woman who had been like a mother to her these past days. Bettina had been strange, but she'd really *cared* about Lorraine. The child had sensed that from the start, and had felt marginally safe with her. Now she had no one, no place to go.

Something dripped on her head—water from an air conditioner. Sucking in a deep, shaky breath, Lorraine stood up and looked carefully up and down the block. She was alone. She kept to the shadows as she moved on, afraid someone might pass by and take notice of her. The little girl was too tired to run; the suitcase had grown heavier somehow. She knew she'd have to find a place to spend the night, but where? Could she hide out in a big box the way Bettina had that first night? Or could she stay hidden in another doorway?

The answer came to her at the next corner. She suddenly found herself looking at a brightly lit building. People were coming and going from it at a busy pace. There were all kinds—younger and older people, even kids. Not as young as herself, but young enough. Lorraine saw a crowd she could blend into and, with a surreptitious look behind herself, crossed over to the Port Authority Bus Terminal.

Lorraine had found a way to get out of the city, but as yet she didn't know where she was going. She passed a bagel stand and realized she was hungry. Carefully she reached into the pocket of her red sweater and pulled out a handful of change. She went up to the counter and bought a cinnamon-and-raisin bagel and an orange juice.

The man behind the counter was big and black, with a mouthful of crooked teeth that flashed a bright smile at her.

"You sure are a big lady to buy that all for yourself," he said.

Lorraine thought quickly. "It . . . it isn't for me. I'm sharing with my daddy."

The black man nodded.

"A little snack for the road, huh?" he asked.

Lorraine did not get a bad feeling from him, but still she didn't want to talk to anyone.

"Uh, yeah," she said. "My daddy's waiting for me. 'Bye!"

"Where are you headed?" the man called out.

Lorraine ignored him. Where, indeed? She found a place to sit, careful to choose a seat beside a sleeping man in case the bagel man looked up and saw her. Then, opening the orange juice and unwrapping the bagel, she looked up at the night's schedule: Teaneck, Bayonne, Elizabeth; the names meant nothing to her.

She took a bite of the bagel, but hardly tasted it. Suddenly the room around her seemed to grow blurry. Voices grew louder, but all masked together, so that individual words were incomprehensible. Out of it all, deep inside her mind, came the familiar voice of a boy.

Marty! Where were you?

I . . . They were busy with me. I'm sorry, Lorraine. Are you okay?

I'm scared. Bettina is dead!

Oh . . .

And a strange man is after me.

Don't let him catch you, Lorraine. He's dangerous. Something very bad is happening here, and he's part of it. You have to get out of that city.

I don't know where to go.

You have to come down to Jersey. Atlantic City is as

close as you can get to me tonight. Buy a ticket for that line.

What do I do when I get there?

We'll figure it out then. But, Lorraine . . .

Yeah?

You can't open that suitcase full of money in front of all those people. You might get robbed by a mean person, or a nice person might tell a transit cop.

Lorraine hadn't considered this. She realized how close she'd come to making a terrible mistake, and her heart began to flutter.

It's okay. I'm here to help you now. Find a bathroom and take the money out in there.

Lorraine did as she was told. She stood up and began to search for the ladies' room, finding one just past a row of ticket booths. The stalls were completely enclosed, right down to the floor. It made it easy for her to hide.

Take out five ten-dollar bills. That will give you more than enough for a ticket.

I've got it.

Then go buy your ticket. No, buy two tickets. It'll throw them off the track. You're too young to travel alone.

What do I do with the other ticket?

Just leave that up to me. Go on, get in line.

Lorraine headed for one of the ticket booths. She tried to look as if she belonged there, as if she wasn't scared to death.

A loud conversation cut into her thoughts.

"What do you mean, it isn't there? You had it five minutes ago!"

"I know I did, Donny! But it's gone! Someone must have stolen it!"

Lorraine looked back over her shoulder to see a young couple, no older than seventeen, standing nearby. The girl's long red hair was hanging down around the purse she had opened on her lap. Her hands moved quickly through it, shoving things out of the way. Her boyfriend leaned close, looking inside himself. Lorraine watched as the girl shook her head. She looked up at the boy with tears filling her green eyes.

"It's gone, Donny! What'll we do?"

Donny threw up his arms, his denim jacket coming open to reveal an Ozzy Ozborne T-shirt.

"Oh, this screws us up royally, Sandy! You know we were goin' down to Atlantic City to apply for work! You know we wanted to beat the summer rush!"

Lorraine immediately realized what had happened. No one had stolen the girl's ticket. Somehow, Marty had made it disappear. She tried to call him in her mind, but he was gone again. Taking a deep breath for courage, she got out of the line and walked over to the teenagers.

"Hello," she said uncertainly.

The boy snarled at her. The girl gave her a weary half-smile.

"I heard what you said," Lorraine went on. "Uhm, if you can do me a favor I can buy you another ticket."

"Oh, right . . ." the boy said doubtfully.

The girl shushed him.

"What do you mean, kid?" she asked.

Lorraine rubbed the back of one leg with the front of her sneaker.

"Well, see, I'm going to . . . Atlantic City too," she explained. "But I don't think they're going to let me on the bus by myself."

Sandy nodded in agreement.

"But if you say you're my sister," Lorraine went on, "then we can go together and no one will say anything."

"Gee, I don't know," Sandy said. "You're really young. We could get in trouble."

"How?"

"Well, if someone starts asking questions . . ."

"We'll say we're on our way to our father's house," Lorraine said. "Our parents are divorced, and Daddy is a . . ."

"He works in one of the casinos," Sandy offered, warming up to the idea. Her eyes sparkled.

Donny snorted. "Forget it, kid. We don't need any hassles."

"You want to get to Atlantic City, or don't you?" Lorraine snapped. She didn't see any other way to solve her own problems, and she wasn't going to "forget it."

Sandy leaned over and whispered something in the boy's ear. Then she looked at Lorraine.

"Are you running away from home?"

Lorraine shook her head. "Are you? I won't ask questions if you won't. It's too hard to explain, okay? You just gotta trust me."

"Trust a five-year-old?" Donny said.

"I'm eight," Lorraine lied with a glare in her gray-green eyes. "I'm just little. Come on, the bus leaves in half an hour. Do you want a ticket or don't you?"

"Donny, please . . ."

"All right!" Donny cried. "I give up. Go on and get your tickets, kid."

Lorraine grinned in triumph.

"Wait," Donny said. "Sandy, you go with her. It'll look better that way."

Playing the big-sister role to the hilt, Sandy took Lorraine by the hand and walked up to the line. The ticket man hardly glanced twice at them as they purchased two bus tickets. Sandy returned to where Donny was waiting and waved the ticket triumphantly.

"We'll be there in about two hours," she said.

"Let's get going," Donny replied. "We want a seat together."

He regarded the small child who still held fast to Sandy's hand.

"All of us," he said. "I don't know what you're up to, kid, but thanks."

Fifteen minutes later they were boarding the bus. As she was about to walk through the door, something made Lorraine turn and look behind her. Intelligent as she was, she could never have explained the feeling. Perhaps the closest analogy would be the feeling a gazelle might have when the lion is close behind.

Lorraine sensed danger.

She stopped and turned.

"What's wrong, kid?" Donny asked. "Go on . . ."

Lorraine didn't hear him. She was staring through the crowd of people, into a pair of dark and familiar eyes. The stranger had caught up to her.

Joe Trefill locked eyes with his quarry. Then he began to run, one hand reaching out, ready to grab the child.

23

IN ONE OF his dreams that night, Steven found himself standing in a timberland of tall leafless trees. The trunks and branches were so gnarled they seemed to take on the qualities of facial features. If Steven had understood the concept of animism, he would have believed it existed in this dream forest. He walked without fear among the trees. They were powerful beings, but benevolent ones. He reached toward one particularly old tree, wanting to draw courage from the antiquity of it.

But someone was pressing a hand on his shoulder, urging him to do . . .

. . . something.

Go 'way.

Wake up. It's time to go now.

The trees faded and Steven was disjointedly aware of being in Tatiana's bedroom. The pressure remained on his shoulder, the shaking persisted.

Wake up!

"N-no," Steven mumbled, half into his pillow. "S'dark out."

You have to leave tonight. You're going to come to us, Steven. We need you.

Marty?

Steven was suddenly completely awake and aware. He realized there was no one touching him.

Get dressed. If you don't come, we'll die. We are a unit, and without you we are incomplete.

Earlier in the day, when he'd been more alert, he'd been able to argue with Marty. But now, driven by a force too powerful to resist, he got up and did as he was told. Moving as if still in a dream, he was ready to leave the house in twenty minutes. Carrying his suitcase, he crept downstairs.

Money, you're going to need money.
I don't have any.
Find some.
I don't want to steal!
You can mail it back someday. This is an emergency!
Do you know where you can get some?

Steven thought, and remembered that Helga kept money in a jar in the kitchen. She used it for emergencies. He went there and was surprised to find one hundred eighty-six dollars, a few quarters, and one dime. He shoved it all into his pocket.

What do I do now?
You have to get to the airport. When you arrive, I'll tell you what to do next.
Marty, I'm scared.

But Marty was gone again. It disturbed Steven how easily the other boy faded in and out of his mind, but not enough to make him go back upstairs and forget this whole idea. With a sigh of resignation, he opened the back door and walked out onto the patio. He carefully closed and locked the door behind him. Then he walked as quietly as he could around to the front of the house. The street was shadowy and deserted, as asleep as the people in the houses that ran down either side of it. Still, Steven expected that any minute someone would catch him. A dog would start barking, or someone who was up late would glance out a window, or . . .

Panic began to overtake him. He started to run, heading toward the main road.

He no longer thought of resisting the call to join Marty and the "others."

24

SAMANTHA SAT CURLED up on the couch in her living room, one of Julie's paintings spread out on the coffee table. The lamp beside the couch cast a softly bright glow over the paper. Julie had been in bed for over an hour, and Samantha felt somewhat lonely without her presence. It was a strange feeling, after living by herself for so long, but she didn't like the quiet in the house. She had turned on the eleven-o'clock news, just to hear another voice. For some reason, she didn't want to be alone this night, even if company meant an impersonal image on the television.

But Samantha wasn't really paying attention to the news. Her eyes were fixed on the painting, studying every detail. Somewhere in that picture was the answer to her questions. It seemed impossible that a child's primitive artwork could conjure up feelings of vague memories, but Samantha had had enough experience with emotions over the past few days to trust her basic instincts.

Julie, albeit subconsciously, was sending her a message. It had to do with a beach, and a place named Haybrook's, and a little girl with a broken pail. Somehow, that was all connected to Julie's presence here, and to whatever had happened in her garage.

No matter how long she stared at the picture, however, nothing came to her. She got up off the couch, grabbed a sweater from the closet, and went outside. The wind blowing down from the mountains was chilly, filled with the promise of rain. The dogs barked a few times, but she called out to hush them, and they quieted at once.

She moved along the path to the garage. In the distance an owl called out a warning that it was on the hunt. The wind rustled the wisteria vines, tapping them against

143

the split-rail fence. Samantha reached the garage. She pulled the door open. Reaching inside, she switched on the light.

The Bronco II sat quietly waiting for another day of work. Samantha went to the driver's side and got in. She held the steering wheel, trying to bring back some kind of memory.

She heard the door going down.

Samantha turned, half-expecting to see the door descending behind her. It was closed tightly, as it was supposed to be. Samantha sat in the truck a few more minutes, then hopped out again. She went to the bypass switch and pressed the button. A new memory came back to her. She recalled having trouble opening the door again.

It opened just fine now.

No, it wasn't just the big door. There had been something wrong with the lock of the back door. She retraced her steps as she might have taken them that night. The lock on the back door was broken now, smashed by the ax Samantha had found on the floor when she arrived home with Julie. She'd put the ax back up on the wall. She looked at it, trying hard to remember.

Her head was beginning to ache from all the brain activity it was being forced to deal with. Samantha rubbed her forehead and yawned. Nothing was coming to her tonight. Maybe all she had to do was sleep. In the morning she might see things more clearly.

Upstairs in her bedroom, she drifted off to sleep, and did not dream anything significant that night.

When she woke up, she didn't think of the previous night at all. She could hear Julie getting dressed, singing a song about the sunshine. Samantha pushed her covers aside and leveraged herself out of bed. She felt achy all over. Passing Julie in the hall, she mumbled good morning and went to take a shower.

Refreshed and awakened completely, Samantha dressed herself in jeans and a madras shirt and went downstairs. Her place was set with two pieces of toast with butter and jelly and a glass of orange juice.

"What a nice surprise," she said. "Thanks, Julie."

"I would have made you coffee," Julie said, "but I never really watched you use the coffee maker."

"That's okay," Samantha said, reaching for the toast. "I don't feel like coffee today anyway."

Julie sat down and began to put jelly on her own toast.

"Are you going to work today?"

"No, honey," Samantha said. "My vacation starts today."

Samantha ate some toast. Remembering Wil's thoughts that Julie might have been brought in from another state, she decided to bring up the subject.

"Julie, I'd like to ask you some more questions today," Samantha said. "It's just a way that might help your memory come back."

"Sure," Julie said. "But I don't remember anything more since yesterday."

Samantha believed this, but she had to try.

"Have you ever been to Utah?"

"I don't know."

"How about Arizona?"

A shrug.

"New Mexico?"

"Why are you asking?" Julie said.

Samantha explained how Wil Sherer had been unable to find any orphanages in Colorado that had sheltered a child named Julie.

"So you might have come from another state," she said. "I know that sounds crazy, but we have to try every possibility. How about that Mr. Henley you told me about the first time we met? Think hard again, Julie. Can you picture him in your mind?"

Julie closed her eyes and thought a few minutes. Finally she shook her head.

"I'm sorry," she said in a small voice. "He was only in the motel room for a few minutes. Then he left, and we spent some time together in Durango. How come you don't even remember the train ride?"

"I wish I knew," Samantha said wearily.

She reached across the table to take the child's hand.

"It'll come back to us, I'm sure. We'll work together—you, and me, and Wil."

She pushed her chair back and brought her empty dishes to the sink. Julie did the same.

"Speaking of Wil," Samantha said, "he asked me to take a picture of you. You're dressed so pretty right now, in those tulip pants and that short top. Can I take your picture outside, by the flowers?"

"How about in front of the little adobe?"

"Great idea!" Samantha said. "You go on ahead. Unlock the kennels and let the dogs out. I'll be out as soon as I get my camera."

Samantha found her Polaroid. Miraculously, it still had two pictures left in it. She carried it outside, down the columbine-laden path to the playhouse. Julie was playing "fetch-the-stick" with the dogs. She turned and smiled at Samantha.

"Stand right outside the door," Samantha said. "That's great!"

Samantha looked up at the trees, frowning.

"It's a little shady here," she said. "But I guess the picture will be okay."

"Why does Mr. Sherer want my picture?" Julie asked.

"Oh, just to keep it on file," Samantha said. She saw no reason to tell Julie it was going to be placed in the missing-persons file.

She aimed her camera. "Ready?"

"Ready," Julie said. She posed, giving a pretty smile.

Samantha snapped the picture. The automatic flash went off, filling in the dark spaces made by the shade of the trees. And instantly Julie doubled over, her hands covering her eyes.

She screamed, her voice like the high-pitched keening of a bird. Samantha dropped the camera, running to her.

"My eyes! My eyes are burning!"

"Julie, what . . . ?"

She tried to pull the child's hands away from her face, unable to understand what had happened. Julie went on screaming, her arms stiff as Samantha moved them to look at her face. She had her eyes squeezed tightly shut. Her face was bright red and tears were streaming down her cheeks.

Without understanding what was wrong, Samantha lifted the child into her arms and ran back to the house with her. The dogs followed, barking in confusion. Samantha brought Julie into the kitchen, threw open the cold-water faucet, and flushed away whatever it was that had gotten into Julie's eyes. The child struggled, but Samantha held fast. All her emergency-room training came into play as she tended to the child's injuries. At last Julie's screams diminished to a quiet whimpering.

Samantha hugged her close.

"Oh, God," she gasped. "What happened?"

"The light hurt my eyes," Julie said. "The flash—it burned my eyes."

Samantha sat the child down and knelt to take a good look at her. Julie's eyes were open now, but bloodshot. Samantha held up a few fingers.

"What do you see?"

"Three fingers."

Julie was seeing all right. Samantha thanked God for that. She knew of people who had gone temporarily blind from flashbulbs popping in their faces. The little Polaroid could never have done such a thing. Why had Julie's eyes reacted in such a way? She'd been in terrible pain!

"Close your left eye."

Samantha checked each eye individually and found out that, despite Julie's obvious suffering, her eyes seemed perfectly normal.

"I'm going to take you to a friend of mine," Samantha said. "Just to be sure everything is okay."

"I don't want to see another doctor!"

"Julie, I think—"

"No!" Julie cried out. "I'm okay. Really, I'm okay!"

Julie got up and ran out of the room. As if nothing at all had happened, she began to romp around the backyard with the dogs. Samantha decided to let the incident pass, with plans to watch Julie's vision very carefully.

She went back to the playhouse to retrieve her camera. Julie's picture was on the ground. Samantha picked it up and looked at it. She'd managed to catch the young girl while she was still smiling. It was a clear picture that would certainly be of help to Detective Sherer. And it was a good thing, because obviously she wouldn't be able to take any more pictures of Julie.

25

JOE TREFILL had to bite his lower lip to keep from swearing out loud. He was inches away from the exit to the bus, held fast from behind by a security guard who seemed half his size.

"Let me go," he said. "I need to get on that bus!"

"You so desperate to lose your money down there that you have to knock people down?"

Trefill did not know what "down there" meant until he read the sign for the departing bus: "ATLANTIC CITY." He was vaguely aware of crashing into someone, but he hadn't been paying much attention. He had missed catching Lorraine by a few seconds. Now she was safely on the bus, and he was entertainment for a gathering crowd.

"Sir, I'm gonna letcha go now . . ."

Trefill didn't cause any more trouble. There was no point in it, now that Lorraine had made her escape. But she wouldn't get too far ahead. All he had to do was follow her. Atlantic City was a big place, but a fat little kid with black hair should be easy to spot.

He turned to walk away, and found that people were still staring at him. He wanted to shout at them, to curse them for being so intrusive, to take out the gun under his jacket and say:

Mine's bigger than the guard's.

But that would draw more attention, and Walter LaBerge had made him swear he wouldn't draw attention to himself.

"Not like that job I gave you in Orlando, Joe. Remember Disney World? Remember standing up on the trolley and screaming because someone cut you off and that guy got away from you?"

Remember? LaBerge had never let him forget.

But he had a second chance now, and all he had to do

148

was calm down and buy a ticket. Keeping his eyes fixed on the counter ahead, he pushed through the crowd. He took a quick glance behind himself to see that they had dispersed, finally realizing there was nothing left to gawk at.

He went up to the counter and pushed a bill forward. "Atlantic City," he said.

The man behind the glass window looked at him through wire-framed glasses.

"I can sell you a ticket," he said, "but you missed the last bus of the night. Next one leaves seven-o-five A.M."

Trefill's fist clenched. The little freak had nearly ten hours' head start!

"I'll take it," he said.

He paid for the ticket, then left the terminal. There was no point in spending the night in this place, among the ragged homeless and the druggies. He'd rent a room for the night, and in the morning he'd head down into Jersey. There he'd find Lorraine, and this time nothing would stop him. If he had to waste the two kids who were helping her, then he'd do it.

Trefill didn't realize he was smiling with the idea that he might get to use his gun for real this time.

The 9:45 bus from Manhattan pulled into Atlantic City close to midnight. Sandy had shaken Lorraine awake, but the ordeal she'd been through made the child as limp as a rag doll. Grumbling, Donny lifted her up and carried her off the bus.

"Don't be such a creep," Sandy said. "That little kid saved our necks, and you know it."

"We have to find a place to spend the night," Donny said.

"We can sleep under the boardwalk," Sandy said. "No one will see us there."

They walked down New Jersey Avenue, heading toward the lights of the casinos. Climbing onto the boardwalk, they found themselves near the Showboat Casino. Sandy gazed around in awe at all the activity she was seeing. The boardwalk was sixty feet wide, stretching as far as her eyes could see, and it was full of people. Bright lights and laughter and loud noises were a sharp contrast to the virtually silent bus ride.

"Wow, it's barely midnight," she said. "And there's people all over the place."

"I heard they don't have clocks," Donny said. "That's to keep the suckers gambling at all hours."

They walked along the boardwalk, passing casinos with ritzy names like Taj Mahal and Caesar's, until at last they had come to the end of all the activity. They found stairs leading down to the beach. Donny shifted Lorraine to his other shoulder. She moaned in protest.

"Where should we set up camp?" he asked.

"Anyplace," Sandy said. "I'm exhausted."

They walked for some distance. Then they ducked under the boardwalk, tucking themselves into a deep shadowed area so that no one passing by would see them. Donny took off his jacket. Sandy took off hers and laid it down just below her boyfriend's. It made a small bed, but nothing big enough for either of them. With a sigh, Donny and Sandy exchanged glances. Then they laid Lorraine down on the makeshift bed.

Using the suitcases for pillows, the teenage couple cuddled together and fell fast asleep.

26

THE BLARE OF a truck's horn made Steven jump, pulling him from the walking reverie he'd been in for the past half-hour. He'd stopped running as soon as he reached the nearest main road to the Freleng house. Without any guidance from Marty, but by his own instincts, he'd followed the darkened streets until he came to the main highway. It had taken him over an hour to get this far, and weariness was taking its toll. Steven had begun to daydream, thinking of Rachel and Eric's argument. He'd lost track of both time and direction, but the rambling eighteen-wheeler had set him back on the right path.

He realized that the sky wasn't quite as dark as it had been when he left the house. He also knew that he couldn't stay well hidden once the sun came up. He moved into the shadows created by the trees alongside the road, and began to walk in double-time. He didn't let himself think again how tired he was. There was no time for that.

Despite the predawn hour, there was a lot of activity on the highway. Steven knew that he had to get across it to reach the airport, and so he began to watch for a break in the traffic. When he found one, he raced as fast as his legs could carry him to the other side. Then he followed the road until he reached the entrance to the airport.

I'm here now, Marty. What do I do?

But Marty did not answer him. Steven wondered if his mysterious friend was sleeping.

Huge signs offered directions to the main terminal. Steven followed them, finally coming to the front entrance. Business people in dark suits hurried by him, briefcases firmly in hand. A few other people had also arrived for early-morning flights. Steven noticed there

151

were no children. He followed a group of people inside, walking close to a black man so that anyone who looked at him would think he was with his father.

The airport was relatively quiet. Only the restaurant and newsstands had opened. Steven could smell something cooking. He thought of the wonderful breakfasts Helga had made over the last few days and began to feel hungry. His stomach growled. But there was an even more urgent pressure in his bladder. He looked around, finally locating a sign for the men's room. Steven went inside, relieved himself, then freshened up by splashing water on his face.

When he came into the lobby again, he could see the sky was as bright and blue as midday. The sun seemed to have come up virtually instantaneously, although Steven knew the light had taken eight minutes to get here. The sudden appearance of morning helped push away the last vestiges of weariness he felt. It was a false energy that overcame him, but he didn't realize this. Steven didn't worry that he'd probably collapse from exhaustion. He could only think about how hungry he was.

He reached into his pocket and took out the roll of bills. Satisfied he had not lost it, he went into the restaurant. There were some businessmen sharing a preflight breakfast at one table. Steven sat as far away from them as possible. As a result, it was nearly fifteen minutes before the waitress even realized he was there.

"Oh, my goodness," she said with a Midwestern twang. "You must think I've been ignoring you. Well, I don't suppose you want a cup of coffee?"

Despite his nervousness, Steven couldn't help laughing.

"No," he said. "Could I have a cup of hot chocolate, please? And then I'd like a stack of pancakes."

"You bet," the waitress said. "Are you travelin' all by yourself?"

Steven nodded. His explanation came so quickly it surprised even him.

"Mom and Dad work all day," he said. "They couldn't get off. So they dropped me off. I'm taking a flight into Newark to see my grandma."

He leaned forward and spoke in quasi-conspiratorial tones.

"See, if I had to wait for my folks to get a vacation," he said, "I'd only see Grandma once a year. But this is my fourth visit."

The waitress's eyebrows went up.

"Well, a frequent flier! You just wait there and I'll be back with your breakfast in no time flat."

It wasn't exactly that fast, but Steven took the time to try to call Marty. He still didn't answer.

"Here you go," the waitress said, setting Steven's breakfast in front of him. "Enjoy. You need anything, you holler."

"Thanks," Steven said.

He searched a rack of syrup bottles for one marked "Strawberry," then drowned his pancakes in the red liquid. As he ate, he thought how nice it would be if everyone on his journey was as accepting of his story as the waitress had been. When he finally finished his meal, he did some lightning-fast mathematics in his head and left her a little bit more than the average tip. Then he went up to the register to pay for his breakfast. He handed the man behind the counter the exact change.

"But we haven't handed you the check yet, young fellow," the old man said. "How did you know the right amount?"

"I'm good at math."

"Well, that's an understatement if I ever heard one," the man said.

He watched Steven return the rest of the money to his pocket.

"Listen, you shouldn't be flashing twenties around like that," he said. "I mean, this ain't New York, but there's bad types everywhere."

"Oh," Steven said. "I'll be careful."

"You got your ticket in a good safe place?"

Steven's heart skipped a beat, but before his face could react with a stricken expression, he swallowed and said, "Safe and sound. G'bye!"

"So long," the old man said. "Nice flight!"

Steven hurried from the restaurant. The lobby was five times more crowded than it had been forty-five minutes ago. Steven hoped no one would see the look of panic on his face.

A ticket! How could he have forgotten about a ticket?

How could Marty have forgotten?

I can't afford a ticket! he thought. *What am I going to do?*

Everything will be okay. Just sit down in one of those chairs and wait.

Marty! Where've you been?

I was sleeping. Sorry, but they were doing so many . . . I was working so hard I was just exhausted.

Marty, I forgot to get enough money for a ticket.

Don't panic. I told you to trust me. Just go sit down and leave everything to me.

Steven found a comfortable seat in the waiting area. He placed his suitcase on his lap and rested his elbows on it. His chin dropped into his hands. He didn't have any idea what Marty was going to do, but he knew he had to trust him.

Around a corner, where Steven couldn't see, a ticket clerk was preparing herself for the start of a new, busy day. Janie Barkley, late of the Summersun Travel Agency, had been on the job only six months. She worked with eager efficiency, always ready to do her best for her customers. Most days the job was enjoyable, even those days when overbooked flights or bad weather brought countless people up to her desk. She could change a flight or issue a ticket with her eyes closed.

I'd like a one-way ticket to Newark.

"Of course, sir," Janie said, flashing a smile that hung like a hammock between two apple cheeks. "Will that be . . . ?"

She realized there was no one in front of the counter.

Janie, do as I tell you.

Janie felt an icy cold draft winding around her body. Instantly she was transfixed by the computer terminal in front of her. Its screen had changed without any human interference.

Type up a ticket for Steven . . . Steven Freleng. A one-way ticket to Newark. First class.

Without protest, Janie did as the voice in her mind commanded. Then she leaned into the microphone on her desk and began to page Steven.

It took a few calls before Steven realized *he* was Steven Freleng. He felt himself fill with an overwhelming sense of panic. They'd found him! Eric and Rachel had come after him!

"Please pick up your ticket at the Mattituck Airlines counter."

Steven sighed with relief. Now he understood what Marty had been up to. He wasn't sure how he'd gotten hold of a ticket, but he didn't ask. He simply walked until he found the desk and took the folder from the clerk.

She was smiling, but her eyes had a weird, glassy quality about them. Her "Have a nice flight, thank you for flying Mattituck Airlines" was unusually forced.

The moment Steven walked away from the counter, Janie snapped to. She blinked a few times, looking around herself. A feeling that she'd lost some time came over her, but she couldn't explain it. Then someone came up to her counter and the incident was completely forgotten.

Steven opened the folder and read the information about his flight. He gasped, realizing he was to take off in twenty minutes.

I saw no need to waste time.

Boy, you sure didn't. Are you sure this will work?

Just tell them the story you told the waitress. The one about your parents working.

You were awake! Steven's tone was accusatory.

Sort of. Go on, they're calling your flight.

Steven hurried to find the right gate. He followed a line of passengers, mostly business people, through a safety check-in. He held his breath as he passed the security guard, certain the man would reach out and grab him and make him explain what he was doing there all by himself.

But as he boarded, the flight attendant gave him the same friendly greeting as everyone else. He found his seat and tucked his bag in the overhead compartment. The big comfortable seat made him realize how tired he was. He took off his jacket and rolled it into a pillow. Lifting the armrest, he laid himself down as best as he could. He felt a tap on his shoulder and sat up to see the stewardess smiling at him.

"Here's a pillow, honey," she said. "Is your seat belt fastened?"

"Uh-huh," Steven said groggily.

The stewardess smiled again. If she had any questions about him traveling alone, she didn't voice them. Steven didn't know if it was because she'd seen many children travel alone or if it was Marty's influence.

He closed his eyes and listened as the captain welcomed them aboard Mattituck Airlines flight 6072 to Newark. By the time the plane was taxiing into position, he was nearly asleep.

But he came awake very suddenly.

Marty!

I'm here! Why are you yelling?

Steven quieted the voice in his mind.

Marty, you made Tatiana see something in the woods, didn't you?

Go back to sleep, Steven.

Didn't you?

But either Marty wasn't answering or Steven really did fall asleep, because there were no more thoughts in his head.

27

SAMANTHA AND JULIE were playing Scrabble when the sound of a car's engine made Julie jump from her chair and run to the window.

"There's a red car outside," she said. "A man's getting out."

Samantha went to the window herself. Wil Sherer had parked his sixty-nine Firebird at the end of the driveway. As they watched, he stopped halfway to the house and called to the dogs. They bounded up to him, wagging their tails in the friendly manner typical of Labs. Wil rubbed their heads briskly, then picked up a stick and threw it. True to their second name, "retriever," the dogs bounded after the stick. Lady brought it back.

Samantha went to the back door and opened it.

"I hadn't expected to see you so soon," she said.

"Hadn't expected to have information this fast," Wil replied.

He came inside. He'd shaved that morning, and Samantha thought he looked much nicer without the beard. From the front, his short haircut made him look conservative. It wasn't until he turned profile that you saw the longer tresses dangling down his back.

His smile was genuine when he looked at Julie. Samantha could tell at once he was a man who really liked children. Julie warmed to him immediately. Like the dogs, she seemed to know he was someone she could trust.

"Hi, pretty," he said. "You must be Julie."

Julie giggled. "Uh-huh."

"I'm Wil Sherer," the detective said, holding out a hand. Julie took it shyly, then let go. "I'm a detective. Do you know about me?"

157

"I told her you were helping us find her family," Samantha said.

"That's exactly what I intend to do," Wil said.

Julie put her arms around Samantha. Wil watched the gesture, then looked at Samantha.

"She really likes you," he said. To Julie: "Samantha's a special person to you, isn't she?"

"Yeah," Julie said. "I love her."

"But you've only known her for a few days," Wil pointed out in a gentle tone.

"I still love her," Julie insisted.

"That's nice," Wil said. "Julie, I'd like to talk privately with Samantha, okay? For just a few minutes?"

"Okay," Julie said, letting go of Samantha. "I'll go upstairs and draw."

Samantha led Wil to her office. He sat down in an armchair, tossing a throw pillow to the rug. Samantha took the seat behind her desk.

"Something happened last night," she said. "When I went to pick up Julie at my friend's house, she was drawing pictures of that yellow house I told you about."

"Did you remember anything new?"

"No," Samantha said in a disappointed tone. "I just had a stronger feeling that it was a place I had been once, a long time ago."

"Might be some kind of vacation home," Wil suggested. "I'll see if I can locate this Haybrook's place."

Samantha reminded him that he'd come with information.

"I found Mr. Henley," Wil said without prelude.

"What!"

"It was easy enough," Wil said. "Just a matter of going back to that hotel in Durango. Raoul Henley used a credit card to pay in advance for your room. I traced his home to an address in Union Fort."

Samantha thought about this.

"That's about halfway between here and Durango," she said.

"Right," Wil answered. "I'm going to be checking into Mr. Henley. So far I know he's single, drives a 1981 Reliant, and rents a house at 358 Maple Avenue in Union Fort."

"How do you know all that?"

"It's a matter of public record," Wil said. "People think there's a great deal of mystery to detective work, but mostly it's just knowing where to find information that's available to anyone who wants it. Raoul Henley is listed, as is everyone else, in the Union Fort city directory."

"The phone book?"

"It's a little more detailed than that," Wil said. "You can find one in the library. All I had to do was take a ride to Henley's town and look him up."

"But we still don't know anything more," Samantha said. "Did you talk to him?"

"Not yet," Wil said. "I'm sure he'll deny everything anyway. I need more solid information before confronting him."

Samantha got up and went to look out the window. A crow was attacking a caterpillar just outside.

"What about Julie?" she asked. "Did you find an orphanage?"

"Sorry," Wil said. "So far, I've only come up with dead ends."

Samantha turned to face him with a concerned expression. Wil held up a hand, the silver-and-turquoise ring he wore flashing under the track lights.

"Don't worry," he said. "Henley will be more than happy to talk to me."

There was a menacing quality to his tone that suggested he wouldn't stop until Henley *did* talk.

"I want to come with you," Samantha said.

"I can't allow that," Wil replied. "You hired me because you need help. Don't play amateur detective. It's dangerous."

"You made it sound rather mundane a few minutes ago," Samantha pointed out.

"It is, to a degree," Wil said. "But there's a lot of danger too. If I feel I need you, you'll know right away. At the moment, I'd rather handle things myself."

He rolled up the cuff of his pants to reveal an ugly red scar that ran from his knee around to the back of his ankle.

"That's a bite from a pit bull," Wil said. "One of the people I was trying to interview for a case sicced him on me."

Samantha made a face, although she'd seen plenty of gore in the emergency room. Most of those incidents had been accidental. But someone had purposely turned his vicious dog on this man!

Wil pushed the pants leg back down again.

"I've been driven away at gunpoint too," he said. "Fortunately for me, no one ever fired a shot."

"Do you carry a weapon?"

Wil shook his head. "Only on certain cases, under special circumstances. Guns aren't the protection they're cracked up to be. Of course, as an ex-cop I'm licensed, and in my early days as a detective I did carry one at all times. But I found that one of two things usually happened: some bully would try to provoke me into using it or would try to wrestle it away from me. I had a few close calls before realizing it wasn't worth it. To tell you the truth, people are a lot more cooperative than you realize. Most of them are good citizens who want to help. And I can handle myself well enough without a gun."

Samantha did a quick, almost unconscious scan of his body. His muscular build told her he wasn't kidding.

"All right," she said. "I'll leave it up to you."

She remembered the picture just then, and picked it up from the pile of papers on her desk. She handed it to Wil. He studied it, not speaking for such a long time that Samantha wondered what he was thinking. Finally he put it into his file.

"It's a good shot," he said. "I'll put it through Missing Persons."

"You seemed very interested in it," Samantha said.

"A thought had occurred to me when I met Julie in the kitchen," Wil said. "I was studying the picture to see if it happened again."

"Did it?"

"Yes," Wil replied. "You haven't mentioned this, so I'm sure it never crossed your mind. Julie looks a little bit like you."

Samantha leaned back, a look of surprise on her face. "Really?"

"Especially around the eyes and nose," Wil went on. "The eye color isn't the same, but the shape is. And you both have very straight brows. It's almost as if you're related."

Samantha brought a hand to her forehead, shaking her head. This new revelation was almost too much to consider on top of everything else.

"Coincidence," she said. "I don't have any relatives. I'm an orphan myself."

"Then you don't have any relatives you know about," Wil said thoughtfully. "But it isn't impossible they know about you."

Samantha closed her eyes and rubbed them.

"I hope you're wrong," she said. "The idea of having lost relatives is more than I can bear right now. I don't think I could handle another shock like that."

"Fine," Wil said to appease her, although he intended to keep the idea in his own mind.

He stood up.

"I have some other avenues to go down on this case," he said. "I'll keep you posted. In the meantime, maybe you should let up on the kid a little. It's possible that something will come back to her if she isn't pressured."

"You're right," Samantha said. "I have been pushing her."

"Why don't you take her someplace special?" Wil asked. "I hear there's a great new water ride at Rocky Point Park."

Samantha smiled. "What a great idea! A day of fun is just what that little girl needs."

Wil returned the smile. "Seems to me she isn't the only one who needs it."

He and Samantha walked to his car together. When he turned to her, there was so much concern in his deep blue eyes that Samantha half-expected him to put his arms around her. And she wanted him to, wanted to feel affection from a virtual stranger, because right now she needed someone as much as Julie needed her. But theirs was a business relationship, barely a few hours old, and she had no right to expect such a thing. Unconsciously she backed up a step.

"Please, trust that I'll do my best for you," Wil said. "Put your worries out of your mind. Whatever's going on here, I promise I'll find some answers."

Samantha nodded. "Thanks. I really feel good about having hired you."

"Remind me to thank John Brightman for the referral."

They exchanged good-byes. As Wil drove away, Julie came running up to Samantha.

"I like him," she said. "He's a nice man."

"He sure is," Samantha said, watching the car disappear down the road.

"Do you like him?"

Samantha laughed. "You mean, like a boyfriend? For heaven's sake, Julie, I just met him."

But she had also noticed a strange stirring inside herself when Wil was there. Embarrassed to think she had a crush at her age, she turned the topic away from the detective.

"Would you like to do something extra special today?"

"What?" Julie asked eagerly.

"Wil says there's a new water ride at Rocky Point Park," Samantha said. "It's just a half-hour's drive from here. Why don't we spend the afternoon there?"

"It sounds great!" Julie said.

Twenty minutes later the dogs were kenneled and Samantha and Julie were on their way to the amusement park. Samantha was determined not to think for a moment about the strange things that were happening. She would follow Wil's suggestion and give Julie an afternoon that was pure fun.

28

LORRAINE WAS THE first to be awakened as sunlight broke through the clouds and seeped through the wooden planks overhead. She sat up slowly, one elbow resting on the makeshift bed Donny and Sandy had made out of their jackets. Donny had a protective, warming arm around his girlfriend. Lorraine thought it would be nice to have someone to hug her too. She thought of Bettina, but for now there was only a vague sense of longing.

She rubbed her eyes with the backs of her hands. Then she stood up and felt an urgent pressure in her bladder. She reached down and shook Sandy.

"Sandy? Sandy, I have to go!"

Sandy bolted upright, jerked out of a dream. For a moment she gazed at her surroundings as if she didn't know where she was.

"Sandy," Lorraine whined, "I *need* to go."

She held herself between the legs. Sandy yawned.

"Don't do that, kid," she said. She turned onto her knees and shook Donny. He grumbled at her. "I'm taking Lorraine to a bathroom. It's morning. You better get up."

Donny sat up and grimaced. He spit sand from his mouth.

"My back hurts," he complained, after a night on the soft beach.

Sandy stood up, brushing sand from her jeans. Then she took Lorraine by the hand and headed for the nearest staircase up to the boardwalk. At this early hour, it was virtually deserted. The concession stands were boarded up, and only a few early-morning joggers passed them by.

They found a bathroom in a nearby hotel, ignoring the hard stares of the concierge. There was a separate powder room, with a gilt-edged mirror and three gleaming white sinks. Sandy pulled a clip from her pocket and tied back her red hair. Then she made a face at her reflection, sticking out her tongue.

"Gawd," she said. "Worst case of moose-mouth I ever had! I wish I had brought my toothbrush in here."

"I'm hungry, Sandy," Lorraine said.

Sandy looked down at the child. In the light of day it suddenly dawned on her how ironic it was that she had been "assigned" to care for this strange small girl. Little kids were precisely the reason she left home in Pennsylvania, making her way first to Manhattan and now Atlantic City. She'd been sick and tired of her nagging parents making her baby-sit her bratty seven little brothers and sisters.

I'm seventeen! she'd cried. *I have a right to a social life, you know!*

But they'd only laughed at her, asking what kind of social life a kid could have.

She looked into Lorraine's gray-green eyes and sighed.

"Yeah, kid," she said. "You and me both."

They went outside again, passing through an ornate lobby, all glass and gilt with a central fountain and thousands of hanging plants. Through an archway they could see a dining room set up with white linen tablecloths and fresh flowers. Breakfast was being cooked for the hotel guests and for those in the neighborhood who could afford it. Sandy pulled on Lorraine's hand, hurrying from the hotel before the smells of bacon, sausage, pancakes, and the like could make her drool like a rabid dog.

Donny was waiting for them, burdened with all three suitcases and the jackets. His dark hair flipped wildly in the ocean breeze.

"We're hungry," Sandy said. "I can't think until I eat. Look, there's a little coffee shop over there. Let's have breakfast."

"Sandy," Donny said in a warning tone, "we don't have a heck of a lot of money."

Lorraine looked from one teen to the other.

"Don't worry," she said. "I'll take care of it."

"No, kid," Sandy said. "You bought me a bus ticket last night. That's enough."

"It's okay!" Lorraine insisted. "I don't want to argue, do you?"

" 'Course not," Donny said.

"Then let's go have breakfast," Lorraine said, leading the way.

Donny leaned closer to Sandy and whispered, "Did she say she was eight, or forty-eight?"

Sandy giggled.

In the coffee shop Lorraine remembered Marty's warning not to flash her money around. She wondered where he was now. She waited until they were given a booth, then excused herself.

"Didn't you just use the potty?" Sandy asked, talking to Lorraine as she would speak to one of her younger siblings.

"I have more inside me," Lorraine said, picking up her bag.

"You can leave that here," Donny said.

Lorraine shook her head vehemently and walked away.

"I wonder what she has in that thing?" Sandy said.

"We won't be around long enough to find out," Donny said. "As soon as breakfast is done, we find a place to clean ourselves up real good so we can start job-hunting."

"Oh, Donny," Sandy said, "you can't mean we're gonna leave that baby on her own?"

Donny leaned back as a waitress put glasses of water in front of them.

"Seems she did pretty well on her own before she ran into us," Donny said. "I don't know what her case is. It isn't my business, and I don't want to get wrapped up in it. It could get us in a hell of a lot of trouble, Sandy."

Sandy stared out the window. A ship appeared over the horizon, moving slowly along the water.

"We're already in trouble, Donny," she said.

In the bathroom, Lorraine took out another thirty dollars. She started to close the bag, but had an idea. She took out an additional one hundred dollars, wrapped it in a paper towel, and tucked it deep into a pocket. Then she left the restroom. When she came to the table, the waitress was taking their order.

"I want French toast and orange juice," Lorraine announced.

"Sounds good to me," Sandy said.

"Make mine scrambled eggs with a side of bacon," Donny said. "And a cup of coffee."

As Lorraine enjoyed her breakfast, she thought that she had left the frightful stranger behind. Unknown to her, Joe Trefill was boarding a Greyhound to Atlantic City at this very moment.

After breakfast, Donny bought a newspaper, and the three walked out onto the boardwalk. By now it was beginning to show signs of the crowds that would fill it before noon, and it was with some effort that the trio found a bench.

"So what are you going to do now, kid?" Sandy asked.

Lorraine shrugged. "I'm waiting for someone. He promised to meet me here. I don't think he should see you with me."

"You didn't tell us someone was waiting for you," Donny said, annoyed. "Why didn't he pick you up last night?"

"He couldn't," Lorraine said. "But don't worry, he'll be here soon."

"I wish I knew why you—"

Sandy cut herself off. She'd been ready to ask for more information about why Lorraine was wandering around by herself. But something in the child's expression made her think better of the idea.

"Well, listen," she said, standing, "if that guy doesn't show up, you find us, okay? We'll take care of you."

You can hardly take care of yourselves, Lorraine thought. She wondered what they'd do if they had Marty to help them.

Well, she thought with a secret smile, they'd be pleased to find the hundred dollars she'd slipped into Donny's pocket. It might buy only two nights in the cheapest motel around, but at least it was some small payment for their kindness.

"Good luck finding work," Lorraine said.

"Thanks," Donny said. "Thanks for everything."

They parted company without further words, the teenagers heading down the boardwalk. Alone now, Lorraine concentrated much harder on calling up Marty. But though she said his name many times in her mind, sometimes even "shouting" it, he did not answer her.

Well, that was okay. The scary man with the gun was far, far away in New York. She'd just wait here until Marty called her, and then everything would be okay.

As the morning passed, she entertained herself at a nearby amusement park, played on the beach, and generally explored her surroundings. No one paid much attention to her; she was grateful for that. At last she decided she was hungry enough for lunch. She walked up to one of the concession stands and bought a hot dog and soda.

When she turned around, she let out a gasp. It was cut short as a hand pressed to her lips. Lorraine could have screamed, and a thousand people would have heard her. But she didn't dare. She didn't want to attract attention to herself.

She was forced to let the man who terrified her, Joe Trefill, take her roughly by the arm and steer her through the crowds.

29

EAR PAIN BROUGHT on by the change in air pressure woke Steven from his nap just as the pilot was announcing their arrival at the airport in Newark, New Jersey. Steven tugged at his ears, wincing. The young man seated next to him tapped him on the shoulder.

"Try this," he said. He held his nose and made a face as if he was blowing through his nostrils. "It'll help your ears 'pop.' "

Steven tried it. The pressure in his ears released a little, but not much.

"It didn't really work," he said.

The man shrugged. "It does, sometimes. Next time bring gum with you to chew."

Steven wriggled around in his seat and looked out the window. Below him, Manhattan Island presented its skyline. Steven recognized the two giant towers of the World Trade Center, as well as the spiked peak of the Empire State Building. He gazed out at them in awe, amazed that buildings could be so tall. He wondered if Rachel had ever been here.

Thoughts of his "foster mother" made him feel vaguely homesick. What were they doing now? he wondered. Were they worried about him? He was sure Tatiana would be glad to see him gone. Rachel would probably be frantic, but Eric would be happy to have his family back to normal again. He'd made that clear enough— Steven was no more than an outsider, a temporary "guest."

Still, Rachel had been so kind to him. He really liked her a lot, as if she was his real mother. He wondered what it would be like to meet his real mother. Marty had said there was no such person, but maybe Marty was a

168

liar. Not maybe, definitely. Steven was certain he had a mother.

The plane landed so lightly that Steven didn't even feel a bump. Even though the stewardess asked the passengers to remain in their seats until the plane came to a complete stop, many of them were already up and getting their things ready. Steven wondered why they were in such a big hurry. As for himself, he really didn't have a place to go. At least, not until Marty called him. He tried to contact the other boy, but there was no response.

The airplane came to a halt at last.

Swinging his bag over his shoulder, Steven wriggled into the line and made his way off the plane. To his relief, the stewardesses were too busy to notice him. He really didn't want to deal with their questions. He was pretty sure most airlines wouldn't allow a kid his age to travel alone without strict supervision.

He passed through a short tunnel, then walked past a number of waiting areas that led to various gates. When he came out on the other side of the security area, he was overwhelmed by the activity around him. There seemed to be people everywhere! They all looked over his shoulder and around him, eyes focused down the hallway in search of arriving loved ones. Steven watched fathers hug children as they returned from business trips. A grandma made a fuss over a baby she was seeing for the first time. Everywhere, families seemed to be reuniting.

Steven felt an odd pressure around the orbits of his eyes. Combined with the heaviness he still felt in his ears, it gave him quite a headache. He bit his lip—more pain, but enough to keep tears from falling. Anyone who saw him crying would start asking questions. He couldn't handle that.

Instead, he moved as quickly as he could past the group. There was a staircase leading down, marked "EXIT—BAGGAGE-CLAIM AREA." Well, he had no baggage to claim. But he wanted to get as far away from this crowded place as possible.

The doorway out was just a short distance from the bottom of the stairs. Steven paused to look out the big plate-glass windows that cut across the front of the terminal building. There were taxis and limousines and one bus. Cars waited in a parking garage across the street. Steven remembered that Marty had said he was to make his way to Atlantic City. But how, he wondered, was he supposed to do that?

Marty? Are you there now?

Marty didn't answer.

Please! I don't know what to do, Marty! I don't know where to go!

Still there was no response from the enigmatic Marty. Wearily Steven sank into an empty seat in the waiting area, his head resting on his hand. Maybe this wasn't such a good idea, he thought. What if Marty didn't answer him for hours and hours?

He began to wish that he hadn't listened to the other boy, and that he'd trusted Rachel to help him.

Five hundred miles away, as Steven's plane was circling Newark, Rachel stepped out of the shower and began to dry herself. She was pulling a slip over her head when she was suddenly struck by an incredibly powerful dizzy spell. She grabbed for the sink, but her fingers slipped off its steamy surface. She sank to the floor, the room spinning around her. Rachel closed her eyes and tried to let it pass, unable to cry out for help.

It was just a few moments before the floor came to a stop beneath her. When she opened her eyes, she wasn't looking at the bathroom wall. She was looking out a window, at a city skyline. The vision lasted less than a minute, and in that time she clearly heard Steven's voice:

I don't know what to do, Marty! I don't know where to go!

Then it was all over. Rachel pulled herself to her feet and hurried from the bathroom, calling Steven's name. She opened the door to Tatiana's room, but the child's bed had already been made.

"Rachel, what's wrong?" Eric asked as she raced down the stairs.

"Have you seen Steven?"

"Not this morning," Eric said. "Why?"

"I think he's run away!"

Eric followed her to the kitchen.

"Helga, have you seen Steven?"

"No, Mrs. Freleng."

Rachel turned to the girls, but they both shook their heads.

"Where did he go?" Olivia asked.

"How the hell should I know?" Rachel snapped. She swung around and gave Eric a burning stare. "It's your fault. He must have overheard what you said last night. He's run away."

Eric yawned. "Don't be ridiculous, Rachel. Of course he didn't run away. Check the bathroom."

"I did that," Rachel said, as if she was talking to a moron. "I checked the entire upstairs, as well as down here."

A flicker of concern washed over Eric's dark face.

"Rachel, he had no money. Where would he go?"

Helga had been listening to all this in troubled silence. Now she put down the coffeepot she was carrying and said abruptly, "Wait!"

She went into the kitchen and returned with a cookie jar.

"It is empty," she announced. "There was nearly two hundred dollars in here. I was saving it to buy my sister an airline ticket so that she could visit me from Berlin. Now that there is no East or West—"

Rachel interrupted her with a curt wave of her hand, not interested in a modern history lesson.

"So he has enough money to get pretty far," she said. She turned to her husband again, but this time the accusation had gone from her eyes. In its place was an imploring look. "Eric, what are we going to do?"

"Well, first we're going to get the girls to the school bus," Eric said.

"Don't you want us to help look for Steven?" Tatiana asked.

"Oh, Tati," Olivia said, "you know you can't miss school!"

Tatiana snorted. She'd hoped something good would come of all this—at the very least, missing school for a day. Frankly, she didn't want to look for Steven at all.

"I'll walk with them," Helga said.

When they had gone, Eric went on, "Now, I'm going to call the police—"

"No!"

Eric held up both hands.

"Rachel, this sudden police phobia of yours makes no sense," he said. "If Steven's run away, they're our best bet to find him."

Rachel's expression turned almost maniacal. Her teeth were set hard and her eyes were very large as she hissed, "I-will-not-work-with-the-police!"

Eric studied her, unable to believe this was the soft-spoken, loving woman he'd known just a few days earlier. Again he asked himself what might have happened to her when she disappeared.

"Rachel, someone's put this idea into your head," he said in a gentle tone. "Think about it. You've never been afraid of the police before. Now, I don't know if Steven has anything to do with this, but—"

"Of course he doesn't!"

"Whatever," Eric said, forcing himself to stay calm. He was already hatching a plan. "But Nina Blair disappeared, and now Steven is gone. There has to be a connection!"

Rachel's face relaxed again, and tears started forming in her eyes. She pressed the sides of her nose with her thumbs before they could overflow.

"Eric," she said in a very small voice, "what's happening to me? I feel as if . . . as if a door has been opened in my life and there is nothing there but darkness. Steven has something to do with it. I don't feel he's the cause of it, but somehow I think he's the only one who can bring light."

"You've only known him a few days," Eric said, "and you've known the girls most of their lives. Look, I'm no psychologist, but maybe Steven is a substitute for the baby we could never have."

Rachel looked down at the red-and-white spectator pumps she had chosen to wear with her red suit. It had been a long time since they'd discussed their failed attempts to have a baby. They'd been tested and retested and had tried many methods, to no avail. Eric seemed to be fine, but the specialists couldn't be certain about Rachel. There was something odd about her eggs, something they couldn't describe. The bottom line was that the two of them were incompatible when it came to reproduction.

Eric put his arms around his wife. She shuddered once, letting out a long sigh, but she didn't cry.

"We're wasting time," she said.

Eric nodded. "All right. I'll make a call to Children's Services right now."

Rachel left the room and Eric turned to the phone.

"You're saying that this child was registered with us?" a woman asked.

"Just last week," Eric said. "I think it would help if I could talk to Kathy Mayer. Nina Blair handled the case, but Ms. Mayer—"

"I'm sorry," the woman cut in, "I'm a little confused. No one by the name of Kathy Mayer works here."

Eric frowned up at the clock, barely registering that he was nearly late for work.

"Maybe I'm mixing up the name," he suggested. "Mayer or Meyer . . ."

"Not even close," the woman said.

"But I spoke directly with her," Eric said, "the day I went to pick up Steven."

"Do you have a last name for Steven?"

"Sorry, no," Eric said. God, was the world full of incompetents? How could they not know what was going on down there?

"Too bad," the woman said. "It would make it easier. I know—I'll check into Nina's files. As soon as I learn what's going on, I'll call you back. Where can I reach you, Mr. Freleng?"

He gave her his number. When he hung up he made one last call: to tell the school neither he nor his wife would be working that day.

Helga was coming in the front door when he went out to the hall.

"The girls are on the bus," she announced. "Is there anything else I can do?"

"Just man the telephone," Eric said. "I'm heading to the police station."

He paused, thoughtful. "They'll want a description. It's too bad we don't have a photograph."

Helga went off to do her morning chores. Rachel came out of the music room.

"Eric, I'm going to drive around Columbus," she said.

"Maybe I'll see him. Or maybe someone will be able to tell me something."

"Rachel, Columbus is a huge area," Eric said.

Rachel shrugged, and Eric could see there would be no stopping her.

"Okay," he said. "But I think we should have a check-in time."

"Good idea," Rachel said. "I'll call here at . . ."

She looked at her watch.

"At ten o'clock," she said. "That's two hours from now."

"Helga will be our liaison," Eric said.

Eric and Rachel exchanged a quick kiss, then headed in different directions. As she drove away, Rachel tried desperately to call back the picture she'd seen during her dizzy spell. It was a skyline, and she knew that it was the place where she'd find Steven. Somehow, he had sent a message to her that he was in trouble.

Rachel recalled that he'd used the name Marty. Or had it been that? It had happened so quickly that she could easily have misunderstood him.

Maybe he'd said "Mommy."

She pulled to a stop at a red light.

"Come on, Steven," she whispered. "Tell me where you are. Tell me where I can find you!"

At home, Eric opened the door and headed to his own car. In spite of Rachel's fears, he would cooperate fully with the police. Probably Steven would be found within an hour or two.

But deep inside, he sensed this would be far from the case.

30

LORRAINE STUMBLED ALONG as Trefill steered her up California Avenue. As soon as she was certain no one else could see, she stopped short. Trefill stumbled, then turned around.

"What the hell do you think you're doing?"

"I'm not coming with you," Lorraine said defiantly.

"Oh, yes you are," Trefill said.

Lorraine swung her foot forward, kicking him hard just beneath his kneecap. He winced, then swung his arm back.

"You little bitch!" he cried. "I'll teach you . . . !"

Lorraine's scream was cut short as Trefill's hand swung forward, knocking her to the ground. He stared at her for a moment, waiting for her to move. She didn't. He'd struck her so hard that, for Lorraine, Atlantic City had ceased to exist.

Panicked, Trefill looked around him. The street was empty. He picked up the child and slung her over his shoulder. Then he went to find the rental car he'd parked nearby. He dumped Lorraine into the back seat and sped off. He'd head for Connecticut at last, where he'd find the people who were supposed to take Lorraine. Then he would complete his mission, and LaBerge would no longer be angry with him.

He heard a soft moan from the back seat and realized Lorraine was waking up. That was good. He'd been stupid to lose his temper. If his superiors found out he'd struck her, they'd dismiss him for certain. Not because they felt any concern for the child, but because they'd want her "undamaged."

"Take it easy, kid," Trefill said, trying to make his voice sound paternal. It came out more like a growled command. "Don't get up."

He looked into his rearview mirror and saw the child had pulled herself up halfway. Her head hung, but he could see the ugly bruise that was forming on her cheek. A thick line of blood was trailing down the middle of the child's face. It globbed on the end of her nose and dripped a small puddle of red on the seat.

"Shit," Trefill said. Then he said it more forcefully, slamming a fist on the steering wheel: "*Shit!*"

He couldn't bring her to the people in Hartford looking like that. They'd ask questions. And Trefill had a feeling Lorraine wouldn't need to be forced when asked how she got that wound.

He'd have to hide with her for a few days. LaBerge was already pissed as hell at him anyway. Let them think he was still searching. One, two days . . . until the wound healed enough to be hidden by her hair. He'd cut her bangs and . . .

But first he had to find a place to stay. He drove for nearly an hour, and entered the town of Windhaven, a beach town on the Jersey shore. It wasn't hard to find a motel with a vacancy. Summer vacations had not yet come to bring in a crowd of tourists.

He found a room in a twenty-room motor lodge called the Conch Cove Inn.

Leaving Lorraine to "sleep it off," he went into the main office and purchased a room for two days. Then he came outside, checked to be certain he was alone, and carried the little girl into the room. He laid her on the bed and began to work on her injury. He moved with efficiency, not tenderness, using care only because he didn't want to hurt the child any worse than he already had.

Lorraine moved restlessly under his touch, but she did not awaken. He wondered what she was dreaming about. They were all so strange, so different, that group that they'd found. Lorraine had been the most different of all of them. They'd hoped a talk with her parents, combined with a valise full of bribe money, would give them some answers.

And then Trefill had screwed up, losing her. He'd gone nearly crazy trying to find her. It was only by a stroke of luck that he'd come around the corner when that man had run wildly into the street. He'd screamed about monsters, but Trefill had heard only one part of his ranting; something about a child with weird eyes. He knew at once he'd found his prey.

He went into the bathroom to wash blood from his hands. Then he came back inside and turned on the television.

The sound of a loud commercial pushing Toyotas broke Lorraine's spell. She sat up abruptly, then cried out in pain as her head swam. Tears rolled down her eyes. She turned onto her stomach.

"Don't move so fast," the man said. "Just lie still. There's a candy machine outside. I'll get you something. You want something?"

Lorraine did not answer him. She heard him get up and leave the room. She would have tried to escape at that moment, but her head hurt too badly. And where would she go anyway? The bad man had a car. She didn't, of course. She knew he was crazy.

Yet somehow she had to get away again.

Then words that Marty had spoken back in the hotel in New York came back to her.

You have the power yourself, Lorraine. Power. She remembered that he'd told her she had a special power.

And then she remembered the landlord and the stove. . . .

31

ERIC RETURNED FROM the police station believing he had done all he could for now. Helga met him at the door, holding his overnight bag.

"Mrs. Freleng asked me to pack this for you," she said. "She wants you to meet her at the airport."

"The airport!" Eric said with surprise. "Why there? Does she knew where Steven went?"

"She believes he is in New York City, Mr. Freleng," Helga said.

Eric, still standing on the front steps, frowned.

"Did he call here?"

"You'll have to ask her that yourself, sir," Helga said. "You go, now. I'm here to take care of the girls."

"But . . ."

"Mr. Freleng, she is going to get the next flight out," Helga said, "and she'll go without you, I am sure."

Befuddled, but not wanting to lose Rachel, Eric thanked Helga and headed back to the airport. Rachel met him near the entrance, holding two tickets.

"I was lucky enough to get two seats on the next flight to New York," she said. "They aren't together . . ."

"Rachel, why are you going to New York?" Eric asked. "Did Steven call? Helga wouldn't tell me anything."

Rachel paused.

"Eric, Steven sent me a message to go to New York," she said. "I've been trying to pinpoint his exact location, but he isn't communicating with me now."

"Communicating with you?" There was a frown in Eric's voice.

"I . . . I can't explain it," Rachel said. "When I was in the bathroom this morning, I saw an image of New York City as clear as if it were on television."

"Rachel, you've been under a lot of stress lately . . ."

"Don't baby me, Eric," Rachel said. "I'm not crazy. I know what I saw, and I know that Steven needs me. I'm going to New York, whether you come or not."

She glared at him, a challenge in her gray-green eyes. Eric sighed, his big shoulders heaving up and down.

"All right, I'll come," he said, "but only to make sure you're safe. You've never been to New York before."

"Neither have you," Rachel reminded him gently.

Eric pointed to the tickets.

"How much time do we have?"

"Nearly two hours, unfortunately," Rachel said.

"Then why don't we pass the time over lunch?" Eric suggested. "I know airport food isn't all that great, but I don't suppose they could ruin coffee and sandwiches."

Rachel agreed, realizing she hadn't eaten that day. She certainly wouldn't be of any help to Steven if she fell over from hunger. She and Eric went to the restaurant and ordered lunch.

Eric sensed that Rachel really wasn't in the mood to talk, so he respectfully refrained from idle chatter. Instead, he watched her as she watched people passing by, and wondered what was on her mind.

By now Rachel's mind was too tired-out to think of much of anything. In those moments of blank thoughts, completely unexpected, she found Steven again.

She dropped her sandwich with such abruptness that Eric reached across the table and took her hand.

"Rachel, what's wrong?"

Rachel didn't answer him. She didn't even see his arm on the table. Instead of plates and glasses, she saw a miniature view of a boardwalk. It curved along a beach until it was out of her "sight," edging a cluster of large gaudy buildings. It was a daylight image, but she could see thousands of lightbulbs decorting their facades, and knew it would be a brilliant, lively place at night. There were hundreds of people walking along the boardwalk. As clearly as if he were alone, she found Steven sitting on a bench.

He had his eyes closed, and his face seemed troubled.

"Rachel!" There was more force in Eric's voice, and this time she heard him.

"Steven's lost," Rachel said, her voice distant. "He's

gone there looking for someone, but he doesn't know what to do next."

"Gone where?" Eric asked.

Rachel pointed at the table. Eric saw only their lunch. Rachel could hear Steven's thoughts, and once again the name Marty came up.

I'm in Atlantic City now, Marty. I don't know what to do, and I'm scared. Why won't you answer me? Where are you?

Rachel tried to tell Steven that she was there, and coming for him, but he didn't seem aware of her presence.

A voice came out of nowhere, not part of her vision. "Would you like more coffee?"

The holographic image of the boardwalk in Atlantic City vanished in a nanosecond. Rachel looked up at Eric. His eyes were full of concern, and she knew he thought she'd gone over the edge. She quickly averted her gaze to the waitress.

"N-no," she answered. "No more coffee for me."

Eric waved the waitress away, then said, "What just happened?"

"I know where Steven is now," Rachel said, staring into her water glass. "I saw an image of a place with casinos, and a boardwalk."

"That has to be Atlantic City," Eric said. "But, Rachel, how—?"

Her head snapped up.

"I don't know how," she said, tears in her eyes. "I can't explain this. But would you please stop looking at me as if I'm crazy."

"I don't think you're crazy," Eric said.

"Yes, you do," Rachel said. "You think something's been happening to me ever since the night of the concert. Maybe you're right. I know I've been horrible to live with . . ."

"You've just got a lot on your mind."

"I've been a monster to the children," Rachel said, "especially Tatiana. But this is something I can't let go of, Eric. There is a reason we were chosen to take in Steven. I have to find him!"

"You will," Eric promised. "We'll be in Atlantic City by this evening, and we'll find Steven."

Rachel managed a smile for him, grateful for his optimism.

Neither one of them knew that Marty was already communicating with Steven, and moving him even farther away. When they finally arrived in Atlantic City, it was evening, and the bright lights Rachel had imagined were now real. Eric, although doubtful, asked if she felt anything.

"Not now," Rachel said. "If Steven is here, he isn't thinking strong enough thoughts for me to hear him."

In truth, Steven was there. He was sleeping under the boardwalk some distance down the beach, his mind free of dreams.

A breeze blew off the ocean, and Rachel shivered. Eric put an arm around her shoulders.

"Then maybe we should try some old-fashioned detective work," he said. "Let's walk along and see if there are any places that might attract a young boy like Steven."

"Fine," Rachel said, only because she didn't know what else to do. The boardwalk seemed endless, but she decided she could try to bring Steven back into her thoughts while they were walking along.

For the next hours they went into one place after another and asked if anyone had seen the young boy. No one had, and a few merchants pointed out that many families came to the beach during the day. One more little boy wouldn't stand out in this crowd.

Disheartened, Rachel sat down on a bench and stared out at the waves. Tears rolled down her cheeks.

"I know he's here, Eric!" she said. "I'm not mistaken about that! Why won't he call me?"

"Rachel, was he ever really calling you?" Eric asked.

Rachel looked at him. Her wet eyes reflected thousands of colored lights.

"You don't believe me."

"I didn't mean it that way," Eric said. "But it's been hours since you last had a . . . a vision. And you said on the airplane that you've heard the name Marty twice. Maybe he's calling this guy named Marty, whoever that is. Maybe Steven doesn't want you to find him."

That was entirely the wrong thing to say. Rachel burst

into unabashed tears, causing a few heads to turn. Eric quickly put his arms around her.

"I'm sorry!" he said. "Look, let's not sit here. We obviously aren't going much farther tonight. Let's book a room somewhere."

Rachel stopped crying and pulled away from him.

"Where do you suppose Steven is going to sleep tonight?"

"I don't know," Eric said. He thought for a few minutes. "But since you haven't picked up on him, maybe he isn't worried about that. Maybe he's perfectly safe right now."

"I want to believe you're right," Rachel said.

"Then believe it," Eric said, standing. He kept hold of her hand. "Let's go find a place to stay."

While the Frelengs sought an empty motel room, Steven slept soundly on the beach, exhausted after all his traveling.

32

SOMETIMES, WIL THOUGHT, his job was closer to that of an archaeologist than a cop. He drove through the streets of Union Fort, unnoticed in the twilight. When he found Henley's house again, he pulled up to the curb. He'd hoped it was trash night, and he'd been right. A huge bag sat near the street. Swiftly, acting as if he did this sort of thing every day, Wil picked up the bag, threw it into his car, got back in, and drove away.

Like an archaeologist, he would comb through the bag to find clues about Henley's existence. By the time he was through, he would know what Henley ate, whether he shaved or not, who wrote letters to him, and more. And out of that he hoped to move closer to solving Samantha Winstead's mystery.

When Wil arrived at Samantha's place that night, she immediately recognized the hum of his car's motor. This time, she and Julie went out to greet him.

"Your suggestion about the amusement park was great," Samantha said.

"We had the best time!" Julie put in. "Maybe you can come with us next time?"

She sounded so hopeful that Samantha and Wil exchanged smiles. Samantha felt the fluttering in her stomach again, and fought it down. This was purely a business arrangement! She couldn't play damsel in distress to Wil's hero.

"Maybe I can," Wil said.

Julie showed him a paperback field guide to wildflowers.

"Samantha bought it for me," she said. "I'm going to try to name all the flowers around the house tomorrow."

"Sounds like a good idea," Wil said. "In the meantime, I'm going to borrow Samantha."

The adults went into the house while Julie headed for the kennel. Samantha invited Wil to sit at the kitchen table for coffee and fresh-baked blueberry muffins.

"So, what did you find for me today?" Samantha asked.

Wil took a bite of a muffin, opened a file, and pulled out a piece of paper.

"Raoul Henley called you last Wednesday," he said. "Look, your number is on his phone bill."

Samantha looked at the long-distance listings. Sure enough, her own number was there. The time the call was made was in the morning.

"That would have been right before I left for work," Samantha said. "But I swear I don't remember taking any such call."

"You spoke for nearly fifteen minutes," Wil said. "I have a theory that he coerced you into coming to Durango to get the child."

"But I didn't," Samantha said, "at least not then. I went to work a double shift."

"And when you came home, Henley was waiting for you," Wil added. "He was the one who drugged you and drove your truck to Durango."

Samantha studied the phone bill as if it could tell her something more than a bunch of numbers.

"I'm beginning to feel like a crazy person," she said.

"You aren't crazy," Wil said.

"Where did you get the phone bill?"

"From his trash," Wil said matter-of-factly.

Samantha laughed out loud. "You took his trash? Ugh!"

"It was pretty unpleasant," Wil said, "but it's part of the job. You'd be amazed at what people throw away. That phone bill, for instance, was a real stroke of luck. It absolutely connects Henley with you."

He took another muffin, commented on how good they were, and said, "Are you busy tonight?"

"Not at all," Samantha said. "We had such a long day, I thought we'd just hang out here and take it easy."

Wil smiled at her in a sly way. "Want to play detective?"

"You told me yesterday you didn't directly involve your clients."

"I said I didn't endanger them," Wil said. "I want to drive into Fort Union and knock on Henley's door. You stay in the car and take a look at him. Maybe the sight of him will jar your memory."

"I'm willing to try," Samantha said. "But what about Julie?"

"Bring her along for the ride," Wil said. "She's as involved in this as you are, and maybe she'll remember him."

"All right," Samantha said. "We'll get ready and go right now. It's getting late, but I think Julie is too wired from our day out to fall asleep, anyway."

"But listen," Wil said, "it might be helpful if you don't tell Julie where we're going. If she's not prepared, the surprise of seeing Henley may jar her memory too."

Samantha went outside and found Julie filling the dogs' water trough.

"What a thoughtful thing to do," Samantha said.

"I figured the dogs needed fresh water," Julie said. "Did Mr. Sherer leave yet?"

"He's still here," Samantha said. "And he wants us to go for a ride with him."

Julie turned off the faucet, then hooked the hose on its holder.

"Yeah?" she said eagerly. "Are we helping him?"

"Sort of," Samantha answered.

Wil was waiting for them. He opened their doors, then got into his own side. A little more than an hour later, an hour in which Julie beat Wil in a dozen games of "Twenty Questions," they reached Union Fort. Wil drove through the town, but stopped a block away from Henley's place.

"It's important you do as I tell you," he said. "I want you to move into the back with Julie, Samantha. The windows are darkened back there, so he won't be able to see you."

"Who?" Julie asked.

Samantha hushed her.

"I'm going to pretend to be taking a survey," Wil went on. "Even if he refuses, you should have enough chance to get a good look at him. Ready?"

"It sounds easy enough," Samantha said, "but I'm not sure it'll do any good."

"We have to try," Wil said. "Go on, get in the back."

Samantha opened her door, pushed up her seat, and climbed in next to Julie. The child looked completely confused.

"Who are we going to look at?" she asked.

"You'll see," Samantha said. "It's a secret."

Wil drove on until he reached Henley's address. He parked the car, picked up a phony survey from his seat, and got out. Julie unbuckled her seat belt and crawled nearer to Samantha to get a better view of the house. Wil walked up to the door and rang the bell. He waited a few moments, then rang it again. Then he looked back at the car and gave his head a slight shake.

"Where's he going?" Julie asked.

"Looks like he's going to check the back door," Samantha said.

But if he does, I won't see the man.

Wil returned to the car a few minutes later. He opened Samantha's door and leaned down, one hand resting on the frame.

"Would you come with me for a minute?"

"Why?" Samantha said. "I thought . . ."

"There's something I want you to see," Wil said. "Don't worry. He obviously isn't home."

Samantha looked up and down the block. Several children were playing in the street about halfway up, and a man was mowing his lawn.

"Won't the neighbors be suspicious?"

Wil went to his trunk, opened it, and pulled out a package wrapped in brown paper. He took out a pen and quickly scribbled Henley's address on the blank label.

"We're making a delivery," he said.

"What's in the box?" Julie asked.

"Nothing at all," Wil said with a wink.

Samantha got out of the car. Julie tried to follow her, but Wil put a firm hand on her shoulder.

"You wait here, honey," he said. "I need a lookout."

Julie looked disappointed, but she sat back again. Wil shut the door and took Samantha by the arm. He escorted her up the driveway to the back of the house.

"When you told me about Julie's ordeal in the hospital," he said, "you spoke of a glass box."

"Julie seemed to feel she'd been trapped in one," Samantha said.

They'd reached the back of the house. Wil crouched down, pushing at an unlocked basement window.

"Look inside."

Samantha did so. It was a few moments before her eyes adjusted to the darkness, but when they did, she gasped. There on the floor, near a table saw, tool bench, and water heater, lay a pod-shaped box. The top, made of glass, lay broken in large pieces around the floor. The bottom seemed to be made of wood. Wires had been ripped out of it and a small control panel hung loosely from the front.

"Julie's glass box," Samantha whispered. She looked at Wil. "But why does it look like it's moving?"

Wil ran a hand through the spiky strands of his hair.

"I can't imagine," he said. "There may be bugs on it . . ."

"Oh . . ." Samantha felt sickened to imagine Julie had been held prisoner in that coffinlike apparatus. Because that's exactly what it looked like: a glass-topped coffin.

Wil stood up. "Come on, we're going inside."

"But that's illegal!" Samantha cried.

"So's kidnapping and child abuse," Wil said. He fished through his pockets and produced a small bag.

Samantha followed him up the stairs to the back door. He took out a tool, fidgeted with the lock, and within moments gained entry to the kitchen. Samantha held back at the doorway.

"Come on," Wil said. "We don't have a lot of time."

"What if Henley comes back?"

"He has a hell of a lot more explaining to do than we have," Wil said. "Try not to touch anything. We don't want to leave fingerprints."

He looked around the kitchen, but didn't touch anything. Samantha was also careful to keep her hands to herself. In the living room Wil went directly to a table laden with family pictures.

"Anybody here look familiar?" he asked.

Samantha looked down.

"No, not at all," she said.

"Let's take a closer look at that pod," Wil said. "We might get a better idea what it was used for."

The entry to the basement was just outside the kitchen. Wil used a handkerchief to open the door and switch on the light. Samantha followed him down the wooden staircase, trying hard not to touch the banister.

"Over there," Wil said.

"You know, Julie must be getting worried," Samantha said.

"We've only been a few minutes," Wil told her. "I think it's important that you see this."

He knelt down near the box, studying it carefully. The gnarls of wood really did seem to be moving, but only for a moment. Wil rubbed his eyes, letting them adjust better to the dim lighting. Samantha moved to the other side and did the same.

"It's too strange for me to figure out," she said.

"Julie would probably know what it was."

Samantha glared at him over the rim.

"No way," she said. "You aren't bringing that child in here."

"I didn't plan to," Wil reassured her. He got back up again and began to search the basement.

"What are you looking for?"

"Some sign she was down here," Wil said. "Evidence he was holding her prisoner before he turned her over to you."

"He sounds like a maniac," Samantha said worriedly. "Wil, please, I don't want to be here any—"

She had been walking toward him as she spoke, but her words were cut off when she stumbled over something lying on the floor. She backed up and cried out in dismay. Wil hurried to her and knelt back down to look at the body Samantha had discovered. It was dressed in a workshirt, khaki trousers, and workboots. The shadows obscured the features, but they knew at once who it must be.

"Henley," Samantha whispered.

Wil went to the tool bench and found a flashlight. When the beam filled in the shadows, Samantha had to suppress a cry. The face they saw, screaming silently, was a mass of red. Facial muscles were so plainly exposed that Samantha could identify each one individually. The eyes were round and staring.

"My God, he must have been burned by something," she said in a choking voice.

"What could take the skin off a man and leave the flesh?" Wil wanted to know.

He, too, felt sickened at the hideous corpse. Wil had seen death many times in his years as a cop and detective, but never anything like this. There was something strange about it, beyond the missing skin. It took Wil only a moment to realize what it was.

"There's no blood," he whispered. "It's like he was skinned alive, but . . . ."

"Let's get out of here," Samantha begged.

"Agreed," Wil said. He took Samantha's hand and walked back upstairs with her. Outside, they took a moment to collect themselves.

"What's going on?" Samantha asked in a quiet voice.

"I sure as hell don't know yet," Wil told her. "Henley was murdered, that's obvious. But I can't imagine how it was done so . . . cleanly."

Samantha looked at the basement window.

"To think Julie might have been down there."

"She's safe with you," Wil said. "Come on, let's go back home again. We aren't going to learn anything here."

They started for the car.

"Get the scared look out of your eyes," Wil ordered. "You don't want Julie asking a lot of questions."

Samantha breathed in deeply, gave Wil's hand a tight squeeze, then held her head high. By the time she reached the car, she was smiling.

"What took you guys so long?"

"Oh, the man was home after all," Wil said quickly. "He wanted to chat a bit."

Wil and Samantha got back in the car and drove off. Bored with drawing, Julie put her head down on the seat. The instant she closed her eyes, a horrifying image filled her mind. She saw a man lying on a floor, his skin hideously peeled away. Julie sat up straight and stared at the back of Samantha's head.

"That man is dead, isn't he?"

Samantha gasped. Wil's head jerked up, a surprised look reflected in the rearview mirror.

"Julie, how do you know that?" Samantha asked. She had been unable to get an image of Henley's body from her mind.

"I just . . . know. Is it true?"

Samantha sighed, looking at Wil. He nodded slightly.

"I'm afraid so," Samantha said. "We found him in his basement. We don't know how it happened."

Julie looked down at her lap.

"I didn't do it."

"Nobody said you did!" Samantha cried.

"Of course not," Wil agreed. "Honey, you couldn't possibly have done what happened to that man."

"What happened?"

"He was . . ." Samantha paused.

"He was beaten," Wil said. "A little girl like you couldn't do that to a big man like Henley."

Samantha thought for a few moments, then said, "You know, his death may have nothing to do with us. Maybe he was in trouble."

Wil nodded. "That's right. He could have owed money to someone."

Julie didn't say anything for the rest of the drive. She knew they were just trying to make her feel better. She no longer had any desire to play or look out at the scenery, so she put her head down again in an attempt to fall asleep.

Marty's voice filled her mind a few moments later.

I know what happened to him.

He sounded as if he were shouting from the other end of a long tunnel. Julie stirred, but didn't open her eyes or sit up.

Hello, Marty. What happened to him?

He was . . . touching something he shouldn't have. But we can't be certain no one else knew his secret.

What secret?

I can't tell you. But it's time for you to come to us, Julie. The others are on their way. You are farthest from us, and therefore your journey will be the most difficult.

I'm not leaving Samantha!

But she lied to you!

She didn't lie. She just . . . just didn't say everything. She's trying to protect me.

Julie, she can't protect you. You must join with the other children, or we'll all die!

I'm not listening to you! I'm not going to die!

Come with us, Julie. You must come with us! You must come . . .

Julie sat up abruptly, shaking Marty's voice out of her mind. He tried calling her, but she refused to answer him.

Samantha looked over the back of the seat. Julie was staring straight ahead, her lips pressed together.

"What's the matter, sweetie?" Samantha asked. "You didn't have another bad dream, did you?"

Julie shook her head. Samantha smiled kindly at her, and turned her eyes back to the road.

It was very late by the time they arrived home, and Julie announced she was tired. She went upstairs to her room and lay on the bed. She hadn't given Henley much thought, but now she tried as hard as she could to bring him into her mind. But try as she might, she couldn't conjure him up. Instead, a shadowy but familiar image appeared.

Julie?

Go away, Marty. I'm thinking.

You're thinking about Henley. He really has nothing to do with us.

He does! You aren't telling me everything.

There was a long pause. Julie imagined Marty was considering his answer.

All right. There is more. Do you remember how you were scared by the box in the hospital?

Uh-huh.

Henley had a box.

Julie gasped out loud.

The box I dreamed about?

Maybe. But there's danger there for you, Julie. Don't you see? You have to listen to me and believe that the only safe place for you is here!

Where . . . where are you?

There is water all around us. I can see land in the distance, but I don't know what it is.

Then how will I find you?

First, you must find the others who are coming. There are only two in this area. One is a boy. His name is Steven and he was living with a family in Columbus, Ohio. He began his journey a short while ago. They mean to hurt us, Julie. But we must work together to fight them.

I'm tired, Marty. I'm tired and scared.

She turned onto her side and wrapped her arms around a stuffed animal.

There is no other way to survive. Sleep now, Julie. In the morning I will help you on your way.

And then there was silence in Julie's mind. Silence filled with the painful stress of making a very, very difficult decision.

33

NEARLY THREE THOUSAND miles from Colorado, completely unaware that Lorraine wasn't the only one of her kind, Joe Trefill sat in the motel room and stared at the sleeping child. She'd come awake briefly a few hours earlier, just after they'd arrived. She sat on her bed in silence, staring at him with those weird olive-colored eyes of hers. Creepy eyes, Joe thought. It was like she could read everything in your brain. He had wanted to slap her, to make her stop staring. Then he remembered the whole reason he'd rented this room for two days was to give her head wound time to heal. He was grateful when her eyelids began to flutter and she fell back on the bed, asleep again.

Trefill was sitting sideways in one of the room's two chairs, feet propped up on the dresser. An old John Wayne western was on the television, one with a box that promised the latest in movies after the insertion of a certain number of quarters. He had bought a package of peanuts from the vending machine at the end of the building, and now he sat eating them one by one. He'd have to get dinner at some point, he supposed, though he hadn't managed to figure out how he'd do it without someone spotting him.

Damned pain in the neck. Why had she run away, anyway? He hadn't hurt her or threatened her in any way. It was those hoodlums in the city. Or maybe it was the gunshot he'd fired off. It didn't matter. Lorraine had run away, and had been taken in for a few days by that old lady. Trefill was glad she'd died. At least no one could identify him.

He crumpled up the peanut bag, tossed it at the wastebasket, and missed. He didn't bother to pick it up. Instead, he swung himself off the chair and went to the night table. He pulled out a telephone book and opened it to the Yellow Pages. No particular kind of food appealed to him, but he decided on Chinese because that was the nearest place.

Nor wanting the hassle of bringing Lorraine with him, he went into the bathroom and found a large towel. Taking a knife from his pocket, he made slits in the tightly woven ends and then ripped the towel into four equal strips. He carried these into the bedroom.

Lorraine was awakened by the feel of someone pulling at her legs. She tried to sit up, but found she couldn't move. She stared at Trefill as he tied her to the bed with strips of white towel. A strange taste of wet terrycloth made her realize he'd gagged her with a washcloth.

She glared at him, as she'd done before, but he didn't look back. He went about tying her without a word. She'd tried earlier to bring the monster back, the one Marty said she'd created to scare the landlord. She glared, fire burning in her mind, fury making her turn red. Where was the monster? Why couldn't she stop this man?

Where was Marty?

The effort had been too much after her head injury. She'd passed out cold again.

Trefill straightened up. "That ought to hold you. I'm going out for Chinese food. I'll be back in half an hour or so. Don't even think about causing trouble. You think I was lying about this being official government business? I wasn't. And there are people backing me up every step of the way. They're watching the building right now. So if you're a bad little girl and you try to run away, you'll be caught and punished. Understand?"

Lorraine simply glowered at him.

"Be good," Trefill said.

Then he was out the door.

Lorraine struggled against the ties, but they were much too tight. So she lay back and closed her eyes and tried to call Marty. To her surprise, this time he answered.

Where were you? she demanded. *I need help!*

I'm sorry. Sometimes . . . sometimes they do things to me and I can't communicate.

Lorraine moaned, the sound muffled by the gag in her

mouth. She stared up at the ceiling and tried to picture her captor in another setting. But she couldn't. She only knew she was terrified of him.

Marty, what am I going to do?

You have to get away from him.

I can't! He has me tied up! I tried and tried to make a monster come, like in the apartment, but I couldn't.

You are too young to work on your own. You need the combined strength of other minds. I will help you this time, and you'll succeed.

Lorraine did not answer right away. She wriggled a little, trying to get comfortable. Then she thought to Marty:

What were they doing to you?

They put a needle into me. It has some kind of strange medicine inside and it makes me feel weird. I can't communicate when that happens.

Are they going to do that to me?

They aren't going to catch you. When we are all together, we'll be too strong for them.

When are we going to be together?

Soon. You're so close now . . .

At that moment the door opened. Instinctively afraid of Trefill, Lorraine cut off all thoughts to Marty. She stared at the man as he set up cartons of Chinese food on the dresser.

Wait until he unties you. Be ready . . .

Lorraine was too nervous to answer him. Trefill came to the bed and began to unfasten her ties. She wiggled into a sitting position and tried to pull the gag from her mouth. Trefill grabbed her wrist.

"Don't misbehave," he said. "You leave that alone for a minute."

Lorraine stared at him. He began opening the containers. She could smell the food from across the room, and realized she was famished.

"I didn't know what to get you," Trefill said, "but I figured you'd like lo mein. Most kids I know do. Now, I'm gonna take off your gag and give you something to eat. Don't even think of screaming. No one is near enough to hear you, and I'll get mad. You won't like me if I get mad."

He pulled out the gag. Lorraine gasped, sticking her

tongue out to get rid of the horrible taste of wet washcloth. Then she took the food container and began to
eat. Trefill parked himself in front of the TV, his back
to her. He switched on the news.

The weather reporter was just finishing his promise of
rain. Lorraine was watching a commercial about dog
food when Marty came into her mind again.

The time has come to get rid of him. Think, Lorraine.

Instantly Lorraine recalled what had happened to the
hoods in the subway and to the landlord. She directed
her full thoughts toward Trefill, staring hard at him.

Trefill's hand came up to the back of his head and
brushed as if to get rid of a fly. But the sensation that
something was touching him wouldn't go away. He
turned quickly and shot Lorraine a warning look, but
the child only glowered at him. *Freaky little bitch*, he
thought.

He turned back to his food. The pressure on the back
of his head increased, spreading around to his temples.
It was a strange, fizzy sort of feeling—like when your
foot falls asleep. Trefill squinted and rolled his neck; had
to be a headache coming on.

You can't eat the food.

Lorraine's thoughts shot into his brain as if sent by a
hypodermic needle. Trefill gasped and looked wide-eyed
into the container in his hands. He couldn't eat it, not
now! If he ate it, something terrible would happen!

"Stupid," he growled, "it's food, just friggin' food!"

And his eyes didn't see anything but his dinner.

But his mind insisted that the container was full of
danger, of evil, of disease.

Don't eat! Don't eat! Don't eat!

"Damn!"

The room began to sway around him, the fizzing in his
head changing to the buzzing of bees. Bees that stung,
over and over, leaving burning pain behind. Trefill
cupped his hands over his ears, the takeout box falling
to the floor. He screamed in agony against pain that
wasn't even real, a worst-case scenario of "Chinese restaurant syndrome" from lo mein that did not contain
even a dash of MSG.

Lorraine climbed slowly from the bed, staring at him,
unable to believe she'd done this to him.

Lorraine! Get up! You have to run now!

Lorraine didn't argue with Marty. She jumped out of the bed, raced to put her shoes on, grabbed the money valise, and headed for the door. As Trefill struggled with unreal fears and pain, she ran down the dark road to dubious safety.

34

JULIE LAY WIDE-AWAKE in bed long after Samantha herself had retired for the night. She curled herself around a big stuffed bear that Samantha had won for her at Rocky Point Park. It wasn't a fancy toy, just a cheap carnival prize made of magenta plush with felt eyes, stuffed with Styrofoam pellets. But it was special to Julie because Samantha had tried so hard to win it for her. She closed her eyes and remembered the way Samantha had thrown ball after ball at a pyramid of bottles.

Samantha was the best person that Julie had ever known. She was certain of that, even though she could not recollect where she had come from. She knew now that she'd never been to the Cliffside Home, and that Mr. Henley (whoever he was) had tricked Samantha. Julie did not even try to understand why. Maybe Marty would explain it all to her, when she saw him.

She knew she *was* going to see him. No matter how much she protested, there was some power beyond her ability to resist that called her to the place where Marty waited. He had said others were coming too. She had to go. It was the only way to find out who she really was. And she believed Marty when he told her something terrible would happen if they didn't unite.

A single fat tear rolled across Julie's nose and onto the bear. She hugged him more tightly. She didn't want to leave Samantha, but she had to know what Marty knew. She just *had* to know!

It was a long time before sheer exhaustion finally pulled the little girl into sleep. She dreamt of darkness, and brilliant light, and being in something moving very fast. When she woke up she remembered the roller coaster and the fun house at the park. But somehow she had a feeling that the dreams weren't about those rides.

When she closed her eyes again, she heard a familiar voice calling to her. Marty came, and as she was drifting off to sleep again, he told her exactly what she had to do.

Samantha was awakened early the next morning by the sound of the dogs barking. It wasn't their normal "we're hungry" bark, but something closer to howling. It was so unusual that she didn't hesitate to get out of bed and investigate. Pulling on her robe, she hurried down the hallway, glancing into Julie's room as she passed. The bed was empty, and unmade.

Julie always made her bed the moment she got up.

Now Samantha ran, down to the kitchen. She opened the back door and looked out at the yard. The sensation she felt just then was so unexpected, so abrupt, that her breath was taken away. The yard seemed very big this morning; very big, very quiet, and very empty.

Something was wrong.

A chill began to rush through Samantha's blood. It was almost like the anxiety attacks she'd experienced when she'd tried to call the police. But there was nothing here to provoke such an incident.

She tried to fight it, tried to tell herself it was ridiculous. She was just tired from so much activity. That was why the yard seemed to be floating in front of her, through a mist of gray.

Something is wrong with Julie!

Her own mind shouted the words at her. Samantha ran through the house, room by room, trying to find the child.

"Julie?"

There was no response. Samantha fought the sense of panic that threatened to devour her.

"Julie!"

Surely the child had heard her by now. Samantha was being gripped by an overwhelming feeling of terror. Why wasn't Julie answering? Where could . . . ?

The barking had reached a crazy pitch, as if Sunday and Lady had gone mad. Samantha left the house and ran to them. Sunday and Lady cowered around her, whining, their tails tucked underneath them.

They were afraid of something.

Samantha crouched down.

"What is it, kids? What? Has something happened to Julie?"

Oh, God, I don't even want to think. . . .

At the sound of the child's name, both dogs' ears perked straight up. Sunday gave one sharp bark.

"Do you know where she is?"

The dogs ran to the door of the kennel. Samantha got up, opened it, and followed them.

When she saw where they were headed, Samantha realized Julie must have gone to the little adobe. That explained why the child couldn't hear her. But why were the dogs so nervous?

The sense of foreboding fought to come back again, and it was beginning to win the battle. She was certain that, when she opened the door, she'd find Julie lying on the floor, like Henley had been.

Stop it!

Samantha pushed open the door of the little adobe. She was relieved to see that Julie wasn't in here, but it was questionable relief. The dogs were still whining, still sniffing around as if trying to find something.

She knew at once that something was different in here, but it took her a moment to see what it was.

There was an afghan in the middle of the floor, and two pillows from the couch. For some strange reason, it seemed that Julie had come here last night to sleep. Samantha moved the afghan and found an open book. It was an atlas, opened to a two-page spread of the United States. A large red circle had been drawn to the right side, encompassing a portion of the eastern seaboard and part of the Atlantic Ocean. An arrow had been drawn from Ashleigh Creek, Colorado, to this vast area.

Samantha looked around further and found a flashlight. She picked up the blanket to discover her purse. She picked it up. Somehow, she wasn't surprised her wallet was gone.

She was shaking inside, but she forced herself to remain calm. Wherever Julie had gone, whatever the atlas meant, she couldn't have gotten very far. Samantha knew she needed help. She carried the things back to the house and called Wil Sherer.

In his usual manner, he hung up without saying good-bye. But he seemed to arrive at Samantha's house with the same abruptness. Wil was a man who did not waste words or time.

Samantha knew her eyes were puffed and bloodshot from crying. She splashed icy water into them, for what it was worth. But Wil was perceptive enough to see how distraught she was. Once before, Samantha had wanted him to put his arms around her, just because she needed the comfort of another adult.

This time, he did it. Without a word he encircled her in his sturdy embrace, offering her the strength of his support. She held on to him for just a moment, then pulled away. Feelings were stirring inside of her, feelings she did not have time for right now.

She swallowed. "She's taken my money. I was going to do some major grocery shopping today, so there was two hundred dollars in my purse."

"When was the last time you saw her?" Wil asked gently. He was the one who led Samantha into the living room and made her sit down on the couch. He sat beside her.

"Right before I went to bed," Samantha said. "It was nearly midnight. She must have gone out to the play-house sometime after that."

She pointed to the coffee table, where the atlas lay open. Wil reached for it and studied the altered page.

"What do you suppose it means?" she asked. "Where is she headed?"

"You mean, where in the East?" Wil asked. "She's circled a large area. I don't know why it includes so much of the Atlantic. Could just be a child's sloppiness."

"Julie was never sloppy," Samantha said.

Wil was thoughtful for a few moments. Samantha watched him, as if his expression would reveal an answer to her problem. But he shook his head.

"It gives us half the country to search," he said.

"What about the picture I gave you?" Samantha asked, hopeful. "Has anything come of that?"

"Not yet," Wil said. "But it's still early. Look, we have to start somewhere. If she is heading east, someone instructed her to do so. The fastest way to get her there would be by airplane."

"Who'd sell an airplane ticket to a child?"

Wil met her worried gaze.

"Who'd erase a child's memory and leave her with a perfect stranger?" he asked. "Someone's got to be behind this. It wasn't Henley, although he seems to have been a pawn."

Samantha made a face to remember the condition of Henley's body, but quickly lost the expression.

"I haven't had time to read the papers," she said. "Did the police find him?"

"I called them," Wil said.

Samantha looked surprised. "But then they must know we were there!"

"They know *I* was there," Wil said. "I didn't mention you or Julie. I gave the information to an old friend of mine working in that precinct. There's more to the story, Samantha."

Samantha straightened herself. What more could happen?

"Do you remember how it seemed Henley had been skinned alive?"

Samantha's expression told Wil she didn't want to be reminded.

"That isn't what the Union Fort police found," Wil said. "They found a skeleton, in perfect condition. Nothing of the flesh was left."

Samantha turned away, hugging herself.

"Who could be doing these things?" she demanded. "What do they want with Julie?"

Wil reached across the couch to touch her arm. The gesture made her turn to him again.

"We're going to find her," he said. "I think she'd start her journey by airplane. I'll check the nearest airport and see what I can find out. In the meantime, I want you to call your friend Barbara."

"Why?"

"Two reasons," Wil said. "You need a friend right now. And she's known you long enough that she may be able to fill in some blanks."

Samantha looked befuddled. "What does that have to do with Julie?"

"I'm not sure," Wil said. "But somehow I think there is a connection. Find out if she knows anyone in the East. It could help us narrow down the search area."

Samantha stood up. "Barbara is off-duty right now. She's probably sleeping. But I'm sure she'll understand."

Wil stood up and tucked the atlas under his arm. "I'm going to take a closer look at this."

They walked to the back of the house together. Samantha grabbed her purse from the kitchen table, unhooked her car keys from their peg, and led Wil out the back door. He waited for her while she tended to the dogs; then they went to their respective vehicles.

Wil took hold of Samantha's arm.

"Be careful," he said.

She smiled. "I'm not doing anything dangerous."

"I wouldn't be so sure," Wil said. "I wouldn't be too quick to trust anyone."

With that, he walked to his car, leaving Samantha to wonder why he'd given her such a grim warning when she was on her way to the home of her very best friend.

She backed out of her driveway, then followed Wil's Firebird for a few minutes. They parted ways, Wil heading north to the airport. Samantha kept her mind busy as she drove, trying to think how she would approach her good friend. She didn't want Barbara to think she didn't trust her.

In truth, it wasn't that she was worried about Barbara's reaction to her question. It was just that, if she didn't occupy her mind, she'd dwell on Julie and the danger she might be in at that moment. And if she did that, she'd become too upset to do anyone any good.

She reached Barbara's apartment. When she pulled into the driveway, she saw that her friend's car wasn't there. But she knew that Barbara sometimes used the double garage, renting space from the family that owned the house.

As Samantha exited the car and walked up the driveway, she saw a little girl digging in a small garden. A child with rippling dark hair.

"Julie!"

She was so overwhelmed with excitement that her heart nearly stopped when the little stranger turned around. It wasn't Julie at all. Samantha bit her lip.

"Oh, sorry," she faltered. "I thought . . ."

The child was looking at her in a distrusting way. Samantha managed a smile, then went up to Barbara's door and knocked.

"Nobody's there," the girl said.

She stood up and came to stand on the steps. Samantha saw now that she was several years younger than Julie.

"Barbara's out?"

"Ms. Huston's gone," the child said. "She came to Daddy this morning and gave him all the money she owed him and then she put her things in the back of her car and then she drove away."

Samantha knew at once what had happened. Barbara had taken Julie!

"Did she say . . . ?"

She stopped herself. There wasn't much use in talking to a young child.

"Is your daddy home?"

" 'Course not," the child said. "He went to work. Mommy's here."

In a few moments Samantha was talking to the landlady.

"I'm sorry," she said. "Barbara didn't tell us where she was going. But she did seem to be in a hurry."

"Did she have a child with her?"

The woman thought a moment, taking off her glasses to chew on an earpiece.

"Not that I noticed," she said. "But it was so early it was still dark. I couldn't tell."

Samantha mumbled a thanks and turned away. She was filled with confusion and anger. Why had Barbara done this?

"I'm going to find you," Samantha said furiously as she drove away. "I'm going to find you and make you tell me what you did with my Julie."

She was too angry to realize she had used the word "my."

Needing his help, Samantha decided to drive up to the airport to find Wil. It was a small one, just outside Boulder, and it wasn't hard to find him. His unusual good looks and broad shoulders made him stand out in the crowd. His eyebrows went up, his face registering surprise to see her.

"Barbara's gone too," she said breathlessly. "The

landlady said she left very early this morning. She couldn't tell if she had a child with her."

"Julie was seen here a few hours ago," Wil said. "One of the ticket clerks was able to identify her from the copy I made of that Polaroid."

Samantha sighed deeply. They'd just missed her!

"Where did she go?"

"Barbara bought a ticket to Newark, New Jersey."

Samantha grabbed his arm, her eyes full of hope. Wil hated to see that expression. It was the kind of face parents wore when they heard their child had been found, right before they were told the bad news.

But Julie, he believed, was still alive.

"I wish I could tell you more right now," he said, and his heart skipped a beat as Samantha's expression darkened, "but at this point there's no way of knowing where they're headed."

Samantha ran her fingers through her hair.

"There must be millions of people in that part of the country," she said.

Wil took hold of her arms. "We don't have time to worry, Samantha."

She looked up at him, her watery eyes hardening with determination.

"What do we do next?" she asked.

"You know what Barbara's car looks like?"

Samantha nodded.

"It's a good bet she's left it in the parking lot."

"Do you think she plans to come back for it?"

Wil shook his head. "Not if she's kidnapped Julie. She'll try to disappear. I think the car is probably abandoned in one of the short-term lots."

"Then let's go find it," Samantha said.

They hurried out of the building to begin their search. Wil took one half of the lot, while Samantha took the other. Twenty minutes later, exhausted and sweating from the heat of the sun, Samantha recognized Barbara's old Mustang. She shouted, and Wil came running. He had a crowbar in his hand, borrowed from his own trunk.

"Great," he said. "Let's open it and see what we find."

Samantha opened her mouth to ask how he was going to do it, but then she remembered it had been easy for him to get into Henley's house. He had the lock picked in seconds. He pulled the door open, then gestured for Samantha to get inside. Then he went around the back and used the crowbar to open the trunk. Except for a spare tire, it seemed empty.

"I'm going to leave this up to you," he said. "Check every square inch of the car, especially inside the seats. I'll open the trunk too. I want you to bring everything you find to me at my office in an hour."

"Where are you going?"

"To see what I can learn about Barbara Huston," Wil said. "If I can connect her to a city in the East, we may be able to learn where she's going with Julie."

He turned and left without saying good-bye, hurrying to get his job done. This time Samantha didn't ponder his occasional abruptness. She set about her own task, determined to do whatever she could to get Julie back again.

35

SOMETHING COLD WAS tickling Lorraine's bare feet. She woke abruptly, jerking her legs up into her torso. She tasted sand in her mouth and sat up, making sputtering sounds. Groggily she looked around herself at the beach where she had collapsed the night before. Where was she? The nearest building was some distance away, and there was no other sign of civilization.

Slowly she pulled herself to her feet and brushed sand-salted hair from her face. Her eyes felt gritty. She rubbed at them. There was a small pool of water near her, the cold that she had felt on her feet. Some child had dug it the day before, but she hadn't seen it in the darkness.

When had she come here? she wondered? How long had she been walking before sheer exhaustion caused her to collapse on the soft surface of the beach? Marty had guided her only part of the way before she lost contact with him. He had said that sometimes they did things to him. Whoever they were, Lorraine did not want to meet them. That horrible man at the motel had been one of them, and he had wanted to hurt her.

A thought knocked all vestiges of sleep from her chubby little body. Maybe, whenever Marty wasn't able to talk to her, they were hurting him! The only person who could help her! What would she do if he . . . ?

No, she wouldn't let herself even say the word. He would be there for her. She would just have to wait. She'd come this far. There had been kind people to help her. Lorraine wondered about Sandy and Donny. Was Donny all right? The police would find that horrible man, and then she'd be okay. But she wasn't quite certain what condition he'd be in when they did.

She looked around herself, finding her shoes and socks and the valise. Picking them up, she began to head away from the water. She had to fight her way through a quarter acre of sea grass, the sharp leaves cutting at her hands. In a short time she reached a long stretch of road. She saw more houses on the other side, but no one seemed to be moving behind the large plate-glass windows. Lorraine was thankful for that. She didn't want anyone calling the police about a little girl wandering all by herself along a deserted beach road.

But then, maybe there were kind people in those houses who would help her. Maybe they'd be like Sandy and Donny, or like Bettina.

Unexpectedly, a clump of emotion so strong it was painful formed in Lorraine's stomach. She crouched onto the ground, holding herself, and burst into tears. For a long time she cried, thinking of Bettina. Was she still on that fire escape?

It's time to go now, Lorraine.

M-Marty? I was thinking about Bettina.

I know. She'll be found. But you must think of yourself. You're upset because you're alone and hungry. But you won't be alone for long. There is another who is searching for you. He is one of us. He'll help you.

Where is he?

He's coming. His name is Steven. He left a place last night, some eighty miles from here.

But where is here?

You are only a few miles from a place called Westbrook. Listen to me, Lorraine. I'm going to tell you where to go, and when you get there you are to wait until Steven comes. He is a boy with black skin, ten years old. He does not have powers as strong as ours, but when he is near, your minds will touch. Together you will complete the journey successfully.

Slowly Lorraine stood up. She now noticed that someone *was* watching her from a nearby beach house. She began to walk quickly, and then she began to run.

Where, Marty? Where am I going?

Start walking . . . away from the sun. The very first thing you're going to do is get yourself something to eat.

A few miles from the beach, Lorraine found a small cluster of stores. She entered a deli and bought an egg sandwich for breakfast, along with a container of milk. After she finished this, she located a telephone. Marty instructed her how to call a taxi, and in a little while one pulled up to the curb in front of the deli. Lorraine expected the driver to ask what she was doing all by herself, but he didn't. In fact, he had such a strange look in his eyes as he drove that she wondered if Marty had put some kind of spell on him.

I didn't, Marty answered. *He's just had one too many tokes this morning.*

Marty!

Don't worry. He's sober enough to drive. He'll get you to Westbrook in one piece, and he won't ask questions.

It all happened as Marty promised. Lorraine paid the man, then turned away from the cab to find herself facing a charming tree-lined street of exclusive boutiques. The shops were just beginning to open, and early-morning browsers walked along the sidewalks. Lorraine walked up to a window filled with animals, stuffed, wooden, glass, and more. She could almost imagine Sandy working in a place like this.

This is a pretty place, this town.

You won't be able to stay for very long. Steven is on his way. He'll be arriving at the nearest train station in a few minutes, and then it will be only a short time until he finds you. Listen, Lorraine. Do you hear him? He's very near.

Lorraine moved on to the next store, staring at a beautiful flowered sundress as she tried to hear another voice in her mind. At first it did not come. But then, oh so faintly, she heard him.

Steven? Is your name Steven?

Hello, Lorraine. Don't be afraid. I'm going to help you.

I'm waiting for you, Steven. I'm tired of being alone.

I'll be there soon.

His voice faded away, as if the effort of mind contact was too great for him. Marty had said they were not exactly alike. What had he meant? Why were her powers so much stronger than an older boy's?

What do I do now?

Just wait. There are windows to look at, and benches to sit on. You can find a place that sells frozen yogurt if you get hungry.

Okay. But people are looking at me in a funny way.

It was true. Heads were turning surreptitiously. Lorraine realized she must be a sight with her windblown hair and the wrinkled clothes she'd worn for nearly two days. She had to do something about that, to make herself less conspicuous.

Marty, there's a children's clothing store across the street. I'm going there.

Marty did not answer.

Steven?

Her mind was silent. She felt a cold chill, wondering what was happening to the boys, especially to Marty. But she knew she had something to do. She held her head up, ignored the whispers around her, and crossed the street. There was a beautiful white church on the corner, the perfect place to take out some of her money. It was peaceful and quiet inside, but Lorraine didn't give herself time to meditate. She took out two hundred dollars and relocked the valise. Then she left the church, crossed the street again, and found the shop.

Yesterday she wouldn't have expected the salesclerk to cater to her without question. But after what she'd done to the man at the motel, she believed she could do anything. She'd never had the chance to try mental suggestion on anyone, but that didn't mean she never did it in her life. Maybe, in the time she had forgotten about, before Bettina found her, she had used this power frequently.

She stopped at the entrance of the store. A woman turned to her from a display of baby dresses. She was dressed in a yellow jumpsuit, tiny moon globes dangling from her ears. The woman frowned, opening her mouth to speak. Quickly Lorraine tried out the powers Marty had insisted she possessed.

To her delight, and a little to her amazement, the woman's frown turned into a smile.

"Well, hello!" she greeted her. "What can I do for you today?"

"I need some new clothes," Lorraine said, unable to believe how easy it was to keep a lock on someone's mind. If only she'd known this a few days ago!

"Of course, darling," the woman said. "We have some wonderful things in your size right over here."

As she tried on clothes, she had a strong sensation that

others were thinking about her. She knew about Steven, but not about Julie. The other girl was just waking up at a hotel in northern New Jersey. Like Lorraine and Steven, Julie had lost contact with Marty for a long time. But that didn't matter for now, because Barbara Huston was taking care of her.

But Lorraine was not aware of this.

36

WHEN SAMANTHA ARRIVED at Wil's place, she hardly even noticed the mess in his front room. She did, however, register the fact that he'd never unpacked his suitcase. It seemed he had become so involved in her case that everything else was forgotten.

Wil was feeding a gecko when she entered his office. He smiled at her, but it was a sad, almost pitiful smile. Samantha felt her heart constrict. He had bad news for her, she just knew it. She sank wearily into a chair.

"There wasn't a thing in Barbara's car," she said. "Not even a gum wrapper. She was very thorough about clearing it out."

"I'm not surprised," Wil said. "I have a feeling she has some answers to questions that go way back for you. You said she was your best friend at med school, that you roomed together and shared some of the same classes. But there's something wrong here."

"What's that?" Samantha asked.

"I called the St. Francis," Wil said, "hoping to find some connection between what's happening now and the first years you knew Barbara Huston. I found her easily enough in the records. But I didn't find you. There has never been anyone named Samantha Winstead registered there."

"That's ridiculous," Samantha protested. "Of course I went to St. Francis. How could I be practicing in a hospital if I didn't? There must be some mistake."

Wil shook his head. "I'm sorry. I double- and triple-checked, and I even went back a full twenty years. You would have been only fifteen or so at the time, but I thought it was worth a check to see if you were 'lost' in the shuffle of computer work."

"But my professors," Samantha said. "Surely . . ."

"I spoke to several who had known Barbara," Wil said. "None of them had any recollection of you."

Samantha's face looked so stricken that Wil came and crouched down beside her seat.

"It's okay," he said. "Whatever's happened, I believe you're a victim. Maybe Barbara is too."

"But I went there!" Samantha said. "I remember it! It was this big brick building, across the street from a shopping mall. There was a highway in front of it, and a huge wildlife refuge in the back."

She closed her eyes, holding out a hand.

"I can remember feeding deer at the fence," she said. "They were that tame. And then one day . . . one day we found a dead one. And my friend said maybe we should dissect it. I was so angry at him . . ."

"What was his name?"

Samantha opened her eyes again.

"I don't remember."

"It wasn't that long ago, Samantha."

"Do you remember everyone you ever meet?" Samantha demanded.

Wil took her hand and squeezed it. "Samantha, this is some fabrication that has been planted in your mind. I don't know why, but Barbara, and Raoul Henley, and even Julie all have something to do with it."

He stood up and walked back to his desk, opening a drawer.

Samantha shook her head in dismay.

"I . . . I don't understand," she said. "Does this mean I've been practicing medicine without a license? That I'm not a real doctor? But how did I ever get hired by Sangre de Cristo?"

"Someone did a very thorough job of writing this script," Wil said.

"What are they planning next?" Samantha asked. "What are they going to do with Julie?"

"I'm still working on Barbara Huston," Wil said. "I should have my information in a few hours. In the meantime, I want you to go home. You said those pictures Julie's been drawing remind you of something. I want you to concentrate on them, and nothing else. If there's a clue in them, there isn't much more time to find it."

Samantha agreed. Wil walked her out to her truck.

Before she got in, she turned to him and said, "Julie loved me. We only knew each other for a few days, but it was as if we belonged together. Maybe there's a reason you thought she looked like me."

"Maybe," was all Wil said.

Silent, but shaking inside, Samantha climbed behind the wheel of the Bronco II. She drove home, through streets that were, somehow, newly unfamiliar to her. She'd been living here for nearly five years, and she was a respected member of the medical community. But she wasn't a doctor at all! It was all a scam, her degree a phony piece of paper.

"No!" she cried out loud. "I won't believe it! I *know* I'm a good doctor. I studied *somewhere*. And I'll find out the name of the school I went to when I find Barbara."

Samantha had no doubt in her mind she would find her "friend." It wasn't that she knew for certain, but that she was so fiercely determined that nothing would stop her until she and Julie were reunited.

When she arrived home, she pulled the truck into the garage and got out. As she opened the back door an odd feeling of *déjà vu* ran over her. She had felt something strange happen in the garage the night before all these events took place. When she'd come back with Julie, she hadn't experienced the eerie feelings. But now that she was alone, a chill was running up her spine.

She closed her eyes and stood in front of the closed door. She tried to bring back those last moments. A sense of fear filled her. The door. There had been something wrong with the door . . .

She felt her hands go up, and come smashing down. Samantha understood the gesture. She'd found the ax in front of the broken door. She'd been trapped in the garage, and had desperately hacked the wood to get out. But she'd never made it.

She wasn't alone. There was someone else there with her.

With a gasp, Samantha opened her eyes. Her heart was pounding. She was certain now that someone had been in the garage and that that person had done something to her to make her lose her memory. If only she could remember!

The dogs had been barking ever since the truck pulled

into the garage, but Samantha was only now aware of them. She left the garage and the vaguely threatening memories it conjured up, and went to let them back out of the kennel again. Sunday and Lady romped around her, wanting to play, but Samantha had to shoo them away.

She went into the house, straight up to Julie's bedroom. Julie's pictures were stacked in a very neat pile on her desk. Samantha took them to the bed and sat down. She began to look through them, scrutinizing each one very carefully. Julie had drawn some pictures of flowers, copying them from the book Samantha had given her. Samantha put these aside until she came to the beach pictures.

They were virtually all the same, with only a few minor changes in each. There was always a beach where a little yellow house with green shutters stood near a jetty. A child walked on the sand, her hair windblown to hide her face. Samantha studied every detail of the little girl, from her blue sandals to her yellow bathing suit. She carried an old pail and shovel. There was something very familiar about the little white crab painted on the red bucket . . .

"Oh, my God," she gasped. The memory of the bucket had come from nowhere, but it was as clear as if she'd held the thing yesterday. And now she understood.

"It's me," she said out loud. "The little girl on the beach is me!"

Somehow Julie had managed to draw a very detailed representation of a summer home Samantha had visited during her childhood. She'd had a pair of blue sandals just like the child in the picture, and the house had been yellow with green shutters. Overwhelmed, Samantha let the pictures fall to the floor and curled herself up on the bed. She buried her face in the crook of her elbow and cried her eyes out. How could Julie have known about that place? Samantha herself hadn't thought of it in . . . in . . . *years*.

It was some kind of clue, just like Wil suspected. Julie might even have drawn these pictures knowing she would one day have to leave Samantha. Maybe Julia was trying to tell her where she could be found! All Samantha had to do . . .

"I can't remember," Samantha said. Those words had become achingly familiar in the past few days. "I can't remember where we spent our summers!"

And then she realized her amnesia was even worse than she'd ever suspected: the more she thought of it, the more she was unable to conjure up a clear image of her family. She saw a mother figure, a woman with dark hair like her own, but with features so vague she could easily have been part of a dream. There was no picture of her father. Samantha's parents had died when she was a young child, but if she could remember the beach house, why couldn't she remember them too?

She started to sob again. And even though it was the middle of the day, she soon cried herself to sleep.

37

ALTHOUGH STEVEN GAZED intently out the window of
the train, he didn't really see the scenery that rushed by
him. He was tired of all this traveling, of airplanes and
buses and the like. He just wanted to settle down someplace and be finished with . . . with whatever Marty
wanted from him.

Well, at least he was on his way to a destination. It
was much better than sitting on a bench in an unfamiliar
place and trying hard not to start crying. When he'd arrived in Atlantic City, he'd been completely overwhelmed. Steven had never seen crowds like that, or at
least he was pretty certain he never had. Most people
ignored him, but a few glanced back over their shoulders
at him. He wasn't the only young boy there, and certainly
not the only black child. Why did he stand out? he
wondered.

Steven had been unaware that he kept a perpetual expression of worry, and people were just concerned about
him. But there was something about his overall manner
that kept them away, and no one ever did question what
he was doing there by himself.

He didn't know that Rachel and Eric were there too,
having breakfast in one of the hotels.

He'd been squirting mustard on a knish, a strange
breakfast, but all he could really afford, when Marty finally came back to him. It was so surprising that he almost dropped his lunch.

Don't do that! he cried. *Don't sneak in on me like that!*

Sorry, but I only have a few minutes.

What happened to you?

*I've been . . . they've been working with me. I'm sorry
I didn't get back to you sooner.*

Standing there on the boardwalk, knish in hand, Ste-

ven frowned. An old woman gave him a questioning
look, but he ignored her and walked down to the nearest
stairs. He sat on the bottom step and listened to Marty
while he ate.

You did pretty well on your own, Marty said.

*Yeah, well, thanks for leaving me at that airport. Lucky
there was a bus to pick up.*

*You'll have to move on now. You were supposed to
meet someone there in Atlantic City, but she's not there
now.*

Meet someone?

Steven was delighted at the prospect of having a part-
ner in this.

*Her name is Lorraine. She's a little girl, about five years
old.*

Five years old! What good is she going to do me?

*She has great powers. But a man was after her, and he
caught up to her. Fortunately, she used those powers to
get away from him, but now she needs to be with someone. She's in a town called Westbrook, a few hours from
here. You'll have to make your way to the nearest train
station, in Oakville. It will take you directly to Westbrook,
where Lorraine will be waiting.*

So now, after using up the last of his money to hail a
taxi into Oakville and then buy a ticket to Westbrook,
Steven was on his way to meet "one of the others." He
was glad that he'd bought a hot dog before leaving the
beach, because now his stomach was starting to protest
from hunger. A young boy doing all the traveling he'd
accomplished in two days needed more energy than one
small potato cake could provide. In a few minutes the
grumbling turned to pain, and Steven thought with much
chagrin that he was going to be sick.

Oh, please! Not here!

He doubled himself up and begged the pain to go
away, not wanting to draw attention to himself.

But someone *was* suddenly aware of him. Some distance to the north, walking along the boardwalk in Atlantic City, Rachel was struck once more by a feeling that
Steven was in need.

She grabbed Eric's arm.

"Eric!" she whispered, trying not to draw attention to
herself. "I feel him again."

Eric stopped.

"Steven?" he asked. After a night of thinking, he'd decided Rachel's sudden knack for telepathy was no stranger than anything else he'd seen in the past few days.

"He's on a train, I think," Rachel said. "Maybe a bus. Eric, let's find out where the nearest station is. Maybe they can tell us if a child bought a ticket, and where he went."

"Then let's go," Eric said. "There's a security guard over there, maybe he can help us."

He was glad to finally be able to do something concrete.

38

WHEN LORRAINE WALKED down the street now, no one even looked twice at her. She was nicely dressed in an orange-and-yellow-striped shorts set. Her dark hair was pulled into a high ponytail with a bright orange "scrunchee," and she was even wearing new sandals. The woman in the store had accepted her payment without question. But when the little girl left the store, the shop owner jolted slightly as if coming awake. She had the sense that something strange had just happened, but since she couldn't explain it, she simply went back to her work.

Lorraine tried calling Marty, but again he did not answer. She hoped he was all right. Then she called Steven. He didn't answer her with words, but she had a strong feeling he was very, very near. Perhaps he was in town right now, looking for her!

No sooner had she thought that than something made her look beyond the crowd of window-shoppers to the opposite corner. A dark-skinned young boy had just turned onto the block. At once Lorraine knew who he was. She had never felt such an attraction to another human being, at least not in her memory. She wanted to shout to him out loud, but didn't dare attract attention. Instead, she quickened her step.

Steven?

I'm here now, Lorraine. Don't be afraid.

And then they were face-to-face. Impulsively the little girl threw her arms around the older boy. They hugged; *that* drew some discreet stares!

"I'm so happy to see you," Lorraine said. "I'm so glad I'm not alone!"

"We've never really been alone," Steven said. "Marty has been with us."

Lorraine shook her head.

"Not always," she said worriedly. "Sometimes he goes away."

"I know," Steven said. "I wish I knew where he was at those times. Because when he's gone, I don't know what to do."

"I know what to do right now," Lorraine said. "I'm hungry. I hardly had any breakfast."

Steven smiled. "I didn't have any at all. Let's go to that little place over there and have some lunch."

The two started for a small restaurant across the street. But halfway across, Steven gasped, stopping short. Lorraine took hold of his arm.

"Did you feel something?" she asked in a small voice.

People crossing the street looked back over their shoulders in curiosity. Steven noticed the light had turned yellow, and quickly steered Lorraine to the sidewalk.

"I felt . . . like something was tugging at me," he said. He looked at Lorraine. "Someone else must be nearby."

"Marty said there were others like us," Lorraine said. "Other children."

Steven looked down at the sidewalk, thinking. Then he shrugged.

"I don't feel it now," he said. "Let's just get our lunch."

In the restaurant, the children ordered hamburgers and sodas. Over a shared plate of ketchup-soaked fries, Lorraine leaned forward and said:

"What did it feel like to you?"

"Like someone was pulling on me," Steven said. "All over my body."

Lorraine's round head bobbed up and down, her dark ponytail bouncing.

"Me too," she said. "But . . . but there was something else too. I felt kind of sad."

"So did I," Steven agreed. "Whoever it was we felt, that person is very sad."

Lorraine's eyes rounded. "Maybe it's Marty! Maybe they're hurting him!"

"I never felt that way with Marty," Steven said. "I either hear his voice or he isn't there at all. But . . ."

Without warning, a feeling of terrible despair came over the children. Lorraine cried out so loudly that the waitress hurried over. She saw that Steven had dropped the french fry he was holding onto his lap, ketchup leaving a red trail across his jeans.

"Oh, it's okay, honey," she said. "That ketchup will wash right out."

"Thanks," Steven choked, trying to smile even though he felt terrible inside. "I'm okay now."

The waitress gave him a questioning look, then walked away. Behind the counter, she commented to the short-order cook that those two children were plenty strange.

Lorraine bit her lip, tears welling in her eyes.

"What . . . who's doing this?" she asked in a soft voice.

Steven squeezed his eyes shut. His heart was pounding, and he thought if he didn't control himself he'd burst into tears. As hard as he could, he tried to send thought messages to the mysterious person. But he could see only a vast field of empty blue.

"I . . . I can't make contact," he said.

Steven beckoned Lorraine to lean closer.

"We have to work together," he said. "I'm not strong enough."

"Let's wait until we leave," Lorraine suggested. "Too many people are looking at us."

They paid for lunch and walked out of the restaurant. The odd devastating feeling kept coming back, but they were getting better at fighting it. They found a deserted alleyway. Sinking to the ground with their backs against a brick wall, they held hands and closed their eyes.

"Concentrate," Steven said. "Think hard."

Lorraine did as she was told.

. . . taken away. My child . . . I want him back!

Lorraine yelped, but Steven squeezed her hand.

I don't want to be part of this!

Who are you? The question was asked by the children in unison.

But there was no answer. Steven held Lorraine's hand as tightly as he could; she was too entranced to notice the pain in her fingers.

Please, please, tell us who you are!

There was a scream in Steven's mind, and suddenly a picture so clear it might have been projected on the wall opposite them. His eyes flew open.

"I saw," Lorraine said. "It was a lady with dark skin like yours!"

"Rachel," Steven said, bewildered. "Rachel is calling me. But, how . . . ?"

"Who's Rachel?" Lorraine asked.

"When I was lost," Steven said, "a family in Columbus took me in. Rachel was the mother. She was very kind to me, more than anyone else in the family. I felt as if . . . as if I knew her somehow."

His eyes rounded.

"Lorraine," he said, "Rachel must be one of us!"

"But Marty didn't say there were any grown-ups," Lorraine protested. "And if she is one of us, why did Marty make you leave her? It's gotta be a mistake, Steven."

"No!" Steven insisted. "Marty didn't tell us everything. Lorraine, what if Marty is the bad one? What if he's pulling us into a trap, away from those we love?"

"Marty helped me—"

"Do you know what he did?" Steven interrupted. "He almost killed a boy. The kid just started screaming like crazy at nothing, and then there was a big windstorm . . ."

Lorraine's mouth dropped open.

"I saw people who were very afraid too," she said. "But Marty said I made them afraid. But I don't think it's a bad thing, Steven. It's just to scare people who try to hurt us. Like the horrible man who kidnapped me and tied me up."

Steven frowned.

"You made them afraid?" he asked. "I can't do that."

"Marty says some of us have stronger powers," Lorraine said. "That's why we have to get together, away from the adults. So we can use those powers."

"No," Steven said, standing up. "I'm not listening to Marty. Rachel wants me back. She wants me so much it hurts *me* to feel it. And it hurts you too, Lorraine. So I can't be wrong! If she's sending messages like that, she has to be one of us."

Lorraine stood up too. She brushed pebbles from the back of her shorts.

"Except, you know what?" Steven went on. "I don't think she knows it. If she did, she would have told me."

He took Lorraine by the arm.

"I'm tired of running away," he said. "I'm tired of listening to Marty and being lost when he . . . 'disappears.' "

He waved a hand to emphasize the word.

"We need help, Lorraine," he said. "I'm going to call Rachel. I'm going to make her come to us. You have to help me, okay?"

Lorraine sighed. She, too, was tired of running. And just because she had dealt with one bad person didn't mean there weren't others waiting.

"Okay," she said. "Maybe we'll go farther with a grown-up, anyway. It's getting to be a pain the way people stare at me."

Steven took her hand. They sat down again and closed their eyes. The sound around them, traffic, birds, people, faded away until they could hear only their own voices in each other's minds. With all their mental strength, they began to call to Rachel.

In a motel room roughly forty miles away, Julie dropped the pencil she was using to draw with and swung around. Tears were dripping from her eyes.

"Barbara, I feel something," she said. "I feel like somebody nearby is in pain."

Barbara stared at her but didn't say a word. Julie turned away, hugging herself. Why did she think Barbara would offer consolation? The woman hadn't said a word since they left Colorado. She'd acted like an automaton, buying airline tickets, hailing taxis, checking into this motel as if someone else was controlling her. Julie knew that someone else *was:* Marty. He was calling her to him, and using Barbara made it easier.

Marty? Marty, is that you?

Marty did not answer. Julie closed her eyes, but saw nothing. She could hear only sobbing, as if from far away. And then, abruptly, she heard two small voices:

Please, please, tell us who you are.

Marty had said there were others like her. Now they were so close by that she could sense their presence. She had to find out who they were, and where they were! They had done nothing since arriving in New Jersey but sit in this motel room. Julie knew that Marty would contact her, but she could no longer wait for him. She would follow the voices. When they got stronger, she'd know they were nearby.

"Barbara, I have to go now," she said.

Barbara simply nodded. Julie felt a moment of regret, wondering how much control Marty had over the woman. After all, she was a nice person, and she was Samantha's friend.

Julie had never wanted anyone more than she wanted Samantha just then. But the need to find the other voices in her mind was greater.

She turned to the desk and pulled out a piece of paper. Then she began to write a note to Barbara, explaining what she was doing.

39

An alarm ringing jolted Samantha out of a deep sleep. Momentarily disoriented, she didn't realize it wasn't the alarm at all, but the telephone. She took a deep breath to steady herself, said a quick prayer that it might be Julie, and went to answer it.

"It's Wil," the detective told her. "Come over to my place. There's someone here I want you to speak with."

Without another word, he hung up the phone. Samantha knew it had to be important, and wondered who Wil could be talking about. She went into the bathroom to freshen up, put on her shoes, and left the house. The dogs barked at her, but she barely heard them.

When she arrived at Wil's house, the inside door was open. Through the screen door she could hear him talking with someone. It sounded like a man, the voice just barely familiar.

"Come on back, Samantha!" Wil called.

She followed his voice into his office. There was someone sitting in one of his chairs. When he turned around, Samantha gasped.

"Fred Matlin!" she cried. "What . . . what are you doing here?"

Fred made a self-conscious face and ran his hand through his auburn hair. Behind his red-rimmed glasses, his eyes looked full of worry.

"Trying to answer some questions, I guess," he replied.

Samantha looked at Wil, her expression demanding an explanation.

"I asked some questions," Wil said, "and found out Mr. Matlin was one of the last people to see Barbara."

"Call me Fred, okay?"

Wil swung a chair around and indicated it was for Sa-

226

mantha. Slowly she sat down, not taking her eyes off Fred. He turned and pretended to be watching a hamster racing in a wheel, purposely avoiding Samantha's gaze.

"Do you know where Barbara is now?" Samantha asked.

"That was my first question," Wil said.

"I don't know," Fred replied. "I'm sorry. She didn't say anything at all about going away when we were together the other night. I'm just as surprised as you."

Samantha's eyes thinned.

"When you were at Barbara's, you said you went to St. Francis with us," she said. "But Wil tells me there's no record of my attendance. How can you remember me?"

Fred turned his hands palms-up.

"I only said I thought I remembered you," he reminded her. "I could have been mistaken."

Wil held up a hand.

"You know," he said, "it's possible you two did hang around there but never actually registered for classes. That would explain some of your memories."

"It doesn't explain how I've been able to practice medicine all these years," Samantha grumbled. "Fred, do you remember ever actually *speaking* with either one of us?"

"I met Barbara at a few parties," Fred said, looking out the window as if the scene was being played in the yard. "We were introduced, but we didn't talk. And you? I'm sorry, I just can't remember. I'm sure I saw you, but I don't think we ever actually spoke."

He leaned back a little, turning to look at Samantha.

"Although I'm not surprised," he said. "Med students have such crazy, busy schedules."

"Fred," Wil said, "we must find Barbara if we're to get to Julie. I don't know what's going on here, but I don't think you're really involved."

Fred seemed to breathe a sigh of relief.

"I think," Wil said, "that when plans were made for Samantha, you and Barbara, and maybe a few others, were worked into the deal. Listen to what you've said. You remember Samantha, but only vaguely. Her own memories are indistinct, as Barbara's probably are. But there is something you can do to help. Has Barbara ever mentioned knowing anyone out east?"

Fred shook his head. "Not at all. She has a sister in Texas and two brothers in California. Her parents are dead."

"There aren't any more answers here," Samantha said. "Only more questions."

"I'm sorry I can't be of more help," Fred said, "but is there any reason for me to stay?"

"No," Wil said, moving away from Samantha. "But thank you for coming down so quickly."

Fred stood up. Wil held out his arm and the two men shook hands.

"Maybe you couldn't tell us where Barbara went," Wil said, "but you've added a few pieces to a very big puzzle."

"Sure," Fred said.

He turned to leave, his thoughts full of his days back in med school. There was no question in his mind that he had met Barbara. He left Detective Sherer's house wondering what this was all about.

In the office, Samantha had gotten up to go look out the window. Now that Fred was gone, she felt she could speak freely.

"I went over Julie's pictures," she said. "I realized something for the first time. The child she's been drawing in these pictures—it's me. I remember the red pail with the crab on it. And there's a concession stand with dolphins painted on the awning. The one with the name Haybrook's. I'm *sure* I've seen it before. Wil, how could Julie know what I looked like as a child? I never showed her any pictures."

"It may only be coincidence," Wil said, although he didn't sound convinced.

"It's strange how I remembered that time at the beach," Samantha said. "I don't have very many memories of my childhood. My parents died when I was very young, and I don't remember any relatives. I must have lived in some kind of foster home or in an orphanage, but I just don't remember it. Could something bad have happened to me, something so terrible it put holes in my memory? I'm not sure I want those holes filled in, but if Julie is part of them, then I know I want her back again!

She's a link to my past, Wil. Answers to my questions. I can't . . . stand . . ."

She started crying again. Wil hurried across the room and took her into his strong arms. He held her tightly until she calmed down again. He was about to say something when the phone rang.

"I have to get that," Wil said, pulling himself gently away. He picked up the phone. A surprised look came over his face and he handed the receiver to Samantha. "It's Barbara Huston!"

Samantha's eyebrows went up. She took the phone.

"Barbara, where are you?" she demanded.

"I seem to be in a motel in New Jersey," Barbara said. "Do you remember how you felt when you woke up in that motel in Durango? The same thing has happened to me! I don't remember coming here! And I think I've done something terrible. I think I kidnapped Julie!"

Wil had switched the phone to a speaker. He looked up at Samantha and mouthed the words "she thinks?"

"What do you mean?" Samantha asked. "Is she there, or isn't she?"

"She . . . she was here," Barbara said. "She left a note."

"Read it to us," Wil said.

"Oh . . . uh . . ." Barbara's tone indicated she hadn't realized Wil was listening. "Sure. She says: 'Dear Barbara: I am sorry Marty made you bring me here, but it was the only way. Now I must go to find the others like myself. Go home and tell Samantha that I love her and I hope I can see her again. I will be okay. Love, Julie.'

"That's all she writes," Barbara said.

"Marty?" Samantha said. "Who's Marty?"

"Julie never mentioned the name?"

Samantha shook her head. "Never. Barbara, do you know who she's talking about? She said Marty made you bring her there."

"I never met anyone named Marty," Barbara said. "The last thing I remember is being in my apartment. I'm sure the doorbell rang. After that, it's a blank."

Like the night in my garage, Samantha thought.

"Samantha, what have I done?" Barbara asked worriedly.

"I wish you could tell me," Samantha said. "I have a thousand questions for you."

Wil held out a hand.

"But right now we have to find Julie," he said. "Barbara, it will be hours before we can get to New Jersey. Can you stay there in case Julie tries to call you?"

"I . . . I suppose I could," Barbara said uncertainly. "But I have no idea where she's gone."

"Is there anything else in the room besides the letter?" Wil asked. "Anything she left behind?"

"Well," Barbara said, "nothing but some drawings she made. That kid sure likes to draw, Samantha. Especially beaches."

Samantha stood up abruptly.

"Look at the pictures, Barbara," she said. "What exactly is in them?"

There was a pause; then Barbara answered.

"A house with shutters. A girl with a dog. And a jetty. Oh, wait, this looks familiar. Yes, yes, I've seen this place. Where? It's a concession stand with dolphins painted along its awning."

"Haybrook's," Samantha said.

"How did you know?" Barbara said. "Never mind. You must have heard about it sometime. It's pretty famous on either coast. Like Nathan's or Red Lobster. There's one in California, where my brother lives. They sell fried clams and shrimp and stuff like that. But it has a bigger name than just 'Haybrook's.' "

There was another delay as Barbara racked her brain.

"I know," she said. "It's called Haybrook's Seaside Clam Bar. It's a very old business that was established at the turn of the century."

"Can you find out if there's such a place in New Jersey?" Wil asked.

"Sure," Barbara said, confidence suddenly filling her voice. She was happy to be doing something constructive.

"Give us your number," Wil said. "We'll call you back in a little while."

Barbara did so; then Wil hung up. Samantha was staring at the calendar on his bulletin board, lost in thought.

"What's wrong?" he asked gently.

"The concession stand," Samantha said. "When Julie drew the pictures at my house, she drew the snack bar as it might have looked when I was a child. It was in nearly every picture, along with the yellow house. Why would she be so consistent?"

"Because she's giving you a clue to where she is," Wil said. "She may not even be aware of it, but that little girl wants us to find her as much as we do."

Samantha looked up at him with hope in her expression.

"And we will find her," she said. "Won't we?"

Wil smiled, his teeth stark white in a tanned face. "You bet we will."

40

IT WAS NEARLY an hour before Rachel and Eric arrived
at the Oakville train station. The ticket house was a
chunky little brick building with a gray roof, its windows
hidden behind locked blue shutters. Eric tried the door
and found it closed.

"This early?" he asked.

"The sign says the office closes at one P.M. today,"
Rachel pointed out. She was despondent. "Eric, we've
lost him again."

Eric looked around at the parking lot, where a hundred cars waited for their commuters. Several pieces of
newspaper blew across the blacktop, skittling along like
birds that had been shot.

"Maybe not," Eric said. "Come on."

He thought the newspapers might have been bought
right there at the station, and when they rounded the
corner of the building he found his guess to be correct.
There was a newsstand set up on the opposite side from
the ticket window, rows of magazines, papers rimming
racks of candy and cigarettes. A elderly man dressed in
paint-spattered khaki trousers and a plaid flannel shirt
stood trying to latch a wooden board on a hook over his
head.

"Closing up?" Eric asked.

"No use staying open," the man replied.

"Can I help you with that?"

The man glanced quickly at them, then shook his head.

"Been doing it for years," he said, and he managed to
lock the board to its hook. He pushed it into place, then
locked his wares behind the board with padlocks placed
at each corner.

"We just missed the ticket office being open," Rachel
said.

The man turned to her. There was a half-day's growth of white razor stubble on his chin, and he rubbed at it.

"You don't have to pay a penalty on the train," he said, "if the ticket office's closed."

Eric put an arm around Rachel's shoulder.

"We weren't looking to buy tickets," he said. "We're trying to find someone. Our . . . our son."

Rachel did a double-take that Eric pretended not to notice. Then she picked up on his story.

"He's run away from home," she said. "We're so worried about him. We were wondering if you might have seen him."

The man nodded. "Yup, I saw him. Hard to miss a child of color when everyone else on the platform is as white as me."

Rachel reached toward him to grab his arm, but Eric gently pulled her back.

"Do you know where he went?"

"Can't say exactly," the man said. "But he did get on a train to Pearmont. Stops at Verkill, Copiague, Rockling, Westbrook, and Pearmont."

He rattled them off as if he were a conductor himself.

"How do we get to Pearmont?" Eric asked.

"There's a schedule posted—"

"We mean by car," Rachel said.

The man turned and pointed toward the highway.

"Follow it along," he said. "You'll see signs. It'll take you a while, though."

"Let's go, Eric," Rachel said, not wanting to waste time.

Eric thanked the man, and they returned to the car. As he turned on the engine, Rachel rested her head back and closed her eyes. She began to think of Steven.

Lorraine picked up a rock and threw it at the brick wall.

"I'm tired," she said. "I can't do this anymore. Nobody's answering us."

Steven stood up. "We aren't strong enough. Not without Marty, anyway. Come on, let's go for a walk. There isn't anything else to do until he calls us again."

"I hate it when he disappears," Lorraine said.

I'm back again.

Lorraine and Steven looked at each other. Steven answered.

Why did you go away again? Are they hurting you?

Sometimes it hurts. Not always. I think they're curious about me. They do so many strange things to me. Steven, Lorraine, who were you calling?

This time when the children exchanged glances, there was guilt on their faces. How much had Marty heard?

What . . . what do you mean? Lorraine asked.

I could sense that you were trying to contact someone.

We felt someone nearby. Someone so sad that we felt sad too. Steven says it's Rachel, the lady who took care of him.

That's impossible! She can't call to you! She isn't like us!

How do you know? Steven demanded in his thoughts. People passing by barely noticed the look of annoyance on the young boy's face. *I saw her in my mind. She's thinking about me, Marty. We tried to contact her because we're tired of being alone. We need a grown-up to help us!*

You don't need anyone but me!

They'd never heard Marty so defiant. Lorraine felt afraid, and said so.

But I get so scared when you disappear. That man at the motel could have hurt me!

You are strong, Lorraine. Stronger than you know. And with Steven, you're even stronger. When the third child of this area comes to join you, you'll be invincible.

Where is she? Steven asked. *Why haven't we heard from her?*

She is not as strong as either of you. But she heard your calls to . . . to this Rachel. She is on her way. Her name is Julie.

What do we do while we wait? Lorraine asked.

There isn't time to talk, Lorraine. They're coming again. They have strange machines that seem to know when my brain is more active than usual. I don't want them to know about you. I have to go now.

"Marty?"

Lorraine realized she had spoken the name out loud. Steven shook his head.

"He's gone again."

"What did he mean when he said there isn't much more time?" Lorraine asked. "What's going to happen?"

"I don't know," Steven said. "But I think that girl named Julie will probably come here on the train. It's three miles to the station. Let's walk there and wait for her."

The children headed out of downtown Westbrook. A block behind them, a car cruised the streets, the driver searching for a little dark-haired girl. Joe Trefill held the steering wheel so tightly his knuckles were white. Madness had etched red lines in the whites of his eyes, eyes that darted furiously left and right in search of his quarry.

41

AT DENVER AIRPORT Samantha walked away from the ticket counter triumphantly waving two red-and-white envelopes. Wil acknowledged her with a thumbs-up sign, then continued to talk into the public telephone he was using to contact Barbara Huston. He hung up just as Samantha reached him.

"I can't believe how lucky we are," Samantha said. "There are very few seats left on the next flight out. We board in half an hour."

"I told Barbara you got the tickets," Wil answered. "She's going to meet us at Newark airport."

"Did she have any luck finding that concession stand?"

Wil shook his head. "No. But she's still trying. She asked a few people, but my guess is that she's too far away from it for anyone to really know what she's talking about. I suggested heading for the library, or maybe even a local travel agent. They book weekends at motels, you know."

"Well, I hope she finds an answer by the time we arrive," Samantha said. "I think this going to be the longest six hours of my life."

"You'll be amazed how quickly it passes," Wil said. "We'll use the time to plan our strategy once we arrive in New Jersey. And it wouldn't hurt you to rest. You look exhausted."

Samantha looked down at the floor, thinking how she'd somehow fallen asleep earlier that day. What would Wil think if he knew?

"I . . . I'm okay," she insisted. "Come on, let's see where our gate is. This overnight bag is getting heavy, and I'd like to sit down."

"Let me carry it for you," Wil offered.

Samantha smiled at him. "You do enough for me already. I'm upset, and frustrated, and yes, I'm tired. But I'm not weak. I'll carry it myself."

"All right, then," Wil said.

He hooked his arm through hers and they went off to find their plane.

Barbara thought it was no wonder the people around here didn't know about the concession stand. She'd never seen such congestion; so many buildings, cars, and people! They probably saw a beach about three times a year, if they were lucky. But Wil had suggested either the library or a travel agency. She opted for the latter, simply because there was a travel agent within the hotel itself.

The woman gave her a friendly smile and offered her a seat.

"What can I do for you?"

"Well, it's kind of tricky," Barbara said. She had planned this speech already. "You see, I want to surprise my husband by taking him to a place he visited many years ago. I know it's on a beach, but there's only one thing I know specifically about it. There's a snack bar there, named Haybrook's Seaside Clam Bar. It's somewhere on the Jersey shore."

The woman grinned. "How romantic! I'm afraid I don't know where Haybrook's is located, but I've heard of it. I could make some phone calls."

"Oh, I'd really appreciate that," Barbara said.

"Why don't you come back in an hour or so?" the woman suggested. "I should have some information by then."

"I'll do that," Barbara said.

She left the travel agency, then walked out of the hotel. Glancing at her watch, she estimated she had more than five hours before Samantha arrived. She hoped she would have some information to give her friend regarding Julie's whereabouts.

And at the same time, she hoped the clue would lead her to some answers of her own.

Julie had begun her journey in a southerly direction, based on the sensations she was picking up. Sometimes they weakened, but when they grew strong again she would change course accordingly. She wished she could take a train or a bus, but moving on foot was the only way she could keep track of any changes in feeling.

She moved along the Parkway, keeping well hidden in the trees that grew alongside the road. Whenever she'd come to an exit or entrance ramp, she'd hide until she was certain she could make it across without being seen. It slowed her down, but she couldn't afford to arouse the curiosity of passing motorists.

Julie wondered who was sending out the emotions she was reading in her mind. Was it the other children, waiting for her? She wondered if they were in Atlantic City, as Marty had planned originally. Or had they moved on? How long would it take her to find them?

She was hiding in the bushes near an exit ramp when Marty spoke in her mind. His voice was so clear that she gasped, thinking someone had caught her.

It's all right, Julie. The others are waiting for you, but you'll never get there if you walk.

How do you expect me to find them? Julie's tone reflected her annoyance. She was exhausted, her feet burning inside her sneakers. *I can only follow what I sense.*

You can listen to me. I'll tell you where they are.

Why didn't you tell me before I walked a zillion miles? Where've you been, anyway?

Marty did not answer her question.

Julie, two more of us are waiting in a town called Westbrook. If you move on to the exit, you can walk up it into a little town called Rockling. You can take a train there to Westbrook, and you'll arrive in just over an hour's time.

Why not Atlantic City? What happened there?

There were . . . problems. But Lorraine and I fixed them.

Lorraine?

One of us. The youngest of our group, but with strong powers.

Julie saw a chance to get across the exit. She ran as fast as she could, half-expecting to hear the sirens of a state trooper's car. She made it to the other side and began to move along behind the trees.

Marty, when am I going to learn who I really am?

But once again Marty was silent.

42

RACHEL AND ERIC had marked off two towns on their list; they had been told that no little boy had gotten off at those stations. Now Eric drove along the Garden State Parkway in silence, knowing that Rachel would speak when she was ready. It seemed she was asleep, with her head pressed back against the cushion behind it. But the tension in her features told him she was still trying to contact Steven. He still wasn't quite sure about all this supernatural business, but she hadn't been wrong yet.

When she spoke, her voice seemed unusually loud over the quiet hum of the motor. She didn't open her eyes.

"What are we going to do when we find Steven?"

"Take him home, of course," Eric said. "And when we get back, I'm going to raise hell with Children's Services. I don't think they're making enough effort in finding that child's parents."

Rachel sat up now and started to play with her hands, long café-au-lait fingers tipped with pink-polished nails.

"Eric," she said.

"What is it?"

"Eric, I don't think Steven has a family," Rachel said. "I don't think he has anyone but us."

Eric sighed. He checked his mirrors and changed lanes.

"Rachel, I know how much you want to believe that," he said, "but sooner or later you're going to have to face reality. Steven's memory will come back to him, and he'll know who his family is. Whoever they are, they haven't tried very hard to find him. And I condemn them for that. Maybe they aren't fit parents. Maybe they don't want him, but—"

"I want him!" Rachel cried.

"I know that," Eric said gently. "But maybe you can't have him."

Rachel turned to stare out the window at the passing scenery. Tears began to well in her eyes, but she brushed them away. She tried to concentrate on the trees, to push away painful emotions. Anyone else riding along the highway would not have noticed the fine details surrounding her. But Rachel was focused, and she could name almost every tree. The highway was a vast stretch of green.

She noticed a spot of red. It moved quickly through the foliage, nearly hidden by it.

"That's strange," she said. "Someone's running through those woods."

"Probably a hiker," Eric said.

"It looked like a child," Rachel said.

She looked back over her shoulder, but they had long since passed the point of seeing anyone. Rachel settled into her seat. She wondered if Steven had traveled that way, hiding in the trees. Was he alone now? Was he afraid? Oh, she knew the answer to that. She knew that he was very, very afraid.

Rachel closed her eyes. The strange feelings she'd had had come back a few times. Eric didn't believe in telepathy, but she did. She was certain Steven was calling for help. She tried hard to concentrate, tried to send him her own message, her promise that she was on her way to rescue him.

Julie stumbled over a fallen branch, suddenly overcome by a feeling that she was being watched. No, it was more like a tugging at her mind, even stronger than the feeling she had every time Marty contacted her. She got onto her knees and kept hidden behind the trees, one hand gripping the branch that had tripped her. Someone out there was searching, desperate to find . . . what?

She knew that no one here could be looking for her. The people who cared about her were far away, with no idea where she was.

But she couldn't stay hidden like this forever. She had to get up and move on. She started hurrying through the trees again, listening to the sound of passing cars and unaware one of them was headed in the very same direction as she.

Eric drove on, staying in the faster left lane until he saw signs for Copiague. He put on his signal and began to move to the right.

Rachel reached across the seat and clamped a hand around his upper arm.

"No, don't get off here," she said.

"Why?" Eric asked. "There's the first exit for Copiague."

"Steven isn't here," Rachel said matter-of-factly.

"How do you know?" Eric inquired. "We haven't even asked at the train station."

"He didn't get off here," Rachel insisted. Eric took a quick glance at her, then turned his eyes back on the road. She could tell he thought she was a little crazy. "Eric, please, if you love and trust me, don't get off at this exit. We're wasting our time here. I know it seems ridiculous, but it's more than just a feeling I have. Somehow, I know he isn't here."

"All right," Eric said, turning off his signal just as the exit came up. "Then where do we go?"

Rachel stared at the road ahead.

"I don't know," she said. "Just keep driving. I don't think he's very much farther away."

She didn't tell Eric she had a feeling they were heading toward grave danger.

43

THE WESTBROOK TRAIN station stood at the very end of the town's main road, a small brick building situated behind a slightly elevated platform. Steven and Lorraine found a seat on a painted green bench.

"I think Rachel's getting closer," Steven said. "The feeling is stronger."

"Yes," Lorraine agreed, "but it isn't as sad as it was. It's . . . it's sort of cross, I guess."

Steven shook his head. "No, not cross. She isn't angry. She's . . . she's determined. I don't think she'll stop until she finds me."

Lorraine gazed at him with big gray-green eyes.

"I just thought of something," she said. "If you want Rachel, why don't you call home?"

Steven held up two fingers, bending each down as he counted.

"First," he said, "I know she's no longer home. And second, I have to be certain she really is one of us. I want her to be, but if she isn't, she might be dangerous."

Lorraine pouted. "I sure wish I knew what 'one of us' means. Marty says that all the time. I don't think I'm so very different."

"But we can talk with our minds," Steven pointed out. "And you can make people very afraid—of nothing they can see. Are you good at math?"

"Oh, very good," Lorraine said.

That made her think of the time she'd counted the money in the suitcase, and how impressed Bettina had been. And *that* made her wonder if the poor old woman was still sitting on a fire escape in Manhattan. Maybe the crows and rats had found her and were . . .

She gasped.

"What's the matter?"

"I . . . I was just thinking of a friend," Lorraine said, pushing the hideous image from her mind before it could form. "Someone who was very kind to me."

Steven nodded. "Rachel was kind to me too. I guess Eric wasn't so bad either. They had two kids named Tatiana and Olivia. Tatiana didn't like me at all, I'm sure."

"It must have been nice, though, to be with other children."

"I guess it was. I wasn't there very long, though."

At that moment they heard three blasts of a train's whistle. Steven and Lorraine stood up, looking down the track as the big green diesel rumbled into the station. Lorraine squeezed Steven's hand as a strong sensation washed through her.

"Oh, do you feel it?" she asked. "The one named Julie is here!"

Steven nodded. "I know she is. Where do you suppose she'll get out?"

Almost as if they'd predicted it, they found themselves standing at the very door where Julie walked onto the platform. For a moment the three just stood staring. Not a word was spoken until the train rattled away.

Steven and Lorraine took in Julie's pretty face, green eyes, and rippling brown hair. In turn, Julie took in Steven's dark skin, thin frame, and neatly trimmed hair. A smile broke out on Lorraine's round face, her almond eyes sparkling. She pushed away a lock of black hair that had blown across her forehead and said: "You're Julie."

Julie nodded. "And you're Lorraine."

Marty had said she was young, but Julie hadn't expected her to be nearly a baby. How much strength could such a little child offer them?

"I'm Steven," the boy announced, afraid Julie had forgotten him for the moment.

"Marty told me," Julie said with a nod. "I felt you calling to someone, and I knew I had to find you. But what do we do now?"

"Same thing we always do," Lorraine said with a pout. "Wait until Marty shows up."

They walked down the stairs from the platform. Steven led the way to the street.

"I have an idea," he said. "Remember that ice-cream parlor we saw in town, Lorraine? Let's go get a treat."

"That sounds great," Julie said. "I never did eat lunch today."

Together the children walked along the tree-lined street to downtown Westbrook. They were halfway there when Lorraine suddenly let out a cry of dismay. With a jerk, she pulled Steven and Julie behind a big tree.

"What's the matter?" Julie asked.

"It's him!" Lorraine gasped. "The man who took me!"

Steven looked surprised. "But I thought you got rid of him!"

"Who?" Julie said uncertainly.

"I thought I did!" Lorraine said. "He must be stronger than I thought. We can't let him see me here! What will we do? What're we gonna do?"

"Wait," Steven said.

The car cruised by very, very slowly. It was obvious the man was searching for Lorraine.

"How did he find out I was here?" Lorraine wondered.

"Who knows?" Steven said. "But we can't stay. We have to get out of here without Marty's help. Look, he's turned the corner. He must be heading into town."

"We can't go that way, then," Julie said.

"What about the train station?" Lorraine suggested.

Steven shook his head.

"There isn't another train for forty minutes," he said, "and there's no place there we can hide. We just have to go on foot, keeping our eyes open. I'm sorry, Julie. I know you're hungry, but we don't have time to stop."

"I got this far okay," Julie pointed out.

Lorraine finally felt it was safe enough to move away from the tree. She looked all around.

"Which way now?"

"I wish we had a map," Steven said.

"Well, we can't go that way," Julie said. "Not if that man is there. And besides, that's the way down to the water. I know the train tracks run north and south, so that way"—she pointed—"has to be north. I say we cross the tracks and move westward."

Steven looked up at the sky.

"Yes, that is west," he said. "Look where the sun is."

"Come on, then," Lorraine urged. "Let's go."

The three children began to run, bounding across the tracks and onto a street surrounded by trees. It was a street devoid of houses or other signs of humanity, one that seemed to be in the middle of nowhere.

Nowhere, at that moment, seemed to be exactly where they were going.

44

BARBARA WAS WAITING when Samantha and Wil walked off the plane.

"This has been a hell of an adventure," she said. "But at least I have an answer to one of your questions."

"Did you find the concession stand?" Samantha asked.

Barbara nodded. "There are thirty of them in New Jersey, but all I had to do was narrow it down to ones that existed when we were kids. That would be in the early sixties. Once I did that, I only had five to work with. Then I just worked with the ones that were on beaches. That leaves two. Despite its name, Haybrook's Seaside Clam Bar isn't always 'seaside.' "

"So which of the two do we go to?" Samantha asked.

"Well, Julie kept drawing jetties," Barbara said. "So I made two phone calls and asked the obvious question. Only one clam bar, dated over thirty years old, situated near a jetty, was left."

Wil laughed. "You'd make a great detective, Barbara."

"I doubt it," Barbara said without humor, "since it was so easy for someone to screw up my brain."

They exited the airport and went to the car Barbara had rented.

"Is this the car you had when you arrived here with Julie?" Samantha asked.

"I suppose so," Barbara said. "I had a key that identified it, or I wouldn't have been able to find it. It's fortunate the hotel had valet parking."

They got into the car, and Barbara started on her way.

"Then you don't remember renting it?" Wil asked from the back seat.

"I don't remember anything at all," Barbara said. "I only remember being home last night. I think the doorbell rang, but beyond that it's a blank. Like I said, Samantha, now I know how frightened you must have been that night in your garage."

"I still don't know who attacked me," Samantha admitted. "I thought it was that Mr. Henley."

Barbara drove for a few minutes before venturing a question.

"Did you ever consider that it might have been Julie herself?"

"Oh! How did Julie drive a Bronco II all the way to Durango?"

"How did she get clear across the country to New Jersey?" Barbara asked.

Wil leaned forward.

"It's a good point Barbara's making," he said. "I don't think Raoul Henley was the mastermind behind all this. Not the way we found him."

"How did you find him?" Barbara asked solemnly.

"Dead," was Wil's simple reply. "But I also don't believe Julie had anything at all to do with that. I do think there might be a third party involved. And not necessarily an individual."

Samantha breathed in deeply.

"Sometimes I wonder if we're ever going to get any answers," she said.

"Well, I have one answer for you," Barbara said. "The name of the town where Haybrook's is located. It's called Shoaling. Does that ring a bell, Samantha?"

Samantha repeated the name several times, then shook her head.

"It doesn't sound familiar at all," she said.

"Shoaling," Wil said. "Strange name for a town."

"It's a kind of wave," Samantha said. "How far away is it?"

Barbara grimaced, an expression she could see in the rearview mirror.

"That's the bad news," Barbara said. "Even if we speed, and I don't dare, Shoaling is a good five hours away."

"Five hours!" Samantha cried out.

"Sorry," Barbara said.

Wil sat back again. First, six hours by plane, then five hours by car; not to mention all the time it took them to trace Julie's original destination. That gave Julie, or her abductors (and he believed they existed), a big head start.

"Don't be sorry," he said. "Just get us to Shoaling. There's nothing else to be done right now."

"Nothing else to do but pray," Barbara mumbled.

45

JOE TREFILL GLANCED in his rearview mirror just as the three children were crossing the railroad tracks. Swearing loudly, he swung the car around, the screech of the tires made louder by the relative peacefulness of the neighborhood.

"I'll get you now, you little freak," he growled, his voice deep and hoarse. He could see her up ahead, his vision blurred by the onset of madness. *"I'll get you now!"*

She was with two other kids. Little bitch was pretty good at making friends, wasn't she? Like a friggin' puppy, Trefill thought.

He was so determined to catch up to her that he didn't pay attention to the clang of the railroad crossing signals. He bumped onto the tracks just as they were coming down, bringing a series of three warning blasts from the *Coastal Express*. Trefil shot across the tracks, picking up speed as he neared the children. He'd run down the other two. He'd get rid of them so Lorraine had nobody to help her . . .

Up ahead, one of the children turned around. A black kid. What was she doing with a black kid?

He had no chance to find out. The children broke into a run, disappearing into the woods that lined the street. And suddenly, as if it had dropped from the sky, there was a police car in front of him. Red lights flashing, sirens blaring, it cut him off and forced him to a stop.

A police officer exited the car, hand on his gun. Slowly Trefill got out of his own vehicle. It would be okay. He'd spotted the kid and she wouldn't get very far. With a shaking hand he reached into his pocket for his wallet. He opened it to show his ID.

"Off-official government b-business," he gasped.

The look on the cop's face went from cool sternness to wide-eyed shock. Trefill just stared at him, knowing how bad he looked but not caring. He just wanted to get away, to get that little freak before he lost her again.

"What happened to you?" the cop asked after a thorough look at Trefill's driver's license.

"I was . . . mugged," Trefill said. How could he say he'd been attacked by a five-year old kid?

"Your face is all scratched to pieces," the cop said, eyeing him carefully. "Those look like . . . like teeth marks."

Trefill breathed in deeply.

"I have to go," he said. "This is—"

"Official government business," the cop repeated. "You said so already. What branch of the government are you with?"

Trefill only stared at him.

"Come on, fella," the cop urged. "FBI? CIA? Are you in the military?"

"I'm after someone," Trefill said. "You're letting her get away. You'll go to jail for—"

The cop became serious again.

"I saw who you were chasing," he said. "Three little kids. Look, I don't know what happened to you. But you know something? I don't believe you're part of any government agency at all."

Trefill nodded. "Yes, yes. It's a special task force. See, we found these two kids and . . ."

Trefil never finished his sentence. His eyes went very wide and staring. The cop looked at him in confusion, wondering what was wrong.

Then Trefill slumped forward into the officer's arms. The back of his head was half-gone.

"Oh, damn," the cop wailed, dropping the man to the ground.

Then, as he grabbed for his gun and dived for cover: "Oh, *damn!*"

He crawled on his belly until he was safely behind his squad car. He could tell from the wound on Trefill's head the direction from which the bullet had come. Carefully he reached up into his car for his radio mike.

"This is Car Seventy-one at the Westbrook Junction,"

he said. "I need backup here, now! There's been a shooting!"

"A what, Seventy-one?"

"You heard me, Betty," the cop said, recognizing the dispatcher's voice. "A shooting! Possible sniper! Get someone down here!"

Betty mumbled something into the airwave; then an announcement went out to all available cars—in this little town, that amounted to just two. In moments, sirens filled the air as other cops headed to their colleague's location.

There was no need for backup, because the cop wasn't in any danger. The shooting, a first in Westbrook's history, was finished.

Walter LaBerge had had a ringside seat at the shooting, in the back of a van. He climbed to the front and got into the passenger seat.

"Go that way," he said to the driver. "There's a path that cuts through the woods. We'll get them ourselves."

They drove in the opposite direction from the incoming police cars.

"I don't get it," the driver said. "Why'd you wait so long to shoot him?"

"I should have got him after he lost her the first time," LaBerge said. "I was an idiot to let an incompetent handle such an important job. But I knew he'd lead me to her."

"What do you suppose she was doing with those other kids?"

LaBerge shrugged. He was a massively big man, nearly three hundred pounds, with small eyes that gave him the appearance of a hog. There was anger in those eyes, anger at himself for letting Trefill go as far as he had, anger at the kid for running away.

The driver of the van, though he thought LaBerge was the ugliest man he'd ever seen, had nothing but respect for the man's intelligence.

"You don't think they have something to do with her?"

"Maybe," LaBerge said. "We'll find out, won't we? The most important thing to do is find out what *she* has to do with that little monster we've got back at headquarters.''

With that, the driver turned into the path that cut through the woods. After he'd driven a short distance, LaBerge ordered him to stop and cut the motor. Then the fat man jumped out of the van and began to run. The driver was amazed that someone that big could move so fast.

LaBerge was on the three children before they had a chance to see him.

46

"ERIC, STOP!" Rachel cried.

Instantly Eric's foot moved toward the brake pedal. It was only years of driving habit that kept him from screeching to a halt in the middle of the Garden State Parkway. Instead, he swung into the right lane, barely missing a truck that was rumbling by.

"Rachel, don't do that!"

They had each been lost in thought for the past two hours, and Rachel's voice was like a jolting siren.

"Eric, he's here," Rachel said. "I know Steven's here somewhere, very nearby!"

Eric didn't argue with her, although he still didn't buy the telepathy bit. But he thought it was only right to do things the way Rachel wanted them done, to humor her. It certainly couldn't put them any further off-base than they might be already.

"Fine," he said. "There's the exit for a town called Westbrook. We'll take a look."

"We'll find him," Rachel insisted. "'I know we will. He's *here*. And, Eric, he's in trouble."

Eric nodded. "Don't worry. We'll get to him before anything happens."

He wished he was right about that, but even more, he wished Rachel was right about Steven being here. He drove off the highway, then followed a curving road that eventually took him over the railroad tracks. Rachel turned around and gazed out the window.

"The woods," she said. "Something about the woods. Eric, Steven might be there . . ."

Eric didn't hear her. His eyes were drawn to a place that had been roped off with yellow plastic ribbon. "PO-LICE AREA" was the message repeated over and over.

"Look at that," Eric said, driving by. "What do you suppose happened there?"

Rachel wailed. "Eric, there's blood on the street. And I know something's wrong with Steven. What if—?"

Eric cut her off. "Don't even think that. Let's go to the police and ask—"

Instantly he knew he'd said the wrong thing. Rachel reacted as vehemently as ever.

"No!"

"All right, all right," Eric said. "I'm sorry I mentioned that. But why don't we just ask around town? I haven't seen another black person since we got off the exit. If Steven was here, he was surely noticed."

They were right about that, and found out when they parked the car and walked into a local coffee shop. Eric had chosen it as a logical place to start because he figured Steven would have stopped for something to eat. They took seats at the counter and ordered cups of coffee. The waitress spoke to them as she polished glasses. At this hour of the day there were few other customers.

"Sure I saw him," the waitress said. "Strange kid."

She looked sad. "I'm sorry. I don't mean that in an unkind way. But his behavior . . ."

"What do you mean?" Rachel asked. "Steven's a perfectly normal little boy!"

"Well, I guess he was just upset 'cause he ran away from home," the waitress said, tucking a glass into a plastic tray. "You have a fight or something? Where are you from?"

"Ohio," Eric told her.

The woman's eyebrows went up.

"Wow, you're a long way from home."

Eric had no patience for small talk. He pressed on.

"What do you mean about his behavior?" he asked. "What was he doing, specifically?"

"Well, when I came over to the table he was sitting there with his eyes closed," the waitress said. "He and his little friend seemed very upset about some—"

"Little friend?" Rachel said.

The waitress held her hand up at about waist level.

"Cute little girl," she said. "Black hair and light skin and the most startling eyes—gray, with green in them. I heard him call her Lorraine."

Eric frowned. Rachel stared out the window, watching a young man pedal by on a bicycle.

"I don't know who that is," she said.

"Maybe he just made a friend," Eric suggested.

The waitress lifted the tray full of glasses and put it on a back counter. Then she began to check the salt and pepper shakers.

"I don't know about that," she said. "I saw them holding hands one time. And the way they were whispering to each other, you'd think they had a big secret."

Maybe they do, Eric thought.

"Uhm, I was wondering," he said, "if you could tell me about that police barricade we saw driving into town."

The waitress's eyes lit up. She'd been on her break at the time and had seen the whole thing, albeit from a distance.

"Oh, that's the most exciting thing that's happened in this town!" she cried. "One of our police officers stopped a man for driving crazy. I saw him—he was all over the road. Must of been drunk. Anyhow, they were talking, and suddenly the guy fell. I could see the blood from two blocks away."

That was an exaggeration, but she felt it made the story sound good.

"Anyway," she said, "I heard he was shot! There were cops all over the place a while ago, but it's quieted down since then."

"Do you know who the man was?" Eric asked.

The woman shrugged.

"Sorry," she said. "I was taken to headquarters to answer some questions because I was an eyewitness, of course. But they didn't tell me who he was. Not from this town, I know for certain. There aren't very many people around here, so you get to notice strangers."

"What about the little girl?" Rachel said. "Have you ever seen her before?"

"No," the waitress replied. "And I know everyone in this town."

Rachel pushed her coffee cup away. She'd drained it dry, welcoming the jolt from the caffeine.

"Eric, I don't think we should be sitting around," she

said. "I don't know who that little girl is, but we have to find Steven."

The waitress rested her forearms on the counter.

"You think that dead man has anything to do with those kids?" she asked.

Rachel got off her stool without answering. Eric sighed.

"I hope not," he said. He paid for the coffee. "Thank you for your help. Did you happen to notice which direction he went?"

"Sorry," the woman said. "Why don't you try the train station? You might be able to learn something there."

"Good idea," Eric said with a half-smile. He'd had enough of train stations that day, but if he had to, he'd head for another. "Thanks."

He took Rachel by the arm and led her out of the diner. They got back into the car and followed the waitress's suggestion. In a few minutes they learned that Steven had not gotten on a train.

"I didn't think he had," Rachel said as they exited the station house. "I still feel him nearby. Eric, there was something about those woods. I want to look there."

"Oh, God, Rachel . . ."

Rachel swung around, meeting his eyes.

"I'm not letting myself think anything, Eric," she said. "Steven is alive. I'm sure of that. But I think he was in the woods. And maybe there's a clue . . ."

"Then let's have a look," Eric said. "It's starting to get dark. We'd better hurry."

He opened the car door, but stopped before getting in.

"If we park on the side of the road, we'll attract too much attention," he said. "I'm not sure if the man who was shot has anything to do with this, but you can bet the police are on the alert for anything suspicious. As out-of-towners, we'd be subject to major questioning."

Rachel nodded. "You're right. Let's walk to the woods."

They held each other's hands like high-school kids, crossing over the tracks that Steven had crossed just a short while earlier. They had no way of knowing that Steven was far, far away, locked in a secret room.

47

SAMANTHA AND HER friends arrived in Shoaling just as the sun was going down. It was a charming community, established in colonial times as a fishing port.

"Does anything look familiar?" Wil asked.

"Not at all," Samantha said. "I suppose I only came here for a short time when I was very young."

Barbara pulled into the beach parking lot. It wasn't nearly as full as it would get in a few weeks, when summer vacation started. She parked and everyone got out. A cool breeze was blowing off the ocean, scenting the air with salt and seaweed perfume. Samantha tucked her Dutch-boy hair behind her ears, but it still flapped at her eyes.

"Well, here we are," she said.

Wil looked around.

"We don't know which way to find Haybrook's," he said.

"Let's just walk," Samantha suggested. "I'm tired of sitting after such a long drive."

"It'd be a good way for you to see if you remember anything," Wil agreed.

He put his arm around her shoulder. A small road led away from the parking lot, following the coast. The beach ran along one side, and tiny summer cottages sat on the other. Samantha looked at each one, but they meant nothing to her.

"Maybe we'll find that house Julie kept drawing," Barbara said.

"Yellow with green shutters," Samantha reminded her.

When they came to a turn in the road, she noticed twinkling lights down the beach. Samantha, Wil, and Barbara plodded across the sand and found Haybrook's.

Samantha sighed. "Not a bit of this rings a bell."

Wil pointed, his voice full of encouragement. "Samantha, look, there's the jetty!"

Samantha gave a half-smile; at least she knew the concession stand and the jetty were real places. But what about the house?

"You know, I have a great idea," Barbara said. "Is anybody up for dinner?"

"I don't think I can eat until I find Julie," Samantha said.

"Of course you can," Barbara insisted. "What kind of shape will you be in if you collapse from starvation? When I looked up Haybrook's, I read they have a great menu. In this town, you can bet the clams were dug up this morning."

"Barbara's right," Wil said, steering Samantha toward the clam bar. "Dinner's on me."

"I won't argue with you on that one," Barbara said. Between the mysterious flight out here and the cost of renting a car, she was nearly broke.

The blue-and-white awning surrounding the building flapped in the ocean breeze, giving the illusion that the dolphins were dancing. They walked up three wooden steps to a pair of glass doors.

A man in a white captain's uniform greeted them in the waiting area.

"Good evening," he said. "Table for three?"

"Yes," Samantha said. She added quickly: "Nonsmoking."

They were led to a table dressed with a blue-and-white-striped cloth. A blue candle had been set in the middle, held in place by an arrangement of seashells.

Although it was just sundown, the restaurant was already crowded. Wonderful smells filled the air, mixing with the sea air that blew in through the open windows. The awnings at the back of the building were rolled up, affording a view of passing boats. Their tiny lights moved slowly along the water, like little fireflies.

The maître d' told them the specials of the night, then started to walk away. Wil stopped him.

"Mind if I ask you some questions about the town?"

"Sure," the maître d' said. "What would you like to know?"

Wil looked at Samantha, then back at the host.

"Well, we visited here when we were very young children," Wil said. "We thought it might be fun to find the house where we stayed. It's yellow, with green shutters. I thought it was near the jetty, but we weren't able to see it."

"I suppose because it's too dark," Samantha put in.

The maître d' gazed out at the water, thinking.

"I'm sorry, I don't remember any such house," he said. "But you know who might? Our cook. Gordon Freeman's lived in this town for sixty years."

"I'd like to talk to him, then," Wil said.

"Why don't you take a look at the menu?" the maître d' suggested. "I'll talk to Gordy and send him out when he has a few minutes."

He walked away. Barbara opened her menu, and her eyes widened.

"Wow," she said.

"I told you I'm paying for it," Wil reminded her.

"It isn't the prices," Barbara said. "Look at this menu. I'm in heaven! Steamed lobster, marinated swordfish, striped bass in sorrel sauce . . ."

"Must have gotten the sorrel from our own desert," Wil said.

"Well, I was under the impression it was just a little concession stand," Barbara said. "Fish and chips, that sort of thing. This is a lovely menu."

"Maybe the material you looked up about Haybrook's was dated," Wil suggested.

Samantha's eyes quickly scanned the menu. She found something right away, and closed it.

"That was quick," Barbara said.

"I guess I'm more hungry than I expected," she said.

It didn't occur to her that she had read the menu ten times faster than either Wil or Barbara, and hadn't skipped a word.

Barbara and Wil finally closed their menus. Barbara rested a hand on her chin and stared out at the night.

"It sure is different here," she said. "I hadn't expected the East to be this pretty."

Wil laughed. "And everyone here thinks we westerners spend all our time kicking around in cowshit."

Samantha couldn't help laughing at that, and Barbara

joined her. For just a moment both women put aside all thoughts of mystery and allowed themselves to enjoy their surroundings.

A waitress came by and took their orders. Moments later, steaming bowls of seafood chowder were placed before them. Wil bombarded his with oyster crackers and pepper.

They had finished the soup and were starting on salads when a frail little man in white appeared at the table. He politely took off his chef's cap, revealing a head covered with white fuzz. He bowed just slightly to the women. They smiled up at him. Wil stood and shook his hand.

"You must be Mr. Freeman."

"Call me Gordy," the old man said. "You don't mind if I sit down, do you?"

"Sure, go ahead," Wil said.

Gordy settled himself. He winced as a quick pain shot through his back.

"Can't be on my feet so much these days," he groaned. When he spoke to the others, something made his eyes focus directly on Samantha. "Now, what is it you want to know?"

Samantha shifted uncomfortably. Did Gordy recognize her, even after many years?

Wil mentioned the summer house.

"It was nearby," he said. "Close to the jetty."

"Well, I know of a place that once stood down the road a bit," Gordy said. "It was yellow with green shutters. But I'm afraid you won't be able to see it."

"Why not?" Samantha asked.

"Because that house burned to the ground ten years ago," Gordy said. "Sorry."

Samantha looked down at her salad, her eyes sad. Another dead end.

"Just one more question," Wil said. "By any chance, are there any government buildings in the area?"

Samantha's head came up. Barbara's eyebrows furled.

"Not here in Shoaling," Gordy said. "But there's a factory about a mile outside of town. They make parts there. You know, things for airplanes and ships. It's all fenced in, with a guard at the front gate. Some of the people here in town go to work there. In fact, if you don't work for the tourist trade in Shoaling, you work at the factory."

The waitress appeared with their dinners. Gordy stood up.

"Well, is there anything else I can tell you?" he asked.

"Not right now," Wil said. "But thanks."

Gordy gave Samantha one last look, then turned and walked away.

"That man was staring at you, Samantha," Barbara said.

"I noticed," Samantha said. It made her very uncomfortable.

Wil began to cut up his order of soft-shell crabs.

"He might have thought you looked familiar," he said. "I suppose it's possible he remembers you from when you visited here."

"But I don't remember him," Samantha said.

She was starting to cry. Barbara, who was nearer to her, quickly reached across the table and squeezed her hand for support.

"It'll be okay," Wil said soothingly. "We're on the right track. I'll talk to Gordy again before we leave, find out why he was looking at you."

Samantha dried her eyes. "Wil, why did you ask if there are any government buildings here?"

Wil took a drink from his water glass, then set it down again.

"I've been going over the things you've told me," he said. "Let's start with that night in your garage, when someone attacked you. Next, finding yourself in a hotel room with a strange child, who just happens to have some amazing talents. Not the least of which is a knowledge of human anatomy and an understanding of certain medical terms."

"Too creepy for coincidence," Barbara commented.

"Right," Wil said. "This remarkable child starts drawing pictures that remind you of a place you visited when you yourself were a child. Then you start finding out that great big holes have been cut out of your memory. There's no record of you ever attending med school, although you've been a practicing doctor for several years now."

Samantha winced. "I'm worried about that. What if

I have to go to jail for practicing medicine without a license?"

"Don't worry," Wil said. "You won't have to answer to any charges if my hunch is right. You aren't the guilty one."

Samantha's eyes rounded.

"You think the government has something to do with this?" she asked.

"You bet I do," Wil said. "It must have taken an exorbitant amount of money to pull all of these tricks, to brainwash several people, to ruin lives, and to commit murder."

Samantha sighed. "Raoul Henley. He's an innocent victim in all this."

"So are you, and so is Julie," Wil said.

They ate in silence for a while, Samantha trying to absorb all that Wil had just said. A government conspiracy! But why? Why was she chosen?

"What are we going to do about it?" she asked finally.

"First of all, we're going to get into that building," Wil said.

Barbara grunted. "Huh! What do you plan on doing? Knocking at the gate?"

"No, but I have an idea," Wil said. "Don't worry. I'll be in there before the day is over."

He looked at his watch. "Let me make a phone call. I'll be back in a few minutes."

Samantha watched him leave, wondering what he had in mind.

"That's some fella you got there," Barbara commented.

"What?" Samantha asked distantly.

"Your new boyfriend!" Barbara cried. "Why didn't you tell me? He's absolutely gorgeous!"

Samantha faced her now.

"You didn't seem very happy about my calling a private detective," she said.

"That's just because I was worried for you," Barbara said. "But now that I've met Wil Sherer, I think you're going to be okay. You're lucky to have found a man like that, Samantha."

"I really wasn't looking, Barbara," Samantha said. "And I think Wil is just a naturally warm person."

Barbara tapped her arm. "Here he comes."

"It's all set," Wil said. "I'll go in tomorrow morning."

"How did you manage that?" Samantha asked in wonder.

"About two years ago," Wil replied, "the wife of the CEO of a big insurance company disappeared. Kidnapping—you might have read it in the papers?"

Both women shook their heads.

"I missed that story," Barbara said.

"I found her," Wil went on. "Her husband was so grateful that not only did he pay me double my fee but also swore he would help me in any way he could. I just called in that favor. He's going to fax some paperwork to the motel, and tomorrow I enter Shoaling Aerospace as William Sherer, safety consultant."

"I don't understand," Samantha said.

"All big factories have insurance," Wil reported. "Most of them have several carriers. In order to keep premiums at a minimum, they have to abide by certain safety rules. Luckily, it's been two years since my CEO's company sent an inspector over there. Unfortunately, I won't be able to see all of the building. And I'll be escorted every step of the way. But if I play my cards right, I might be able to learn if anything unusual is happening there."

Samantha looked worried.

"Do you have to go in alone?"

"No," Wil said. "I'm getting two sets of papers. You'll be going in with me as a trainee."

He looked at Barbara. "Sorry, but bringing one person with me is pushing it. I can't risk both of you."

Barbara smiled. "I'll wait in the getaway car."

"I hope it doesn't come to that," Wil said.

48

JULIE WAS THE first to awaken. She was lying on a cot in a small room with concrete walls. Shakily she swung herself around and put her feet down on the floor. The feel of cold tiles made her realize she wasn't wearing shoes, and jolted her into complete wakefulness. She looked around herself. The room's only window was a hand-size rectangle cut into the large gray door. She knew at once she was in a prison cell. Terrified, she went to the door and began banging her fists against the metal.

"Let me out! Let me out! Let me oooouuuut!"

Her cries awakened her friends, locked in individual cells across the hallway.

"Julie! Are you okay?"

No, Lorraine. Use your thoughts! Steven's voice came through as clearly as if he were actually speaking aloud.

In her own cell, Lorraine bit her lip. She closed her eyes, sat down on her cot again, and began to communicate with her friends.

Where are we? Julie asked.

I don't know, Lorraine replied. *But Marty is very nearby. Can you feel him?*

The other two children concentrated on their mysterious acquaintance. They *could* sense him, but though they tried in unison to call him, he did not answer.

Maybe he's right here, Steven thought. *We have to make him aware of us!*

We have to get out of here, Lorraine answered. *Steven, maybe we can—*

The sound of steel rubbing on steel silenced them at once, although they were pretty certain no one could read their minds. Footsteps came down the hall, and Julie and Steven each heard another door open. Someone spoke softly, a voice easily picked up by the children's sensitive ears. It was a woman's voice, and she said:

"Come on, Lorraine. Don't be afraid, honey. We'll get this all straightened out."

Julie breathed in deeply. If the woman was calling her "honey," maybe she wasn't a bad person. Maybe Lorraine wasn't in danger.

At least not now, she heard Steven say. He'd read her thoughts.

Julie was too afraid to answer him.

"What are you going to do to us?" Lorraine asked. "Why don't you let my friends go?"

"We really just want to ask you some questions," the woman said.

They were silent again. If they began to speak a few minutes later, neither Julie nor Steven could hear.

They've taken her too far away, Steven said. *But if she needs us, she'll call us.*

What good would it do? Julie said worriedly. *How could we help her?*

In his cell, Steven laughed. But there was no humor in the sound, and it sounded eerie as it bounced off the flat gray walls.

Believe it or not, he said, *that little kid is better at taking care of herself than either one of us. She has a special . . . talent.*

What kind of talent?

Steven told her about the monsters both Lorraine and Marty had created.

I can't do that, he admitted.

Neither can I, said Julie. *I'm glad I didn't see that bird-thing at the house in Ohio.*

The problem is, Steven said, *that Lorraine shouldn't try doing that here. I'm afraid she'll reveal too much about us to these people.*

Julie sat down on the edge of her bunk and buried her head in her arms.

Maybe they already know, she said. *Maybe they did this to us, and that's why they want us back.*

Marty said we'd be strongest together, Steven said. *We have to wait for him to call us again, and then we can fight.*

How long has it been since we heard from Marty?

Steven thought awhile, and came up with an exact figure. But he said: *A very long time.*

What do you suppose is happening to Lorraine?

*She must not be in trouble yet, Julie. She hasn't called
to us.*

I'm going to think about her, Julie said. *I'm going to
tell her to be brave. I don't care if she can make monsters
happen. She's just a baby.*

Three floors above them, the woman who had escorted
Lorraine to another room was thinking exactly the same
thing. Lorraine sat on an examination table, sipping a
can of soda. Marianne Scott had gotten it for her from
a refrigerator. She watched her now, studying her strange
eyes as they looked around the room. Lorraine's hair
was dirty, but Marianne thought it must be beautiful
when freshly washed. The poor baby needed some TLC.
Not that this was the place she'd get it.

The door opened behind them, and before either one
could turn, a voice boomed:

"What the hell are you doing?"

And suddenly the soda can was flying across the room.

"Hey!" Lorraine cried, annoyed.

"I . . . I thought she might be thirsty, Mr. LaBerge,"
Marianne said, her eyes round.

Lorraine glared at the huge man who had just entered
the room. She had caught only the briefest glimpse of
him in the woods, but she knew this was the man who
had brought her here. She also sensed that, while he had
acted violently, he was mostly just talk. Not like the man
who'd taken her to the motel, or even the landlord at
Bettina's place. Those men were crazy enough to kill.

"You're not to do a damned thing without being told,"
LaBerge snapped. He glared at Marianne, his subordi-
nate, with piggy little eyes. "She can't be filled up with
substances like sugar when she's to be given a thorough
examination."

"I'm sorry," Marianne replied. "But I thought all that
was done when we first got her here."

Lorraine's eyebrows went up, keen interest lighting her
round face. She'd been here before!

LaBerge cleared his throat, a very ugly sound to Lorraine's little ears.

"Because of that fool Trefill," he said, "it's necessary

to start again. I don't know what happened to her out on the road before Trefill found her again. Or what damage he did to her himself."

He reached over and brushed back the lock of hair that was hiding Lorraine's cut. She flinched away from him.

"We can't return her to her . . . her 'family' in less-than-perfect condition," LaBerge said. "We don't even know who those people are until the child tells us. But thanks to Trefill, she's got amnesia."

"She had it when she first came here," Marianne pointed out.

LaBerge's voice was even, an odd contrast to the raving maniac who had entered the room.

"Don't tell me things I already know, Scott."

"Yes, sir."

"You can go now. Send Dr. Blanely in here."

He turned to Lorraine and said in a very clinical manner, "Get yourself undressed."

"No!"

Lorraine wasn't afraid they'd hurt her, but she had no intention of cooperating with these people.

"Don't argue with me," LaBerge said. "I'm stronger than you. If we have to, we'll strap you down. Just take off your clothes. I'll be back in a few minutes."

Lorraine felt anger rising in her, anger enough to conjure up an imaginary demon. It was so strong that even without words Steven and Julie both picked up on it.

No, Lorraine! Steven called. *Don't do it!*

But they're going to do an examination on me! I don't want that!

Lorraine, even if you get out of that room, Steven said, *we don't know enough about this building to make an escape. You might not get away.*

Yes, and then they'd know what you can do, Julie added.

I don't want anyone touching me!

Steven and Julie were silent. For the moment they did not know how to change Lorraine's fate. Then Steven had an idea.

Do you remember how Marty influenced all those people during our different journeys?

Like the train clerks and shopkeepers? Lorraine asked.

Maybe we can do the same. Julie, Lorraine, listen to me. We have to work together. Lorraine, you tell us when the others are there. Then we'll help you stop them.

I don't know if I can do that, Julie said. *I can't even make monsters.*

But Marty said we were strongest together, Steven said again. *We have to try.*

Here they come! Here they come! The big fat man is angry because I didn't get undressed.

Stare at him, Lorraine. Stare into his eyes.

Okay, Steven.

Julie, Lorraine, think this with me: Leave her alone. Leave her alone.

They repeated the command over and over. Dr. Blanely reached for Lorraine's chin, shining a light into her eyes. She stared at him, and tried with all her might to make him stop. But he worked on, silently and efficiently, as if their thoughts were having no effect on him at all. He poked the speculum of an otoscope into her ear, not too gently.

It isn't working!

Keep trying!

Blanely did a few more basic tests, then turned to LaBerge.

"So far, I see no resemblance between her and the other subject. But of course these are only preliminary findings. I suggest several scans, as well as a sonogram and blood tests."

Lorraine glowered at the men, but they acted as if they weren't aware of her.

"Get her to room C-6," Blanely said. "The equipment is already set up for a sono. It's a logical place to start."

"Fine," LaBerge said.

The two men left the room.

They didn't even flinch! Lorraine reported. *I guess we can't do that, and Marty can. We need Marty!*

What's happening now, Lorraine? Julie asked.

They left the room. They're going to do a sonogram. I'm not afraid of that. I know it won't hurt. But I don't want them sticking me with needles or anything!

We have to stop them before they get that far, Steven said. *And I think the only way to do it is with Marty's help. So here's what we have to do. We have to concen-*

trate on calling him. He's here somewhere, I'm sure of it. I don't know why he's not calling us, but maybe if he knows how close we are, he'll respond.

The three children, each locked in a different room, closed their eyes in unison and began to call to Marty. But their friend could not answer them at that moment. He was far too weak.

Alone in his own secret chamber, Marty was dying.

49

IT WAS WELL after midnight when Rachel directed Eric to turn off the highway and enter the town of Shoaling. The ocean mist hovered like softly glowing clouds under the streetlamps. Most of the beach houses, as yet unoccupied, were dark.

"Are you sure this is the place you want to be?" Eric asked, driving slowly through the quiet streets.

Two glowing orbs gazed up at the car, then disappeared into the overgrown grass of a forgotten bungalow.

"I can feel Steven," Rachel said. "He's stronger here than anywhere else. I know he's somewhere very near."

A well-lit sign caught Eric's attention, and he turned the car down a side street. A few moments later he was on another of the town's main roads, pulling into the parking lot of Shoaling's single motel.

"I believe you," he said. "But we aren't going to do anything at this hour. Let's get a room and rest for the night."

"Eric, what if he's in danger right now?" Rachel asked.

Eric parked the car and turned off the engine. He turned and looked directly into her eyes.

"Do you sense that he's in danger?"

"No, not right now."

"Then that settles it," Eric said, opening his door to get out.

Although he and Rachel had taken turns behind the wheel, Eric himself had been driving for the past two hours. It felt good to stretch his legs. He breathed in the invigorating ocean air.

Rachel came out of her own door. The ocean air was not invigorating for her, but made her yawn widely.

"We both need a rest," Eric said, putting his arms around her. She felt small in his embrace.

They entered the motel, where they had to wait a few minutes before someone showed up at the desk. The bespectacled old man yawned himself, making Rachel yawn again. Eric had to bite his lip to keep from picking up the habit.

"Double?" the man said.

"Yes, for two nights," Eric replied.

Rachel looked up at her husband, wondering why he was asking for another night. She didn't expect to be here that long. She expected to get hold of Steven and go home by tomorrow afternoon.

"Getting a vacation in before the crowds?" the manager asked in a friendly way. He's been dozing in the back office, but had come wide-awake now.

"Yes . . . yes, that's it," Eric said. "Only time I could get away from work."

"You and a few others," the man replied. "Funny, I haven't seen much business in a month, then I get five people here in one night."

Eric took the room key, thanked the man, and walked to the elevator. He didn't care much about whoever might also be renting a room tonight. All he cared about was sleep.

Rachel seemed to think the same way, because moments after she climbed into the bed, she was off. Eric cuddled up next to her and fell asleep himself.

The sun was so bright when Eric woke up that his first reaction was to grab his watch off the night table and check the time. To his surprise, it was only seven-thirty. He guessed that being on the coast made the sun more obvious.

He rolled onto his back, debating whether or not to wake Rachel. Oh, he'd let her sleep, he thought. Poor thing needed her rest. She'd been through so much in the past week.

But his movements had stirred Rachel awake. She turned and smiled weakly at him. They kissed, mumbled greetings, then each rolled off the bed.

"I love the way hotels have double sinks," he said as they washed up together. "We ought to do this at home."

He caught Rachel's reflection in the mirror. Her eyes were bloodshot.

"How do you feel, honey?" he asked gently.

"He's still here," was Rachel's reply.

"That's not what I meant."

Rachel brushed her teeth, then set the brush into a plastic cup provided by the hotel.

"I'm rested," she said. "Ready to face the day. But I'm also frustrated, and hungry."

"Frustrated I can't help you with," Eric said. "But we can get some breakfast. Did you notice if there's a place to eat in this motel?"

"I saw a coffee setup in the lobby," Rachel said. "Probably the doughnuts route. I need something more substantial than that."

Eric went to the bed and sat down, picking up the phone. First he called the front desk and learned there was a diner across the street. It served a buffet breakfast. Next he asked to make a long-distance call. He put his hand over the receiver.

"Tatiana and Olivia would be getting ready for school right now," he said. "I just want to check in on them."

Olivia came on the line first.

"Did you find Steven?" she asked. "Are you coming home?"

"Not yet, sweetheart," Eric apologized. "But we're close, I'm sure. Are you okay?"

"Helga's taking good care of us," Olivia said. "But we miss you. Please hurry home!"

"I'll try, baby," Eric said. "Is Tatiana there?"

"Right here."

Tatiana came on next.

"When are you coming back?" she asked bluntly. There was an accusing tone in her voice.

"Soon as we can, Tati," Eric said. "Not too long."

"How come you didn't say good-bye?"

Eric could hear the crack in her voice, and imagined tears welling up in her big brown eyes.

"Oh, Tati," he said, "there was no time. I—"

"I have to go now," Tatiana said. "The school bus is coming."

She hung up without saying good-bye. Rachel read the stricken look on her husband's face and knew what must have happened. But she didn't say a word. Instead, she suggested they go off to find the diner.

So they got dressed and left the motel. They entered the restaurant and waited to be shown to a seat. There were about twelve other people in the place, which would seat nearly eighty during the high season. Even so, the buffet tables were well-laden. Once seated, they both refused menus, asking for the buffet instead. Eric led the way, enticed by delicious smells of bacon and sausage and fresh coffee and more. A chef stood behind three skillets, each on a blazing fire and each filled with eggs. Eric ordered a western omelet and waited as it was being prepared.

Rachel had moved on to a table of pastries and fruits. Suddenly she dropped her tray, the metal making a loud thud on the carpet. Eric quickly took his plate from the chef and hurried to her.

"Rachel, what is it?"

Someone else was already picking up Rachel's tray for her. Eric took it and thanked him without actually meeting his gaze.

"Rachel?"

His wife was staring over the room full of people, her eyes focused on a table near the back corner.

"They know about Steven," she said in a voice that did not seem to be her own.

Before Eric could question her or stop her, she moved around him and hurried by the tables of people. Eric quickly followed her. The table she stopped at was occupied by a man and two women. The man had a rugged look about him, countered by the punky way he combed back his hair. One of the women was a tall blond with green-rimmed glasses. The other was smaller, her dark hair cut in a Dutch-boy. It was this latter one that Rachel focused a pair of glaring eyes upon.

"You've got my child," she accused. "What have you done with my child?"

In her chair, Samantha leaned as far away from this crazed black woman as she could. Her eyes went round with fear.

"Wh-what are you talking about?"

"Rachel, people are staring."

Rachel didn't hear her husband. She lowered her voice of her own accord.

"I can feel his presence here," Rachel said. "You know something about him. You've taken Steven, and I want him back!"

"Who's Steven?" Barbara asked, looking from Wil to Samantha and up to Eric.

"I don't know anything about your boy," Samantha said. She'd had a terrible, almost sleepless night, and really wasn't up to an altercation with a stranger. Tears filled her eyes. "I don't care about your boy. I care about my own little girl. I'm here looking for my child."

Eric mumbled a surprised expletive. Rachel stared down at Samantha, tears coming into her own eyes. For a moment they were all frozen in a tableau.

It was Wil who finally spoke.

"You're also looking for a child?" he asked.

Rachel nodded.

"His name is Steven," she said. "He's my . . . well, not my son, but . . ."

"But he feels like he should be your son?" Samantha asked, understanding.

"We took him in as a foster child," Eric said.

At this, Samantha turned to Wil, as if the detective could explain the coincidence. He didn't reply, but quietly offered the Frelengs a seat.

"My name is Eric Freleng," the big black man said, shaking Wil's hand in a firm grip. "This is my wife, Rachel. We're from Columbus, Ohio. We had taken in a foster child, who ran away a few days ago. We have reason to believe he's here somewhere."

"I'm Samantha Winstead," Samantha said. She almost added "Dr." out of habit, but since she wasn't sure of her right to that title, she left it out. "This is Detective Wil Sherer, and this is my good friend Dr. Barbara Huston."

She didn't feel it was right to take away Barbara's title.

"Where are you from?" Rachel asked. Her voice had calmed considerably, although she was still shaking inside.

"Colorado," Samantha said. "A little town called Ashleigh Creek."

"How we got here is a long story," Wil said. "But I

think we should all tell what we know. It's too strange that both our groups are looking for lost children and that we're both from out-of-state."

He took out his pad and pen in order to write everything down.

"Who wants to start?"

"I will," Rachel said, and she began with the night at the school when she'd "blacked out."

"Nearly the same thing happened to me," Samantha said in amazement.

By the time they had all given their version of the story, Wil had a list of unbelievable parallels. Loss of memory, foster children who seemed to come from nowhere, the strange bondings between Samantha and Julie, between Rachel and Steven.

"There's something I don't get," Barbara said. "What attracted you to Shoaling? Julie left clues in her paintings. Did Steven leave something behind?"

Rachel looked at her husband, her expression almost guilty. She wasn't sure she wanted to tell these virtual strangers about the visions she'd had.

"I just . . . just . . ."

"It's okay," Samantha said. "Whatever you want to say, it's okay."

Rachel breathed in deeply and plunged on. "I *felt* him. Something was drawing me to this place. I think, somehow, Steven has been calling to me."

"I don't feel Julie at all," Samantha said sadly. "I feel empty inside."

Rachel shook her head. She didn't understand this newfound talent herself.

"Do you have any plan of action?" Eric asked.

Wil explained his idea about entering the factory as a safety inspector. Eric agreed it was a good idea.

For the next half-hour they enjoyed their breakfasts, not speaking of the subject on all their minds. It was as if they needed the reprieve to gather strength for whatever might be forthcoming.

Wil checked his watch. "I don't have to be at the factory until ten. That gives us some time to work. Does anyone have any ideas?"

"Look, I don't believe much in spooky stuff like telepathy," Barbara said, "but this whole thing is weird. I say we take a leisurely walk through town. Maybe Rachel will be able to sense something more."

"I agree," Wil said. "Barbara's got the right idea for a starting point. Let's check out the town now that it's daylight."

As they walked down the street toward the beach, they looked no different from any other tourists. No one knew that Wil had belted a gun under his jacket, that Rachel's mind was filled with thoughts of Steven's presence, that Samantha was taking in every detail under the morning sun and trying, trying to remember.

50

ALTHOUGH IT WAS a great temptation, Lorraine managed to hold back her powers throughout the examination Dr. Blanely performed on her. He worked in a very efficient manner, never smiling. He never looked into her eyes; except, of course, when he examined them. Others might have been moved by such a sweet baby face as Lorraine's, but Hartford Blanely saw her only as a specimen. She wasn't even a very interesting one, as far as he was concerned. Not at all like the subject they'd nicknamed Marty.

But it was Blanely's job to find out what her connection was to the older boy.

So far, none of the procedures hurt her, so Lorraine was able to take them in stride. She didn't like them at all, but she understood Steven's suggestion that she keep her powers to herself. At that moment she wondered why she'd suddenly lost contact with her two other friends. They'd been working together to call Marty, unsuccessfully, until Lorraine was brought in for the sonogram. For a few moments she'd still heard them in her mind. It made her worry that something might have happened to them. But curiosity was a stronger emotion, and soon all her concentration was aimed at the small televisionlike apparatus to her right side.

A nurse walked into the room. Without saying a word to the child, she picked up a device that reminded Lorraine of a microphone. She lifted up Lorraine's shirt and rubbed a clear gelatinous liquid on her stomach. The little girl squirmed at the cold, tickly feeling. The nurse made no attempt to comfort her. In fact, she didn't smile at all. She just left the room without a word, replaced in a few moments by Dr. Blanely. Lorraine didn't like him, but she lay still for the entire procedure, watching in

277

fascination as the sonogram revealed her insides in pie-wedge sections on the screen. She recognized her sternum and clavicles and various other bones. She saw her own heart beating.

Dr. Blanely spoke into a tape recorder.

"So far, the subject shows no anomalies of the internal organs," he said. "Bone structure is consistent with a child of this age, organs are functioning properly."

Of course they are, Lorraine thought. *There's nothing wrong with me.*

He punched a few buttons, and moments later sonogram "snapshots" came rolling off a printer.

"I'll be right back," he said, as if Lorraine might try to go anywhere.

Lorraine pulled her shirt back down. She jumped off the table and went to the still-working printer, holding out the row of black-and-white prints. It fascinated her so much that she hardly heard the voice in her mind. When it called her name a second time, she dropped the printout.

Steven? Is that you?

But it was Marty who had suddenly, finally, spoken up in Lorraine's mind. She closed her eyes with relief to know he was there.

Lorraine, there's danger . . . You have to get out of there!

Something was wrong. This wasn't the Marty she knew. Before, his urgency was born of strength. Now it seemed full of desperation.

Marty? Where have you been? Are you all right?

No, no. You must get away from them. They'll kill you. Do you hear me? They'll kill you, and Julie, and Steven. I've seen what they can do!

I lost contact with Julie and Steven. Did something happen to them?

They were given sedatives, but they're all right. The danger right now is to you.

Marty, they keep trying to see if I look like you inside. Why would they be doing that? Of course I don't look like you inside! I'm a girl, and you're a boy!

That . . . that isn't what they mean. Lorraine, listen to me. You must get away from them.

But Steven told me not to use my powers! He said it would reveal too much!

You have to take the chance. Lorraine, save yourself!

Lorraine heard footsteps from down the hall. She hurried to climb back up on the exam table.

I can't do it alone! You said we were strongest together. That's why you called us all here!

Lorraine, I'm . . . sick. I can't help you right now. You have to do the same thing you did at the motel room. You . . .

Blanely had just entered the room, followed by the nurse. Lorraine turned quickly toward him, her eyes wide. He stared back at her, and for a moment it almost seemed as if he knew what was in her thoughts. But then he broke eye contact and turned to a table. He had brought a small plastic bag with him, which he hooked onto a stand behind the table. At the same time, the nurse slid a needle under the back of Lorraine's wrist. It was done so efficiently that it didn't hurt.

"What's that?" Lorraine demanded.

"Nothing that will hurt you," Blanely reassured her, although there was no kindness in his voice. "It's just something to help you relax. We're going to do some . . . tests."

No! Don't let them do that!

But Marty's words came too late. Already Demerol was dripping into the child's blood, at just the right dosage for her weight. It was only seconds before the medication took effect. Suddenly everything in the room seemed to be floating. Voices sounded farther away, stationary things began to move.

Marrrteeee . . .

Lorraine, you have to fight it!

But his words came out all stretched and distorted, and Lorraine hardly understood them.

It didn't really matter, though. She kind of liked this feeling. At least it was better than being scared. Funny, now she wasn't scared at all. She was just getting sleepy.

She heard Blanely and the nurse talking, but their words made no sense. Walter LaBerge suddenly came into the room. He reminded Lorraine of a big fat walrus, and she began to laugh. LaBerge glowered at her. She fixed her eyes on the lapel pin he wore. It seemed to float down the front of his chest, but when she blinked, it was right back where it belonged. LaBerge spoke in a way that sounded as if he was giving orders, then left the room.

She felt herself being lifted. Moments later she was on a gurney, the screech of the wheels sounding like sirens in her drugged mind.

No, that wasn't sirens. It was screaming. Marty screaming.

Lorraine! You have to wake up!

MAAARRTEEEE . . .

They want to cut into you, Lorraine! They're wheeling you into surgery! Snap out of it! You have to wake up!

It was the bright lights of the operating room that finally broke through the cloud that had wrapped around the little girl's mind. Though the Demerol still dripped into her, she became fully aware that something horrible was about to happen.

"No!"

No one paid attention to her. She tried to move, but found she was too weak and dizzy.

You have to get the needle out of your arm!

Lorraine did as she was told, a line of blood trickling down her wrist. Blanely had his back to her, preparing himself for . . . something. The nurse was busy setting up tools. Lorraine glanced quickly around the room, her eyes finally settling on the stethoscope Blanley wore around his neck. She could just make out the white ear tips beneath his shirt collar. She stared at them, hard.

Blanely winced, and brought his hand up to rub the back of his neck. He felt a tremendous pressure there, a very sudden headache. Well, it was no wonder, he told himself, the way LaBerge treated everyone around here. The headache would go away in a few moments.

But it didn't go away. The entire back of his skull seemed to press harder and harder against his brain, so hard he was certain that any more pressure would cause his head to explode. He shut his eyes and rolled his head, trying to find a position that would make the pain go away.

"Dr. Blanely?"

He heard the nurse, but he couldn't answer her. Right at that moment he was certain he was going to die.

"Dr. Blanely, what's wrong with you?" The nurse sounded near hysteria.

He rubbed at his neck and felt the tips of the stethoscope pushing into his neck, pinching nerves. It was as if they had a life of their own.

If he didn't get rid of them right away, he'd *surely* die.

"No!" he shouted firmly, ripping the instrument from around his neck.

He threw it on the floor and stared at it. The nurse, in turn, stared at him and wondered if he had lost his mind. But Blanely wasn't aware of her gaze. Instead, he felt the child glaring at him, and when he turned to look at her, her eyes were full of triumph.

"Did you do that?" he demanded of Lorraine.

She only stared at him, the effects of the Demerol still slowing her reflexes.

"She's taken the IV out," the nurse said suddenly.

"Get it back in!" Blanely said. "We have work to do!"

It didn't work, Marty! It wasn't enough!

You need something stronger! Give it back to them!

Lorraine knew at once what Marty meant. She concentrated on the IV tubing the nurse was trying to reattach to her arm. It jerked out of the nurse's hand and whipped around like a snake, the needle at its end like a tooth. The little girl put all her effort into moving the thing in the right direction, slamming it hard into the nurse's arm even as the woman called Blanely for help.

The nurse was injected with such a large dose of the drug that she collapsed to the floor. Lorraine forced herself to sit up, watching all this in fascination. She had been unaware of any knack for telekinesis, but there was no time to ponder the thought. Blanely was coming at her. Without as much effort as before, she made the tubing jerk out of the nurse's arm and aim for Blanely. He stopped in his tracks.

"You little . . . *monster!*" This last word was spat out with all Blanely's might.

He turned and hurried from the room in search of help. Lorraine heard him lock the door. As soon as it closed, the giant worm became no more than a four-foot length of tubing.

She wriggled down off the table, landed on wobbly legs, and had to sit down on the floor.

You can't rest, Lorraine! You have to get out of there before they come back!

How? They . . . they locked the . . . door.

Are there any windows?

Lorraine looked around.

There's just a big one in the door.

Break it!

Lorraine didn't waste time. Moving as if in a dream, she picked up a blood-pressure gauge and threw it with all her might. Glass flew in all directions. Instinctively Lorraine looked behind her to see if the nurse had come around. She still lay on the floor, drugged. Dizzy herself from the medication, Lorraine had to make three tries before she could crawl through the window frame. She was small enough to miss most of the shards of glass that surrounded it, but one caught her along her bare thigh and left a long cut. She was too doped up to realize she was in pain, trailing blood along the floor.

Run! Run!

Marty's command sent her flying. She raced down the hall, in the opposite direction from the way Blanely had gone. When she saw someone turn a corner, she ducked into a bathroom. She waited a few minutes, then opened the door and carefully looked out. The hall was empty. She hurried down it, glancing back over her shoulder every few feet. Lorraine was certain they were coming after her. She wasn't certain if she could conjure up another "helper."

Three sharp turns led her into a short corridor. A sign marked "STAIRS" glowed above the door at the end. Lorraine hurried to them, opened the door, and disappeared just as someone was coming out of a laboratory. She ducked down and waited a moment. Then she tried to remember being taken from her "cell." Had she been brought upstairs or downstairs? She had to choose the right way.

But Marty had said to get away. And she knew she couldn't help her friends if they were locked up and sedated. So Lorraine chose to go downstairs, to what she hoped would be an exit. She moved as fast as she could, the drug wearing off a little more with each step. By the time she had gotten down five flights, she was completely sober, and not the least bit winded. It didn't even occur to her that no young child should have been able to do what she had just done.

She had passed by several floors because she could tell there was just too much activity. But on this floor the hallway was darkened. There were only two flights to descend, but she decided to take her chances and see what was here. For the first time in over twenty minutes, she called to Marty.

It's dark down here. And cold. What is this place?

I think they . . . things up there.

Up there? Where are you? Are you lower than this?

All the way down, Marty told her. *They keep me well-hidden.*

Why?

Lorraine, I can't explain that now. You don't have time to listen. Go into the dark hall. There's a way out there. I'm not sure what it is, but it is behind a large curtained area. I don't think they want anyone to know about it.

A secret exit?

I think so. Try to find it, and hurry!

What . . . what do I do when I find it?

There are others looking for you. Good people. You'll find them.

Who are they?

Marty did not answer.

Marty, who are they?

There was still silence in her mind. Lorraine sighed deeply, frustrated at having lost contact again. She wanted to go deeper into the structure, to find the enigmatic Marty, but she knew she had to follow his orders. Whoever these others were, she'd find them. They were her only hope.

The entire floor was empty, and very, very cold. Lorraine did not hurry through the corridors. She could sense that, five floors up, Blanely and LaBerge were feverishly searching for her. They could never believe she would have gotten this far this fast. But she didn't let herself give in to a false sense of security. It was only a matter of time before they caught up with her.

Most of the doors along the hall had windows, something like classrooms in a grammar school. Lorraine peered into each one in search of the curtained area Marty had mentioned. She found it at last at the very opposite end of the building. It was in the back of a large room that appeared to be a storage area. Cobwebs, a thick layer of dust, and a musty smell all told Lorraine no one had been here in a long time. She went to the curtain and pulled it back to reveal a knobless door. To her surprise, it wasn't even locked. She pushed, and it swung away easily, revealing a black void.

Lorraine had no idea where the exit led, but still she plunged into it, more afraid of the bright rooms upstairs than the darkness ahead. She steadied herself against the wall as she walked, the feel of concrete cool and rough beneath her hand. There was a salty smell in here, like the ocean breeze outside, making her guess it must lead out to the beach.

She could hardly believe it would be this easy to get out of here. Surely an alarm had been sounded throughout the complex and dozens of people were looking for her right now. She hoped they'd think she wasn't clever enough to have found this secret passageway. That might buy her some much-needed time.

Every once in a while Lorraine would look behind herself. She could barely make out the dim light of the room. When it faded altogether, she concentrated her efforts on moving forward. She wasn't afraid of the dark, because she did not have the experience to fear it. There were no thoughts of rats or spiders. Lorraine had seen real monsters, and not just the kind she created with her own mind. Trefill, LaBerge, the gang of thugs that had attacked in the subway—these were all true monsters. Trefill and the gang were far away. LaBerge might be looking for her right now, but she had a feeling the big man couldn't move very well in this small tunnel.

Her hand passed over a round hard lump at even intervals. Lorraine guessed they were light sockets. How long had it been since they'd been lit?

She walked for a long time, until the air began to grow colder. Lorraine hoped to see light at the other end, but accepted the possibility that that, too, was blocked off. She only hoped it would be easy to remove the barricade.

More than that, she hoped no one would be on the other side.

In the dark, there was no way of seeing where she was going, and suddenly her foot plunged ankle-deep in water. Lorraine stopped short. She had guessed she was heading to the water, but what if the way out was *under* the water?

She stepped back a yard or so, until the floor was dry again, then sat down to rest. Water! Lorraine racked her young mind, trying desperately to remember if she could swim. Was that a talent that was simply lost in her forgotten time? If she found herself in over her head, would she panic? Would she drown?

What am I going to do? she wailed in her thoughts. *Marty, please help me!*

It wasn't Marty who answered, but Steven.

Lorraine, where are you?

In a secret tunnel! Steven, there's water! I think the way out is under the water! I'm trapped!

Maybe not, Steven answered. *I don't think Marty would have led you that far to get you into trouble. Lorraine, I can feel Rachel very, very close. You have to find her! That's the only way we're going to get out of here.*

I'm afraid of the water!

Now Julie piped in with her own words of encouragement.

Don't be! We'll stay with you. Go on, Lorraine. It's our only chance!

Yeah, Lorraine, Steven prompted. *Try it. You can get through!*

There really was no other choice. The thought of returning to the complex and facing her captors was more terrifying than the thought of drowning. Lorraine stood up and waded into the water.

Tell us what's happening, Julie suggested.

It's up to my knees. Now my hips and now my tummy and now . . .

There was a moment of silence.

Lorraine?

I'm okay, Steven! I'm under the water. And guess what? I can swim!

Good for you! Julie answered.

Don't talk to us now, Steven said. *Save your strength. We don't know how far you have to swim.*

Lorraine groped through the water, finding it easy to hold her breath. She actually enjoyed the swimming, even though it was cold and pitch-black dark. She moved through the water as if she'd been born to it.

But then her hand struck a wall. Thinking she'd taken a wrong turn, she moved back and forth, groping. There was the rough feel of the concrete on two sides, but the wall in front was smooth.

I found a door!

Great! Can you open it?

Lorraine fumbled around for a latch, but couldn't find one. Her fingers felt a seam where two pieces of wood met, but though she tried, she couldn't make it budge.

Now she began to panic.

I can't open it! It's getting harder to hold my breath! I'll have to go back!

No! Lorraine, use your mind!

Lorraine banged on the wood, but the water slowed her efforts. She hardly heard what Steven was trying to tell her.

Lorraine, your mind is strong. You can do anything!

This time, Lorraine heard him. She directed all her thoughts to the door, hoping to find mental power strong enough to blast right through the door and whatever was holding it shut on the other side. But the effects of the medication she'd been given had tampered with her abilities to bring imaginary creatures to life. Dizziness began to fill her head, and her lungs begged for an intake of oxygen. She'd been under the water for nearly three minutes.

Lorraine had no choice but to turn and swim back until her head was above water.

It didn't work, she told the others. Her tears mixed with the salt water on her face. *Oh, it didn't work at all!*

Rest, Lorraine, Julie said. *You can try again in a few minutes.*

I need Marty!

I'm here, Lorraine. I'm back.

Marty! All three children shouted it in their minds.

Marty, I'm trapped. I can't get through the door.

Yes, you can. We can. I'll help you, Lorraine. Go back under the water.

With Marty to help her, and with the encouragement of her friends, Lorraine plunged into the water without hesitation. This time, when she tried to push the door, she had the power of Marty's mind working with her. The force within her radiated into the surrounding water, making it glow with a phantom electricity. For the first time since she entered the tunnel, Lorraine could see.

But there was no time to look around herself. She heard pounding and knew that something—some energy—was striking the wooden door with incredible force. Instantly sunlight poured into the water. Clouds of sand billowed around Lorraine's head. She squinted and watched as the door bulged open, straining against the sand. The electric glow was replaced at once by sunlight.

Lorraine swam through the door, then up another five feet until she broke the surface of the water. She was hidden in a garden of tall beach grass.

I'm out! Marty, Steven, Julie! I'm out!

Hooray! Steven shouted.

Good for you! Julie praised.

There were no words from Marty. The effort had been too great, and now he was unable to respond.

But Lorraine, encouraged by the amazing thing she'd just done, waded through the waist-high water and up onto the beach. She glanced in all directions, making sure she wasn't being watched. The beach was empty. Lorraine sank down on the sand and let herself rest for just a moment.

Then she stood up and went to look for help.

51

DURING THEIR WALK around town, Rachel and Samantha shared what little memories they had of their childhoods. Samantha mentioned Julie's beach drawings, most especially the yellow house near the jetty.

"I'd like to see that jetty," Rachel said. "Perhaps there's a clue."

"We looked," Samantha said. "I'm afraid nothing was familiar."

"That's because you were seeing it with your eyes," Rachel said. "I'm experiencing it with . . . well, with whatever's making me feel Steven."

Samantha looked so downtrodden that Wil put his arm around her shoulder.

"I wish I could 'feel' Julie," she said.

Barbara pointed. "The jetty's in that direction, just beyond Haybrook's. I don't suppose you have any memory of that place?"

She directed the question to Rachel, who shook her head.

They headed toward the jetty. The very moment she was near it, Rachel let out a cry. Her eyes widened, and she pivoted to face Samantha.

"You said the yellow house burned down years ago," she said. "And it was near a jetty."

Samantha only nodded in reply. Eric looked concerned.

"What is it, Rachel?" he asked.

Rachel closed her eyes, her expression tightening as she concentrated.

"A gateway," she said. "Some kind of dark tunnel. I don't know where it leads, or how to get there, but it will take us to the children."

288

"This is the only jetty," Wil said. "The house had to be in this area."

"Another house must have been built on the site," Samantha added. She looked down the beach at Haybrook's, still quiet at this early hour. Then she broke into a determined stride. "Come on, everybody. I know where we can get some answers."

Gordy's whole life was the clam bar, and he spent most of his waking hours there whether he was actually working or not. They found him in the kitchen, shucking clams for the upcoming lunch crowd. He looked up, but didn't seem surprised to see them. His eyes cast a questioning look in Samantha's direction for just a second, but he didn't move quickly enough for her not to notice.

"Hello," he said simply. "Looks like your party grew a bit."

"Gordy, we have to ask you some questions," Wil said.

"You seem to enjoy asking questions," Gordy replied. " 'Course, I suppose as a detective-type, that's your job. What is it you want to know?"

"The yellow house . . ." Wil began. "Was another structure put up in its place?"

"No," Gordy said. "That property has stood empty for decades. Don't make much sense, being prime waterfront real estate. Some say it belongs to the government."

Barbara grumbled: "That figures."

"Could you tell us where to find the lot?"

"You already know," Gordy said. "It's near the jetty, like you said. You can't miss the spot. It's the only property on the block overgrown with weeds—even at this time of the year."

"I remember that place," Eric said. The others agreed with him. "It doesn't look like anyone's taken care of it in years."

"You're probably right," Gordy said. "But I can't blame people for staying away. Strange things happened in that house just before it burned down. People said they saw glowing orange lights behind the windows."

"Flames," Eric suggested.

"Not that color orange," Gordy said. "Weird lights—magical."

He stared down at his hands, wet with clam juice.

"I always wondered about that," he said. "Wondered if it had anything to do with the explosion."

"What explosion?" Samantha asked.

"Out at sea," Gordy said. "It happened just a day before the house burned down. Big enough to light up the whole sea and sky. Then this big navy ship showed up, probably investigating."

"Did they ever explain what it was?" Wil asked.

"Oh, sure," Gordy said. "They said it was an oil tanker. But you saw what that tanker did up in Alaska, spilling those millions of gallons of oil. There wasn't a drop out there, not a drop. You tell me how an oil tanker explodes and doesn't leave a bit of its cargo."

"Do you have any theories?" Wil asked.

"Yeah," Gordy said. "I think it was some kind of enemy submarine, maybe Russian. I don't think they wanted people to know how close they got, so as not to start a panic."

"You thought it had something to do with the yellow house burning down," Samantha reminded him.

"Oh, probably just coincidence," Gordy said. "There sure were a lot of things happening that summer here in Shoaling. That's the same year Shoaling Aeronautics went up."

All the while he was speaking, he stared very intently at Samantha. When he finished, he seemed to realize what he'd been doing, and turned away.

"Why do you keep doing that?" Samantha demanded.

Gordy did not deny that he'd been staring.

"I'm wondering why you don't remember me," he said.

Samantha's eyebrows went up. Wil took a step closer to her.

"What . . . what do you mean?" she asked. "I came here as a child. Of course I don't remember you!"

Gordy shook his head. "I don't know what you did when you were a kid. I remember you from the night of the explosion. You came wandering in here, all straggly with seaweed and sand. Seemed you'd swum a good distance. I thought you might be a Rusky because you wouldn't say a word. But you seemed like a sweet, scared kid. So I fed you hot soup and tried to get you to a hospital, but you'd have none of it."

"That's crazy!" Samantha cried. "I wasn't here ten years ago! I was never even on a boat!"

"Maybe you're mixing her up with someone else," Wil suggested, although he didn't believe this.

Gordy's white head swung back and forth with vigor.

"No, I don't forget faces," he said. "You're definitely the woman I saw. Maybe you were hurt badly in that explosion—whatever it was—and it affected your memory."

Samantha turned to hug Wil, completely bewildered. Gordy's reference to memory hit a little too close to home. When was this going to end?

Barbara's yellow brows furled.

"What happened next?" she asked Gordy. "I mean, after you found Samantha?"

"She just took off," Gordy said. "Spooky. I'm sorry, lady. But that's the right word for it. You were like the waking dead."

"Walking dead," Eric corrected.

Gordy looked at him. "I mean 'waking dead.' She acted like she'd been dead asleep for a long time, then just woke up."

"I was here ten years ago," Samantha said distantly, as if she hadn't heard anything else.

Wil looked at Samantha, who was staring out the window at a distant boat. Barbara was concentrating on her friend, while Rachel and Eric held each other. He made a decision to make his next move on his own, fearing he might put the others in danger if they joined him.

"Wait here," he said. "I'll be right back."

Samantha seemed to become aware of him at that moment.

"I'm coming with you!"

"No," Wil said. "I'll only be a few minutes. If what I'm doing is safe, I'll come back for you."

He hurried off before anyone could question him. The others followed, moving more slowly as a group. They respected Wil's instincts as a former cop. A few moments later he reached the property. On the off-chance that this place was under surveillance (provided it *was* connected with that explosion at sea), he didn't want anyone else seen here.

Gordy had been right, the place was overgrown. Wil was grateful for the workboots and long-sleeved shirt he wore, protecting him from tics. Not that tics were any great problem when compared with secret government agencies.

He kicked around the weeds, his eyes searching for any clue at all. There were a few burned chips of wood, some broken dishes, and a doll that had been distorted in the heat. None of it offered any answers. Wil was about to give the whole thing up as a wild-goose chase when something caught his eye. He pushed aside stacks of sea grass as tall as himself and reached down to pick up a broken, rusted bucket. A little bit of the paint showed through, and he could tell it had once been red. There was a white spot in the middle of its side, and after careful study he realized it was a baby crab. His eyes widened.

This was the bucket Samantha had said Julie put in her pictures.

Wil tucked it under his arm and hurried back to the others.

"Why did you make us wait?" Barbara asked.

"Did you find anything?" Samantha wanted to know.

Wil answered Barbara first. "If that is government property, it may be under surveillance. They probably have a picture of me right now. It's safer not to get you involved."

"I think we're pretty involved right now," Eric said.

Wil answered Samantha's question now, by handing her the bucket.

"I found it on the property," he said.

"Oh, it's the one from the pictures!" Samantha cried. "The one I must have had as a child!"

Eric shook his head. "Whoa, wait a minute. You said you thought you had come here thirty years ago. That isn't thirty years' worth of rust on that thing. Besides, if it was yours as a child, it would have disintegrated by now."

"I don't think she was here as a child," Wil said.

Samantha looked up at him, the bucket held tightly in her hands.

"What do you mean?" Barbara asked, as if speaking for her friend.

"I mean, I think Gordy's right," Wil said. "I think you really were here ten years ago. I think you're connected with that explosion somehow."

"But Julie's drawings!" Samantha protested. "And the bucket . . ."

Wil shook his head. "I don't know what the explanation is for all that. But I do think we're getting closer to an answer. It's twenty minutes of ten. I'm going to head over to the factory now."

"I'm ready," Samantha said.

"No, Samantha, I've changed my mind," Wil said. "Yesterday, it was a good idea to bring you as my assistant. But now that Rachel's shown up, and has exhibited . . . extraordinary powers, I think it makes more sense for her to come. She'd be the one who could tell me if there's anything to be found in the factory."

Samantha was disappointed, but couldn't argue with Wil's logic.

"What are we supposed to do?" Barbara asked. "Just hang out?"

Wil was about to answer when Rachel tapped his arm and pointed down the beach. The adults turned to look, and saw a small figure stumbling toward them. This particular section of beach was privately owned, so there were no other people blocking their view.

"That looks like a little child," Rachel said. "She's coming to us."

Wil was about to ask how she knew this, but dropped the question.

"I don't think it's Julie," Samantha said, although she hoped she was wrong.

"I know it isn't Steven," Eric said.

"Maybe it's just some kid who got lost," Barbara said. "I feel sorry for her, but we've got our own problems. Wil, you're going to be late."

Rachel held up her hand. "Please, wait."

She hurried across the sand to the child. The others watched from the road as she fell to her knees. The little girl threw herself into Rachel's arms. Her hair was dripping and full of sand. Her wet clothes soaked through Rachel's.

"Rachel," she whispered in a choking voice. "Your name is Rachel."

Rachel pulled back. She beckoned the others with a wide arc of her arm.

"How do you know that?" she asked.

"Steven . . . told me," Lorraine said. "We were calling to you. Did you hear us?"

Rachel hugged her close again. "Yes, yes! I heard you!"

Lorraine held fast to Rachel, hardly able to believe she'd found her. The Demerol had worn off, but the effort of escape had left her as weak as a baby.

The others had arrived. Rachel looked back over her shoulder.

"She knew my name! She knows about Steven!"

"They've got them locked up!" Lorraine wailed. "They tried to hurt me! I don't know what they want!"

"Are there others?" Samantha asked.

"Just Julie and Marty," Lorraine said. "He's bigger than the rest of us. Older. But I've never seen him."

Samantha held fast to Wil's arm. "Julie's okay!"

"I think she is," Lorraine said.

Wil knelt down to her level. "Lorraine, how did you get away?"

"Marty told me about a secret tunnel."

"A secret tunnel?" Samantha repeated with surprise.

"Can you show it to us?" Wil asked.

Lorraine nodded. "Come on, follow me."

But when she tried to walk, her weak little legs gave out and she stumbled. Wil lifted her up into his arms. Lorraine pointed, and they started down the beach together. The adults were full of questions, but the tired look on the child's face told them the questions would have to wait. They walked for nearly half an hour, until Barbara grew impatient enough to ask:

"Is it much farther?"

"It's right over there," Lorraine said. "See all that beach grass? There's a pool of water there, and a secret entrance underneath."

"Water?" Samantha said. "You mean you swam out?"

"Why would they build a tunnel under the water?" Barbara asked, not really expecting an answer.

They reached the grass, and Lorraine showed them the

pool of tidewater. They could barely make out the entrance to the tunnel.

"I'd bet it wasn't always underwater," Wil said. "It must have been built for a purpose, and when they were done with it they covered it up. Nature took its course and finished the job."

Samantha touched Lorraine's arm.

"How far did you have to swim?"

"Not too far," Lorraine said. "I can hold my breath a few minutes."

She said this with some measure of childish pride.

"But there was a door blocking the way," Lorraine went on. "I got scared, but the others helped me. Marty helped me the most of all."

The adults looked confused.

"How did he do that?"

They expected to see another child emerge from the water.

"He helped me . . . in my mind," Lorraine said.

Suddenly she clammed up. She wasn't sure how much she was supposed to reveal.

Everyone turned to Wil, who had become the unofficial leader of this expedition. He asked another question.

"Could you give us an idea how big the building is?"

"I went down a lot of stairs," Lorraine said. "Maybe six or seven."

Wil thought about this. It seemed there might be secret subbasements in the factory.

"What now?" Barbara asked.

"First of all," Wil said, "we get this little girl away from here. I'm sure they're looking for her, and it won't take them long to find out she got out this way."

"I can handle that," Barbara said. "I'll take her back to the motel."

"No, that isn't safe," Samantha said. "Take her to Haybrook's. I'm sure Gordy won't mind."

Barbara nodded, and took Lorraine into her arms.

"Now, I have to stick to my original plan to enter the building as a safety inspector," Wil said. "But two of you need to get in this way. Do you swim?"

"I do," Eric said. "I was a lifeguard years ago, and I've kept it up."

"I don't know if I can swim," Samantha said.

"I can," Rachel said. "Do you think I let Eric run off to the Y without me?"

Wil nodded. "Then that's that. You two go in this way. I have a feeling you won't get caught, since Lorraine managed to get this far without being seen."

"Maybe it's been so long since the tunnel was in use that they forgot about it," Samantha suggested.

"I hope you're right," Wil said. "But it won't be forgotten for long. We'd better get moving."

They agreed on a rendezvous point, then went their separate ways. Eric and Rachel stripped down to their underclothes, using their belts to tie the bundles of their clothing to their backs. With a deep breath, they both plunged into the water.

52

FROM ALL OUTWARD appearances, Shoaling Aeronautics was not any different from any other factory. It was housed in a long brick-face building with a row of windows along each of its two stories. Armed with the phoney ID's faxed to them by Wil's former client, Wil and Samantha approached the front gate. Samantha's heart beat so hard that she swore the man could hear it as he handed her a clearance badge. They were told to wear the badges throughout the building and to return them on their way out. They went inside, where they were greeted by a man named Wesley Kane.

"You'll only be allowed in certain areas," he said. "Of course, you understand that in a place like this we do some very . . . specialized work."

"I'll bet you do," Wil mumbled.

Kane looked at Wil strangely. Then he led the two down the hallway. As they walked, Samantha wondered if the children really were somewhere in here. Did Wil have some kind of plan?

They entered a room, where another guard took a look at their badges. Samantha noted a green border around the ones she and Wil wore, and immediately connected it to the green trim around the door. She wondered if this meant they would enter only rooms with green doors.

Even though Wil and Samantha were authorized, everyone in the room hunched over his or her work to try to hide it. Some people actually stopped working, pushing parts aside and busying themselves with odd jobs like sorting nuts and bolts.

"Why do the people in these places always stop work when I arrive?" Wil asked, as if he'd been doing this for years. "If I can't see what they're doing, I don't know if they're working within industry standards for job safety."

Kane gave an apologetic shrug.

"I guess you do the best you can," he said.

He led Wil and Samantha through the room. Wil pointed out a few things that needed change, and jotted some notes. His former client had even gone so far as to send him the proper blank forms.

At last the tour came to an end. Samantha felt disappointed as they headed toward the front of the building. She hoped Rachel and Eric had gotten through the secret tunnel and that they'd found out more than she and Wil had. As far as she was concerned, this whole episode was a waste of time.

But Wil had a surprise in store. Although there were guards in the building, they weren't everywhere. As soon as the three of them were alone, he pulled out a gun from beneath his jacket, as smoothly as a magician produces a scarf. Kane was so stunned that he stood staring at the gun barrel, blubbering.

"Not a word," Wil said. He tossed his head to the side to indicate an unoccupied room, a supply closet he had "inspected" just moments before.

Kane moved inside. Samantha shut the door behind them. If her heart had been pounding loudly when they first entered the factory, it was ready to burst now.

"Who are you?" Kane demanded.

Wil didn't say a word to him. He waved the gun at some rubber tubing and instructed Samantha to tie Kane up. With shaking hands she did so, in knots so tight it would take scissors to open them. Then she gagged him with packing tape.

Wil removed his ID badge and pulled it out of its green-rimmed holder. He had noticed other badges on the shelf, and chose the one with the most colors. Samantha did the same. They now had access to any part of the building.

"Come on," Wil said. "We don't have a lot of time."

Wil took Samantha by the hand, and the two hurried down the hall. They reached a door marked "STAIRS" and entered a darkened stairwell. Wil finally tucked his gun back into its holster.

"I didn't know you had that with you," she said.

"Like I said," Wil replied, "sometimes I need it."

He looked down the stairwell.

"That little girl said there were at least six or seven floors here," he said, "but these only go down one more flight. There must be a secret set of stairs."

"Lorraine said she found the entrance to the tunnel in a storage room," Samantha said.

The complex had been built according to a plan, and it was only a matter of minutes before they found an entrance to a new set of stairs behind some dusty old crates in a supply closet.

"The tunnel must lead to one of these floors," Samantha said as they descended. "I wonder if we'll find Rachel and Eric."

"We won't have the chance for that," Wil said. "We can't explore every story of the building. My guess is that if they've got anything to hide here, it would be in the lowest possible level."

They went down the rest of the way without speaking. On each floor they stopped to carefully look out the glass window on the door. They could see people moving quickly about, some with guns out. Samantha knew they were looking for Lorraine, but doing so in such a quiet manner that the people on the upper floors weren't aware of the escape. Those people probably were no more than locals from the town. Kane might have been one himself.

As she followed Wil, Samantha kept looking back over her shoulder, expecting to see someone coming behind them. But so far they were alone. No doubt these stairs were used only in emergency situations.

When they reached the bottom floor, Wil pulled her back into the shadows and carefully looked out the window. The hall was brightly lit, and occupied by people in white space suits. Wil and Samantha had to wait five minutes before the way was clear for them to walk into the hallway. The sight of people hidden under helmeted white suits alerted them that they'd found something quite important. It also gave them a chance to take a look around incognito. Wil guessed that, like the floor where Kane was held prisoner, the storage room was right near the stairs. He found a pair of white suits, and they both pulled them on.

"Wil, what if there's some kind of disease down here?"

Samantha asked worriedly. "What if we put these suits on wrong?"

Wil showed her one of the valves.

"This is set for exhaust," he said. "That means that the outside air is being protected from whatever germs might be emanating from you."

"From me?" Samantha echoed, staring at the helmet in her hands.

"That's right," Wil said. "It's a cleanroom suit. Air going out is filtered, not air coming in."

Samantha looked toward the door.

"What are they trying to protect out there?" she wondered.

Wil pulled on his helmet and latched it as easily as a man who had done this hundreds of times. Samantha made a mental note to ask him about this at a later date. She fumbled with her own, and Wil helped her. It gave her a slightly claustrophobic feeling, and memories of being locked up by her mother fought to surface. Samantha fought back, and they disappeared.

Wil helped her with her gloves. In moments they looked like astronauts. More important, they looked no different from anyone else on the floor.

"Can you hear me?" Samantha said.

Wil answered, his voice sounding gravelly inside her helmet.

"Yes, how about you?"

"Just fine," Samantha said. "Wil, how will you get your gun if you need it?"

"I couldn't use it anyway," Wil said, holding up the fat fingers of his glove.

They exited the storage room together. They could see two other people down the hall, but neither one turned to look at them. For the next ten minutes they explored as best they could, avoiding anyone else in case questions might be asked. Finally they came across a room marked "AUTHORIZED PERSONNEL ONLY."

"I wonder why there isn't a guard," Samantha asked.

She saw Wil's helmet shake back and forth. Carefully he pushed at the door. It was locked.

"I hear someone coming," Samantha said.

They ducked into a broom closet. Wil watched a figure

go by through the crack in the door, a white-suited figure like himself.

The guard unlocked the door to the mysterious room and went inside. Guiding Samantha with a gentle push, Wil led the way back to the hall. This time the door that had stopped them stood slightly ajar.

"What are you waiting for?"

The voice inside his helmet did not sound like Samantha's. Wil turned to look at her, or at what he could see through the dark visor that covered her face. There was someone else with them, standing to Samantha's side. Wil didn't need to see Samantha's face to know she had a stricken expression. He could read it in the stiff way she stood.

"Come on, doctors," the third person, sounding female, said. "Marty's due for his next test."

Marty! The boy Lorraine had mentioned.

"Yes, yes, of course," Samantha said.

Without hesitation she hooked the fat arm of her cleanroom suit through Wil's and walked past the "NO ADMITTANCE" sign.

They entered a short hallway and followed it to a small room. In here, red lights glowed warmly. Wil and Samantha looked around themselves in wonder.

"Must be some kind of decontamination unit," Wil guessed.

"Let's go," Samantha urged. "I want to see who Marty is. Maybe he can lead us to Julie."

Now they entered another hallway. The guard they had seen stood outside the next door. If he had even glanced at their ID badges, they couldn't tell. But obviously these people had been expecting someone. Wil thought that was a terrible blunder, proving security wasn't as tight in this place as all its locked doors and secret rooms might make it seem. Well, he thought, a tiny little kid like Lorraine got away easily enough.

He opened the door at the back of the hall and entered a large sterile white room. Flashing lights drew his attention to computers that ran along the back wall. A large table in the room's center held lab equipment. There were steel drums filled with God-knew-what, oxygen tanks, and EKG monitors. The four or five other people in the room worked busily, their backs turned to the newcomers. Samantha leaned toward Wil.

"What do we do now?"

"Let's just look around," Wil said. "I have a feeling we'll know Marty when we see him."

Samantha felt a tap on her shoulder and almost screamed. At the last moment, she caught the sound in her throat. Someone beckoned them to a back corner of the room.

"We've prepped him for you," he said. "I'm afraid his vital signs have slackened off since the last time he was examined."

"Let's have a look at him," Wil said.

They walked toward a partition at the back of the room. It was a glassed-in room, the windows covered now by drawn curtains. But suddenly Samantha stopped dead in her tracks. Her hands came up, shaking, to point at something in a large Plexiglas case. Wil looked in that direction and whispered:

"Oh, damn . . ."

It was a wooden box shaped almost like a coffin, and with a glass top.

"That's the newest one," the man in the other suit said. "Just dug it out of the gulf a few days ago. It's the most intact pod we've ever found. That's why LaBerge wanted it protected."

Within the helmets, his sigh sounded like a windstorm.

"Ten years of work," he said, "and we still haven't been able to pinpoint exactly what they're made of."

Ten years, Samantha thought. Gordy had said she'd been here ten years ago. On shaking legs Samantha neared the case. Someone was using robotic arms to scrape tiny pieces off the wood at the side of the pod. "He" carefully placed the splinters on slides. Samantha's eyes were immediately drawn to an unusual knot in the wood. For a split second she thought she saw a tiny face turn to her with a silent, pleading scream.

Their escort tapped her shoulder and pointed to a monitor. An electron microscope stood near the case, and when the slides were placed within it, a strange image appeared on one of the screens at the back of the room. It looked like a chain of long knotted-up balloons.

"Not like any wood I've ever seen," the man said. "How about you?"

"I . . . I've never seen wood under a microscope," Samantha stammered.

With a firm but gentle tug, Wil steered her away. They went to the glass-walled room and went inside.

Marty turned to gaze up at them. Samantha met his eyes, and she began to scream.

Then she began to remember.

53

RACHEL AND ERIC emerged from the tunnel, dripping wet and smelling of seawater, while Wil and Samantha were tying up Wesley Kane. They found themselves in an office filled with file cabinets. Taking the clothes off their backs, they wrung them out as best they could and dressed. Rachel shivered.

"It's so cold," she said. "I don't see how that little girl made it out so easily."

"I don't think it was easy for her," Eric said. He took Rachel into his arms for just a moment, and they tried to draw warmth from each other's bodies.

"Are you ready?"

Rachel took a few steps. Squeaking noises filled the room like a blaring Klaxon.

"We'll have to go barefoot."

Eric and Rachel removed their shoes and hid them behind one of the cabinets. Rachel glanced at the files, wishing she could take the time to look at them. What secrets would they reveal?

She followed Eric into the hall. It was darkened, as if this floor of the building was not currently in use. Still, she and Eric moved quickly and carefully, always on the alert for others. They left a wet trail for a few yards, but eventually their clothes stopped dripping. Rachel worried someone would see the trail. She was grateful to see it end just before a fork in the hallway. Anyone who came after them would have to decide which way to turn.

There seemed to be nothing on this floor but supplies. Then Eric found something strange in one of the darkened rooms. Rachel looked at the triangular-shaped wheeled piece of equipment. There was a pulley and chain attached to it, rusted now after years of disuse.

"What is that?" she asked.

Eric touched it. "A winch. The kind of thing you use to pull boats out of the water. This is a strange place to store something like that."

Rachel looked toward the door, as if she could see down the hall to the secret passageway.

"Maybe not," she said. "Maybe that wasn't an escape tunnel at all, Eric. What if they were using it to pull something *into* the building?"

Eric nodded eagerly. "Of course! Something they couldn't bring through the town because they didn't want it to be seen. When the job was finished, they destroyed that loading dock out there and covered up the opening to the tunnel with sand. Nature took its course, and the tides came in over it."

"At a different time of day," Rachel added, "we may not have been under the water for so long."

Eric took her by the arm.

"Let's get going," he said. "I have a feeling we're going to find something very important on this floor."

Rachel hurried along with him. She looked around herself in wonder.

"Why aren't there any other people on this floor?" she asked. "If it's so secret, where are the guards?"

"I have a feeling there may be only one or two other means to get in here," Eric said. "The guards are probably based at the stairs and elevator. They might not even know about the tunnel."

Rachel pointed down the hall. All the other doors had been simple wood ones, some with glass windows. But this was a double door, made of metal. Even from this distance Rachel could read the sign:

"DO NOT ENTER! DANGER OF CONTAMINATION BEYOND THIS POINT! NO UNAUTHORIZED PERSONNEL!"

Again Rachel looked for a guard.

"Whatever they had in that room," she said, "it must be gone now."

"Let's have a look anyway," Eric suggested.

They were only half-surprised that the door was unlocked. It was true—whatever had been stored here had been moved away. The room, as huge as an airplane hangar, was empty. Disappointed, Eric turned to leave the room. But Rachel tugged at his wet sleeve.

"Wait!" she cried. "Look over there! Do you see how

that panel of the wall is slightly different from the others?"

Eric looked in the direction she was pointing. He squinted his eyes and studied the back wall, but it all looked the same to him.

"Not at all," he said.

"Well, it is," Rachel said. "We've found another secret room. Let's take a look."

She went to the panel and pressed her hands against it. Eric's eyebrows went up when it slid around like a revolving door. There was blackness beyond it.

"Another secret passageway?" Eric whispered. Something about the darkness warned him to be careful.

Rachel did not answer. She reached inside the room and felt along the wall until she found a switch. When the lights went on, she gasped.

The room was filled with metal boxes, at least thirty of them. They were neatly stacked, carefully numbered, and padlocked. Eric went to one and pulled on the lock.

"What do you suppose is inside here?"

"I don't know," Rachel said. "But I want to find out. Eric, I saw some tools in one of the rooms we entered. Let's go back for them."

They turned off the light, replaced the panel, and hurried to the room Rachel had mentioned. When they found the tools they needed, they returned to the secret room. As they entered and turned on the light, Rachel whispered:

"Eric, I don't think we're alone."

"Is it Steven? Are you feeling his presence?"

Rachel's head swung back and forth. "No. Eric, someone is watching us."

Eric felt a chill rush through his body, and it wasn't from his damp clothes. He looked around himself, but the whole area seemed empty.

"I don't think there's anyone here," he said, although he couldn't be certain. Rachel had been right about her other "feelings." "If they were, they would have come out by now."

"You're right," Rachel agreed. The feeling of being watched wouldn't go away, but still she went on with her task. She took a hammer and crowbar and began to work at the back of the metal box. In a few minutes it popped open.

There was another box inside, a wooden box with no lid. Rachel gazed at it in wonder, taking in the strange whorls of the wood, patterns that resembled living things. Eric leaned over and looked inside.

"Weird," he said. "Someone carved faces into that. I wonder what it is."

Rachel just stared at it. Something was very, very familiar. She reached in and ran her hands along the wood.

"Look, there's an empty space at the front," Eric said. "Some kind of wires are sticking out. Do you think it could have been a probe of some kind? Gordy said there was an explosion at sea ten years ago. Maybe there was a submarine, and they launched these one-man probes to let spies enter our country without being caught. Only they were caught, and here are their vessels."

He scratched his head. "Is that what this is all about? Does this have something to do with enemy spies? Maybe this whole setup is to study these pods, to see how it was done."

"I don't have anything to do with spies," Rachel whispered. "But, Eric, I've seen this before. Those faces in the wood—"

The sound of a quiet sneeze made them swing around. There was a muttered curse from a dark corner of the room.

"Who's there?" Eric demanded.

Suddenly a man appeared, armed with a rifle. He aimed it at the two.

"How long have you been standing there?" Rachel cried.

"Long enough," the man said. "Did you think it would be this easy to move around on this floor? We were aware of your presence from the moment you opened that panel. You might have gotten away if you hadn't been so resourceful."

He looked right at Rachel as he spoke.

"I wanted to shoot you down on sight," he said. "But the fat man wanted me to hear what you had to say. You've got something to do with those other two, don't you?"

Rachel stiffened. Eric put an arm around her.

"I don't know what you're talking about," he insisted.

"Sure you do," the man said. He waved the gun at the opening in the wall. "Move on out. You'll be with your friends in a few minutes. And then you'll all have a lot of explaining to do."

Rachel was tempted to retort that the man's superiors would have explaining of their own. But she decided this was one of the times when silence was best.

54

SAMANTHA SAT ALONE in a cell very similar to the one which held Julie captive. She'd been separated from Wil minutes after her breakdown, dragged yelling and struggling off the floor where Marty lay strapped to an examination table.

Marty.

Samantha kept looking at her hands, trying to see beyond the pinkish flesh and five fingers. These were not her hands at all, but "borrowed" appendages, part of an overall metamorphosis from her true identity. Seeing Marty had brought back memories of her real self.

"I'm not human," she whispered, not even caring if she was being monitored. "My name is Ch'Mrazi and I am Ixtauran."

When Marty had turned to look at her, it had been with aquamarine doe's eyes. His eyes were twice as large as a normal human's, the focal point of a bald, rounded head. His nose was small, his mouth lipless, his ears tiny. The overall effect was that of a baby.

This is what Samantha knew herself to be like; at least, it was what she had once looked like long ago. As a female, her head had been different in that her ears were bent downward and her cheekbones were more pronounced. Like Marty, she did not have five fingers, but eight, and they had been almost six inches long. Like Marty, she had also had a tail.

She was humanoid, but very definitely not human. She was beyond human.

And the others? Were the children also Ixtauran? Was Rachel, or Eric? Where did Barbara and Wil fit into this?

Some memories had come crashing to the surface when

she looked at Marty, but not all. There were still many unanswered questions.

She brought the back of her wrist up to her eyes and wiped away tears. As far as she could recall, Ixtaurans did not cry tears.

Samantha heard rattling in the metal door, which swung open to reveal an armed guard.

"Come on, lady," he said. "LaBerge wants to talk to the lot of you."

He waved his gun into the hall, then followed her after she'd exited the cell. He did not seem afraid, or even curious. Samantha guessed he'd never been down to the lowest level, and had never seen Marty.

Or . . . he had seen the young alien and had no idea that Samantha was supposed to look like that. This revelation gave her strength. If no one knew who she really was, perhaps there was some way out of this.

She was led to a large windowless room. There was an oval table down its center, surrounded by black chairs. She saw Rachel and Eric sitting with a young boy between them. A dark-haired child swiveled in another chair, her back to Samantha. But it was the trio standing at the back of the room that caught her attention. She was sorry to see Barbara here, because it meant her friend had been caught. She saw now that the other child was Lorraine, swinging back and forth in her chair and pouting. But she ignored them and called to the child who meant most to her.

"Julie!" she cried.

Julie turned away from Wil and Barbara and ran the length of the room in just a few strides. Samantha caught her in open arms and hugged her fiercely.

"Oh, it's so good to see you!" she cried.

"Samantha!" Julie said.

Samantha pulled back and looked at her.

"Are you okay, sweetie?" she asked. "Did they hurt you?"

Are you another like me?

Julie frowned, staring at her. She had heard Samantha's words.

I . . . I don't know who we are.

Samantha gasped at the sound of Julie's voice in her mind. Why hadn't she been able to hear her before?

Was this what Rachel had meant by "feeling" Steven's presence?

Barbara and Wil had joined them.

"She seems okay," Wil said. "I understand they've been treated decently, other than being locked up."

"Being locked up cuts out the 'decently' part, in my opinion," Barbara said.

Samantha stood up, keeping an arm around Julie. She looked at Wil, seeing him differently than she had when she'd thought they were of similar origins. The feelings of love and affection still stirred within her, but now there were doubts about the "rightness" of those emotions.

She didn't have time to dwell on it. Julie was tugging at her sleeve.

"Come meet my friends," she said.

Samantha went to the table.

"You must be Steven," she said to the young black boy.

"Hello, Samantha," Steven said politely.

"We were reunited with him after we were caught," Rachel said, not revealing news about the room she'd found.

She wanted to correct him, but stopped herself. If she was the only one who knew of their true nature, they might become as upset by the truth as she had been; as she still was.

"Hi, Samantha," Lorraine drawled. "They caught us."

"Yeah," Barbara said. "We didn't get as far as Haybrook's back door. I'm glad, too. The creeps that pointed guns at us and brought us back here were nasty SOB's. I'm glad Gordy wasn't involved."

Samantha gazed into Lorraine's eyes and realized now where their gray-green irises had come from. Her eyes were meant to be lapis-colored, like Marty's. When she had been changed, a little of the original tint had remained, showing through the green of her "new" eyes.

Lorraine was definitely one of her own kind. But how had that change taken place?

"Samantha, what's going on here?" Wil asked gently, as if he had read her mind. "When you saw that . . . thing down there, you acted as if you'd finally remembered something."

Samantha turned on him. "Don't call him a thing! He's a child! A sentient being with as much right to respect as any of us!"

Wil's eyebrows went up, and he backed up a step.

"You're right," he said. "Of all people, I should be open-minded. I've certainly seen enough in my life."

Will you be open-minded about me?

What about us?

She looked around at the others. That hadn't been Julie, but she couldn't decide who had spoken to her.

"Please, Samantha," Wil said. "Tell me what you remember. Does it have something to do with that crash? With the yellow house?"

Samantha nodded. It would be okay to reveal that much, for now. But then again, what if someone was listening?

"Are we being monitored?" she asked.

"Probably," Wil said. "But I checked everywhere and can't locate a bug. I think you'll be okay if you whisper."

Samantha lowered her voice and began her story. If they were bugged, it didn't matter. She was not telling all she knew.

"Gordy was right," she said. "I am a survivor of a . . . shipwreck. I traveled through the water to land in a pod like the one we saw in Marty's room."

Rachel gasped. Wil turned to her.

"Do you know something about that?"

"We found a whole room full of them," she said. "Behind a secret panel."

"They're kept in metal crates," Eric said. "About thirty. When we broke into the room, it set off a silent alarm. That's how they caught us."

"What are those things?" Rachel asked.

Samantha wasn't exactly sure, but she thought it was the entire reason for their being here on Earth.

"When I came near enough to swim under my own power," she went on, "I disembarked and sank the pod. The ones you found may have resurfaced accidentally."

She didn't dare think of the horrible alternative: that her comrades had been captured and imprisoned ten years ago, perhaps even allowed to die.

"What did you do when you got on land?" Barbara

asked. She had taken a seat on the tabletop and was leaning forward to catch every softly spoken word.

"It was dark, and I could see the glow of the ship's explosion just along the horizon," Samantha said. "I made my way down the beach, looking for a place to hide and rest."

Looking for a place to change.

"I found an empty house near the jetty," she said.

"The yellow house with green shutters?" Wil guessed.

Samantha nodded.

"I never spent a childhood in there," she said. "I think I must have picked up some false memories in the time I was hidden away. I'm sure I was hurt, and exhausted; maybe even in shock. The house had been deserted, but earlier that summer a family had stayed there. A child must have used that pail and shovel you found in the ruins, Wil. In my hurt mind, I made that toy my own."

Rachel stood up and walked across the room to the door. She looked out the small window and saw they were under heavy guard. Then she turned back and said:

"It still doesn't explain where these children came from, or why we feel so drawn to them."

"I think I know who can answer those questions," Samantha replied. "The child they're still holding prisoner—Marty."

She looked at Wil.

"He called the children to this place," she said. "He must know everything."

Wil was about to reply when the door opened. Then a huge man walked in, fixing his piggish eyes on each of them in turn, and Lorraine backed up into Wil's arms. He put his hands on her shoulders.

"Who are you?" he demanded.

LaBerge glared at him.

"You are in no position to ask questions," he said. "However, I will tell you my name is Walter LaBerge. Now, you tell me who you are."

"Wil Sherer," the former cop replied. "I'm a detective, from Ashleigh Creek, Colorado."

"I didn't ask where you were from," LaBerge snapped. "Although I might have. What right do you have to be here in New Jersey?"

"I'm a private detective," Wil amended. He nodded

toward Samantha and Julie. "Samantha Winstead and the child named Julie are my clients."

LaBerge looked at them. Julie turned her face into Samantha's arm.

"I see," he mumbled. He looked at the black family. "I know who you are. Your wallets told me. Eric Freleng and Rachel Freleng, of Columbus, Ohio."

He rocked back on his heels.

"You're from all over the map, aren't you?" he said. "But it isn't residents of the USA I'm interested in."

He looked down at Lorraine.

"What do you know of Marty?" he asked. "What connection could a human child have with that creature?"

"Marty's my friend!" Lorraine wailed. "I already told you that!"

"Yes, I know," LaBerge said. "And I think you've been lying. I think you're all liars. You know something, don't you? *Don't you?*"

Lorraine hugged Wil tightly.

"I'd suggest you stop terrorizing little children, La-Berge," Wil said. "You're holding us prisoners against our will. That's a federal offense, although I have a feeling you understand all about things that are 'federal.' "

LeBarge turned his attention to the detective.

"Don't play cop with me," he said. "Have you forgotten we confiscated your gun?"

Wil didn't give him the courtesy of an answer.

The fat man turned to Samantha.

"And you," he said. "What do you know of our alien specimen? I'm told you put on quite a show when you saw him."

Samantha stiffened. It wasn't right to call a sentient being a "specimen"! she thought.

"I have an idea," LaBerge said. "I'm going to bring you all downstairs. Maybe if you meet Marty as a group, you'll be more willing to answer my questions."

Lorraine whispered into Wil's ear, "Why does he keep talking about Marty in such a funny way? What's wrong with Marty?"

"Nothing," Wil whispered back. "He's exaggerating."

LaBerge wasn't exaggerating at all, he thought. But he did hope there was nothing wrong with Marty. He'd never seen anything like that in his life, and he respected

Samantha's belief that Marty deserved respect. He also deserved the same rights as any other living being—mainly, the right to his freedom.

No one protested as they were escorted from the room under armed guard. LaBerge should have wondered about their sudden silence, but he was too caught up in what would happen when they all saw Marty to think about it.

In truth, only their voices were silent.

Samantha, tell us about Marty, Rachel requested.

He is . . . not like us, Samantha began, wondering how best to approach the subject. Now that they were actually going to see him, the shock of meeting Marty would be softened if Samantha prepared them. *At least, he is not the way we are now.*

What do you mean "now," Samantha?

It was Steven asking the question.

Steven, does the name Ixtaura mean anything to you?

Steven thought a moment, staring at his sneakers as they were hustled down the hallway. The others were also lost in thought. Only Wil, Barbara, and Eric kept their eyes on LaBerge.

It's a little familiar. Like a place I went to once, long ago.

I think so, too, said Lorraine.

Sorry, Rachel put in. *Nothing here.*

Me neither.

You'll remember in time, Julie. Don't worry. Listen, everyone. You have to prepare yourselves for a real shock. It was so sudden to me that I could not control my emotions. That's how I was caught. I think your only hope of escape is to make them think you are normal human beings, just caught up in all this by accident.

Aren't we "normal human beings"? Julie asked.

Samantha swallowed. They were entering the elevator that would take them to the lowest level. It was her last chance to reveal the truth before they all found out in the cruel way that she had.

No, Julie. I'm sorry I don't have time to say this more gently. But we are not humans at all. We're from a planet called Ixtaura.

That's crazy! Steven cried in his mind.

Rachel put an arm around him. Wil noted the gesture, and wondered if they were somehow "communicating."

Maybe not so crazy, Steven, Rachel said. *We already know we're different from others. The way we can talk with our minds, for instance.*

The elevator door opened. They were led to the same supply closet where Wil and Samantha had found cleanroom suits.

"We don't have any that will fit the children," a guard said.

LaBerge looked from the white suit in his hands to his group of captives.

"I don't think it matters now," he said. "There's no need to use the suits."

"But, sir!" the guard protested. "The danger of contamination—"

"I'm well aware of that!" LaBerge answered. "The subject has already been contaminated! He had contact with this little one . . ."

He indicated Lorraine. She moved closer to Wil, whom she had unofficially adopted as her new guardian.

". . . and these others know something about him," LaBerge went on. "They have answers, and I mean to get them!"

He reached for Julie, who just happened to be the closest person to him. Holding her upper arms tightly, he shook her and shouted:

"Or I will kill the whole lot of them!"

Julie screamed.

"Let her go!" Samantha cried, stepping forward.

Wil and Eric both moved in to save the little girl, but three guns suddenly rose to the level of their heads.

"What's the point of hurting her?" Eric asked.

But LaBerge wasn't listening. He dragged Julie, screaming, into the back room. A half-dozen white figures turned to them in surprise. LaBerge pulled Julie along. The others hurried after them, stopping when they reached the curtain. With a curt gesture, he ordered everyone else out of the room. The guards hesitated, but LaBerge's silent order was clear. When they were alone, LaBerge began to speak.

"Look now!" LaBerge said. "Look now and give me the answers I've been wanting these past ten years!"

With that, LaBerge jerked back the curtain that had kept Marty hidden. His eyes were wild as he scanned the group, ready to gloat at their reactions. Wil and Samantha, who had already seen Marty, only stared. Barbara uttered a loud curse. Eric instinctively jerked Rachel away, and in turn she pulled Steven into her arms.

"Lorraine, are you doing that?" Steven cried, forgetting to use his mind in his excitement.

"No!" Lorraine protested.

"Doing?" LaBerge echoed. "Doing what?"

He turned around, and when he saw what was lying on the table, he let out a scream that rattled all the glass in the room. There was no sickly alien boy there at all, but a hideous beast with bright red eyes and a tooth-lined mouth that ran vertically from the middle of its "face" to the bottom of its belly. It was covered with hair, shaped something like a fat snake that had been split open. It reared up on multiple hind legs, letting out a high-pitched keening sound.

"What the hell is that?" Eric demanded.

"Don't be afraid!" Steven cried. "It's only make-believe."

"It's real enough for me!" Barbara cried, racing to the door.

Wil stopped her just in time. "You'll alert the guards!"

They turned to see the "thing" flop forward, just as LaBerge's fat form stumbled. Moving with unusual grace, LaBerge rolled away, saving himself in the nick of time. He went on screaming, but no one moved to help him. The room was soundproof, so the guards had no idea what was happening.

"Make it go away!" he screamed like a frightened child.

"We can't," Steven said. "We didn't bring it here."

It must be Marty! Julie thought.

Where is he? Rachel asked. *Where did he go?*

There seemed to be no sign of the boy anywhere in the room. But there was no time to look for him. The "beast" was pulling itself up to its full height now, an amazing ten or twelve feet. It swung itself around, looking very much like a lasso. This time it caught LaBerge by his legs. The fat man screamed in horror.

"Stop it! Stop!"

And then a strange voice filled the room.

I'll make it stop. I'll make it stop when you set my people free.

That doesn't sound like Marty! Lorraine cried.

"Who is that?" Wil asked.

Everyone turned to him.

"You heard that?" Samantha asked. "But how?"

"It's coming over the intercom system," Barbara said, looking up and around.

"Yeah, I heard it too," Eric said.

The creature was thrashing back and forth, flopping LaBerge about as if he was light as a feather. They noted he had stopped screaming.

"He's passed out," Rachel said.

"Maybe he's dead?" Barbara asked.

Instantly the horrible creature vanished. There were no signs that it had existed at all. LaBerge lay unconscious on the floor, but his pants legs weren't even crumpled.

For a long time everyone stood in eerie silence.

Then Samantha moved slowly forward to the partitioned area where Marty had been a short time earlier. She reached for the doors of a closet and pulled them open.

Marty sat inside, his body folded up into a ball. Gently Samantha reached in and pulled him out. Cradling him in her arms, she carried him out for the others to see. Barbara's mouth fell open. Eric shook his head in wonder.

"I've never seen anything like that before," he said.

"Marty isn't a 'thing,' " Samantha said. "He's an Ixtauran child. He is what we all—with the exception of Eric, Wil, and Barbara—look like."

Marty regarded them all with huge aquamarine eyes. He did not speak, or even try to communicate with his mind. He was too weakened to do so.

"Hello, Marty," Lorraine said in a soft voice. She came forward and touched him, completely without fear.

As if they'd been well-prepared for this moment, the other aliens also surrounded Marty.

"How did you know he was in the closet?" Wil asked.

Samantha smiled at him. "Some of your detective's talents must have rubbed off on me. I realized that Marty couldn't have left this room without being seen. The only place he could have hidden was the closet."

The others gazed at the young male alien, the children touching him in gentle wonder.

"He doesn't look strong enough to have created that monster," Rachel commented.

"I think he's hurt," Lorraine said. "Sometimes, when he would talk to us through our minds, he would stop. He said they were doing things to him."

Rachel shuddered visibly. Eric put his arms around his wife, feeling a little unsure about all this "alien" business.

"If he didn't do it," Steven said, "then who did?"

They all looked at each other. Then Samantha said in a soft voice:

"There must be others."

"But how did they get in here?" Barbara asked. "Where are they?"

Eric looked toward the door.

"I don't know about that," he said, "but those guards are bound to come back in here at any moment."

He turned to Marty. Samantha had laid him back down on the examination table, and his eyes were drooping toward sleep. Eric had never seen anything more amazing than this young alien, but he did not have the luxury of time to be either fascinated or repulsed by him. Instead, he leaned toward the being's tiny ear and said:

"Is there another way out?"

Only one way.

When he didn't hear Marty, Eric stood up.

"He said 'only one way,' " Lorraine told him.

"That means we're trapped," Barbara said.

Just then the door opened and two white-suited figures entered. The children moved toward the adults. Wil instinctively reached for the gun that was no longer at his side. The figures did not acknowledge the group, but went to LaBerge's prone figure and knelt down to examine it. Then they stood up and took off their helmets.

There was a man with a crewcut and a woman with black hair and porcelain skin. The woman gazed at Lorraine while the man spoke.

"He's alive."

Samantha guessed at once who the woman must be.

"You . . . Lorraine belongs with you, doesn't she?"

"Vrodrani is our child," the woman said. She went to the little girl and knelt down to her.

"How did you get in here?" Wil asked. "Where are the guards?"

The man grinned broadly. "Sleeping it off. They won't awaken until we're long gone."

Lorraine put her hands on the woman's face, staring into her eyes.

"I wanted to find you," she said. "But I had to come here when Marty called."

"I know, dear," the woman said.

She stood up and looked at the group.

"My true name is Morgana," she said. "Here on Earth I'm called Judy. This is my husband, Kalor."

"My Terran name is George," the man said. "In fact, until we know we are safe, it would be best to use our Earth names."

Barbara held up her hands.

"Whoa!" she cried. "All this alien stuff is really bothering me. Would one of you guys like to explain what's going on here?"

"Please sit down," George said. "It's going to be a very long story. It began nearly a hundred years ago . . ."

Everyone took a seat and listened intently. They were so caught up in George/Kalor's words that their minds did not pick up the signals coming from LaBerge's body. He was coming into wakefulness, but he played possum, and listened to every word that was said.

55

"OUR RACE ACHIEVED the ability of interstellar flight many Earth centuries ago," George said. "In the time since then, we've made just a few 'first contacts.' We became aware of Earth only recently in our history."

"One can't simply land on a planet and say, 'Hello, we're here!' " Judy said.

She held Lorraine on her lap. The child's head had dropped to her chest, and she was sound asleep. Her ordeal in the operating room, and then in the tunnel, had been too much for her.

"It takes years to prepare for a meeting with another species," Judy went on. "Years of study, of acclimating to that new race's way of life."

"You've been among us for nearly a century?" Wil asked, recalling George's earlier words.

"Yes," George said. "We first sent a small group to orbit your planet and study you from afar. At that time, of course, you did not have the tracking devices you employ today. We were able to cruise around Earth's atmosphere without being detected."

Barbara swung a hand, indicating the structure around them.

"You sure were detected this time," she said.

"Yes, we were," George acknowledged. "That was a mistake, but I'll get to that later. Our first attempts to study your culture told us that as a general rule you would be unable to withstand the shock of knowing there are other life forms in the universe. We realized this would take time. More important, we were able to learn of your different cultures, your styles of dress, methods of work, and so on. With this information, the next wave was sent to Earth at the turn of the twentieth century.

Disguised as humans, we joined with your societies all around the globe."

Judy nodded. "We served in your wars, worked in your factories, and generally lived the lives of humans."

"How many of these 'waves' have arrived so far?" Wil asked.

"The children would be the tenth," Judy said.

"In this plan," George said, "we had never sent anyone but individuals. We felt it was time to begin studying Earth's cultures as family units. Ten Earth years ago, a group including Morgana and me was sent to prepare for lives as families. We had . . ."

He stopped a moment to consider the right word.

"We 'deposited' reproductive cells in a laboratory," he continued. "These were cultured, and the resulting babies raised for one purpose only—to be the first children to travel from our planet."

"Wow," Steven said.

Eric looked at the little boy.

"Wait a minute," he said. "Let me make sure I understand this. Are you saying Rachel came with the ninth group and that Steven was raised in a test tube to be sent to her at a later date?"

"In a manner of speaking," George said.

"Then Steven is my son," Rachel said, her voice softened in awe. "That explains why I felt so drawn to him."

"And Julie is my daughter?" Samantha said, a hint of hope in her tone.

"Yes, she is," Judy said with a smile. "Your natural daughter."

Julie looked over at Samantha and grinned happily. Samantha smiled back, but only momentarily.

"But if she is my child," she protested, "why don't I remember creating her? You said we 'deposited' cells in a lab. If I'd given away some of my eggs, I would surely remember it. And I sure as hell would remember traveling across a galaxy to a new planet. Where are all these memories? What happened to us?"

George sighed deeply. "It has always been the policy of this project to send Ixtaurans to Earth with no memories of their home planet. That way, no one could be influenced by what he already knew. Your minds were *tabla rasa*, ready to absorb all new data."

"Well, not exactly," Judy said. "You were given enough information to function in this society, but most of what you know now you've taken in since your arrival."

"Why were we chosen, in particular?" Samantha asked.

"You weren't chosen, Ch'Mrazi," Judy said, calling Samantha by her real name. "You volunteered. We all did. This is the most important thing that ever happened to Ixtaura, our major reason for living."

"This is incredible," Samantha mumbled. She felt Wil's hand on her shoulder and put her own on top of it.

"Okay, I get it so far," Barbara said. "First there were eight other groups. Then group number nine came along to prepare for the coming of these children. But there's another thing I don't get. You and George are a couple, both Ix . . . Ixtauran. But I get the impression Eric isn't Ixtauran. And where's Samantha's husband, or mate, or whatever you call him?"

George breathed in a deep, melancholy sigh. "Dead," he said. "Killed when the last ship landed just off this very coast."

"I was on that ship!" Samantha cried.

"You came with your husband," Judy said. "You were chief medical officer and he was head of the biological sciences. This is why you were able to join this society as a doctor."

"You can explain all that later," Barbara said. "In the meantime, where do I fit in?"

"It would not have made sense to send our people here cold," George said. "So the previous wave of Ixtaurans prepared certain 'receptive' individuals. You were prepared, subconsciously, to be Samantha's friend."

"Was I also 'prepared'?" Eric asked, gazing at the wife he loved so dearly. It would break his heart to think he had fallen in love with her only because some other being had "arranged" it.

Judy gave him a sympathetic look. "I don't know. It would be impossible for me to know everyone's story."

"How do you know these stories?" Wil asked. "Why weren't your minds erased?"

"In every generation," George explained, "there were

a privileged few who were allowed to retain their full memories. This was a precautionary matter, in case anything went wrong."

"Are you those people?" Samantha asked.

Judy and George shook their heads simultaneously.

"No," Judy said. "That man came here fifty years ago, and lives in a remote part of India. He was aware of the crash which took your husband's life, Ch'Mrazi. But there was no way of knowing where the remains of the ship and crew were taken."

Samantha looked at the examination table, where Marty lay asleep.

"No way until Marty started calling to our children," she guessed.

"We felt the signals," George said. "We knew Lorraine was calling for help, but we did not understand them until the man came from India. He has the most powerful of all our minds, and he 'heard' Marty. He traveled to America to speak with us and reveal the truth. Once we knew, we came here. We have been following you as a group for days, to make certain you are on our side."

"But what about Marty?" Samantha asked. "Why didn't he 'change' like the rest of us?"

"There was another accident," Judy said. "Shortly before the ship bearing the children landed, the crew experienced equipment failure. The children had been placed in special pods, each destined to a different part of the Earth. You yourselves were sent in similar pods a decade ago."

George continued the story.

"The crew was able to launch almost all the pods," he said. "Only two remained: Lorraine and Marty. Lorraine, perhaps because of her small size, somehow changed before she was found. But something went wrong with Marty's pod. It must have floated until he was found, looking exactly as he had when he left our planet."

Eric walked over to LaBerge and looked down at him.

"That's why he kept asking Lorraine what she knew of him," he said. "They were found together, and LaBerge was crazy to know what an Earth child had to do with an alien."

"Or what he *thought* was an Earth child," Wil said.

"It makes me wonder," Rachel said. "Maybe other children landed in different parts of the world and did not change."

George shrugged. "We were not told of them."

Samantha reached toward Julie and brushed back her hair.

"I'm glad Julie found me," she said. "I don't understand, though, why we weren't just told about our children. Did our superiors think we'd reject them?"

"Of course not," Judy said. "But remember, your minds were blanked. You had no recollection of creating your offspring."

"Were you afraid of the police?" George asked.

Both Samantha and Rachel nodded excitedly.

"That's because it would have been unsafe for you to involve any authorities," George explained.

"Seems like you built in a lot of protective devices," Wil said. "I'd hate to imagine what a mind-blanking session is like."

Barbara huffed. "They didn't build in enough to keep some of them from getting caught. And what about Raoul Henley?"

"Who?"

Samantha told Judy about the man who had supposedly given Julie to her, and what had happened to him. Rachel mumbled something.

"We also lost someone mysteriously," she said. "Nina Blair was a social worker. She practically begged me to take in Steven. Then she was killed, her body burned beyond recognition by some kind of chemical. Do you suppose she suffered the same fate as your man?"

"It's possible," Samantha agreed.

"The pods are set to help us change," George said. "But in human hands . . ."

They all looked to the Plexiglas case, where the pod hung suspended. It was no more threatening than a carved-out piece of wood.

"But what about all those pods we found?" Eric asked. "Do you mean someone died horribly each time one of them was exposed?"

"I think they lose their potency after a time," George said.

Wil walked over to the display case.

"I don't see much in the way of technology here," he said. "Just a few controls at the front. Hardly the kind of thing to keep someone alive through space."

"But the lack of technology is precisely the reason it works," Judy said. "Those pods aren't manmade . . . or should I say Ixtauran-made. They *are* Ixtauran."

"I don't get it," Wil said.

"They are the reason we were able to travel through space," George said. He looked at the pod, and a sort of reverence came into his voice.

"We all strive toward the highest level of physical and spiritual existence," he said. "The *Cetacu* achieved these aeons ago, when they became one with nature. They gave up their corporeal forms and, shall we way, 'linked' with various types of flora. In doing so, they were able to find the answers to questions all beings have been asking since the beginning of time."

"It was the *Cetacu* who discovered the secret to 'faster-than-light' speeds," Judy added. "They are the ones who allowed us to break free of our own planet and explore the galaxy."

On the floor, LaBerge had been quietly listening to every word. His heart began to pound now. Ten years of research, and at last he knew the answer! It was the pods! All the time, he thought, it had been those strange wooden "boats" they'd found floating in the ocean. And he was lucky enough to have a new one, one that was almost completely intact.

Suddenly the room filled with the blare of sirens. Everyone looked around in confusion, except for George and Judy. Samantha turned to them.

"What's happening?"

"Not to worry," George said. "We set the alarm system to go off at this time. It's to clear everyone out of the building."

"But why?" Eric asked. "What are you going to do?"

"We've come to rescue you," George said. "But we can't just leave this place as it is. No one must know we are here. The entire complex must be destroyed."

No! LaBerge shouted in his mind. *You can't destroy all my work!*

Still, he didn't dare move.

"But so many have seen all this," Rachel pointed out. "Surely they'll talk."

"We can erase certain memories from their minds," Judy said, "as easily as our own memories were erased. But we want to give them the chance to escape. We aren't murderers."

"Tell that to Raoul Henley," Wil said.

No one answered him.

"But how are we going to destroy this place?" Steven asked.

The wails of the sirens woke Lorraine up, and she began to fuss. Judy rocked her back and forth.

"We must all work together," she said. "Lorraine? Lorraine, listen to me."

"Yes, Mommy?"

Samantha gasped. It was the first time one of the children had acknowledged an adult as her parent. For a moment she wondered what it would be like for Julie to call her the same.

But there was no time for that.

"Lorraine," Judy was saying, "think of that secret tunnel you found. Think of the water at the doorway."

Lorraine nodded. She closed her eyes and imagined the place. It came to her mind as clearly as if she were right there. She could even feel the cold water on her body.

"Everyone, concentrate on that tunnel," Judy commanded. "Concentrate on bringing the water into the building."

"You're going to flood the place!" Eric said. "How will we get out? Last time I looked, Barbara and Wil and I didn't have magical powers."

"We'll get out," George promised. "The building will be empty when the water crashes through. It will destroy everything, and everything above will collapse and bury these lower floors."

All the Ixtaurans in the room did as they were told, calling for the flood to come even as they readied themselves to evacuate.

Eric pointed to LaBerge.

"What about him?"

Everyone looked at the fat man on the floor. They

hated him for what he had done, and yet they were too peaceful a race to let him die.

"We should wake him up," Rachel said.

"Somebody better get Marty too," Samantha said.

"I've got him," Wil said, hurrying to pick up the little alien being. By now he was neither fascinated nor afraid of him. He cradled Marty in his arms like a baby.

George and Eric went to LaBerge and attempted to shake him. Suddenly LaBerge rolled onto his back, thrusting their hands away.

"Don't touch me!" he screamed. "Don't touch me, you alien freaks!"

"He wasn't asleep!" Julie cried, turning to Samantha. "He heard everything!"

LaBerge was on his feet now, moving back toward the display case.

"Yes, I heard everything!" he said. "It was the pods! The pods are my answer! You aren't going to obliterate all my work! If they gave you power, they'll give it to me!"

With that, before anyone could stop him, he picked up an oxygen tank and threw it at the case.

"Don't do that!" Samantha cried, thinking of what had happened to Raoul Henley.

Wil and Eric rushed for the man, but he was already climbing into the case. He moved with a grace that seemed impossible for such a big man, reaching into the pod and fumbling with the controls. A few hours earlier, he would never have allowed anyone to have direct contact with the structure. But he was beyond control now, desperately trying to finish his work before it was taken away from him. He turned knobs and pushed buttons and frantically ran his fingers over the control panel. The others tried to stop him, but no one could.

A bright orange glow filled the broken display case. Samantha felt something tighten in her stomach. She remembered the glow. She had seen it surrounded by darkness, under the water. It was the glow that had changed her into a human being.

For some reason, the power had been delayed in Marty's pod. What should have happened days ago to change him into a human boy was now doing something horrible to Walter LaBerge. His screams filled the room, competing with the sirens.

Julie covered her ears and turned to Samantha.

"Make it stop!" she cried.

Lorraine was wailing loudly. Steven hurried to her and knelt beside Judy.

Don't be afraid.

They all heard the voice. They turned to Wil, who felt Marty stirring in his arms.

Don't be afraid. We'll be all right. But we . . . we have to get out now!

"Come on!" Rachel shouted. "Let's go!"

George opened the door. The hallway was empty—the guards had been mesmerized to leave with everyone else. Already they could hear rumbling from the floor up above.

"The water's coming!" Samantha shouted over the din of the sirens.

"Marty knew it first!" Steven cried. "He warned us!"

Eric was the last one out of the room. He turned to look at the orange glow. Like a man running from an inferno, LaBerge suddenly emerged from the display case. Through the orange mist that surrounded him, Eric saw a sickening sight. LaBerge's skin was gone, his flesh and muscles exposed. Some weird noise came from his mouth—or what was left of it.

He collapsed, a bloodied hand reaching for Eric's ankle.

"Eric!" Rachel cried from down the hall.

Eric broke free and raced to the others. As fast as they could, they hurried up eight flights of stairs. Wil glanced quickly through the window in the door and saw water flooding into the halls. It would be only a matter of minutes before everything was destroyed.

When they reached the top, everyone immediately headed for the doorways. But Wil stopped short.

"What about Marty?" he cried.

Everyone else stopped and turned.

"He's right," Samantha said. "There must be two hundred people out there. We can't let them see Marty!"

Barbara ducked into a closet and pulled out a tarpaulin. Quickly she helped Wil wrap this around the alien.

"It's okay," she told him soothingly. "We're almost out."

I'm not afraid. I'm with friends. It did not matter to him that Barbara couldn't pick up his message. His large expressive eyes told her what he was thinking.

Finally they opened the door and walked out into the sunshine.

A huge crowd was milling about the parking lot. Some were still dressed in white cleanroom suits, and were drawing stares from the townspeople who worked in the factory above.

"Who are those people?" a woman asked. "They look like astronauts."

"I sure never saw them before," the man next to her commented.

The guards drew enough attention to keep it away from the escapees. They had all taken their helmets off, and a few were scratching their heads in wonder. They only remembered hearing the Klaxons and running from the building.

But none could remember what they'd been doing in there.

"What's happening?" someone yelled. "Is it a fire?"

"I don't see any smoke!"

"Maybe it was a false alarm!"

"Someone should check!"

Wil leaned toward George, who was standing closest to him.

"I think we'd better leave while we can," he whispered.

"You're right," George said.

He jerked his head slightly and the group followed him through the throng of people. A few were heading back to the building, curious to see what was going on.

Stop! You'll be killed!

Marty, they can't hear you! Julie cried in her mind.

We have to stop them! Work harder. Put all your mind power on the water inside! We must hurry!

The group huddled together, staring at the brick building. All other thoughts but its destruction flew away from their brains. The power that suddenly emanated from them was so strong that Wil and Barbara looked at each other. Somehow, they had felt it too.

"Stop!" yelled a man in the crowd.

"Look at the water! Look at the water!"

Like a tidal wave, a huge gusher came shooting out of the front doors of the building. People ran in all directions, crying out in fear. As others watched in wonder and horror, the entire structure collapsed, sinking into a deep, deep hole in the ground.

And just as suddenly, it stopped, leaving a large quiet pool of ocean water.

"Wow," someone whispered.

It was suddenly so quiet that his word was heard by everyone.

"Let's leave now," Lorraine said.

"Yes, let's," Rachel said, taking Steven by the hand. "It's over."

They walked toward the town, leaving the crowd to wonder about what had just happened. Even the least scientific-minded of them knew that no natural thing had just happened. But even after years of study, there would be no answers. No one would ever really explain where enough pressure came from to drive the water of the ocean through a tunnel and into a building two miles away, completely destroying it in a matter of minutes.

Epilogue

One Month Later

STEVEN SWUNG THE baseball bat with all his might, but he still missed the ball that Olivia had pitched to him.

"Strike one!" Tatiana yelled.

"Be nice, Tati," Olivia called. "Steven's never played baseball before."

"I *am* being nice," Tatiana said. "That's what you're *supposed* to say."

She put her hands on Steven's elbows and pressed down.

"A little lower," she said.

Behind the fence, Eric and Rachel sat holding hands at the top of the bleachers. Eric turned to look at his wife, for perhaps the thousandth time since they'd come back from Shoaling. He tried as hard as he could to imagine her to be the same creature as Marty, but his deep love prevented it.

"It's hard to believe that's the little girl who wouldn't hug you at the airport," Rachel commented.

Eric turned back to the game. Poor Steven had struck out three times, and now it was Tatiana's turn. She whacked it with all her might and went racing around the bases, reaching home plate even before Olivia could retrieve the ball.

"Go, Tati!" Eric yelled.

"I couldn't really blame her for that," he answered Rachel. "After all, I did run out on her without a word of good-bye."

"No, it's more my fault," Rachel said. "I was a terrible bitch that week Steven arrived. It must have been a nightmare, living with me."

Eric put his arm around her and pulled her closer.

"It wasn't your fault at all," he insisted. "Something

was planted in your brain to make you reject everyone else in favor of Steven."

"Tatiana realized something was wrong," Rachel said. "I wonder if she still thinks I'm 'different.' "

"You've changed again," Eric said. "Back to the mother she had always known. Kids are very forgiving. Just look how she gets along with Steven now."

Rachel was thoughtful for a few moments.

"I'll have to tell her the truth someday," she said. "And then what will she think?"

"She'll still love you," Eric said. "You're her mother. In the end, I think that's all she ever really wanted."

"Well, I'm going to try to make up for what happened," Rachel said. "I don't know if I'm ever going back to my . . . to that planet. I still can't think of it as 'home.' This is my home, with you."

Steven was up to bat again. He struck out once, twice . . .

"Come on, Steven . . ." Rachel encouraged softly.

On the third swing, the bat hit the ball with a crack like a snapping branch. Eric and Rachel got to their feet, watching it sail clear across the park and out onto the road, hundreds of yards away. Steven raced around the bases, cheered on by Tatiana and Olivia.

"All *right*, Steven!" Eric shouted.

Steven's sisters hugged him, jumping up and down. Eric plunked on the bench again and grinned at his wife.

"And you said he couldn't play baseball. Did you see that? Did you see how far that went?"

Rachel laughed. "We're multitalented, I guess."

Eric caught his breath. "It makes me wonder what other amazing things you can do."

With a flirtatious smile Rachel put her arms around him.

"Why don't we go home and find out?"

They began to kiss.

"Ewww!" Tatiana yelled. "Cut that out, you two! There's people here."

Eric and Rachel ignored her.

Samantha watched Julie as she romped with the dogs, chasing them around Samantha's backyard in Colorado. Wil and Barbara sat in lawn chairs with her, each one holding a frosty mug of beer. Samantha, Wil and Julie had just returned that morning from a week in Mexico. Barbara, who had had to return to work at the hospital, had come here to meet them. Her friends had spent the past two hours telling Barbara what had happened.

"I'm glad we found Marty's parents," Samantha said. "They were able to heal him, and now he has a real home."

"But how will he get along?" Barbara asked. "He can't very well go walking the streets looking like he does."

"George and Judy promised to contact the man in India," Samantha said. "He will see to it that Marty is properly 'changed.' I understand he's that powerful."

"Some of you seem more powerful than others," Wil pointed out. "Marty was strong enough to call the children from all points of the country. But you told me you didn't make contact with Julie until you were with her."

Samantha nodded. "Yes, we do have different groups on Ixtaura. But it is not like a caste system. Those with great powers don't frown on those with few. We all help each other, and as a group we are invincible."

"Well, you sure proved that in Shoaling," Barbara said in awe.

Samantha looked at her. There were dark circles under her eyes, proof she hadn't really slept since learning the truth.

"Don't praise us," she said. "We made some terrible blunders. People died because of us."

"That's unfortunate," Wil said, "but you can't blame yourselves. You only wanted to meet a new race, and did it in the best way you knew how."

"You're still doing it," Barbara said. "George and Judy said no one in Shoaling would remember what happened. Stage Ten of your work can continue now."

Wil smiled at Samantha.

"Maybe by the time the Eleventh Wave comes," he said, "we Earthlings will be ready for you."

Samantha couldn't help a laugh.

"Don't say 'Earthlings,' " she told him. "It sounds like a low-budget science-fiction movie. Call yourselves 'Terrans.' It's more dignified."

"I'm glad you think we're dignified," Wil said. "We

have light-years to go before we reach the heights that you have."

Samantha shook her head. She stared at Wil, her eyes filling with tears.

"Oh, no," she said. "You're wonderful people. You, and Barbara, and Gordy, and everyone who helped us. I can't wait until we do make contact."

"And don't forget that bag lady," Barbara said. "Bettina, that was her name. If it wasn't for her, Lorraine might not have found us."

Neither Wil nor Samantha heard her. They were staring very intently into each other's eyes.

"What's wrong?" Wil asked softly.

"I love you so much," Samantha said, a choke in her voice. "But how can I love you? We're . . . we're so different. And I don't know what to do about it!"

She hung her head and began to sob. Wil got out of his chair and went to kneel in front of her, taking her hands in his.

"I know exactly what to do about it," he said. "George said the whole purpose of Julie being sent to you was to acclimate yourselves to our society as a family unit. Well, all you need to complete this family unit is a father for Julie."

Samantha stopped crying. Her head came up abruptly, and she stared at Wil through wide, disbelieving eyes.

"Wh-what?"

Barbara laughed out loud, enjoying the romance she was witnessing.

"He's asking you to marry him."

"Oh . . ."

The word came out like a squeak. Samantha tried to talk again, but Wil was pulling her down to him. As they kissed, Barbara got up from her chair. She walked across the field to Julie and the dogs.

Aliens and Terrans, she thought in amazement.

Sunday came running up to her. She picked up a stick and threw it.

Maybe we'll do okay in this universe, she said. *Maybe we won't. But I sure am glad to be a part of a new world!*